CARTOMANCY

Also by Mary Gentle in Gollancz

Ash
Orthe
White Crow
Ancient Light
1610: A Sundial in a Grave

CARTOMANCY

Mary Gentle

Cartomancy Parts 1 and 2 © 1991, first published in *Villains*,
The Logistics of Carthage © 2002, first published in *Worlds that Weren't*,
Kitsune © 1998, first published in *Odyssey*, *The Road to Jerusalem* © 1991,
first published in *Interzone*, *Orc's Drift* © 1997, first published in *Valkyrie*,
The Tarot Dice © 1988, first published in *Scholars and Soldiers*, *The Harvest of
Wolves* © 1983, first published in *Isaac Asimov's Science Fiction Magazine*,
Anukazi's Daughter © 1984, first published in *Tomorrow's Voices*, *What God
Abandoned* © 1990, first published in *Weerde Vol. 1*, *The Pits Beneath the World*
© 1983, first published in *Peter Davison's Book of Alien Planets*, *Cast a Long
Shadow* © 2004, *A Sun in the Attic* © 1985, first published in *Despatches
from the Frontier of the Female Mind*, *A Shadow under the Sea* © 1983, first
published in *Isaac Asimov's Science Fiction Magazine*, *Human Waste* ©
1994, first published in *Interzone*

The right of Mary Gentle to be identified as the
author of this work has been asserted by her in accordance
with the Copyright, Designs and Patents Act 1988.

This collection first published in Great Britain in 2004 by
Gollancz
An imprint of the Orion Publishing Group
Orion House, 5 Upper St Martin's Lane, London WC2H 9EA

A CIP catalogue record for this book is
available from the British Library

ISBN 0 575 07532 5

Typeset at The Spartan Press Ltd,
Lymington, Hants

Printed and bound in Great Britain by
Clays Ltd, St Ives plc

Contents

CARTOMANCY: An Introduction

Viewed from the dragon's back, five hundred feet up, sunlight bleaches all colour from the city of Huirac.

Greatest city of the Twenty-Four Kingdoms, it bathes in the southern noon that whitens palaces, tenements, river bridges, docks, and plaster-walled mansions. The cries of street-vendors echo up from the alleys, and the crash of cartwheels splintering against each other in narrow streets, and carters settling down to a good curse. The stenches of middens rise in the heat.

The dragon circled in a holding pattern. Elthyriel peered down from its scaled back.

Beyond the town quarter, by the river bridge decorated with the statues of heroes, the tall ramparts of the Citadel of Virtue brood. There is an aqueduct running from Huirac's royal palace to the Citadel, which is no aqueduct but a walkway wide enough, in an emergency, to gallop an armoured horse down, full tilt. For, strategically, he who holds the Citadel holds Huirac, and there have been enough quarrels between Huirac's royalty and the villainous of this world – or even Huirac's poorer citizenry – for the Order of Virtue's Citadel to be a king's refuge. Virtue is beleaguered, always. But Virtue will, Elthyriel reflects, win in the end; doubtless it is so appointed . . .

The blue dragon hovered above the Citadel's inner courtyard. Its filigree wings beat up a storm of dust. Squire-acolytes scurried about with heads bent to avoid the wind-blast. Elthyriel, Elected Pontiff and Knight-Patriarch of the Order of Virtue, sat with his armoured hands folded in his lap, in the howdah attached to the great wyrm's back.

Esquires with silken scarves bound across their mouths wheeled out a set of wooden steps covered with purple velvet. The dragon's hovering wings cast spiked shadows against the fortified inner walls of the Citadel. Having it land in the small deep courtyard, with no runway room, would mean a grounded dragon.

Elthyriel unbuckled straps and cords and sprang alertly from his howdah seat. He strode down the steps, dismissing the flocking military aides. The beat of the hovering dragon's wings blew his mane of azure hair about his pointed, pale ears. He swept hair back from his aquiline face, securing it with a knight's headband. His golden eyes shone brighter than the sun on his cusped and spiked armour, brighter than the white surcoat with the Key and Blade of the Order of Virtue embroidered on the breast. Tall, slender; as sharp-edged as his own blade, the elvish Knight-Patriarch stood for a moment still.

The first touch of his boots on the Citadel's flagstones was, despite his elven powers of magery, always something of a relief. Flight made Elthyriel sick.

A flick of his race's magic dismissed the fire-wyrm from its eye-watering, dust-cloud-raising, ear-splitting hover.

A voice called, 'Sieur-Father Elthyriel! Wait!'

The elven Knight-Patriarch strode across the heat-soaked courtyard and into the shadow of the cloisters. The noise of beating wings faded.

'No!' He spoke sharply in elvish. In the common tongue, he added, 'I must face this alone.'

He let his golden eyes rest on the human squire-acolyte until she bowed, clashed sword-hilt to breastplate in salute, and stood aside to let him enter the Citadel.

Inside the fortified bastions, the marble walls shone like cream.

The elven Elected Pontiff let his armoured fingers brush the cool stone as he walked through the galleries. The patterned marble beneath his knightly feet – red, green, cream, brown – reflected the painted ceilings and friezes in the airy halls. Elthyriel quickened his pace. In passing stone statuary he caught polished fragments of his reflection: tall and slender in cusped silver armour, his surcoat whirling about his ankles. With pricked ears and long eyes: the first of his race to wear the Blade and Key.

He paused at the foot of a curving flight of marble steps, and drew an unsteady breath. He walked up the narrowing gyre of the stairs. Tapestries on the walls were figured with constellations as they would appear from the Drowned Lands, and elven maidens playing multi-stringed instruments beneath forgotten or mythical Trees. No rustle from the cloth, now, only the clash of the Knight-Patriarch's steel sabatons.

'*O rider of the martial steed,*' a voice husked in one of the Far South's barbaric tongues, '*behold!*'

The Elected Pontiff turned to face the entrance to the Long Gallery. He lowered his gaze. Huirac's sunlight fell through high windows, bringing a sallow glow to the skin of the being before him.

'Sieur-Father: the work is complete!'

The flaring, bushy mane of her hair shone brown and red, pinned back from her face with the carved bones of small animals; and her eyes were large and lustrous enough to make him suspect some lamia ancestry. Her miniature bronze lips curved. As she strode forward, the minuscule leather-and-chain coverings of her generous breasts and groin clinked. Leather bands and golden torcs bound her upper arms, and she wore calf-strapped sandals, and the empty sheath of a blade that, for her, would have been a greatsword, but that Elthyriel could have wielded as a dagger.

The halfling barbarian stood, hands on her hips, and shoulders proudly back, some three feet and six inches tall.

'All honour to you, Sieur-Father.' Her voice sounded low and musical as she switched to the common tongue.

Averting his eyes from her barely covered breasts, Elthyriel looked over her head into the airy gallery. A hulking form blocked most of the archway; its low-ridged brow, gleaming piggy eyes, and leathery greyish skin marking it as one of the northern orcs. The red headband of a mercenary was knotted about its misshapen skull.

'We done it good! Mistress and me.' The orc beamed dimwittedly. Its swinging knuckles brushed the marble floor tiles. One gristly, powerfully-clawed thumb jerked in the general direction of the gallery walls. 'I done dat.'

The halfling barbarian grinned and reached up to give the orc's bulging loincloth a playful tweak. 'You think I can't do without you, don't you? Muscle, this is the Head of the Order of the Knights of Virtue. You remember the nice elf, Muscle.'

'Duh . . .'

'You can see to it that the Sieur-Father and I are not disturbed.'

'Yur.' The orc shifted its muscular bulk to one side as Elthyriel walked into the gallery, and then sat down firmly on the floor at the entrance. Elthyriel raised one doubtful, elegantly arched brow, in no doubt as to who the orc thought it guarded. He returned his attention to the halfling (or semi-halfling) barbarian.

'Well, Zerra?'

'Well enough.' She whirled with a movement reminiscent of the jungles beyond the Mines of Sulphur, a great-cat swiftness in her small step. Copper coins clanked in her hair and the odour of musk trailed dizzily behind her. 'Who better than a traveller between the worlds to make your maps for you, Eminence? And who better than I, uncivilised and barbaric—'

Glancing back and up, she caught his eye. The Pontiff opened his mouth to contradict her, remembered the Oath of Verity, and closed his mouth again.

'—I, who do not fear to get my hands dirty, to make maps such as these?'

She threw her small arms wide.

Gauze covered the high windows so that the sunlight entered into the gallery as a pale glow and not a searing whiteness.

The air shone with the blue of seas.

From floor to ceiling, twenty feet in height, the gallery's walls were covered in vast frescoed maps.

To Elthyriel's left and right, maps gleamed like great portals. The seas shone a royal blue, the lands rich green and ochre, lettered in gold.

He took a few steps down the gallery.

The maps had the property of seeming to grow sharper in detail the closer one came. Elthyriel felt himself tense; threatened. Twenty feet high, intricately drawn, each map seemed to centre on a single realm or aspect of a world – mountains drawn with snow-capped peaks, each river with its oxbow bends, each port with its outgoing ships, each city with its buildings of great name . . .

'Here is what lies beyond the world of the Twenty-Four Kingdoms,' the barbarian halfling said softly. 'Upon your left hand, the worlds of *magia*. Here is the White Mountain and Prague, whose mercenary soldiers do not know they fight in lands that hide more than the Hermetic knowledge of the Rose . . . And here, the World's Edge, made all of city; where subversion is lit by naphtha flares, and gamblers tell fortunes with bone dice. There is the war-savaged coast of Tunis, where men live on the edge of that Darkness called the Penitence, and disguises and visions of Time abound. Here are the shamen and stone beehive-huts of Tulkys, among islands where the Kraken does not sleep . . . Here, Bazaruk and the Hundred Isles – Keshanu – Orindol and Zu— Oh, and *there*, a fort held by warriors much like my companion—'

Elthyriel snorted.

The halfling hesitated. He waved her to continue, taking a further step between the towering high maps as he did so.

Zerra's rich lilt sounded behind him:

'On your right hand lie the worlds of *scientia*. Silver ships that make their descent upon an azure grassland, where gifts of spun glass do not ensure safety . . . Flesh that is made subject to artifice, and cities may be grown and tended, though some creations are less – wise – than others. Here is Tekne, where ships ride the air, and marriages are made between many. And here, in a half-collapsed city that you could not fly across in a single day, there is betrayal in a single room. And more . . .'

The elf Pontiff bent closer to the painted wall, scrutinising the miniature merchant ships in Carthage's sunless harbour. Someone with knowledge of ropes and prevailing winds had painted this – or (he glanced at the barbarian halfling's sword-callused hands, the orc's paws) somehow caused it to take pictorial shape.

'And is the information in these maps . . . reliable?'

Zerra pushed her hands through her dark sunburst of hair. The movement of her arms lifted her scantily covered breasts. 'Sieur-Father, they can tell only the truth, as it happens, where it happens. I sought far and wide for such magicks – from a nine-tailed fox spirit, and a brother and sister far too much akin, to those philosophers who play with the art of shadows, and women and men who suffer, nameless, under the tyranny of grey armies. From children; from lovers; from solitary survivors. Now all is done.'

'It must tell the truth.'

The female halfling paced onward down the gallery, cat-like; passing from shadow to dim sun and back. The metal bangles on her ankles flaring. 'For what you are offering as reward? Sieur-Father, you have it. These maps are truth-tellers. If the dimensions, planes, and strata of existence are different from those that you yourself know – if hearts are strange, and bodies alien – truth is still truth, within those minds. And you have truth here.'

Elthyriel straightened, only then conscious of how close to the frescoed surface he had been leaning. It seemed that the gold-edged wavelets lapped, the boreal cloud-winds blew, the endless alien grasses on the great Plains of Talinor rippled under two differently-coloured suns, and the stews and slums of New Cabotsland heaved with painted humanity. He swallowed, his mouth dry. Magery prickled in the tips of his inhumanly long fingers.

The Elected Pontiff turned, his hand reaching for the wheel-pommel of his sword.

'And this map-magic works – how?'

The barbarian halfling drew a pin from her hair. The end glinted: a two-centimetre miniature blade. 'Draw blood, Sieur-Father, and shed it on the corner of each map. Then you have but to say *I name thee* – whatever world it shall please you – and you will immediately witness what happens there. And because it is your blood, you shall be the only one who can witness these people. You will see as they see, feel as they feel, know what they know.'

Elthyriel slowly unbuckled the spiked steel gauntlet from his left hand. He dropped it with a clash on the marble tiles. Noon's city heat, ever different from the Forest's shadowed leaves, baked him even through the Citadel's stout walls.

With an old campaigner's disregard for minor pain, he slashed the pad of his seventh finger and slowly went down one side of the gallery and up the other, anointing each great map.

'Cartomancy is one of the neutral magics,' he acknowledged as he came back to where Zerra stood beside the orc at the entrance, 'but I dislike blood-magery, it often has an evil taint.'

The air shimmered blue and gold. Muscle lifted his almost neckless head, tusks glinting, and crooned in a husky bass, 'Pretty . . .'

Still speaking the formal tongue of the southern cities, Zerra said, 'We have endeavoured to serve the Sieur-Father as well as we may.'

'You will have served Virtue,' Elthyriel corrected her. He turned, bare and armoured hands clasped behind his back, to survey the long bright perspective of the gallery. 'We are increasingly besieged by evil – the Horde of Darkness gathers its battalions, east of the Twenty-Four Kingdoms, and prophecies of the Last Battle abound. But that is not our greatest danger. Were it but battle, we might stand on the virtue of good swords and true hearts. But there is a dangerous corruption at work within our borders. We are beset! In friendly fields, in our own streets, in our own houses and hearts – evil conquers the best of us, before we even see its face.'

The silence of the Citadel pressed down on the bright gallery.

'We must have knowledge. Here.' Elthyriel's fist struck his breastplate over the Key and Blade embroidered on his surcoat, and over his heart. Steel clanged dully. 'Forewarned is forearmed. Evil knows us, but we do not know Evil! As Head of this Knightly Order, I take it upon myself to learn. And when I have learned the weaknesses of Evil, that knowledge I will pass on, and so the Darkness in our hearts will be defeated.'

The curvaceous barbarian halfling bowed, flesh shifting, jewellery and empty scabbard chinking. 'A wise and cunning plan, Sieur-Father.'

Elthyriel turned briskly. The elven Elected Pontiff's surcoat swept the marble, hissing; and his armoured feet clanged. His long golden eyes narrowed, looking down at the barbarian cartographer and up at her orc assistant.

'It is an intelligence-gathering technique.' Elthyriel stood with inhuman grace and a swordsman's balance, drawing the authority of a knightly campaigner and an elven mage suddenly about himself.

A snap of his fingers brought the sound of halberds grounded to attention on the marble flagstones one floor below.

'There are at least three hundred of the Knights of Virtue in residence here,' Elthyriel said. The diminutive barbarian and the orc exchanged glances. Elthyriel smiled grimly. 'I am utterly defended against all evil magic. I am also a veteran of the eastern wars, and I have more combat experience, madam, than you and your over-muscled friend put together. I do not particularly think I am unaware of the nature of those who provide magic at a price – for anyone may pay, and you will have had dealings with Evil as well as Virtue.'

'Sieur-Father . . .' The halfling's long-lashed eyes widened. She, unconsciously it seemed, ran her hands down her tiny naked flanks and all-but-naked hips.

'And you may spare me the tricks learned from your succubus mother! If I were to succumb to the temptations of debauchery, I would have done it before now – besides which, the trials for election to Knight-Pontiff remove not only the temptations of the flesh, but the means by which to satisfy them. And as for you—'

Elthyriel gazed at the orc as it rose menacingly to its clawed feet.

'—*sit down.*'

Helplessly responding to authoritative magery, the orc sat down squarely on its rump and regarded its mistress with bewildered anguish. Zerra put her diminutive fists on her hips and glared up at Elthyriel.

'Don't you bully him!'

The elvish Pontiff drew his sword. It caught the gallery's blue light and shone. A smile touched Elthyriel's thin, ascetic lips.

'This is no game. I am no pigeon to be plucked or fool to be drawn into Evil's grasp. Now you will sit quietly, madam, until I have tested your cartomancy. Either it will be the greatest weapon in Virtue's armoury, exposing the secrets of evil to me, or it is a snare and a delusion. And if it is a cheat, or corrupt, then you will face the anger of Virtue – which, you may believe me, is more terrible to the wicked than the wrath of Darkness.'

The halfling barbarian's gaze shifted for the first time away from Elthyriel's face. Her dark eyes fixed on the sword's point. She backed away until the edge of the arched entrance caught her shoulder, and shivered at the touch of bare skin against marble. From below came the sound of Knights of Virtue drilling.

'I have been honest, Sieur-Father, I swear! Give me my payment and let me go – take the orc if you will, they're creatures of Evil, and he's but a hod-carrier after all!' She looked wildly up through dishevelled hair. 'Pay me and spare me!'

'Neither, yet. You must wait. If you are virtuous, you have nothing to fear.'

Elthyriel turned his back on the halfling and the orc. Pacing the length of the gallery, feeling the tingle of cartomancy along his drawn blade, he spoke as if to himself:

'Which first? Which shall it be? There is always Evil – so much, so much of it . . .'

The noon sun shone into the gallery, as bright and warm as the sensation of cartomancy in the air.

'There.' The Pontiff Elthyriel lifted his slender elven blade and pointed it at one of the intricately drawn and painted maps, and spoke the first name:

'North Africa's barren shore . . .'

The Logistics of Carthage

I have put this document together from the different sources included in the Ash papers, and have again translated the languages into modern English. Where necessary, I have substituted colloquial obscenities to give a flavour of the medieval original. Let the casual reader, expecting the Hollywood Middle Ages, abandon hope here.

PIERCE RATCLIFF, AD 2010

'Most women follow their husbands to the wars . . . *I* followed my son.'

Yolande Vaudin's voice came with the grunt and exhalation of physical effort. Guillaume Arnisout looked at her down the length of the corpse they were carrying.

He grinned. 'Your son? You ain't old enough to have a grown-up son!'

She appeared a wonderfully perverse mix of male and female, Guillaume thought. The clinging of her belted mail shirt, under her livery jacket, showed off the woman's broad hips. Her long legs seemed plump in hose, but were not: were just not male. Shapely and womanly . . . He got a kick out of seeing women's legs in hose: entirely covered, but the shape so clearly defined – and hers were worth defining.

She had her hair cut short, too, like a page or young squire, and it curled sleekly onto her shoulders, uncovered, the rich yellow of wet straw. *She* had been able to slip her helmet off before the sergeant noticed: it was buckled through her belt by the chin strap. That meant he could see all of her wise and wicked face.

She's willing to talk, at least. Can't let the opportunity go to waste.

He put his back against the Green Chapel's doors and eased them open without himself letting go of the corpse's ankles. Yolande held her end of the dead woman's body tightly under

the arms, taking the weight as he backed through the door first.
The blue-white flesh was chill against his palms.

Not looking down at what she held, Yolande went on, 'I had
Jean Philippe when I was young. Fifteen. And then, when he
was fifteen, he was called up in the levy, to be a soldier, and I
followed.'

The partly open door let in the brilliant sunlight from the
barren land outside. It glittered back off the white walls of the
monastery's other buildings. Guillaume twisted his head around
to look inside the chapel, letting his eyes adjust, unsure of his
footing in the dimness. 'Didn't he mind you being there?'

Her own sight obviously free of the morning glare, Yolande
pushed forward. The legs of the body were stiff with rigor, and
they shoved against him. Bare feet jabbed his belly. There was
black dirt under the toenails.

He backed in, trying to hold one door open with his foot while
Yolande manouevred the dead woman's shoulders and head
through it.

'He would have minded, if he'd known. I went disguised, I
thought I could watch over him from a distance . . . He was too
young. I'd been a widow five years. I had no money, with his
wages gone. I joined the baggage train and dyed my hair and
whored for a living, until that got old, and then I found I could
put a crossbow-bolt into the centre of the butts nine times out of
ten.'

The chapel's chill began to cool the sting of sunburn on the
back of his neck. His helmet still felt excruciatingly hot to wear.
Guillaume blinked, his sight adjusting, and looked at her again.
'You're *not* old enough.'

Her chuckle came out of the dimness, along with the shape of
the walls and tiled floor.

'One thing a woman can always look like is a younger man.
There's her.' Yolande said, with a jerk of her head downward at
the rigid dead body between them. 'When she said her name
was Guido Rosso, you'd swear she was a beardless boy of
nineteen. You take her out of doublet and hose and put her in
a gown, and call her "Margaret Hammond", and you'd have
known at once she was a woman of twenty-eight.'

'Was she?' Guillaume grunted, shifting the load as they
tottered toward the altar. He walked backward with difficulty,

not wanting to stumble and look stupid in front of this woman. 'I didn't know her.'

'I met her when she joined us, after the fall.' Yolande's fingers visibly tightened on the dead woman's flesh. There was no need to specify which fall. The collapse of Constantinople to the Turks had echoed through Christendom from East to West, four years ago.

'I took her under my wing.' The woman's wide, lively mouth moved in an ironic smile. Her eyes went to the corpse's face, then his. '*You* wouldn't have noticed her. I know what you grunts in the line fight are like – "Archers? Oh, that's those foulmouthed buggers hanging around at the back, always saying 'fuck' and taking the Lord their God's name in vain . . ." I dunno: give you a billhook and you think you're the only soldier on the battlefield.'

Guillaume liked her sardonic grin, and returned it.

So . . . is she flirting with me?

They staggered together across the empty interior of the Green Chapel. Their boots scraped on the black and white tiles. He could smell incense and old wood smoke from the morning's prayers. Another couple of steps . . .

'I used to help her back to the tents, drunk. She was never this heavy. There!' Yolande grunted.

Just in time, he copied her, letting the stiff ankles of the body slide down out of his dirty grip. The body thunked down onto the tiles at his feet. No one had cleaned it up. The bones of her face were beaten in, the mess the same colour as heraldic murrey: purple-red.

His skin retained the feel of hers. Stiff, chill, softening.

'*He Dieux!*' Guillaume rubbed at his back. 'That's why they call it *dead* weight.'

He saw the dead Rosso – Margaret – was still wearing her armour: a padded jack soaked with blood and fluids. Linen stuffing leaked out of the rips. Every other piece of kit from helmet to boots was gone. Either the jacket was too filthy and slashed up to be worth reclaiming, or else the charred and bloodstained cloth was all that was still holding the body's intestines inside it.

Yolande squatted down. Guillaume saw her try to pull the body's arms straight by its sides, but they were still too stiff. She settled for smoothing the sun-bleached, blood-matted hair back. She wiped her hands on her peacock-blue hose as she stood.

'I saw her get taken down.' The older woman spoke as if she was not sure what to do next, was talking to put off that moment of decision – even if the decision was, Guillaume thought, only the one to leave the corpse of her friend.

The light from the leaf-shaped ogee windows illuminated Yolande's clear, smooth skin. There were creases at her eyes, but she had most of the elasticity of youth still there.

'Killed on the galley?' he prompted, desperate to continue a conversation even if the subject was unpromising.

'Yeah. First we were on one of the cargo ships, sniping, part of the defence crew. The rag-heads turned Greek fire on us, and the deck was burning. I yelled at her to follow me off – when we got back on our galley, it had been boarded, and it took us and Tessier's guys ten minutes to clear the decks. Some Visigoth put a spear through her face, and I guess they must have hacked her up when she fell. They'd have been better worrying about the live ones.'

'Nah . . .' Guillaume was reluctant to leave the Green Chapel, even if it was beginning to smell of decomposing flesh. He felt cool for the first time in hours, and besides, there was this woman, who might perhaps be an impressed audience for his combat knowledge. 'You never want to leave one alive under your feet. Somebody on the ground sticks a sword or dagger up and hits your femoral artery or your bollocks – Ah, 'scuse me.'

He stopped, flustered. She gave him a look.

Somewhere in his memory, if only in the muscle-memory of his hands and arms, is the ferocity with which you hack a man down, and follow it up without a second's hesitation – *bang-bang-bang-bang!* – your weapon's thin, sharp steel edges slamming into his face, throat, forearms, belly; whatever you can reach.

He looked away from the body at his feet, a woman to whom some soldier in the Carthaginian navy has done just that. Goose-pimples momentarily shuddered over his skin.

'Christus Viridianus! I couldn't half do with a drink.' He eased his visored sallet back on his head, feeling how the edge of the lining band had left a hot, sweaty indentation in his forehead. 'Say, what *did* happen to your son? Is he with the company?'

Yolande's fingers brushed the Griffin-in-Gold patch sewn

onto the front of her livery jacket, as if the insignia of their mercenary company stirred memories. She smiled in a way he could not interpret. 'I was a better soldier than he was.'

'He quit?'

'He died.'

'Shit.' *I can't say a thing right!* 'Yolande, I'm sorry.'

Her mouth quirked painfully. 'Four months after he went to war. What was I thinking, that I could *protect* him? He was carrying shot in the first siege we were at, and a culverin inside the castle scored a direct hit on the powder wagon. When I found him he'd had both his hands blown off, and he'd bled to death – before his mother could get to him.'

'Jeez . . .' *I wish I hadn't asked.*

She's got to be ten years older than me. But she doesn't look it.

He guessed Yolande had not, like 'Guido Rosso', even temporarily tried to pass as a man.

Because she's a woman, not a girl.

'Why did you stay with the company?'

'My son was dead. I wanted to kill the whole world. I realised that if I had the patience to let them train me, the company would let me do just that.'

In his stunned silence, Guillaume could hear goat bells jingling outside and some shuffling noises closer to hand. A warm breeze blew in through the Green Chapel door, which had lodged open on a pebble. The smell of death grew more present now, soaking into the air. Like the back of a butcher's shop in a heat wave.

'Shit.' He wiped at his mouth. 'It's going to get hot later in the morning. By evening . . . she's going to be really ripe by Vespers.'

Yolande's expression turned harsh. 'Good. Then they can't ignore her. She's going to smell. *That* should get the bloody ragheads moving. The captain's right. This is the only thing to do.'

'But—'

'I don't care what the fucking priests say. *She's going to be buried here like the Christian soldier she is.*'

Guillaume shrugged. For himself, he would as cheerfully have chucked all the bodies overboard, to go with the Carthaginian Visigoths and feed the fish; evidently this wasn't the thing to say to Yolande right now. Especially not if you want to get into the crossbow woman's knickers, he reminded himself.

'If the abbot can ignore the stink she's going to make . . .' He let his grin out, in its different context. 'What do you bet me he'll send for the captain before Sext? Hey, tell you what . . . I bet you a flagon of wine she's buried by midday, and if I lose, I'll help you drink it tonight. What do you say?'

What she would have answered wasn't clear from her expression, and he didn't get to hear a reply.

The scuffling noise that had impinged on his consciousness earlier grew louder, and he spun around and had his bollock-dagger out of its sheath at his belt and pointing at the altar a full second before a boy rolled out from under the altar cloth and sat staring down at the woman soldier's corpse.

'Aw – shit!' Guillaume swore, exasperated.

He saw the thin iron ring welded around the boy's throat. Some slave skiving off work. Or hiding from the big bad Frankish mercenaries – *not that I blame him for that.*

'Hey, *you* – fuck off out of here!'

The youth looked up, not at Guillaume, but at Yolande. There was a quiver about him that might have been fear or energy. He looked to be anywhere in his early or middle teens, a pale-skinned Carthaginian Visigoth with dark hair flopping into his eyes. Guillaume realised instantly, She's thinking he's fifteen.

'I wasn't listening!' He spoke the local patois, but it was plain from his ability to answer that he understood one Frankish language at least. 'I was foreseeing.'

Guillaume flinched, thought, Were we saying anything I don't want to hear back as gossip? No, I hadn't got round to asking her if she fucks younger men— And then, replaying the kid's remark in his head, he queried: 'Foreseeing?'

Silently, the young man pointed.

Above the altar, on the shadowed masonry of the wall, there was no expected Briar Cross. Instead, he saw a carved face – a Man's face, with leaves sprouting from the creepers that thrust out of His open mouth.

The carving was large: perhaps as wide as Guillaume could have spanned with his outstretched hands, thumb to thumb. There is something intimidating about a face that big. Vir Viridianus: Christ as the Green Emperor, as the Arian Visigoths prefer, heretically, to worship Him. The wood gleamed, well polished, the pale silvery grain catching the light. Holm oak, maybe? The eyes had been left as hollows of darkness.

'I dream under the altar,' the young man said, as hieratic as if he had been one of the monastery's own priests, and not barefoot and with only a dirty linen shirt to cover his arse.

Guillaume belatedly realised the scrabbling noise hadn't ceased with their stillness. The hilt of his bollock-dagger was still smooth in his hand. He stepped back to give himself room as the altar cloth stirred again.

An odd, low, dark shape lifted up something pale.

Guillaume blinked, not processing the image, and then his mind made sense both of the shape and of the new smell that the odour of the corpse had been masking. A pale flat snout lifted upward. A dark hairy quadruped body paced forward, flop ears falling over bright eyes . . .

The young man absently reached out and scratched the pig's lean back with grimy fingers.

A pig-boy asleep under the Green Man's altar? Guillaume thought. Sweet dead Jesus on the Tree!

'I had a seeing dream,' the young man said, and turned his face towards the living woman in the chapel; towards Yolande. 'I think it is for you.'

Yolande glanced down at the dead body of Margaret Hammond. 'Not in here! Outside . . . maybe.'

She caught the billman's nod, beside her. He said, 'Yeah, let's go. We don't want to be in here now. We got this place under lockdown, but there's going to be *plenty* of shit flying before long!'

The pig's sharp trotters clicked on the tiles, the beast following as the Visigoth swineherd walked to the left of the altar. The young man pushed aside a wall hanging embroidered with the She-wolf suckling the Christ-child to disclose a wooden door set deep into the masonry. He opened it and gestured.

Yolande stepped through.

She came out in the shade of the wall. The world beyond the shadow blazed with the North African sun's fierceness. A few yards ahead was a grove of the ever-present olive trees, and she walked to stand under them, loving their shade and smell – so little being green after the company's previous stopover in Alexandria.

She heard Guillaume stretch his arms out and groan, happily, in the sun behind her. 'Time enough to go back to Europe in the summer. *Damn*, this is the place to have a winter campaign! Even if we're not where we're supposed to be . . .'

She didn't turn to look at him. From this high ridge of land she could see ten or fifteen miles inland. Anonymous bleak rock hills lifted up in the west. In that direction, the sun was weak. The blue sky defied focus, as if there were particles of blackness in it.

The edge of the Penitence. Well, I've been under the Darkness Perpetual before now . . . We *have* to be within fifty or sixty leagues of Carthage. Have to be.

Guillaume Arnisout sauntered up beside her. 'Maybe Prophet Swineherd here can tell us we're going to wipe the floor with the enemy: that usually pays.'

She caught the billman's sardonic expression focused on the pig-boy. Guillaume's much better looking when he's not trying so hard, she thought. All long legs and narrow hips and wide shoulders. Tanned face and hands. Weather-worn from much fighting. Fit.

But from where I am, he looks like a boy. Haven't I always preferred them older than me?

'If you're offering to prophesy,' Yolande said to the swineherd, more baldly than she intended, 'you've got the wrong woman. I'm too old to have a future. I haven't any money. If any of us in the company had money, we wouldn't be working for Hüseyin Bey and the goddamn Turks!'

'This isn't a scam!' The boy pushed the uncut hair out of his eyes. His people's generations in this land hadn't given him skin that would withstand the sun – where there was sun – and his flush might have been from the heat, or it might have been shame.

She squatted down, resting her back against one of the olive tree trunks. Guillaume Arnisout immediately stood to her left; the Frenchman incapable of failing to act as a lookout in any situation of potential danger – not even aware, perhaps, that he was doing it.

And how much do I do, now, that I don't even know about? Being a soldier, as I am . . .

'It's not a scam,' the boy said, patiently now, 'because I can show you.'

'Now look – what's your name?'

'Ricimer.' He'd evidently watched more than one Frank trying to get their tongues around Visigoth pronunciation and sighed before she could react. 'Okay – Ric.'

'Look, Ric, I don't know what you think you're going to show me. A handful of chicken bones, or rune stones, or bead-cords, or cards. Whatever it is, I don't have any money.'

'Couldn't take it anyway. I'm the Lord-Father's slave.'

'That's the abbot here?' She held her hand high above the ground for theoretical illustration, since she was still squatting. 'Big man. Beard. Loud.'

'No, that's Prior Athanagild. Abbot Muthari's not so old.' The boy's eyes slitted, either against the sun off the white earth or in embarrassment: Yolande couldn't tell which.

She frowned suddenly. 'What's a *priest* doing owning slaves?'

Guillaume put in, 'They're a load of bloody heathens in this monastery: who knows what they do? For fuck's sake, who cares?'

Ric burst out, 'He owns me because he saved me!' His voice skidded up the scale into a squeak, and his fair skin plainly showed his flush. 'I could have been in a galley or down a mine! That's why he bought me!'

'Galleys are bad.' Guillaume Arnisout spoke after a moment's silence, as if driven to the admission. 'Mines are worse than galleys. Chuck 'em in and use 'em up. Lucky if you live twenty months.'

'Does Father Mu—' she struggled over the name, '—Muthari know you go around prophesying?'

The boy shook his head. The lean pig, which had been rootling around under the olive trees, paced delicately on high trotter toes up to his side. Sun glinted off the steel ring in its black snout. Yolande tensed, wary.

The vicious bite of the pig will shear off a man's hand. Besides that, there is the stink, and the shit.

The pig sat down on its rear end, for all the world like a knight's hound after a hunt, and leaned the weight of its shoulder against Ricimer's leg. Ric reached down and again scratched through the hair on its back, and she saw its long-lashed eyes slit in delight.

'Hey!' Guillaume announced, sounding diverted. 'Could do

with some roast pork! Maybe the rag-heads will sell us a couple
of those. 'Lande, I'll go have a quick word, see what price
they're asking. Won't be much; we got 'em shit-scared!'

He turned to go around the outside of the Green Chapel,
calling back over his shoulder, 'Kid, look us out a couple of fat
weaners!'

The thought of hot, juicy, crunchy pork fat and meat dripping
with sauce made Yolande's mouth run with water. The memory
of the smell of cooked pork flooded her senses.

If you burn the meat, though, it smells exactly the same as the
Greek fire casualties on the galley.

'Demoiselle!' Ricimer's eyes were black in a face that made
Yolande stare: his skin gone some colour between green and
white. 'Pigs are unclean! You can't eat them! The meat goes
rotten in the heat! They have tapeworms. Tell him! Tell him!
We don't eat—'

Yolande cut off his cracking adolescent voice by nodding at
the long-nosed greyhound-pig. 'What do you keep them for,
then?'

'Garbage disposal,' he said briefly. 'Frankish demoiselle,
please, tell that man not to ask the Lord-Father!'

So many things are so important when you're that age. A year
or two and you won't care about your pet swine.

'Not up to me.' She shrugged; thought about getting to her
feet. 'I guess the fortune-telling is off?'

'No.' Still pale and sweaty, the young man shook his head. 'I
have to show you.'

The determination of a foreign boy was irritating, given the
presence of Margaret Hammond's dead body in the chapel
behind her. Yolande nonetheless found herself resorting to a
diplomatic rejection.

Young men need listening to, even when they're talking
rubbish.

'If it's a true vision, God will send it to me anyway.'

The boy reached out and tugged at her cuff with fingers dusty
from the pig's coarse hair. 'Yes! God will send it to you *now*. Let
me show you. We'll need to sit with Vir Viridianus and pray in
the chapel—'

The face of the woman came vividly into her mind, as it had
been before the bones were bloodied and the flesh smashed.

Margie – Guido – grinning as she bent to wind the windlass of her crossbow; mundane as a washerwoman wringing out sheets between her two hands.

'Not with Margie in there!'

'You need the Face of God!'

'The Face of God?' Yolande tugged at the leather laces that held the neck of her mail shirt closed. She fumbled down under the riveted metal rings, between her gambeson and linen shirt and her hot flesh, and pulled out a rosary. 'This?'

Dark polished beads with a carved acorn for every tenth bead; and on the short trailing chain, carved simply with two oak leaves and wide eyes, the face of the Green Christ.

The boy stared. 'Where'd you get that?'

'There's a few Arians in the company: didn't you know?' She laughed softly to herself. 'They won't stay that way when the company goes north over the seas again, but for now, they'll keep in good with God as He is here. Doesn't stop them gambling, though. So: you want me to pray to this? And then I'll see this vision?'

He held his hand out. 'Give it to me.'

Reluctantly, Yolande passed the trickle of beads into his cupped palms. She watched him sort through, hold it, lift the rosary so that the carved Green Man face swung between them, alternately catching shafts of sunlight and the darkness of shade. Swinging. Slowing. Stopping.

A pendant face, the carved surface of the wood softly returning the light to her eyes.

Where I made my mistake, she thought later, was in listening to a boy. I had one of my own. Why did I expect this one to be as smart as a man?

At the time, she merely slid under the surface of the day, her vision blurring, her body still.

And saw.

Yolande saw dirt, and a brush. Dusty dirt, within an inch or two of her face. And it was being swept back with a fine animal-hair brush, to uncover—

Bones.

Yolande was conscious of sitting back up on her heels, although she could not see the bits of one's body one usually sees out of peripheral vision. She looked across the trench, conscious that she was in an area of digging – someone throwing up hasty earth-defences, maybe? – and not alone.

A woman kneeling on the other side of the gash in the dirt sat up and put a falling swath of dark hair back behind her equally dark ear. Her other hand held the small and puzzling brush.

'Yes,' the woman said thoughtfully. 'I suppose you would have looked just like that.'

Yolande blinked. Saw cords staked a few inches above the ground. And saw that what also poked out of this trench, blackened in places and in some cases broken, were teeth.

'A grave,' Yolande said aloud, understanding. 'Is it mine?'

'I don't know. How old are you?' The brown woman waved her hand impatiently. 'No, don't tell me; I'll get it. Let me see . . . Mail shirt: could be anywhere from the Carthaginian defeats of Rome onward. But that looks like medieval work. Western work. So, not a Turk.' Her shaped thick eyebrows lowered. 'That helmet's a giveaway. Archer's sallet. I'd put you in the fifteenth century somewhere. Mid-century . . . A European come over to North Africa to fight in the Visigoth-Turkish wars, after the fall of Constantinople. You're around five and a half centuries old. Am I right?'

Yolande had stopped listening at *helmet*. Reaching up, startled, she touched the rim of her sallet. She fumbled for the buckle at her jaw.

Why do I see myself dressed for war? This is a divine vision: it's not as though I can be hurt.

The helmet was gone. Immediately, all the sounds of the area rushed in on her. Crickets, birds; a dull rumbling too close to be thunder. And a clear sky, but air that stank and made her eyes tear up. She ruffled her fingers through her hair, still feeling the impress of the helmet lining on her head. The cool wind made her realise it was morning. Early morning, somewhere in North Africa . . . in the future that exists in God's mind?

'Is that my grave?'

The woman was staring at her, Yolande realised.

'I said, is that my—'

'Don't know.' The words bit down sharply, overriding her own. The dark eyes fixed on her face in concentration, evidently seeing more of it now the sallet was off.

Yolande drew composure around her as she did before a fight, feeling the same churning bowel cramps. *I thought it would be like a dream. I wouldn't be aware I was having a vision. This is terrifying.*

'I won't know,' the woman said, more measuredly, 'until I get to the pelvis.'

That was curious. Yolande frowned. *Some of this I will only discover the meaning of by prayer afterward. Pelvis? Let me see: what do I remember of doctors – is that what she is, this woman, grubbing in the dirt? Odd kind of medic . . .*

'I have borne a child,' Yolande said. 'You don't need to find my bones: I can tell you that myself.'

'Now that would be something.' The woman shook her head. 'That would be really something.'

The woman wore very loose hose, and ankle boots, and a thin doublet with the arms evidently unpointed and removed. Her Turkish-coffee skin would take the sunlight better, Yolande thought. *But I would still cover up long before Nones, if it were me.*

The woman sounded sardonic. 'Finding a female soldier who was a mother – what kind of an icon would that be?'

Yolande felt a familiar despair wash through her. *Why is it always the women who don't believe me?*

'Yes, I've been a whore; no, I'm not a whore now.' Yolande repeated her catechism with practised slickness. 'Yes, I use a crossbow; *yes*, I have the strength to wind the windlass; *yes*, I am strong enough to shoot it; *yes*, I can kill people. Why is it so hard to believe? I see tradeswomen in butcher's yards every day, jointing carcasses. Why is it so difficult to think of women in a similar trade? That's all this is.'

Yolande made a brief gesture at what she could feel now: her mail shirt and the dagger and falchion hanging from her belt.

'It's just butchery. That's all. The only difference is that the animals fight back.'

She has been making the last remark long enough to know that it usually serves only to show up any ex-soldiers in a group. They will be the ones who laugh, with a large degree of irony.

The dark-haired woman didn't laugh. She looked pained and disgusted. 'Do you know what I was before I was an archaeologist?'

Yolande politely said, 'No,' thinking, *A what?*

'I was a refugee. I lived in the camps.' Another shake of the other woman's head, less in negation than rejection. 'I don't want to think there has been five, six hundred years of butchery *and nothing's changed*.'

The wind swept across the diggings, which evidently were not defences, since they made no military sense. They more resembled a town, Yolande thought, as one might see it from a bluff or cliff overlooking it from a height. Nothing left but the stumps of walls.

'Every common man gets forgotten,' Yolande said. 'Is that what this is showing me? I – Is this her grave, not mine? Margie's? I know that few of us outlive our children's memories. But I – I need to know *now* that she's recognised for what she is. That she's buried with honour.'

Margaret would have died fighting beside any man in the company, as they would have died at *her* shoulder. This is what needs recognition, this willingness to trust one another with their lives. Recognition – and remembrance. *Honour* is the only word she would think of that acknowledged it.

The woman reached down and brushed delicately at the hinge of a jawbone. 'Honour . . . yes. Well. Funerals are for the living.'

'Funerals are for God!' Yolande blurted, startled.

'If you believe, yes, I suppose they are. But I find funerals are for the people left behind. So it's not just one more body thrown into a pit because cholera went through the tents, and it was too dangerous to leave the bodies out, and there was no more wood for pyres. So they've got a grave marker you can remember, even if you can't visit it. So they're not just – one more image on a screen.'

Screen? A little sardonically Yolande reflected, We are not the class of people who are put into tapestries, you and I. The best I'll get is to be one of a mass of helmets in the background. You might get to be a fieldworker, while the nuns spend all their skills embroidering the lord's bridle and all his other tack.

'If you believe?' Yolande repeated it as a question.

'If there was a God, would He let children die in thousands just because of dirty water?'

If the specifics evaded Yolande, the woman's emotion was clear. Yolande protested, 'Yes, I've doubted, too. But I see the evidence of Him every day. The priests' miracles—'

'Oh, well. I can't argue with fundamentalism.' The woman's mouth tugged up at the side. 'Which medieval Christianity certainly is.'

A voice interrupted, calling unintelligibly from somewhere off in the destroyed village settlement.

'I'm coming!' the woman shouted. 'Hold on, will you!'

The settlement's layout was not familiar, Yolande realised with relief. It was not the monastery.

So if I am fated to die on this damned coast, it isn't yet.

The woman turned her head back. There was an odd greediness about the way she studied Yolande's face.

'They'll put it into the books as "village militia". Any skeleton with a female pelvis who's in a mail shirt must have picked up armour and weapons as an act of desperation, defending her town.'

There was desperation in her tone, also. And self-loathing; Yolande could hear it.

And this mad woman is not even a soldier. What can it matter to her, *digging in the dirt for bodies, whether Margie and I are remembered as what we were?*

The woman pointed at her. Yolande realised it was the mail shirt she was indicating. 'Why did you do this! War? Fighting?'

'It . . . wasn't what I intended to do. I found out that I was good at it.'

'But it's wrong.' The woman's expression blazed, intense. 'It's sick.'

'Yes, but . . .' Yolande paused. 'I enjoy it. Except maybe the actual fighting.'

She gave the woman a quick grin.

'All the swanning around Christendom, and gambling, and eating yourself silly, and fornicating, and *not working* – that's all great. I mean, can you see me in a nunnery, or as a respectable widow in Paris? Oh, and the getting rich, if you're lucky enough to loot somewhere. That's good, too. It's worth risking getting killed every so often, because, hey, *somebody* has to survive the field of battle; why not me?'

'But killing other people?'

Yolande's smile faded. 'I can do that. I can do all of it. Except the guns. I just choke up, when there's gunfire. Cry. And they

always think it's because I'm a woman. So I try not to let anyone
see me, now.'

The dark-skinned woman rested her brush down on the
earth.

'More *sensitive.*' The last word had scorn in it. She added,
without the ironic tone, 'More sensible. As a woman. You know
the killing is irrational.'

Yolande found herself self-mockingly smiling. 'No. I'm not
sensible about hackbuts or cannon – the devil's noise doesn't
frighten me. It makes me cry, because I remember so many dead
people. I lost more than forty people I knew, at the fall.'

The other woman's aquiline face showed a conflicted sadness
difficult to interpret.

Yolande shrugged. 'If you want *scary* war, try the line fight.
Close combat with edged weapons. That's why I use a crossbow.'

The woman's dignified features took on something between
sympathy and contempt.

'No women in close-quarters fighting, then?'

'Oh, yeah.' Yolande paused. 'But they're idiots.'

Guillaume's face came into her mind.

'*Everybody* with a polearm is an idiot . . . But I guess it's easier
for a woman to swing a poleaxe than pull a two-hundred-pound
longbow.'

The other woman sat back on her heels, eyes widening. 'A
poleaxe? *Easier?*'

'Ever chop wood?' And off the woman's realisation, Yolande
gave her a *there you are* look. 'It's just a felling axe on a long
stick . . . a thinner blade, even. Margie said the axe and hammer
were easier. But in the end she came in with the crossbows,
because I was there.'

And look how much good *that* did her.

'Not everybody can master the skills of crossbows or arque-
buses . . .' This was an argument Yolande had had before, way
too often. 'Why does everybody think it's the *weapons* that are
the difficult thing for a woman fighting? It's the guys on your
own side. Not the killing.'

The fragments of bone and teeth in the earth had each their
own individual shadow, caused by the sun lifting higher over
the horizon.

'The truth is important.' Yolande found the other woman watching her with wistfulness as she looked up. Yolande emphasised, 'That's the *truth*: she was a soldier. She shouldn't have to be something else just so they can bury her.'

'I know. I want proof of women soldiers. And . . . I want no soldiers, women *or* men.' The woman recovered her errant lock of hair and pushed it back again. Yolande saw the delicate gold of an earring in the whorl there: studded barbarically through the flesh of the ear's rim.

'Of course,' the woman said measuredly, getting to her feet, 'we have no idea, really. We guess, from what we dig up. We have illuminations, dreams. I visualise you. But it's all stories.'

She stared down at Yolande.

'What matters is who tells the stories, and what stories never get told. Because people *act* on what the histories are. People live their lives based on nothing better than a skull, a fragment of a mail ring and a misremembered battle site. People *die* for that "truth"!'

Moved by the woman's distress, Yolande stood up. She rubbed her hands together, brushing off the dust, preparatory to walking forward to help the woman. And it was the oddest sensation possible: she rubbed her hands together and felt nothing. No skin, no warm palms, no calluses. Nothing.

'Yolande! *Yolande!*'

She opened her eyes – and that was the most strange thing since she had not had them shut.

Guillaume Arnisout squatted in front of her, his lean brown fingers holding her wrists in a painful grip. He was holding her hands apart. The skin of her palms stung. She looked, and saw they were red. As if she had repetitively rubbed the thin, spiky dust of the courtyard between them.

A cool, hard, flexible snout poked into her ribs, compressing the links of her mail shirt. Yolande flinched; turned her head. The sow met her gaze. The animal's eyes were blue-green surrounded by whites: unnervingly human.

What have I been shown? *Why?*

A yard away, Ricimer lay on his side. White foam dried in the corners of his mouth. Crescents of white showed under his eyelids.

Yolande turned her wrists to break Guillaume's grip on her

forearms. The sow nosed importunately at her. *It will bite me!*
She knelt up, away from it: leaned across, and felt the boy's face
and neck. Warm, sweaty. Breathing.

'Kid had a fit.' Guillaume was curt. ' 'Lande, I met your sergeant: the Boss wants us. The report on Rosso. I had to say you
were praying. You okay? We got to go!'

Yolande scrambled up onto her feet. It was cowardice more
than anything else. There was no assurance that the boy would
live. She turned her back on him and began to walk away, past
the chapel.

Visions! Truly. Visions from God – to *me*—!

'No. I'm not okay. But we have to go anyway.'

'What did you see? Did you see anything? 'Lande! Yolande!'

The captain's wiry brass-coloured beard jerked as he bellowed at
the assembled monks.

'She will have a soldier's burial!' His voice banged back flatly
from the walls of the monastery's large refectory. 'A Christian
burial! Or she stays where she is until she rots, and you have to
bury her with a *bucket*!'

Johann Christoph Spessart, the captain of the company of the
Griffin-in-Gold, was the usual kind of charismatic man. Guillaume would not have been in his company if he had not been.
He was no more than five feet tall, but he reminded Guillaume
of a pet bantam that Guillaume's mother had kept – a very
small, very bright-feathered cock that intimidated everything in
the yard, chicken or not, and gave the guard mastiffs pause for
thought.

He was a lot more magnificent back in France, Guillaume
reflected, when he wore his complete, if slightly battered,
Milanese harness. But even highly polished plate armour
doesn't lend itself to the hot sun of the North African coast.

Now, like half his men, Spessart was in mail and adopted a
white Visigoth head cloth and loose trousers tucked into tough
antelope-hide boots.

Still looks like a typical Frankish mercenary hard case. No
wonder they're shitting themselves.

'You. Vaudin.' The Griffin captain pointed to Yolande. The
woman's head came up. Guillaume's gut twisted at her blank,
bewildered stare.

Dear God, let the captain take it for piety and think she's been praying for her dead friend! What *happened* back there?

'Yes, sir?' Her voice, too, was easily recognisable as female. The monks scowled.

Spessart demanded, 'Is Margaret Rosso's body laid out before the altar of God?'

Guillaume saw Yolande's mouth move, but she did not correct the captain's mangling of the dead woman's name. After a second, voice shaking, she said, 'Yes, sir.'

It could have been taken for grief: Guillaume recognised shock.

'Good. Organise a guard roster: I want a lance on duty at the chapel permanently from now on, beginning with yours.'

Yolande nodded. Guillaume watched her walk back towards the main door. *I need to talk to her!*

He found himself uncomfortably on the verge of arousal.

'Arnisout?'

'Yes, Captain.' Guillaume looked down and met the German soldier's gaze.

'What does the Church say about Christian burial, Arnisout?'

Guillaume blinked, but let the sunlight coming off the refectory's whitewashed walls be the excuse for that. 'Corpses to be buried the same day as they die, sir.'

'Even a foot soldier knows it!' The Griffin captain whirled around. 'Even a billman knows! Now, I don't go so far as some commanders – I don't make my soldiers carry their own shrouds in their packs – but I keep to the Christian rites. Burial the same day. She died *yesterday*.'

'I appreciate your point of view, *qa'id*.' The abbot of the monastery hid his hands in his flowing green robes. Guillaume suspected the man's hands were shaking, and that was what he desired to hide. 'I hesitate to call anyone damned for heresy. Christ knows who worships Him truly, no matter what rite is used. But we *cannot* bury a scandalous woman who dressed as a man and fought – killed.'

Guillaume found himself admiring the small spark of wrongheaded courage. The abbot spoke painfully, from a bruised and swollen mouth.

'*Qa'id*, the answer is still no.'

And now he calls Spessart *qa'id*, 'general'!

Guillaume grinned at the plump abbot: a man in his early middle age. *Not surprising, given what happened yesterday* . . .

Guillaume had been up on the ramparts, squinting across the acres of sun-scalded rock to see what progress the hand chain was making. From up here, the men had looked tiny. A long line of figures: crates and barrels being passed or rolled from one man to the next, all the way up the chine from the desolate beach. Food. And—

One of the men ducked out of line, arms over his head, a sergeant beating him; shouting loudly enough that Guillaume could hear it. A water barrel had splintered and spilled. *Okay, that's down to nine hundred-odd* . . .

Guillaume, squinting, could just see part of the hull of the beached galley. The round-bellied cargo ships were anchored a few hundred yards offshore, in deeper water; the side boats ferrying the stores ashore as fast as they could be rowed. White heat haze hung over the blue sea and islands to the north.

A shadow fell on Guillaume's shoulder. *The corporal, of course: he has to catch me the one minute I'm not doing anything.*

'If we're really lucky, there could be any number of Visigoth galleys out there, not just the two that bushwhacked us . . .' Lance Corporal Honoré Marchès came to stand beside Guillaume, gazing satirically out to sea. 'Not like we're up the Turkish end of the Med now, with their navy riding shotgun on us.'

'We could do with the Turkish shipwrights.' At Marchès' look, Guillaume added, 'Carpenters say they were right, sir. Patching up the galley is going to need skilled work. They can't do it. We're stuck here.'

'Oh, Boss is going to love that! How's the unloading coming along, Arnisout?'

'Good, sir.' Guillaume turned around, away from the coast. It was obvious to a military eye: the monastery here had taken over an ancient Punic fort. One from the days when it had been a forested land, and any number of armies could march up and down this coast road. Now the fort was covered with monastic outbuildings as a log is covered with moss, but the central keep would be still defensible in a pinch.

'I've got the lances storing the cargo down in the deep cellars, sir.'

A large enough cargo of food that it could feed an army – or at least a Turkish division coming up from Tarābulus, somewhere to the east now, which is what it's intended for. And *water*. On this coast, water. The days when you could bring an army up the coast road from Alexandria to Carthage without resupplying by sea are gone with the Classical age.

'Yeah, that should do it.' Marchès turned, signalling with a nod, and led the way down the flight of stone steps from the parapet to the ground. Over his shoulder, he remarked, 'Fucking lot of work, but the Boss is right: we can't leave it on board. Not with no galley cover. Okay, Arnisout, get your team and come along with me, Boss is going to have a little talk with the abbot here.'

Guillaume nodded obedience and bellowed across to Bressac and the others who shared the ten-man tent that made them a team. Bressac waved a casual hand in acknowledgement.

Marchès snapped, 'Now, Arnisout! Or do you want to tell the Boss why we kept him waiting!'

'No, sir! Bressac!'

There was some advantage in having one's officer be part of the captain's command group, Guillaume thought as he yelled at his men, pulling them out of the chain of sweating mercenaries swearing with all apparent honesty that physical labour was for serfs and varlets, not honest soldiers.

One is never short of news to sell, or rumours to barter. On the other hand – we get to be there when Spessart proves *why* he's a mercenary captain.

Guillaume had arrived sweating in the big central hall the monks used as their refectory, and not just because of the heat. A barked order got his men into escort positions around the captain – a round dozen European mercenaries in jacks and hose, most with billhooks resting back across their shoulders in a gleam of silver-grey, much sharpened metal.

'Nothing until the Boss says so,' Marchès warned.

The familiar tingle of tension and the piercing feeling in the pit of his belly began to build into excitement. Guillaume halted as Spessart did. A great gaggle of entirely unarmed men flooded into the hall from the door at the far end, wearing the green robes of the heretic Christianity practised here. All uncertain, from their expressions, whether these Franks considered them proper clerks and so a bad idea to kill.

The hall smelled of cooking. Guillaume's gut growled as he stood at Marchès' shoulder. The older man kept his gaze on the hefty oak doors by which they had entered, in case someone should try to interrupt the captain during his deliberations. A wind blew in from the arid land outside, smelling of goats and male sweat and the sea.

Guillaume was conscious of the stiff weight of the jack buckled around his chest and the heat of plate leg harness, articulations sliding with oiled precision – and of how *safe* one feels, ribs and groin and knees protected. A delusional safety, often enough; but the feeling obstinately remains.

'I understand there's trouble with the burials,' Spessart rasped. His eyes swept over the African priests as a group, not bothering, evidently, to concern himself with who exactly might be their Father-in-Christ. 'What's the problem? Bury the bodies! We're not working for your masters, but common Christian charity demands it. Even if you are the wrong sort of Christians.'

Ah, that's our tactful captain. Guillaume bit his lip to keep his smile from showing.

A tall man with a black-and-white badger beard stepped forward. waving his arms. 'She isn't a man! She is an abomination! We will not have her soil the rocks of the graveyard here!'

'Ah. It's about Rosso. Now look, Father Abbot—'

A shorter, plumper man, perhaps five and thirty years old, stepped past the bearded man to the front of the group. He interrupted.

'I am abbot here. Prior Athanagild speaks for us all, I am afraid. We will bury no heathen whores pretending to be soldiers.'

'Ah, *you're* the abbot. Tessier! I ordered you to find this man for me before now.'

'Sir.' The knight who was the officer of Guillaume's lance glared at Corporal Marchès.

Before there could be recriminations, which was entirely possible with Tessier – the Burgundian knight was not a man to keep his mouth shut when it was necessary – Spessart turned back to the plump abbot.

'You, what's your name?'

'Muthari,' the monk supplied. Guillaume saw a flash of annoyance from the man's eyes. 'Abbot Lord-Father Muthari, if we are being formal, Captain.'

'Formal be fucked.' Spessart took one step forward, reversing the grip he had on his war hammer. He slammed the end of the shaft into the abbot's body between ribs and belly.

The monk sighed out a breathless exclamation, robbed of air by sheer pain, and dropped down on his knees.

'How many messengers have you sent out?' Spessart said. He stared down, evidently judging distance, drew back his boot, and kicked the gasping man. It would have been in the gut, but the abbot reared back and the boot caught him under his upper lip. Guillaume bit his own lip again to keep from laughing as the captain nearly overbalanced.

'How many of your rats have you sent off to Carthage?'

Blood leaked out of the abbot's mouth. 'I – None!'

'Lying shitbag,' Spessart announced reflectively. He shifted his grip expertly on the war hammer, grasping the leather binding at the end of the wooden shaft, and lightly stroked the kneeling man's scalp with the beaked iron head. A streak of blood ran down from Muthari's tonsure.

'None, none, I haven't sent anybody!'

'All right.' Guillaume saw the captain sigh. 'When you're dead we'll see if your prior's any more cooperative.'

Spessart spoke in a businesslike tone. Guillaume tried to judge if that made it more frightening for the abbot, or if the chubby man was decoyed into thinking the captain didn't mean what he said. Guillaume's pulse beat harder. Every sense keyed up, he gripped the wooden shaft of the bill he carried, ready to swing it down into guard position. Constantly scanning the monks, the hall, his own men . . .

'Tessier.' Spessart spoke without looking over his shoulder at the down-at-heels knight. 'Make my point for me. Kill one of these priests.'

Guillaume's gut cramped. Tessier already had his left hand bracing his scabbard, his thumb breaking the friction seal between that and the blade within. His other hand went across to the hilt of the bastard sword. He drew it in one smooth movement, whipping it over and down, aiming at a tall skinny novice at the front of the group.

The skinny novice, not over twenty and with a badly cropped tonsure, froze.

A tall monk with wreathes of grey-white curls flowing down

his shoulders and the face of an ex-*nazir*, a Visigoth corporal, straight-armed the skinny guy out of the way.

The novice stumbled back from the outstretched arm—

Tessier's blade hit with a chopping, butcher's counter sound. Guillaume winced. The *nazir's* arm fell to the floor, cut off just below the elbow. Arterial blood sprayed the six or seven men closest. They jolted back, exclaiming in disgust and fear.

The ex-*nazir* monk grunted, his mouth half open, appalled.

'*He Dieux!*' Tessier swore in irritation. He ignored the white-haired man, stepped forward, and slammed the yard-long steel blade toward the side of the skinny novice's head.

Guillaume saw the boy try to back up, and not make it.

The sword's edge bit. He dropped too fast and too heavily, like a falling chunk of masonry, smacking facedown into the flag-stones. A swath of red and grey shot up the whitewashed wall, then dripped untidily down. The young man sprawled on the stone floor under it, in widening rivulets of blood.

There is no mistaking that smell.

Tessier, who had brought two hands to the hilt on his stroke, bent and picked up a fold of the dead man's robe to clean his sword. He took no notice of the staring eyes a few inches away from his hand, or of the shouting, screaming crowd of monks.

Two of them had the white-haired man supported, one whipping his belt around the stump, the other talking in a high-pitched voice over the screaming; both of them all but dragging the man out – towards the infirmary, Guillaume guessed.

In the silence, one man retched, then vomited. Another made a tight, stifled sound. Guillaume heard a spatter of liquid on the flagstones: someone involuntarily pissing from under their robes.

The tall, ancient prior whispered, his voice anguished and cracking. 'Huneric! *Syros* . . .'

It looked as if he could not take his eyes off the young novice's sliced, bashed skull and the tanned, freckled forearm and hand of the older man.

The limb lay with the body on the stone floor, in wet blood, no one willing to touch it. Guillaume stifled a nauseous desire to laugh.

He saw Tessier glance back at the captain, face red. Anger and shame. *Messy. Not a clean kill*. The knight sheathed his sword and folded his arms, glaring at the remaining monks.

Guillaume understood the silence that filled the refectory. He had been on the other side of it. *Men holding their breaths, thinking. Not me, oh Lord God! Don't let me be next!* One of the slaves back at the kitchen door snivelled, crying wetly. His own chest felt tight. *The captain of the Griffin-in-Gold has long held to the principle that it's easier to kill one or two men at the beginning to save hassle later on.*

Guillaume wiped his mouth, not daring to spit in front of the captain. *He's right. Of course. Usually*.

'Now.' Spessart turned back briskly toward Abbot Muthari signing to Tessier with his hand.

'*Wait!*' The Lord-Father sprawled back untidily on the floor, his bare legs spread and visible under his robe. 'Yes! I sent a novice!'

'Only one?'

The man's eyes were dazed. Muthari looked as though he could not understand how he came to be on the floor in front of his juniors, undignified, hurt, bleeding.

If he had any sense, he'd be grateful. Could be him *dead or maimed. The captain is only keeping him alive because his men are used to him as their leader.*

'No! Two! I sent Gauda, but Hierbas insisted he would go after.'

'That's better. Which way did you send them?'

'Due west,' the abbot choked out. *Not with pain or fear,* Guillaume saw, *but shame. He's betraying them in front of his congregation.* 'I told them to stay off the main road from here, from Zarsis—'

Ah, is that where we are? And is it anywhere near where we should *have dropped the supply cache?*

Close enough to Tarābulus for the Turks to get here in time?

Guillaume kept his face impassive.

'They will be aiming for the garrison at Gabès. But travelling slowly. Because it is so far.' The Lord-Father Muthari sat motionless, terror on his face, watching Spessart.

'There. I knew we could come to a mutual agreement.'

The German soldier bent down, which did not necessitate him bending far, and held out his hand.

Too afraid not to, the fatter and taller man reached up and gripped it. Guillaume saw Spessart's face tense. He hauled the monk up onto his feet with one pull and a suppressed grunt of effort.

'This place will do as well as any for us to wait for our employers. Tessier, take your men out and find and capture the novices.'

'Sir.'

Tessier beckoned Marchès. Guillaume glanced back and got his team together and ready with only eye contact.

'You cannot behave like this!' he heard Athanagild protesting; and Muthari's voice drowning the bearded man out: 'Captain, you will not harm any more of us; we are men of God—'

Three or four hours' searching in the later part of the afternoon had brought them up with the fleeing novices. To Guillaume's surprise, Tessier kept them alive. Guillaume, mouth filled with dirt by far too much scrambling up rocky slopes and striding down dusty gullies, was only too happy to prod them home with blows from the iron-ferruled butt end of his billhook.

He had seen the fugitives as he marched back into the refectory today. One, his gaze full of hatred, had whispered loudly enough to be heard. 'I'll see you in Hell!'

Guillaume had grinned. 'Save me a seat by the fire . . .'

Whether or not it was deliberate, today the German captain halted on the spot where the skinny, tall novice had been killed eighteen hours earlier.

The flagstones were clean now, but the whitewashed wall held a stain, the scrubbed, pale outlines of elongated splashes.

'I have no more patience!' Spessart snapped.

'Captain . . . *qa'id* . . .' Muthari blinked soft brown eyes as if in more than just physical pain. 'Syros is dead. Huneric has now died. There must be no more killing – over a *woman*.'

At the mention of the ex-*nazir* monk Huneric, Guillaume saw Tessier assume an air of quiet satisfaction. Vindication, perhaps.

'I don't want to kill a monastery full of priests,' the captain remarked, his brilliant gaze turned up to Muthari. 'It's bad luck, for one thing. We're stuck here until the Turkish navy turns up with expert carpenters, or the Turkish army turns up as reinforcements. Meantime, I'd rather keep you priests under lockdown than kill you. I *will* kill you, if you put me in a situation where I have to.'

The abbot frowned. 'Who knows who will come first? Your Turkish masters – or a legion from Carthage?'

'Oh, there is that. It's true we won't be popular if some *Legio* turns up on the doorstep here and finds an atrocity committed.'

Johann Spessart smiled for the first time. Guillaume, as ever, could see why he didn't do it that often. His teeth were yellow and black, where they were not broken.

'Then again, if Hüseyin Bey and his division come up that road . . . they'll want to know why we didn't crucify every last one of you on the olive trees.'

Prior Athanagild looked appalled. 'You would kill true Christians for a Turkish bey?'

'We'll kill anybody,' Spessart said dryly. 'Turk, Jew, heathen; Christian of whatever variety. I understand that's what they pay us for.'

Abbot Muthari stiffened.

The fat priest is getting his balls back, Guillaume thought. *Bad idea, Abbot.*

Abbot Muthari said, 'We *are* priests. We *are* gifted with the grace of God. You cannot force us to perform the small miracles of the day here. *You* may not need them. Can you know that all your men feel the same way?'

'No.' Spessart's voice dropped to a harsh rasp. 'I don't care. They're my men. They'll do what I tell them.'

The captain raised his head to gaze up at the monks. It might almost have been comic. Guillaume would have bet Johann Christoph Spessart couldn't even be seen from the back of the crowd. He would be hidden below other men's shoulders. *But that isn't the point.*

Guillaume felt his chest tighten with disgust. *Ashamed,* he thought, *On the field of battle, yes. But killing in cold blood turns my gut. Always has.*

Spessart raised his voice to be heard all across the refectory. The voice of the commander of the Griffin-in-Gold was used to carrying through shrieks, trumpets, gunfire, steel weapons ripping into each other, the screams of the dying. Now it eradicated whispers, murmurs, protests.

Spessart said, 'Understand me. I know very well, the sea is

only a half mile from here. There are caves under this fort. Plenty of places to dispose of an embarrassing corpse. *Don't do it.*'

Spessart paused. An absolute silence fell. Guillaume could hear his own heart beat in his ears.

The mercenary captain said, 'If her corpse is moved, if you even attempt the sacrilege of touching her body except to inter it, *I will kill every human being over the age of thirteen in this place.*'

Yolande's lance handed over to Guillaume's at the Green Chapel without any opportunity for him to speak to her.

He fretted away three hours on guard, while Muthari and his fellow monks celebrated the offices of Sext and Nones, the abbot with his nose screwed up but singing the prayers all the same, carefully walking around the blackening, softening body of Guido Rosso/Margret Hammond, as if she could not be deemed to share in the previous day's prayers for their own dead.

Guillaume and the squad occupied the back of the chapel, restless, in a clatter of boots, butt ends of billhooks, and sword pommels rubbing against armour.

'Spessart'll do it,' the gruff northern *rosbif*, Wainwright, muttered. 'Done it before. But they're *monks.*'

'Wrong sort of monks!' Bressac got in.

Wainwright scowled. 'They're Christian, not heathen. I don't want to go to Hell just because I screwed some monks.'

The Frenchman chuckled. 'How if it were nuns, though?'

'Oh, be damned and happy, then!'

It was, to give them credit, ironically said. *And I have a taste for gallows humour myself.* Guillaume allowed himself a glance down the chapel at the celebrants: all white-faced, many of them counting out prayers on their acorn rosaries. 'He's left us no choice now.'

There were murmurs of agreement. No man as reluctant as one might hope; long campaigning numbed the mind to such things.

All of the priests sang as if they were perfectly determined to go on this way through Terce, Sext, Nones, Vespers . . . all through the long day until sunset, and beyond. Compline, Matins, Prime. Every three hours upon the ringing of the carved hardwood bell.

I could pray, too, Guillaume reflected grimly, but only that they'll have given in before my next shift on guard. This place is getting *high*.

When Nones was sung – with some difficulty, down by the altar, because of the clustering flies – the Lord-Father Abbot paced his way back up the chapel, and stopped in front of Guillaume.

Before the Visigoth clerk could speak, Guillaume said grimly, 'Bury Margaret Hammond, master. All you have to do is say a few words over her and put her under the rocks.'

The boneyard was just visible through the open chapel doors – distant, away on the southern hill slopes. Cairns, to keep jackals and kites off. Red and ochre paint put on the rocks, in some weird Arian ceremony. But nonetheless a sort-of-Christian burial.

'Tell me, *faris*,' the abbot said, 'if we were to offer the heretic woman's heart in a lead caskct, to be sealed and sent home to her family and buried there, would that content your captain?'

Guillaume felt an instant's hope. The Crusaders practised this. But . . .

'No. He's put his balls on the line for a burial here. The guys want it. *Do* it.'

'I would lose my monastery – the monks, that is.'

Guillaume had an insight, staring at Muthari perspiring in his robes: power always appears to lie with the leaders. But it doesn't. Under the surface, they're all trying to find out what the men need, what the men will leave for if they don't have it . . .

Guillaume shrugged.

The abbot pulled out a Green Emperor rosary, kissed it, and returned to the altar.

When Guillaume's shift ended and he came out into the blazing afternoon sun, he thought: Where the hell is Yolande!

His mind presented him with the sheer line of her body from her calf and knee to her shapely thigh. The lacing of her doublet stretched taut over the curves of her breasts. He felt the stir and fidget of his penis under his shirt, inside his cod-flap.

'Good God, Arnisout,' the lanky blond billman, Cassell, said, walking beside him toward the tents. 'We know what *you're* thinking! She's old enough to be your grandmother.'

'Yours, maybe,' Guillaume said dryly, and was pleased with himself when Cassell blushed, now solely concerned with his

own pride. Cassell was a billman very touchy about being seventeen.

'Catch you guys around.' Guillaume increased his pace, walking off towards the area where the camp adjoined the old fort.

Yolande Vaudin – oh, that damn woman! Is she all right? Did
she really have a *vision?*

He searched the clusters of tents inside the monastery walls,
the crowded cook wagon, the speech-inhibiting clamour of the
armourers' tent, and (with some reluctance) the ablutions shed.
He climbed up one flight of the stone steps that lined the inner
wall of the keep, with only open air and a drop on his right
hand, and stared searchingly down from the parapet.

Fuck. He narrowed his eyes against the sun that stung them.
Where is she?

Yolande walked down the shadow of the western wall, in the
impossible afternoon heat. She pulled at the strings of her coif,
loosening it, allowing the faint hot breeze to move her hair. Off
duty, no armour, and wearing nothing but hose, a thin doublet
without sleeves, and a fine linen shirt, she still sweated enough
to darken the cloth.

The rings in their snouts had not been sufficient to prevent
the pigs rootling up the earth here. Fragments, hard as rock,
caught between her bare toes. She paused as she came to the
corner of the fort wall, reaching out one arm to steady herself
and brushing her hand roughly across the sole of her foot.

As she bent, she glimpsed people ahead under a cloth awning.
Ricimer. The abbot Muthari. Standing among a crowd of sleeping hogs. She froze. They did not see her.

The priest swiftly put out a hand.

What Yolande assumed would be a cuff, hitting a slave in the
face, turned out to be a ruffle of Ric's dark hair.

With a smile and some unintelligible comment, the Lord-
Father Muthari turned away, picking his way surefootedly
between the mounds that were sleeping boars.

Yolande waited until he had gone. She straightened up.
Ricimer turned his head.

'Is that guy Guillaume with you? Is he going to kill my pigs?'

'Not right now. Probably later. Yes.' She looked at him. 'There
isn't anything I can do.'

He was white to the thighs with dust. Yolande gazed at the lean lumps of bodies sprawled around him in the shade cast by linen awnings on poles. Perhaps two dozen adult swine.

'You have to do something! You owe me!'

'Nobody owes a slave!' Yolande regretted her spite instantly. 'No – I'm sorry. I came here to say I'm sorry.'

Ric narrowed his eyes. His lips pressed together. It was an adult expression: full of hatred, determination, panic. She jerked her head away, avoiding his eyes.

Who would have thought? So this is what he looks like when he isn't devout and visionary. When he isn't meek.

The young man's voice was insistent. 'I gave you God's vision. You left me. You owe me!'

Yolande shook her head more at herself than him as she walked forward. 'I shouldn't have left you sick. But I can't do anything about your pigs. We won't pass up fresh pork.'

One of the swine lifted a snout and blinked black eyes at her. Yolande halted.

'I want to talk to you, Ric,' she said grimly. 'About the vision. Come out of there. Or get rid of the beasts.'

The boy pushed the flopping hair back out of his face. The light through the unbleached linen softened everything under the awning. She saw him glance at her, at the pigs – and sit himself down on the earth, legs folded, in the middle of the herd.

'You want to talk to me,' he repeated.

Yolande, taken aback, shot a glance around – awnings, then nothing but low brick sheds all along the south wall, driftwood used for their flat roofs. Pig sheds. Stone troughs stood at intervals, the earth even more broken up where they were. A *dirty, dangerous animal*.

'Okay.' She could not help her expression. 'Okay.'

She stepped forward, ducking under the awning, her bare feet coming down within inches of the round-bellied and lean-spined beasts.

The boar is the most ferocious of the wild animals: that is why so many knights have it as their heraldry. And what is a pig but a tame boar?

And they're huge. Yolande found herself treading up on her toes, being quiet enough that she heard their breathy snorts and snores. What had seemed no more than dog-sized, walking with Ricimer, was visibly five or six feet long laying down on its side. And their heads, so much larger than human heads. It's not right for a *face* to be so big.

'Now – you can tell me about the vision.' Yolande kept her conciliatory tone with an effort. 'And I mean *tell* me about it. No more putting visions in my head! I don't know what I'm meant to make of that. What God wants me to do. But I do know it scared me.'

The young man ignored her.

'I'm getting a farrowing shed ready.' Ric nodded across to the huts against the wall.

Yolande saw one with the wooden door standing open, and bracken and thin straw piled inside on sand used for litter.

So those strip fields do yield a grain or two – I thought we were never going to eat anything else but tunny.

'Screw your goddamned farrowing shed! I want to know—'

'So I ought to be working,' he interrupted, glancing around, as slaves do. '*I* want to speak to *you*.'

'What about?'

Another nod of his head, this time taking in the sprawled and noon-dozing swine. 'These. They *have* to be safe!'

'Ric, they're . . . *pigs*.' Yolande took her courage in both her hands and squatted down. This close, there was a scent to the pigs – more spicy and vegetable than those back home. Particularly the boars'. And they were not dirty. A little dusty only.

Mud – that's what I'm missing. I expected them to be covered in mud and shit . . . Maybe they have dust baths here, like chickens.

She felt the shaded earth cooler under her hands, and sat down nervously, shifting her gaze from one to the other of the large animals. 'Your church is different; Leviticus, I suppose. "Unclean flesh". We just . . . eat them.'

'*No, not these!*'

His vehemence startled the animals. One of the younger swine got up from a heap of gilts, with much thrashing and rolling, and stood with its head hanging down, peering directly at Yolande. It began to move towards her, agile now it was on its feet.

About to jump back, she felt Ric's large hand grip her upper arm. If she had not been so disturbed, he would not have come that close. She restrained herself only an instant from smashing her elbow into his nose.

'You can stroke her.'

Held, Yolande was motionless on the ground for just long enough that the pig ambled up to her, wrinkled its slightly damp snout forward and back, scenting her.

The boy's hand pushed her arm forward. Her fingers touched the sow's warm flank. She expected it to snap; tensed to snatch back her hand.

It slowly moved, easing itself down towards the earth – and fell over sideways.

'*What?*' Yolande said.

The boy's hand released her. 'Her name is Misrātah – like the salt marshes? Scratch her chest. She likes that.'

Misrātah had her eyes closed. Yolande sat, more terrified by the animal's proximity than by the fight on the deck of the galley. It shifted its snout closer to her thigh and – eyes still closed – gave a firm and slightly painful nudge.

'Hell!' she yelped.

Ricimer's strained face took on a grin. 'You don't want her to rootle you hard! Scratch her!'

Yolande reached out again to the slumped, breathing body of the pig. She encountered a warm, soft pelt. She dug her fingers into the coarse hair over the pig's ribs. The body rolled – leaning over, disclosing the teat-studded belly. A grunt made the flesh vibrate under Yolande's fingers. The dense, solid body shifted. She startled.

'You just got to be careful. They're big and heavy.' The young man spoke with a quiet professionalism, as if they were not in the middle of a quarrel. 'She would only hurt you without meaning it.'

'Oh, that's a comfort!'

The sow's long body rolled over even further onto its side, with a resonant short grunt. Misrātah stretched out all four long legs simultaneously, as a dog stretches, and then relaxed.

'It's solid.' Yolande pushed the pads of her bare fingers against meat-covered ribs. 'Hard.'

'It's all muscle. That's how come they move so fast? *Bang!*' His illustration, palms slammed together, made a couple of the larger boars lift their heads, giving their swineherd a so-human stare.

'One minute they're standing, next second they're in your lap. All muscle. Three hundred pounds. You can't force them out of the way. If they want something, they'll push their way to it.' Ric gave her a mock malicious grin of warning. 'Whatever you do, don't stop scratching . . .'

There was something not entirely unpleasant about sitting on the dry ground, surrounded by breathing clean animals, with her fingers calling out a response of satisfaction from Misrātah.

'Oh . . . I get it.' Yolande ran tickling fingers down the hairless skin. The pig in front of her let its head fall back in total abandon, four legs splayed, smooth belly exposed. It grumpled. 'They're like hounds.'

He pounced. 'So how can you *eat* them!'

'Yeah, well, you know what they say about hounds – eight years old, they're not fit to do more than lick ladles in the kitchen. Nine years old, they're saddle-leather.'

'*Shit.*' Ric put his hand over his mouth.

'No one's going to listen to me, frankly,' Yolande said. 'If I go to Spessart . . . He's over in the command tent right now, thinking, "Rosso's giving me trouble even when she's *dead.*" What's he going to say if another woman comes in and asks him to please not slaughter the local swine? I'll tell you what he'll say: "Get the fuck—"'

'All right!'

Her thoughts completed it: Get the fuck out of here and back to the baggage train; quit using the crossbow, because you're plain crazy.

Prostitution again, at my age?

Ric glared at her, rigid and angry. His fury and disappointment stung her in a raw way she had thought could no longer happen.

'Ask Guillaume Arnisout.' The words were out of her mouth before she thought about them. *But it isn't that stupid an idea.* 'Guillaume's a man. He might get listened to. If you can get him to speak for you. Wouldn't the abbot try to speak for you? He's your master?'

'My master—'

He broke off. A different pig heaved herself up, walked forward, dipped her snout to Ric's knee where he sat, and with slow deliberation let herself fall down with her spine snug up against his leg.

'Lully . . .' The boy slid his fingers down behind her ear, into the soft places. Yolande thought, Dear God, I recognise a *pig*. This is the one he had at the chapel.

'I've been here since I was eight.' Ric's girl-long lashes blinked down. 'I don't remember much before. A banking house. The men used to travel a lot. I used to hold the horses' reins for them.'

Yolande could picture him as a page, small and slender and dark-haired. He would have been attractive, which was never an advantage for a slave.

I wonder how much the fat Lord-Abbot paid for the boy? And how much he would ask for him now?

She caught herself. No. Don't be a fool. The most you can afford is a few derniers for someone from the baggage train to help armour you up. You can't pay the price needed to get a full-time page or varlet.

Maybe I could borrow the money . . .

'And then,' Ric said. 'And – then. The Lord-Father came. Abbot Muthari. I have to know!'

Her expression must be blank, she realised.

'My *master*. Your *qa'id*'s going to kill him, isn't he?'

'If he doesn't bury Margaret.'

'He won't do that.' Ricimer wiped at his face, leaving it white with dust, his eyes showing up dark and puffy. 'He won't. I know he won't.'

'Look, you'll be all right; you can pass for under thirteen, if you try—'

'That's not it!' His anger flashed out at her. 'The Lord-Father – he mustn't be killed! You're not *going* to kill him. Please!'

'Muthari?' Yolande found herself bewildered. 'You want *Muthari*'s life, too? Your master?'

'Yes!'

He spoke vehemently, where he sat, but with a restraint unlike such a young man. Certainly her son Jean-Philippe was never prone to it.

He doesn't want to startle his animals.

'I'll tell.' His eyes fixed on her. 'I'll tell my abbot and your *qa'id*. You had a vision. You did sorcery.'

Yolande stared. A threat? 'You said it was from God! That's what I came here to ask – what it means – what I'm supposed to do with – *Sorcery?*'

'It was from God. But I'll say it wasn't.'

Slaves have to be shrewd. She had seen slaves in Constantinople who manoeuvred the paths of politics with far more skill than their masters. Being able to be killed with no more thought than men give to the slaughter of a farmyard animal will do that to you. Slaves listen. Notice. Notice what Spessart says to Muthari, and how the Lord-Father reacts, and what the mercenary captain needs right now . . . because knowledge, information, that's all a slave has.

Ric said, 'I counted. There's a hundred of you. There are seventy monks here. Your *qa'id* needs the place kept quiet. If he hears about a woman having visions from God . . . that's trouble. He can't have trouble.'

Well, damn. *Listen* to the boy.

Yes, the company's no larger than a *centenier* right now. And, yes, he can threaten to tell Spessart. The captain's always been half and half about women soldiers: wants us when we're good, doesn't want any of the trouble that might come with us.

'I'll tell them you made me do it,' he added. 'The sorcery. They'll believe it.'

'They will, too.' Yolande gazed down at him. *Because I'm old enough to be your mother.* 'They probably would burn me. Even Spessart wouldn't tolerate a witch,' she said quietly. 'But Spessart doesn't have any patience. He solves most problems by killing them. Including heretic priests who have heretic visionaries in their monastery.'

Ric stared, his face appalled.

Yolande put her hands in the small of her back, stretching away a sudden tension. 'The Griffin-in-Gold is a hard company. I joined to kill soldiers, not noncombatants. But there's enough guys here who just don't care who they kill.'

A crescent of light ran all along both underlids of the boy's eyes. A gathering of water. She watched him swallow, shake his head, and suppress all signs of tears.

'I *won't* have the Lord-Father die. I won't have my pigs *eaten*.'

'You may not be able to stop it.' Yolande tried to speak gently.

'I had another dream.'

For a second she did not understand what he had said.

His voice squeaked: adolescent. 'I don't understand it. I didn't *understand* the *first* one.'

Yolande's breath hitched in her throat. No. He's lying. Obviously!

'Another dream for me?'

Another vision?

This is some kind of threat to strong-arm me into protecting his pigs and Muthari's arse. . . . *Muthari*. His master. His pigs.

He's just trying to look after his own.

Without preamble, not stopping for cowardice, she demanded, 'Give me this second vision, then!'

The wind blew the scent of rock-honey, and pigs, and she was close enough to the young man to smell his male sweat. Ric's dark eyes met hers, and she saw for the first time that he was fractionally taller than she.

He said, 'I *have* to! It's God's. If I could hold it back any longer, until you promise to help . . . I *can't*. We have to go to the Green Chapel!'

There's no time. I'm on duty again in an hour. And how can I sneak him in there to have a vision – *if* I do – with the captain's guard on the place?

The next thought followed hard on that one, and she nodded to herself.

'Meet me outside the chapel. Two hours. Vespers. We'll see if you're lying or not.'

A young voice emerged from the depths of the dimly lit Green Chapel. 'Christ up a Tree, it stinks in here!'

Guillaume grinned as he entered from checking the sentries. 'Cassell, I think that's the idea . . .'

Ukridge and Bressac snickered; Guillaume decided he could afford not to hear them. *The more bitching they do about this duty, the less likely they are to slide off to the baggage-train trollops and make me put them up for punishment detail in the morning.*

Bressac got up and paced around on the cold tiles, evidently hoping to gain warmth by the movement. He did not look as though he were succeeding. Now that it was past Vespers, it was cold. Guillaume pulled his heavy lined wool cloak more securely around him. The other Frenchman walked over to the woman's body, where it lay swollen and chill in front of the altar, under a lamp and the face of Vir Viridianus.

'You'd think she wouldn't smell so much in this cold.'

'This is nothing. You want *real* smell, you wait until tomorrow.' Guillaume, feeling the tip of his nose numb with cold, found it difficult to remember the blazing heat of the day. He kept it in his memory by a rational effort.

Bressac paced back to the group. 'I went to an autopsy once. Up in Padua? Mind, that corpse was fresh; smelled better than this . . . They were doing it in a church. Poor bitch had her entrails spilled out in front of two hundred Dominican monks. And she was some shop owner's wife: doubt she even showed an ankle in public before.'

'Some of those Italians . . .' Ukridge gave a shrill whistle at odds with his beef-and-bread English bulk. 'Over in Venice, they wear their tits out on top of their gowns. I mean, shit, nipples and everything . . .'

'So that's how you know the Italian for "get your tits out for the lads"?' Cassell's chuckle spluttered off into laughs and yelps as the big man got him in a headlock and ruffled his coarse brown hair.

A voice over by the door exclaimed, 'Viridianus! I prefer the company of *real* pigs to you guys.'

Yolande! Guillaume saw Bressac look up and chuckle with an air of familiarity as Lee and Wainwright, outside, passed the crossbow woman in. *She certainly picks her moment.*

Bressac called, 'Come on in, 'Lande. Bring a bit of class to the occasion.'

Guillaume managed to stop himself from bristling at the other Frenchman's informality. It was no more than the usual way of treating her: somewhere between a whore and a friend and a mother. For a moment he felt shame about his desire for the older woman.

A shorter figure emerged from the dark shadows behind the crossbow woman. Ric's still alive, then, Guillaume thought sourly.

Not that much shorter, he abruptly realised. Is she really no taller than a youth?

'You ought to be pious,' the boy said, with an apparent calm that Guillaume found himself admiring. It took courage to face down heavily armed Frankish mercenaries. 'If she's your friend, this dead woman, you don't want to disgrace her.'

'Little nun!' Ukridge jeered, but it was *sotto voce*.

Guillaume judged it time to speak. 'The boy's right. Rosso's still one of the company. This is a dead-watch, no matter why the Boss put her here. Let's have a little respect.'

There was muttering, but it seemed to be in general agreement, with no more than the normal soldiers' dislike for being told to do something.

'She's still working for the company,' Guillaume added. 'Or she will be, when the sun comes up.'

Bressac snickered approvingly.

Guillaume nodded to Yolande, feeling awkwardly formal in his command role – *even if it is only five grunts and the metaphorical dog . . . hardly company commander*. He studied her as well as he could in the light of two pierced-iron lanterns. Even with the door of one lantern unlatched – he leaned over and unhooked the catch – it was difficult to read her expression by a tallow candle's smoky, reeking light.

Yolande's mouth seemed tightly shut, the ends of her lips clamped down in white, strained determination. Her eyes were dark and they met his with such directness that he almost flinched away, thinking she could read his lust.

But she doesn't seem to mind that.

She's afraid, I think.

'I might need you to bring me back, Guillaume.'

Ignoring the puzzled remarks of the other men, Guillaume exploded. 'You've come here for that? You're not letting that damn pig-boy practise sorcery on you again!'

She flinched at the word. 'It isn't sorcery. He has grace. It's prayer.'

'It's dangerous.' Guillaume blinked a sudden rolling drop of sweat out of one eye. The moisture was stingingly cold. 'You were somewhere else, 'Lande. Your spirit was. What happens if you don't come back? What happens if he has another fit! What if you do? What if God's too much for you?'

The holm-oak carving over the altar was only a collection of faint highlights off polished wood, not distinguishable as a face.

With a shudder he would have derided in another man,

Guillaume said, 'I believe in God. I've seen as many miracles as the next man. I just don't believe in a *loving* God.'

'It's all right.' Her smile suggested that she was aware of his reasons for being overprotective. He searched for signs that she was angry. He saw none.

'I'm going to pray now.' She walked to the altar. Guillaume saw her reach for the lantern there. She bent down, holding it close to the corpse.

'*Shit* . . .' The stench made Yolande clamp her hand over her mouth.

By the lantern's light, Guillaume saw that Margaret Hammond's bare hands and feet were white on top, purple underneath, flesh shrinking back to the bone. On duty here, you could watch her flesh shrink, swell, bubble. The front of her head, where her face had been, was black, lumpy, wriggling with mites. Her slim belly had blown out, and contained by the jack she wore, it made her corpse look ludicrously pregnant.

Yolande's voice sounded low, angry. 'She should have been buried before we saw her like this!'

She knelt down clumsily on the cold stone tiles by Margaret Hammond's reeking body. The knees of her hose became stained with the body fluids of her friend. She closed her eyes, and Guillaume saw her place her hands across her face – across her nose, likely – and then bring them down to her breast, where she still wore the mail shirt over her gambeson and doublet.

Layers of wool, for the cold nights . . . under which would be her breasts, warm and soft.

Breasts pulled with the suckling of one boy who would be older now than Cassell, if he had lived. *I need to forget that. It's – confusing.*

'What's she doing?' Cassell asked in a subdued voice.

'The boy gets visions. *Gives* visions,' Guillaume corrected himself.

A mixture of respect and fear was in the air. God has His ways of sending visions, dreams, and prophecies to men. Usually through His priests, but not always. It is not unusual for someone born a peasant, say, in a small village near Domremy, to rise to be a military prophet by God's grace.

Guillaume shivered. And if Ricimer is that, too? The Pucelle put the king of France back on his throne. The last thing we need is a male Pucelle out of Carthage, knocking the Turks arse over tit. Not while we're signed up with the Bloody Crescent.

The young man brushed past Guillaume, towards Yolande, catching his gawky elbow against the heavy wool cloak. Guillaume watched Ric's back as he walked up behind her. His voice was gruff, with the cracks of young manhood apparent in it.

'I still have your rosary.'

'Yes. Yes, of course.' Yolande put her hand to her neck. She let it fall down onto her thighs, where she knelt. 'Show me more.'

'But – these men—'

'Show me more.'

It's nothing but the repetition of the words in a different tone. Guillaume doubted she even knew she was doing it. But her voice carried the authority of her years. And the authority that comes with being shot, shelled, and generally shat on, on the field of battle. *The pig-boy doesn't stand a chance.*

'I need to pray first.' Ric's thinner frame was silhouetted against the altar, where the second lantern stood. He knelt down beside the crossbow woman. Out of the corner of his eye, Guillaume saw that Bressac and Cassell had both linked their hands across their breasts and closed their eyes. Sentimental idiots.

Ukridge put his water container to his lips, drank, wiped his face with the back of his hand, and suppressed a loud belch to a muffled squeak.

The pig-boy sat back on his heels and held up the woman's rosary. The dark wood was barely visible against the surrounding dimness of the chapel.

'Look at the light.' Ric's voice sounded more assured. 'Keep looking at the light. God will send you what is good for you to know. Vir Viridianus, born of the Leaf-Empress, bound to the Tree and broken . . .'

The words of the prayer were not different enough. They skidded off the surface of Guillaume's attention. He found himself far from pious, watching the woman and the boy with acute fear.

Yolande stood up.

She said, very clearly, *'Shit.'*

She fell backwards.

She fell back utterly bonelessly. Guillaume threw himself forward. He got his sheepskin-mittened hands there just in time to catch her skull before it thumped down on the tiles. He yelled with the pain of the heavy weight crushing his fingers between floor and scalp-padded bone. Bressac and Cassell leaped forward, startled, drawing their daggers in the same instant.

Guillaume stared at the pig-boy across Yolande's body. Yolande Vaudin, laid out beside Margaret Hammond's corpse, in precisely the same position.

'*Get her back!*'

Sand had sifted into the gaps between the small flat paving stones so no grass or mould could grow between them. Dry sand. No green grass.

One of the old Punic roads, Yolande thought. Like the Via Aemilia, down through the Warring States, but this doesn't look like Italy . . .

The oddest thing about the vision, she thought, was that she was herself in it. A middle-aged and tired soldier. A woman currently worrying that hot flushes and night sweats mean she's past bearing another child. A woman who curses the memory of her only, her dead, son because, God's teeth, even stupid *civilians* have enough sense to stay alive – even a goddamned *swineherd* has enough sense to stay alive, in a war – and he didn't. He died like just another idiot boy.

'Yeah, but they do,' a stranger's voice said, and added in a considering manner: '*We* do. If shit happens.'

The stranger was a woman, possibly, and Yolande smiled to see it was another woman disguised as a man.

This one had the wide face and moon-pale hair of the far north, and a band of glass across her eyes so that Yolande could not see her expression. Her clothes were not very different from those that Yolande was familiar with: the hose much looser, and tucked into low, heavy boots. A doublet of the same drab colour. And a strange piece of headgear, a very round sky-coloured cap with no brim. But Yolande has long ago discovered in her trailing around with the Griffin-in-Gold that all headgear is ridiculous. Between different countries, different peoples, nothing is so ridiculous as hats.

'This is Carthage.' Yolande said suddenly. 'I didn't recognise it in the light.'

Or, to be accurate, it is not far outside the city walls, on the desert side. A slope hides the main city from her. Here there are streets of low, square, white-painted houses, with blank frontages infested with wires. And crowds of people in robes, as well as more people in drab doublets and loose hose.

And the sky is brilliant blue. As brilliant as it is over Italy, where she has also fought. As bright and sun-infested as it is in Egypt, where the stinging power of it made her eyes water, and made her wear the strips of dark cloth across her eyes that filter out something of the light's power.

Carthage should be Under the Penitence. Should have nothing but blackness in its warm, daytime skies.

This is a vision of the world much removed from me, if the Penitence is absolved, or atoned for.

'What have you got to tell me?'

'Let's walk.' The other woman smiled and briefly took off the glass that shielded her eyes. She had brilliant blue cornflower eyes that were very merry.

Yolande shrugged and fell in beside her. The woman's walk was alert, careful. She expects to be ambushed, here? Yolande glanced ahead. There were six or seven men in the same drab clothing. Skirmishers? Aforeriders? Moving as a unit, and this woman last in the team. They walked down the worn paving of the narrow road. People drifted back from them.

This is a road I once walked, a few years back, under the Darkness that covered Carthage.

And that, too, is reasonable: it's very rare for visions to show you something you haven't seen for yourself previously. This is the road to the temple where she sacrificed, once, for her son Jean-Philippe's soul in the Woods beyond the living world.

A stiff, brisk breeze smelled of salt. She couldn't see the sea, but it must be close. Other people passed their chevauchée, chattering, with curious glances – at the woman in the loose drab hose, Yolande noted, not at herself. The woman carried something under her arm that might have been a very slender, very well-made arquebus, if such things existed in God's world. It must be a weapon, by the way that the passing men were reacting to it.

Topping the rise, Yolande saw no walls of Carthage. There was a mass of low buildings, but no towering cliffs. And no harbours full of the ships from halfway around the world and more.

No harbours at Carthage!

Of the temple on this hill, nothing at all remained but two white marble pillars broken off before their crowns.

A dozen boys were kicking a slick black-and-white ball around on the dusty earth, and one measured a shot and sent the ball squarely between the pillars as she watched.

That's English football! Margie described it to me once . . .

Yolande watched, walking past, trailing behind the team. Children playing football in the remains of Elissa's chapel. Elissa, called the Wanderer, the *Dido*; who founded this city from Phoenician Tyre, eons before the Visigoths sailed across from Spain and conquered it. Elissa, who was never a mother, unless to a civilisation, so maybe not a good place for a mother's prayer.

Nothing left of Elissa's temple now, under this unfamiliar light.

'Is that what I'm here to see?' she asked, not turning to look at the woman's face as they walked. 'Do you think I need telling that everything dies? That everything gets forgotten? That none of us are going to be remembered?'

'Is that what you need?'

The strange woman's voice was measured, with authority in it, but it was not a spiritual authority; Yolande recognised it.

'Is *that* it? That you're a soldier?' Yolande smiled with something between cynicism and relief. 'Is that what I'm being shown? That we will be recognised, one day? You're still disguised as a man.'

The woman looked down at herself, seemingly startled, and then grinned. 'Of course. That's what it would look like, to you. And you'd think my dress blues were indecent, I should think. Skirts at knee-level.'

Yolande, ignoring what the woman was saying in favour of the tone in which it was said, frowned at what she picked up. 'You . . . don't think I'm here, do you?'

The other woman shook her head. 'This is just a head game. Something I do every time we check out the ruins.'

The woman's strange accent became more pronounced.

'We're not over here to fight. We're here to stop people fighting. Or, that's what it should be. But . . .'

A shrug, that says – Yolande fears it says – that things are still

the same as they ever were. Yolande thought of the 'archaeologist', her hands muddy with digging, her face impassioned
with revulsion at the prior behaviour of what she unearthed.

'Why *are* we doing this?' she said.

'You mean: it's such a shit job, and we don't even get the
recognition?' The woman nodded agreement. 'Yeah. Good
question. And you can never trust the media.'

A grinding clatter of carts going past sounded on the road at
the foot of the hill. No, not carts, Yolande realised abruptly. Iron
war wagons, with culverin pointed out of the front, like the
Hussites use in battle. No draft beasts drawing them, but then,
this is a vision.

'Judges, chapter one, verse nineteen!' Yolande exclaimed,
made cheerful. Father Augustine used to read the Holy Word
through and through, at his classes with the prostitutes in the
baggage train. She remembered some parts word for word.
' "And the Lord was with Judah; and he drave out the inhabitants of the mountain; but could not drive out the inhabitants of
the valley, because they had chariots of iron"!'

'K78s.' The other woman grinned back. 'Counter-grav tanks.
They're *crap*. The K81's much better.'

Yolande peered down toward the road. Dust drifted up so that
she could no longer see the pale-painted chariots of iron. 'So
why not use the – K81 – instead?'

The other woman's tone took on a familiar and comfortable
sound. Soldiers' bitching.

'Oh . . . because all the tank transporters are built to take the
K78. And all the workshops are set up for it, and the technicians
trained to repair it. And the aircraft transport bay pods are made
to the width of the K78's tracks. And the manufacturers make
the shells and the parts for the K78, and the crew are trained to
use the K78, and . . .'

She grinned at Yolande, teeth white below her strip of dark
glass. 'Logistics, as always. You'd have to change everything. So
we end up with something that's substandard because that's
what we can support. If we had the K81s, we'd be stuffed the
first time one of them stripped its gears . . .'

Yolande blinked in the amazing Carthaginian sunlight. 'To
change one thing . . . you have to change everything?'

The other woman stepped back from the edge of the bluff,

automatically scanning the positions of the men in her team. 'Yeah. But, be fair: the K78 was state-of-the-art in its day. It just takes decades to get the next version up and running and into the field—'

A black hole appeared on the woman's shoulder, far to the right, just below the collarbone.

In a split second, Yolande saw the woman's white face turn whiter and her hand go to her doublet. Saw her scream, her hand pressing a box fixed to her breast. Saw the neat wound flow out and darken all the cloth around it. And heard, in the dry morning, the very muffled crack that was too quiet, but otherwise resembled gunfire.

Soldiers shouted, orders erupting. The woman took three long, comically staggering steps and ended rolling into the shade and cover of one of Elissa's pillars. There were no children. The slick-surfaced ball remained, perfectly still on the sun-hardened earth.

'Doesn't anything change?' Yolande demanded. She stood still, not diving for cover. 'Why *are* we doing this?'

The woman shouted at the small box as if it could help her.

Not a serious wound, unless things have gravely changed – and yet they may have: obviously have, if an arquebus ball is no longer heavy enough to shatter the bones of a shoulder joint.

Yolande saw puffs of dust and stone chipping kick up out of the old Punic road toward her. The hidden man with the arquebus is walking his shots onto target, like a gun crew with a culverin, sniping, as she does with her crossbow. But the reload time is amazing: *crack-crack-crack!*, all in the space of a few rapid heartbeats.

I can't be hurt in a vision.

The world went dark with a wrench that was too great for pain, but pain would come afterward, in a split second—

No pain.

Dark . . .

It's dark because this is the chapel, she realised.

The dark of a church, at night, lit only by a couple of lanterns.

She was lying on the glazed tiles, she discovered. Or at least was in a half-sitting position, her torso supported against the knees and chest of Guillaume Arnisout. He was shivering, in the stone's chill. His wool cloak was wrapped around her body.

She thought she ought to be warm, with his body heat

pressed so close against her, but she was freezing. All cold – all except what had been hot liquid between her legs, and was now tepid and clammy linen under her woollen hose.

Embarrassed, she froze. Bad enough to be female, but these guys can just about cope with thinking of her as a beautiful hard case: a woman warrior. If they have to see me as a fat, middle-aged woman, cold white buttocks damp with her own pee . . . No romance in *that*.

Ah – the cloak – they can't see—

'You had foam coming out of your mouth.' The youngest man, Cassell, spoke. She could hear how scared he was.

'You had a fit.' Guillaume Arnisout sounded determined about it. 'I warned you, you stupid woman!'

Ukridge peered out of the dark by the door. 'It isn't Godly! It's a devil, in't it!'

Yolande snickered at his expression: a big man wary as a harvest mouse. She extricated her arm from the cloak and wiped her nose.

'It's grace,' she said. 'It's just the same as Father Augustine when he prays – prayed – over the wounded. Calling on God's grace for a small miracle. A vision's the same.'

Guillaume's voice vibrated through her body. 'Is it? 'Lande, you have to stop this!'

She thought Guillaume sounded the least scared so far. And way too concerned. She moved, unseen in the near dark, wrapping the cloak's folds around her now-chilled thighs.

I hope they can't read him as easily as I can. He'll be ribbed unmercifully. And he's . . . well. He doesn't deserve that.

She looked around. 'Where's Ric?'

'Ric is the swineherd?' Bressac enquired, looming up into the candlelight from the darkness by the far door. 'We threw him out. No need to be afraid of him, Yolande. We can keep him away from you.'

'But – did he have a fit? Was he hurt?'

Guillaume shrugged, his chest and shoulder moving against her back, unexpectedly intimate.

She realised she was smelling the stink of meat gone off.

Lord God! That's still Margie, there. Tell me how this vision helps *her*.

'I don't understand,' she whispered, frustrated.

Guillaume Arnisout grinned, mock consoling. ' 'Salright, girl. Me neither!'

Yolande reached her hand up and touched the rough stubble on his jaw.

She would pray, she would sleep, she would question the boy again, and maybe one of the Arian priests, too: she knew that. For this moment, all she wanted to do was rest back against the man who held her, his straggling black hair touching her cheek, and his arms shuddering with cold because he had covered her.

But it's never that easy.

She got to her feet, fastening the cloak around her neck, and walked to the altar. She reached up and took the carved Face down from the wall.

She heard one of the men curse behind her. It came down easily. Someone had fixed the Face there with a couple of nails and a length of twisted wire, and under it, covered but not expunged, was painted a woman's face.

Her nose was flat, and her eyes strangely shaped in a way that Yolande couldn't define. The worn paint on the stone made her skin look brownish-yellow. There were leaves and berries and ferns in her hair, so many that you could barely see her hair was black. Her eyes, also, were painted black – black as tar.

There was no more of her than the face, surrounded by painted flames. Elissa, who died on a pyre? Astarte the child-eater goddess?

'Elissa,' the young man Cassell said, prompt on her thoughts. Still holding the Face in her hands, she turned to look at him.

He blushed and said, 'She founded New City, *Qart-hadasht*, before the Lord Emperor Christ was born. She set up the big temple of Astarte. The one the Arians took over, with the dome? She took a Turkish priest off Cyprus, on her way from Tyre – a priest of Astarte. That's why they think Carthage is their Holy City. The Turks, I mean. Like Rome, for us. Even though there's no priests of Astarte there any more.'

Yolande lifted the carved oak Face and replaced it, with a fumble or two, against the bitter chill stone wall.

'They'll be pleased when they get here,' Guillaume's gruff voice said behind her. 'The Beys. She looks one tough bitch, too.'

'They used to burn their firstborn sons as sacrifices to her,' the Frenchman, Bressac, added. *'What?* What did I say?'

'I'm going back to my tent,' Yolande said. 'Guillaume, if you don't mind, I'll give you the cloak back in the morning.'

Guillaume Arnisout slipped out in the early morning for his ablutions.

If I move *fast,* I can call on Yolande before rollcall . . .

It was just after dawn. The air was still cool. He picked his way among the thousands of guy ropes spider-webbing between squad tents. A few early risers sat, shoulders hunched, persuading camp fires to light. Moisture kept the dust underfoot from rising as his boots hit the dirt. He scratched in the roots of his hair as he walked down past the side of the monks' compound to the lavatory.

It was a knock-together affair – whatever the Arian monks were, they weren't carpenters. A long shack was built down the far side of the compound on the top of a low ridge, so that the night soil could fall down into the ditch behind, where it could be collected to put on the strip fields later.

Best of luck with mine, Guillaume thought sardonically. Usually, with the wine in these parts, I could do it through the eye of a cobbler's needle. Now? You could load it into a swivel gun and shoot it clear through a castle wall . . .

The lavatories were arranged on the old Punic model: a row of holes cut into wooden planks, and a sponge in a vinegar bowl. With a sigh, Guillaume pulled the lacing of his Italian doublet undone. He slid doublet and hose down in one piece, to save untying the points at his waist that joined them together. Slipping his braies down, he sat. The morning air was pleasant, cool with just his shirt covering his torso.

So – am I going to make my approach to Yolande? Because I think the door is unbarred. I *think* so . . .

He sat peacefully undisturbed for a number of minutes, having the place to himself. He listened to the clatter of pans from the monks' kitchen, and heard a rustling of rats here and there across the courtyard and below him in the ditch. There was more movement now the sun was up, but this yard remained deserted.

Abbot Muthari and his monks rang for service every hour

through the night. They *can't* keep that up; they're bound to quit today and plant her . . . she's starting to leak over the floor.

If it was me, I wouldn't worry about a dead archer, no matter how smelly she's getting. I'd worry about the live archer. *Two* visions! You can't tell me she didn't have another one, in the chapel. I need to get 'Lande away from that damned kid . . .

'Ah, *Dieux*!' Guillaume folded his arms across his belly and bent forward a little to alleviate his sudden cramp. A spasm eased him. He sighed with happiness, feeling his body begin another.

A cold, hard object suddenly shoved up against his dilated anus.

It hit with surprising force, lifting him an inch off the plank. Before he could react in any way, something warm and wet wiped itself almost instantaneously from his scrotum down the crack of his arse, and finished at his anus again.

He was not conscious that he screamed, or that his flesh puckered up and shut in a fraction of a second. The next thing he knew, he was hopping out into the courtyard, his hose trapped around his ankles, hobbling him, and the rest of his clothes pulling behind him through the dust.

'It's a demon!' he shrieked. 'It's a demon! I *felt teeth!*'

Two monks came running up at the same time as Bressac and one of the company's artillerymen.

'What?' Bressac yelled. 'Gil!'

His shirt was caught under his armpits and the wind blew chill across his bare arse.

I *knew* we shouldn't have left an unblessed corpse in a chapel, I knew it, *I knew it!*

'It's a demon!'

'Where?' The foremost monk grabbed Guillaume by the arm. It was the abbot, Muthari, his liquid eyes alert. '*Where* is this demon?'

'Down the goddamned shit-hole!'

The abbot goggled. 'Where?'

'Fucking thing tried to climb up my arse!' Guillaume bellowed hauling hopelessly at his tangled hose. He gave up, grabbed the abbot by the arm, and hobbled back across the courtyard toward the long shed. 'You're a fucking *monastery*! You didn't ought to have *demons* in the *lavatory*!'

Once under the tiled roof, the abbot pulled his arm out of Guillaume's grip. Guillaume glared, breathless. The abbot leaned a hand against the wooden pillar that supported the lavatory's roof, and peered down the hole. His shoulders convulsed under his robe. For a split second Guillaume thought the monk was becoming possessed.

Bressac shoved past, pushed the abbot aside, and stared down the hole. A cluster of monks and soldiers was growing out in the yard. Guillaume stood with his clothes still around his ankles. He yanked the tail of his shirt down, gripping it in a fist with white knuckles. The feeling of cold, unnatural hardness prodding at his most vulnerable area was still imprinted in his skin. That, and the warm, wet sensation that followed. He felt he would never lose the belly-chilling fear of it.

'God damn it, let *me* see!' Guillaume heaved his way bodily between Bressac and the Visigoth.

The hole in the plank opened into emptiness.

Beneath the plank was a shallow gully full of rocks and the remnants of night soil. And something else. A recent-looking landspill from the far side had raised the level of the gully here, until it was only a yard or so under the wooden supports.

As he watched, a quadruped shape turned back from waddling away down the slope and lifted its head towards him.

He gazed down through the hole at a brown-snouted pig.

It gazed back hopefully at him, long-lashed eyes slitted against the bright light.

'Jesus Christ!' Guillaume screamed. 'It was *eating* it. *It was eating my fucking turd while I was shitting it!*'

Bressac lost it. The abbot appeared to control himself. His eyes were nonetheless very bright as he waved other approaching monks back from the shed.

'We feed the pigs our night soil.' Muthari raised his voice over Bressac's helpless and uncontrolled howling. 'It appears that one of them was anxious to, ah, get it fresh from the source.'

The faintest stutter betrayed him. Guillaume stared, affronted. The Lord-Father Abbot Muthari went off into yelps and breathless gasps of laughter.

'*It's not funny!*' Guillaume snarled.

He bent down, this time managing to untangle his dusty hose and his doublet and pull them up. He dipped his arms into his sleeves, yanking his doublet on, careless that he was rucking his shirt up under it. He shuddered at the vivid remembrance of a hot, overlarge tongue. A *pig's* tongue.

Taken by surprise by a realisation, Guillaume muttered, 'Oh, *shit*—!' , and Bressac, who had got himself upright, sat down on the plank and wept into his two hands.

'*Shit*,' Guillaume repeated, deliberately. He ignored all the noise and riot and running men around him. Ignored the mockery that was beginning as the story was retold. He stared down the shit-hole again at the thoughtfully chewing pig.

'Shit . . . we were going to *eat* one of those.'

There was no more talk of pork. But there was endless discussion of the incident, and Guillaume glimpsed even Spessart smile when one of the archers yelled 'Stinker Arnisout!' after him.

'Animal lovers are never appreciated,' Bressac said gravely, strolling beside him. 'St Francis himself was exiled, remember?'

'Ah, *fuck* you!'

Bressac whooped again. 'Only – trying – to help!'

Guillaume passed the day in anger and hunched humiliation, going through his duties in a haze. He registered another row between Spessart and the monks – the captain swearing quietly afterward that it would be better to kill every man of the Visigoths here, and that he would do it, too, if the company's only priest had not been killed on the galleys. Guillaume thought ironically that it was not just he who missed Father Augustine.

He stood escort for the captain again after the hot part of the day, when tempers flared in another confrontation at the chapel door, and Spessart knocked down Prior Athanagild, breaking the elderly man's arm. That would have been the signal for a general massacre, if Gabès had not been uncomfortably close to the west, and men difficult to control when they are panicking and dying. Both parties, monks and soldiers, parted with imprecations and oaths, respectively.

Off duty, Guillaume hung about the fringes of the camp as the evening meal was served, and afterward found himself wandering among the ordered rows of tents that led out from the fort's main courtyard to the sand that ran unobstructed towards

Carthage. Tent pegs had been driven hard into the ochre earth. The outer ring of the camp should have been wagons, if this were a normal war, but arriving by sea meant no wagons to place. They had settled for stabling the few knights' horses at that end, knowing that any strange scent would have them bugling a challenge.

Guillaume found Yolande sitting between two tents, in a circle of men, playing at cards round the fire pit. She smiled absently as he sat down beside her. He put his arm around her shoulder, heart thudding. She didn't object. She was playing hard, and for trivial amounts of money, and losing, he saw.

Towards what short twilight there was in these parts, the woman ran her purse dry and threw her cards down.

'Nothing to spend it on here, anyhow,' Guillaume said, trying to be comforting.

She gave him a sharp look.

'So . . . ah . . . you want to walk?' he asked.

A slow smile spread on her face. His belly turned over to see it. He knew, instantly, that she had heard the nickname being bandied about the camp. That she was about to say *Walk with you, Stinker? The idea's a* joke.

'I don't mind,' she said. 'Sure. Let's do it.'

There was no privacy in the tents, and none in the cells of the fort: none, either, down among the packed cargo-cog stores – far too well guarded – and the desert itself would be chilly, snake-ridden, and dangerous.

The woman said, 'I know somewhere we could go.'

Guillaume tried to read her expression by starlight. She seemed calm. He was shaking. He tried to conceal this, rubbing his fingers together. 'Where?'

'Down this way.'

He followed her back past the keep, stumbling and swearing, and quietening only when she threatened to leave him and go back to the tents. She led him to the back of the fort, and a familiar scent, and he was about to turn and go when she grabbed his arm and pulled him down, and they tumbled on top of each other through a low doorway.

'A *pig* shed?' Guillaume swatted twigs out of his hair – no, not twigs. A familiar scent of his boyhood came back to him. Bracken. Dried bracken.

'It's been cleaned out.' Too innocent, the woman's voice, and there was humour in her face when his eyes adjusted to the dimness. 'The occupant doesn't need it yet. It's not going to be in use tonight.'

'Oh, I wouldn't say that . . .' Steeling himself to courage – *I have known women to back out at this stage* – Guillaume reached out his arm for her.

'Now you just wait.'

'*What?*'

'No, wait. We should sort something out first. What are we going to do, here?'

Despairing, he splutterd. 'What are we going to *do*? What do you think we're going to do, you dumb woman!'

He intended it as an insult, but it came out comic, fuelled by his frustration. He was not surprised to hear her snort with laughter. Guillaume groped around in the dark until a white glimmer of starlight on skin allowed him to grab her hand. Her flesh was warm, almost hot.

He pushed her hand into his crotch.

'That's what you're doing to me! And you ask me what we're going to do?'

His voice squeaked with the incredulity that flooded him. She laughed again, although it was soundless. He only knew about it by the vibration of her hand.

'That isn't helping . . .'

'No.' Fondness sounded in her voice, and amusement, and something breathless. Her face was invisible. Her voice came out of the dark. 'I find it helps to sort out these things in advance.'

Guillaume almost made a catastrophic error. *You mean you're arranging a price?* He bit his tongue at the last minute. She used to be a whore – but this isn't whoring.

His understanding of how much hurt the question could inflict on her drained his impatience of its violence.

'Am I going to suck *this*,' her voice continued, out of the darkness, 'and then you lick me? And that would be it? I'm past the age of having a child, but you never know. Or are we going to fuck?'

Guillaume heaved in a harsh breath, dizzy. Her fingers were kneading his crotch, and he could not speak for a moment. He clamped his hand down on top of hers. The throbbing of his penis was all-encompassing, as far as his mind went. His fingers and hers around his cod: oh dear Lord, he prayed, completely unselfconsciously, don't let me spill my seed before I have her!

'I want you,' he said.

He felt his other hand taken, and pressed, and after a second realised that it was pushed up between linen shirt and hot flesh, cupping the swell of a heavy breast. His fingers touched a rock-hard nipple.

'I want you,' Yolande said, out of the dark. 'But is it that easy?'

The sounds of the monastery were muffled: the bells for Compline from the Green Chapel, the groaning chorus of hungry pigs, the rattle of boots outside as men went past to the refectory.

'You can have sex whenever you want,' she said, long-eroded anger in her voice. 'And it doesn't change anything. If I have sex, it changes everything. If I "belong" to a man. Or to many. Whether I'm safe to rape. Whether I'm going to be trusted when we're fighting . . .'

All true, but . . . Guillaume grunted in frustration. In comic despair, he muttered, 'And on the *good* side?'

A chuckle came out of the darkness.

She likes me. She actually likes me.

He felt her rest her arm down in the warm, dry bracken, close to his arm. A sudden shine of silver – moonrise – let him distinguish her face as his eyes adjusted.

'On the good side,' she finished, 'you're not in my lance. You're not another archer. And you maybe won't commit the cardinal sin if we get into combat . . .'

Guillaume kept himself still with an effort. 'Which is?'

'Trying to protect me.'

He stopped with one hand on her shoulder, the other still inside her shirt. Actually stopped. After a second, he nodded. 'Yeah. I get it. You're right. I won't.'

Some expression went across her face, so close now to his, that he couldn't properly make it out. Amusement? Lust? Liking? Respect?

Her nipple hardened under his palm. An immense feeling went through him, which he realised after a moment was relief.

She can't deny she wants me, too.

She wants *me.*

A little too straight-faced, Guillaume said, 'But it's not a problem if you can't have sex often, is it? *Men* want it all the time, but women don't really like sex . . .'

Her anger was only half mockery. 'So it doesn't matter if I have to go without?'

Deadpan, he said, 'Of course it doesn't—'

She threw her arms around his chest. He abandoned caution, tried to kiss her, but she rolled them both over in the bracken. He ended on his back: felt her straddling him.

' 'Lande!'

Her voice came out of the darkness, full of joy. 'You should have listened to the monks – women are *insatiable*!'

'Good!' he grunted, reaching up.

One of her hands clamped down on his groin. The other grabbed his long black hair, holding his head still. She brought her mouth down on his.

Guillaume cradled her against him when she fell asleep in his arms, in the rising moon's light; her clothing half pulled up around her, bracken shrouding her bare shoulders. He was dazzled and aroused again by the glimpse of her rounded belly, striated silver here and there; and her surprisingly large and dark-nippled breasts.

He tightened his embrace and looked down at Yolande's sleeping face. All the lines were wiped out of her face by relaxation. She appeared a decade younger. It was a phenomenon he was familiar with: it happens when people sleep, and when they're dead.

'I *did* know him!' Guillaume exclaimed aloud.

Yolande's eyes opened. She had evidently picked up the soldiers' trick of coming awake almost instantly. She blinked at him. 'Know who?'

'Your Margie Hammond. *Guido Rosso!* Bright kid. All boy!'

The moon's light, slanting into the pen, let him catch a wry smile from Yolande. Too late to explain his definition. *Impulsive, dashing, daring*.

'You know what I mean! I just didn't—' Guillaume shook his head, automatically pulling her close and feeling the sweaty warmth of her body against his. 'I guess there was no way I was going to recognise the face.'

'When we put her in the chapel, she didn't *have* a face.'
Guillaume nodded soberly.

He remembered Rosso now, a young man prone to singing in
a husky boy's voice, always cheerful, even in the worst weather,
who would sit out any dancing on the excuse of his very minor
damage to one hip and thighbone, and use the time to chat up
the women. *I prefer to dance with the enemy*, he'd say, priming the
girls to regard him as a wounded hero – the limp, of course, was
very small; enough to give him a romantic, dashing air, but not
enough to keep him out of the line fight. He had gone to the
archers anyway, and Guillaume had not, at the time, known
why.

'We used to call him Crip,' Guillaume said. 'He limped. And *he*
was a girl? That girl – that woman – we carried into the
chapel . . . ? *That's* Crip Rosso, and he was female?'

'She wouldn't marry the man her parents picked out for her.
Her mother locked her in her room and beat her with a stick
until she couldn't stand. That's where she got the limp.' Yolande
stared past him, into the darkness of the pig shed, apparently
seeing pictures in her mind. 'She limped to the altar on her
bridal day. When she'd had a couple of children that lived, her
husband said he'd let her go to a nunnery, because she was a
bad influence on them. She ran away before she got there.'

Guillaume whistled quietly.

'He – she – always seemed so cheerful.'

'Yes. Well.' Out of the silver shadows, Yolande's voice was
dry. That was not so disconcerting as the feeling of withdrawal
in all the flesh she pressed against him: skin and muscle tensing
away from his body. 'Wouldn't she be? Misery gets no company.'

'Uh – yeah.' He reached over to touch her cheek and got her
mouth instead. Wet saliva, the sharpness of a tooth. She grunted
in discomfort. He blushed, the colour hidden by the dark, but
the heat of it probably perfectly apparent to her.

Does she think *I'm* a boy? he wondered. Or is she – I don't
know – Is this it: over and done with? Do I care, if it is?

''Lande . . .'

'What?'

'Doesn't matter.'

'I'm awake now.' She rummaged about in the dark, and he

felt her haul at something. She pulled the woollen cloak that covered them up around her own shoulders, uncovering Guillaume's feet to the cold. He said nothing.

The moon rose on up the sky. The strip of white light shining in between the hut's walls and roof now barely let him see the shine of her naked flesh in the darkness. He put his hand on her, stroking the skin from thigh, buttock, belly, up to her ribs. Warm. Soft. And hard, under the soft surface.

'So Crip joined the company because no man would have her?' He hesitated. 'Oh . . . *shit*. That was meant to come out as a joke.'

He couldn't distinguish her expression. He didn't know if Yolande heard his rueful truthfulness and credited it.

After a second, she spoke again. 'Margie told me she ran away on the journey to the nuns. I don't know how she got as far south as Constantinople, but she was already dressing as a man. That's why she got raped, before she joined the company. Revenge thing, you know?'

Guillaume froze, his fingers pressing against her warm skin. He heard her voice falter.

'They had the fucking nerve to tell her she was *ugly*, while they were doing it. "Crip." '

The bracken moved under him and crackled. There was a grunt from the next shed over. One of the sows rising, with a thrash of her trotters, and then settling again.

Guillaume winced. 'Nothing I could say would be right. So I'll say nothing.'

There was the merest nod of her head visible in the dim light. Yolande's muscles became tense. 'The name stuck, after she signed on with the company.'

'Stuck?' He felt as if his pause went on for a whole minute. His heart thumped. Incredulous, he said, 'It was one of *us* who raped her?'

'More than one.' She kept her voice deliberately bland. Still she shook, held within his arms.

Guillaume felt cold. 'Do I know the guys that did it?'

'I don't know their names. She wouldn't tell me.'

'Do you *think* you know?'

'How could I tell?'

He almost burst out, *Of course you can tell the difference between one of us and a rapist!* But recalling what she would have seen at sacks of towns, he thought, Perhaps she has cause to doubt.

'We wouldn't have treated her like that,' he said. 'Not when she was one of us.'

Not out of morality – lives depend on loyalty. Men-at-arms and archers together, each protecting the other, and the bows bringing down cavalry before it could ever reach the foot soldiers. And the billmen keeping the archers safe from being ridden down. *Safe.*

Yolande's voice came quietly as her body leaned back against him. 'I guess she didn't think about the rape much, later. We could all die any time, the next skirmish, field of battle, whatever. What's the point of remembering old hurts if you don't have to?'

An obscure guilt filled him. Guillaume felt angry. Why must women always *talk* at moments like this? And then, on the heels of that, he felt an immense sadness.

'Tell that to your Ric,' he said. 'When his master's dead.'

She was silent momentarily. He was fairly sure she thought he had not been listening to her recounting the day's happenings. She confirmed it, a note of surprise in her voice.

'I didn't think you were paying attention.'

'Ah, well. Full of surprises.'

A small, spluttered chuckle; her relief apparent. 'Evidently. You're – not quite what I expected you to be.'

He didn't stop to work out what that might mean. Guillaume hitched his freezing feet up under his cloak. 'His pigs are safe. But . . . Spessart might not kill Ric, but I'd take a bet with you that Muthari won't make it – or I would, if I had any money.'

She gave him a look he couldn't interpret at *money.*

'Yeah. At least the pigs won't die.' She sounded surprised by her own thought. 'These pigs, I mean . . . more like dogs than pigs.'

'All pigs are.' Guillaume could just see surprise on her face. He shrugged. 'We had pigs. My dad always got in a hell of a black mood when it came to slaughtering day. Loved his pigs, he did. Hated his sons but loved his pigs . . .'

'So what happened to you and Père Arnisout and the pigs?'

'What always happens in a war. Soldiers killed my father, raped my mother, and took me away to be their servant. They burned the house down. I would guess they ate the pigs and oxen; it was a bad winter . . .'

Her arms came around him. Not to comfort him, he realised after a second of distaste. To share closeness.

She said dispassionately, 'And now you're on this side of the fence.'

He put his hand up past his head, where his sword lay in the bracken, and touched the cross-hilt. 'Aren't we all . . .'

'I'll have to see Ric again.' The moonlight was gone now, her face invisible; but her voice was sharp and determined.

'About Muthari?'

'About the visions.' Her hands sought his arms, closing over his muscles. 'Two of them, Gil. And I don't understand either. Maybe things would be clearer if I had another.' Her tone changed. He felt her laugh. 'Third time lucky, right? Maybe God believes things come in threes, too.'

'Well, fuck, ask him, then – the pig-boy,' Guillaume clarified. 'Maybe he *can* tell you when the enemy's going to drop on us from a great height. I'd also give money to know who'll turn up first, Hüseyin Bey or the Carthaginian navy. If I had any money.' He grinned. 'Poverty doesn't encourage oracles, I find.'

She sounded amused in the dark. 'A*nd* he might know why God bothers to send visions to some mercenary soldier . . .'

'Or not.'

'Or not . . .'

He depended on sensation – the softness of her waist under his hand, the heat of her skin against him. The smooth, cool wool that sheltered them from the night's cold. The scent of her body, that had been all day in the open air.

He felt his way carefully, as if speech could be tactile. 'What we were saying – about Crip Rosso?'

'Yes.' No hint of emotion in her voice.

'I was going to ask . . . were you ever raped?' Guillaume was suddenly full of raw hatred that he could not express. 'I – hope not. Just the thought's made my prick wilt, and talking about that *isn't* the way to bring it up again. Not in my case. Though I've soldiered with men who would come to attention instantly at the thought.'

His eyes adjusted to starlight. It illuminated shapes – the precise curlicues of bracken, and the crumpled linen mass of his doublet under them, colourless now; and her own hand, where it rested on his chest.

Guillaume whispered, 'I'd take all your hurts away if I could,' and bent his head to nip at her heavy breasts.

'Yes . . .' Yolande smiled.

He felt her body loosen.

Her voice became half-teasing. 'But that's because you're one of the good guys. I think.'

'Only think?' he gasped, mouth wet from trailing kisses across her body, under her pulled-up shirt. He reached down and put her hand on him, to encourage his prick upright again. 'I'm good. What do you want, letters of recommendation?'

She spluttered into a giggling laugh.

'You see? In the dark, you could be sixteen.' He put her remaining hand to his face, and let her fingers trace his grin. 'I knew I could make you happy again.'

With Prime and Vespers always at six a.m. and six p.m. here, it made the hours of the day and the night the same length, which Guillaume found odd.

On the cusp of dawn, he began a dream. Forests where it was hot. Holm-oak woods. Dwarf elephants, no bigger than horses. Men and women in red paint, who burned their children alive – sacrifices to deforestation, so that cities could survive. A scream that was all pain, all desolation, all loss. Then he was lost in the African forests again. And again.

He woke with a start, the nightmare wrenching him awake. Cold draughts blew across the pen, counteracting the bracken's retained heat. Cool blue air showed beyond the half door.

Morning.

'*Green Christ!* What *time* is it? 'Lande.' He untangled himself gracelessly, shaking her awake. His breath showed pale in the cold air. ''Lande! It's past roll call! We're meant to be on duty – oh, shit.'

Running feet thumped past outside. Lots of running feet. Men shouting. Hauling his clothes on, wrenching at knotted points, clawing under the bracken for a missing boot, he gasped, 'It's an attack! Listen to them out there!'

Loud voices blared across the morning. He cursed again, rolling over, trying to pull on his still-laced-up boot.

Damn! Hüseyin Bey's division ought to be a fortnight behind us at most. At *most*. We can stand a siege – if there hasn't already been a battle to the east of us. If Hüseyin's Janissaries aren't all dead.

'Don't hear the call to arms!' Yolande pulled her shirt down and her hose up. She finished tying off her points at her waist, and knelt up in the bracken like a pointing hound.

'What? What, 'Lande?'

'That's at the chapel!'

'*Bloody hell.*'

He struggled out of the pig shed behind her, shaking off bracken, not worrying now if anyone saw them together. It was a bright crisp morning, sometime past Prime by the strength of the dawn. So the rag-head monks would be there, to celebrate mass, and this racket must mean—

'Rosso! Margie!' he grunted out, having to run to keep up with Yolande.

'Yes!' Impatient, she elbowed ahead of him, forging into the crowd of mercenary soldiers already running towards the chapel doors.

He tried to catch a hackbutter's arm, ask him what was the matter, but the other man didn't stop. Guillaume heard the captain's voice way ahead, piercing loud above the noise, but couldn't make out all the words. Only one came through, clean and clear:

'—*sacrilege!*'

Yolande barged through the black wooden doors into a rioting mess of men and – *pigs?*

She reared back from the smell. It hit her as soon as she was through the doors. Hot, thick, rich. Rotten blood, fluids, spoiled flesh. Dung. And the eye-watering stink of concentrated pig urine. Yolande gasped.

In front of her, an archer bent down, trying to stop a sow. The small, heavy animal barged into him and knocked him away without any effort. Yolande caught at his arm, keeping him upright.

'What the hell is this?' she shrieked over the noise of men bawling, pigs shrieking and grunting, metal clattering and scraping against stone.

'The fucking pigs et her!' the archer bawled back. His badge was unfamiliar, a tall man from another lance, his face twisted up in rage or anguish, it was impossible to guess which.

'Ate her?' Yolande let go of him and put one mud-grimed hand over her mouth, muffling a giggle. 'You mean – ate her body?'

The archer swore. 'Broken bones of Christ! Yes!'

Another pig charged past, jaws gaping. Yolande jumped back against the Green Chapel's wall as the gelded boar, mouth wide open to bite, chased a green-robed monk towards the open doors.

'Grab it!' the monk yelled, holding the Host in its holm-oak box high over his head. 'Grab that animal! Help!'

Yolande's hand pressed tight against her mouth, stifling another appalled snicker.

Ten or twelve or fifteen large pigs ran around between her and the altar, screaming and honking and groaning. And two dozen soldiers, easily. And the monks who had come in to celebrate Prime. A sharp smell of pig dung filled the air. There were yellow puddles on the tiles where pigs had urinated in fear or anger.

'Who . . .' she stuttered, 'who let them in here?'

The nearest man, a broad-shouldered elderly sergeant, bellowed, 'Clear the fucking House of God! Get these swine out of here!'

Yolande shoved forward, then slowed. Men moved forward past her. The lean-bodied pigs were not large, but heavy – all that muscle.

A knight had his legs and arms wide, trying to herd a young black sow away from the altar. The animal shoulder-charged past him, bowling him over in a tangle of boots and armour. Yolande realised, on the verge of hysteria, that she recognised the beast – Ric's favoured sow, Lully.

The black-haired pig scrabbled past her as Yolande dodged aside. The tiled floor was covered in dark dust. Boot prints, the marks of pigs' trotters, the prints of bare feet. Dust damp with the early morning's dew.

And something white, kicked and trodden underfoot.

Yolande bent down. She kept close to the wall and out of the way of the struggle ahead – men flapping their arms, clapping, shouting, doing everything to harry the pigs away from their focus, a few yards in front of the altar. She squatted, reached out, and snared the object.

It had a rounded, shiny end. The back of it had a bleached stump, and blackened meat clinging to it. She recognised it all in a split second, although it took moments for the realisation to plod through her mind. It's a bone. A thigh joint. The thigh bone's been sheared off it—

By the jaws of pigs.

That guy was right. They ate her.

She thrust her way between the men, ignoring the skid of her heels in pig dung on the floor. She got to the altar. What was in front of her now were pig backs, lower down than anything else. Hairy sharp rumps. Pigs with their snouts snuffling along the tiles, wrenching and snatching things between them. Heads lifting and jaws jerking as they swallowed.

Bones.

Meat.

There was not enough left to know that it had been a human skeleton.

The pigs had had her for a long time before they were caught, Yolande could see. Almost all of the flesh was gone. *He did say his pigs ate carrion . . . 'garbage disposal'.* Most of the bone fragments had been separated from each other. There was nothing left of Margie's skull or face. Only a fragment of bottom jaw. Pigs can cut anything with their shearing teeth.

'Margie,' she whispered under her breath, not moving her fingers away from her mouth. Her breath didn't warm her stone-cold flesh.

Now there is nothing to bury. Problem solved.

She felt wrenching nausea, head swimming, mouth filling with spit.

I didn't always *like* her. Sometimes I hated her guts. There was no reason we should have anything in common, just because we were two women . . .

The body of Margaret Hammond, Guido Rosso, such as it was now, was a number of joints and bones and fleshy scraps, on the floor and in the jaws of pigs. She saw the captain, Spessart, reach down to grab one end of a femur. He yelled, cursed, took his hand back and shook it. Yolande saw red blood spatter, and then the brass-bearded man was sucking at the wound and swearing at one of the monks while it was bound up.

'You knew this would happen!' Spessart bawled.

The round face of Abbot Lord-Father Muthari emerged into Yolande's notice. She saw he stood back from the fracas. One white hand held his robe's hem up from the mess of rotten flesh and dung on the tiles.

'I did *not* know,' Muthari said clearly.

'You knew! I swear – execute – *every one of you over thirteen—*'

'This is an accident! Obviously the slave in charge of the animals failed in his duty. I don't know why. He was a good slave. I can only hope he hasn't had some accident. Has anyone seen him?'

Yolande stood perfectly still. Memory came back to her. She could hear it. The shrill complaints and groans of hungry pigs. The stock know when their feeding time is. And if they're not fed . . .

We *heard* them. They weren't fed last night. That's why they're so hungry now. That's why they've – eaten everything in here.

Her hands dropped to her sides. She made fists, pressing her nails into her palms, trying to cause enough pain to herself that she would not shout hysterically at the abbot.

Ric would have fed them last night.

And these animals have been locked in here, she thought, dazed, staring back at the door where the crowd was parting. Or they'd be off at the cook tent, or foraging . . .

Someone stabbed a boar, sending it squealing; others, flailing back from the heavy panicking animal, began to use the hafts of their bills to push the swine back and away.

A European mercenary in dusty Visigoth mail pushed through the gap in the men-at-arms, grabbing at Spessart's shoulder, shouting in the captain's ear.

Yolande could hear neither question nor answer, but something was evidently being confirmed.

Spessart swung round, staring at Abbot Lord-Father Muthari.

'You're damned lucky!' the captain of the Griffin-in-Gold snarled. 'What's coming down the road now is the Legio XIV Utica, from Gabès. If the Turkish advance scouts were coming up the road, I'd give them this monastery with every one of you scum crucified to the doors!'

Yolande began to move. She walked quite calmly. She saw Muthari's face, white in the shadows away from the ogee windows, blank with shock.

'So consider yourself fortunate.' The captain's rasp became more harsh as he looked at the fluid pooled before the altar. 'We have a contract now with the king-caliph in Carthage. You and I, Muthari, we're – allies.'

He's going to pull that one once too often one day. Yolande numbly pushed her way between taller men, heading for the small door beside the altar, under the embroidered hanging. *Mercenary companies who change sides in the middle of wars get a bad rep.*

But then . . . six thousand enemies a few miles away, no support for us: time to say 'Hey, we have supplies, and we can tell you where there are food caches farther down the coast . . .'

The handle of the door was rough in her palm. A ring of cold black iron. She turned it, and the heavy bar of the latch lifted. Yolande stepped through.

The air outside hit her. A smell of dry dust, honey, and olive trees. The sun was well up. *Did I just spend so long in there?*

She walked calmly and with no unnecessary speed down past the olives, past the broken walls of this end of the monastery, and down to where the pig shelters stood.

Here, in the shadow of the southern wall, there were still patches of frost on the earth.

She walked up past the first low hut. The boy was lying at the foot of the flight of stone steps that came down the fort's wall. His back was towards her. She stopped, reached down, felt him quite cold and dead.

Dead for many hours.

She manoeuvred his stiff, chill body around to face her. He was almost too heavy. Frost-covered mud crackled underfoot.

It was not the first time she had felt how someone's head moved when their neck was broken. Snapped, with the neck held, the jaw clamped into someone's hand and jerked sideways—

No one will prove it. It looks perfect: he had a fit, and fell.

Spessart will accept it as an accident. It solves all his problems.

No woman's body to bury; no living man to blame.

She heard the voices of men coming after her.

Yolande turned her head away and stared up at the flight of steps, leaving her fingers on Ric's smooth, bitter-cold flesh. How easy to take hold of a young man by the iron ring around his neck. Just get close, inside his guard.

He took this from someone he trusted to get close. He was a slave. He didn't trust many people.

Yolande's thoughts felt as cold as the boy's dead body.

I hope Muthari broke his neck from behind.

I hope he let Ric die without ever knowing he had been killed by someone he loved.

Guillaume Arnisout leaned his hip against the rail on the galley's prow. He braced the burden that he carried.

The thing that had been part of him for so long – his polearm, the hook-bladed bill – was no longer propped beside him, or lying at his feet, or packed in among the squad tents. *Because they won't put me into a line fight now. Not with a broken knee. And I can't say I blame them.*

The warm wood under his hand and the salt air whipping his hair stiff were part of him now, so long had the *Saint Tanitta* been on its way to Italy. The brilliant sun on the waves was still new – the ship having been Under the Penitence as far as Palermo, on the coast of Sicily.

He looked back down the galley, finding Yolande Vaudin. *But nothing fills the gap, after Zarsis monastery – not for her. Nothing.*

Archers sprawled on the deck, their kit spread out around them. Every plank was covered with some mercenary, or some mercenary's gear. Men arguing, drinking, laughing, fighting. Yolande was squatting down with her hand in the crotch of a blond Flanders bowman.

Guillaume could not hear what she said to the big man at this distance. By now, he didn't need to. It was always the same – and one of the reasons for keeping a distance in the first place.

She tries everything . . .

Yolande hauled the man up by his arm. He laughed. Guillaume watched them lurch as far as the butt end of the ship. Yolande touched the man's chest. The two of them vanished behind a great heap of sailcloth and coiled ropes. As much privacy as might be found on shipboard, when all of a mercenary company is crowded into one galley.

He turned back to the rail, shifting his leg under him.

Threads of pain shot through his knee and the bone beneath it.

Better than two months ago in Carthage; at least I can stand up without it giving way.

Guillaume shifted the burden he carried against his chest, moved his shattered and mending knee again, and swore.

Bressac came and leaned on the ship's rail beside him. He had lost a lot of weight. The other Frenchman made a pretence of looking out across the milky blue sea towards Salerno. He sniggered very quietly. 'Got left holding the baby again?'

Guillaume looked down at his burden – the child in its tight swaddling bands, resting against his chest.

The lengths of linen bands bound it to a flat board. He had had the carpenter drill a couple of holes in the wood, and now he had loops of rope over his shoulders to hold the swaddling board against his body. It left the child facing him. All that could be seen of her were her bright eyes that followed his movements everywhere.

'I don't mind. She's all right, for a Visigoth.' Guillaume spoke carelessly, edging one linen band down and giving her a finger to suck. 'Have to find the wet nurse soon. Right hungry little piglet, she is. Ain't you, Mucky-pup?'

'Daah,' the baby said.

Bressac snickered again.

The red tile roofs of Salerno became distinct, floating above the fine blue haze. Birds screamed.

Bressac said, not laughing now, 'She ought at least to come and *look* at the damn brat, after we went to so much trouble to get it.'

Guillaume took his finger back from the hard gums, and the baby gave him a focused look of dislike. He said, 'First time in the entire bloody voyage this little cow hasn't been crying, or puking up all over me. Looks cute enough to get her interested in it again.'

At Bressac's look, Guillaume admitted, 'Well, maybe not *that* . . .'

'She's drinking too much to have the infant. Drop it overboard, probably.' Bressac glanced over his shoulder and then, sentimental as soldiers anywhere, said. 'Give it here.'

Guillaume slid the ropes of the swaddling board off his shoulders and handed the baby over to rest her nose against Bressac's old and smelly arming-doublet. To his surprise, she neither cried nor puked. *Can't win, can I?*

'Yolande's drinking too much,' he said. 'And angry too much.'

Bressac joggled the baby. 'She keeps going on about that pig-boy – "Oh, the abbot killed him; oh, it was murder." I mean, it's been half a year, we've had an entire damned campaign with the Carthaginian legions; you'd think she'd get o—' His voice cut off abruptly. 'Damn! Kid just threw up all over me!'

'Must be your tasteful conversation.' Guillaume took the baby back as she began to wail, and wiped her face roughly clean with his kerchief. The wail changed from one of discomfort to one of anger.

Bressac, swiping at himself, muttered, 'Green Christ! It's just some slave's brat!', and wiped his hands on the ship's rail.

Above him, the company silk pennant cracked, unrolling on the wind: azure field merging with azure sky, so it seemed the gold griffin veritably flew.

Bressac said, ''Lande was *drunk*, remember? Kept saying she wanted a baby and she was too old to have one. She *insisted* we haul this one out of goddamn Carthage Harbour. Now she's bored with it. Green Christ, can't a bloody slave commit infanticide in peace?'

'You think it was a slave?'

'Hell, yes. If the mother had been freeborn, she could have *sold* it.'

'Maybe we should find a dealer in Salerno, for the Turkish harems.' Guillaume was aware he was only half joking.

If she's got bored with the kid . . . so have I.

Merely being honest about moral failings is not an excuse.

It's not boredom. Not for Yolande. It's just that the kid isn't Ric – or Jean-Philippe. Saving this kid . . . isn't the same. And that's not the baby's fault.

'This *isn't* a place for a baby.' Guillaume looked guiltily around at the company. 'Kid deserves better than old sins hanging round her neck as a start in life. What can she ever hope for? Like 'Lande keeps on saying, to change anything—'

The words are in his mind, Yolande repeating the words with the care of the terrifyingly drunk:

'To change anything . . . we'd have to change everything. And I don't have the time left that that would take.'

Blue sea and white foam streaked away in a curve from this side of the galley's prow. He went as far as unknotting the ropes from the swaddling board and sliding them free.

Splash and gone. So easy. A lifetime of slogging uphill gone. When we meet under the Tree, she'll probably thank me.

Bressac's voice broke the hypnotic drag of the prow wave. 'So. You going to talk it over with the master gunner? Ortega will have you for one of the gun crews; they're shorthanded now. Not much running about, there . . .'

There was a look in Bressac's eyes that made Guillaume certain his mind and proposed action had been read. Not necessarily disapproved of.

A seabird wheeled away, screaming, searching their wake for food. The perpetual noise of sliding chains from the belly of the ship, where the rowers stood and stretched to the oars, quickly drowned out the bird's noise.

'Sure,' Guillaume said. 'A gunner: sure. That'd suit a crip, wouldn't it?'

The baby began to wail, hungry again. Guillaume looped the board back on one shoulder and slid a finger under the linen band. He tucked the baby's still white-blonde birth hair carefully back underneath.

'Maybe I could do with a vision,' he said wryly. 'Not that they helped 'Lande. Or the kid. What's the point of seeing things centuries on? He needed to see what that son of a bitch Muthari was like now.'

'One of us would have to have done it,' Bressac observed, his long horse face unusually serious. 'You know that? If there wasn't going to be a massacre?'

Guillaume heard sudden voices raised.

Farther down towards the slim belly of the galley, Yolande Vaudin was standing now, shouting – spitting with the force of it – into the face of the company's new priest.

The priest evidently attempted to calm her, and Guillaume saw Yolande slap his hand away, as a woman might – and then punch him in the face, with the strength of a woman who winds up a crossbow for cocking.

"*Ey!*' The sergeant of the archers strode over, knocked Yolande Vaudin down, and stood over her, yelling.

Guillaume felt himself tense his muscles to hand the baby to Bressac and run down the deck. *And . . . run*? The sergeant abruptly finished, with a final yell and a gesture of dismissal. Guillaume felt frustration like a fever.

Yolande got to her feet and walked unevenly up towards them at the prow. One hand shielded the side of her face.

She halted when she got to them. 'Stupid fucking priest.'

Bressac reached out to move her hand aside. Guillaume saw him stop, frozen in place by the look she shot him.

'Want to take the baby?' he offered.

'I do *not*.' Yolande moved her hands behind her back.

A bruise was already coming up on her cheek. Red and blue, nothing that arnica wouldn't cure. Guillaume didn't stand. He lifted the baby towards her.

Her gaze fixed on its face. 'Damn priest said I was asking him to do fortune-telling. It isn't fortune-telling! I wanted to know if what I saw was *real*. And he won't tell me.'

'Maybe he doesn't know.'

'Maybe.' Yolande echoed the word with scorn. 'He said . . . *he* said none of it was a half-millennium in the future. He said the heathen boy had been telling *my* future – that *I'd* never be recognised. That *I'd* die a mercenary soldier, shot by some hackbutter. And that foretelling my future was witchcraft, and so it was right the abbot should kill such a boy – that's when I hit him.'

Guillaume found himself nodding. The sensation of that possible future being truncated – of it being a translated form of this woman's desires and terrors – eased some fear he had not been aware he still had. Although it had given him nightmares in the infirmary, after his wound.

I don't like to think about five, six hundred years in the future. It makes me dizzy. But then . . .

'Priest might be frightened it *is* true foresight,' Guillaume said quietly. 'Either way . . . as a future, are you so in love with it?'

The old Yolande looked at him for a moment, her expression

open and miserable. 'You know? I can't think of anything better. Recognition. Acceptance. And a better death than disease. I wanted it for so long . . . Now I know I ought to be able to think of something *better* than this. And . . . I can't.'

Guillaume rested the baby back against him. He didn't say anything about families, farms, retirement into city trades.

What's the point? Neither of us are going to stop doing what we do. No matter what. This is what we are now.

No wonder she drinks. I wonder that I don't.

'Been doing it too long.' The other Frenchman's voice was gently ironic. Bressac nodded down the deck towards the sergeant of archers, who was standing with his fists on his hips, talking to one of the corporals, glaring after Yolande Vaudin. 'All the same . . . That isn't the way to behave to a sergeant.'

'Oh, so, what am I supposed to be afraid of?' Scorn flashed out in her tone. 'A black mark against my name on the rolls? It's not like they're ever going to make *me* an officer, is it? A woman giving orders to men!'

So easily caught by those old desires, Guillaume thought. If I could go back into the line fight, as the team's boss . . . How long would I hesitate? A heartbeat? Two?

Bressac grinned. 'You want to do leadership the way Guillaume here does it – he finds out what we're going to do, then he tells us to do it!'

There was enough truth in that that Guillaume couldn't help smiling. Bressac's face clouded.

'As Guillaume here *used* to do it,' Guillaume commented.

The wind smelled suddenly of fish and blood as it veered – the stink of the fish-shambles, in Salerno. A brown-haired woman, the wet nurse, approached from the direction of the other rail. Guillaume noticed she ignored Yolande pointedly.

In a stilted French, she said, 'Master, I'll take the baby; she needs changing now.'

'Oh – sure, Joanie.' Guillaume shifted, grunting with his knee's pain, and handed over the infant. Whatever was passing between the two women was not accessible to him, although he could see there was unspoken communication. Condemnation. On both sides?

He watched the wet nurse kneel down, untie the swaddling bands from the board and then from the child, and coil up the soiled wrappings and set them aside. The smell of baby shit and milk was way too familiar for a billman-turning-gunner.

'Joanie will keep it with her,' Yolande announced, over the other woman's bent head. 'I don't want anything more to do with this.'

' 'Lande—'

'It was a *mistake*. She isn't . . . I'm sorry for the child, but . . . Joan, I'll bring you money, out of my pay; you'll continue to feed it, and keep it by you – yes?'

The brown-haired woman nodded without looking up. 'As long as I'm paid.'

She fumbled down her bodice for clean linen bands. The baby, laid facedown on the warm wooden deck, hitched with elbows and knees and made a slight wriggling progression. Evidently she had not been used to swaddling bands before she fell into the hands of a Frankish nurse.

Guillaume bent down, picked the baby up from under so many feet, and tucked it under his arm. The infant made vague, froglike motions.

'How long will that last?' he demanded.

Joanie got up, dusting her hands on her skirt. 'I have forgot the new bands. Look after it now, master, while I fetch them.' She walked away towards the head of the gangway.

Yolande shrugged.

She turned and leaned her forearms on the rail, beside Guillaume. She had something in her hands – the Arian rosary, he saw. She trickled it from one hand into the other, while the wind and spray whipped her short hair into her eyes.

'Some people have the grace of God,' she said, just audibly. 'Some people can look down the chain of our choices and tell us what might happen in future years.' She held the use-polished Christus Imperator up in front of her face. 'I'm not one of them. Never will be. Ric was. And he . . .'

She opened her hand. The carved holm-oak rosary fell and disappeared, lost in spray and the Gulf of Salerno.

Yolande cast an eye up at Bressac. 'Shall we walk?'

It was an invitation, although not as whorish a one as Joanie had been giving earlier in the day, Guillaume noted. The other Frenchman began to smile.

'See you,' Yolande said neutrally, looking down at Guillaume.

She was more than mostly drunk, Guillaume could see, if he
looked at her without illusion.

Too many months' practice in hiding it, that's all. And now
she's brawling with priests, and fucking who she pleases, and
out of control. She'll cause fights, and bad discipline, and she
wants to.

Someone has to pay for Ricimer – and if it's not going to be
Muthari, I guess she's decided it's going to be her . . .

Yolande walked away across the deck. Bressac gave Guillaume a look compounded both of apology and of disbelief in
his own good luck, and followed her.

The woman wore a pleated velvet doublet against the wind's
chill, and the sunlight illuminated how it nipped in at her waist
and the skirt of it ended just short of her lower hip, so that the
curve of her lower buttocks could be seen as she walked away.
And all the long length of her shapely legs. A woman in doublet
and hose: the cast lead Griffin badge pinned to her upper arm
and even the sunlight showing the worn patches in the velvet
could not spoil her attraction.

She'd still fuck, if I asked.

I think she knows I won't ask.

That's not what I ended up wanting from her.

Guillaume sat back on the oak chest, his spine against the rail,
the infant firmly in the crook of his elbow. He felt her warm,
solid, squirming. If I put her down now, she'd be across this deck
in a heartbeat, no matter how few months she has to her. It's in
her. It's in all of us, surely.

He looked at the carved black walking stick beside him, and
with his free hand eased at the muscles above his knee.

'Well, now.'

With some awkwardness, he shifted the baby out from under
his arm, and plumped her astride his other knee. She kicked
her heels against his old, patched hose. The sun, even through
this fog, would scald her, and he looked up for Joanie's return
– and saw no sign of the wet nurse – and then back at the
baby.

Knowing my luck, it's about to piss down my leg . . .

The master gunner, Ortega, appeared out of the port gangway, two or three of his officers with him, and stood talking
energetically, gesturing.

'Well, why not?' Guillaume said aloud. 'The pay's as good, as a gunner. What do you think?'

The baby, supported under her armpits by his hands, blinked at him with her human eyes. She weighed less than a weaner piglet, although she was weeks older.

'Maybe I'll put a few shillings in, with Yolande,' he said quietly, his eyes scanning the deck. 'A few a month. Joanie'll probably soak me dry, telling me you've got croup, or whatever infants have.' His mouth twisted into a grin he could feel. 'At least until I'm killed in a skirmish, or the Italian diseases get me . . .'

The salt wind blew tangles in his hair. He wiped his wrist across his mouth, rasping at stubble. Joanie, coming back, was accosted by Ortega. Guillaume heard her laugh.

'Fortuna,' Guillaume said, prodding the baby's naked round belly. The infant laughed. 'The chain of choices? It's not a chain, I think. Choices are free. I believe.'

The baby yawned, eyes and nose screwing up in the sunshine. Feeling self-conscious, Guillaume brought the infant to his chest and held her against his doublet, with both his arms around her.

The weight of her increased – becoming boneless, now, with sleep, and trust. She began a small, breathy snore.

'It's not all sitting around in the gunners, you know,' Guillaume lectured in a whisper, watching Italy appear from the mist. 'I'll be busy. But I'll keep an eye on you. Okay? I'll keep a bit of a watch. As long as I can.'

Afterword

1477 AND ALL THAT

Sellars and Yeatman's wonderful book *1066 and All That* says that History is all you can remember from your schooldays. *Ash: A Secret History*, of which 'The Logistics of Carthage' is a piece of flotsam, says that History is all you can remember . . . *and it's wrong.*

The links between alternate history and secret history fiction run deep. With *Ash*, I wanted not only to consider a moment at which history as we think we know it might have turned out differently, but to think about the nature of history itself. History as narratives that we make up – aided, of course, by things we take to be evidence – to tell ourselves, for one or another reason. 'History' as distinct from 'the past', that is.

The past happened. It's just that we can't recover it. History is what we can recover, and it's a collection of fallible memories, inconvenient documents, disconcerting new facts, and solemn cultural bedtime stories.

I went a stage further with *Ash* – the past didn't happen, either, not as we're told it did, and the scholar Pierce Ratcliff uses history to work that out. Well, history plus those inconvenient things upon which history is based: memoirs, archaeological artefacts, fakes, scholarship tussles, and quantum mechanics. It's different for a writer, thinking of an alternate history point of departure in these terms. History is not a road on which we can take a different turning. The road itself is made of mist and moonbeams.

And then there's AD 1477. And AD 416. And between the two of them is AD 1453, which is where 'The Logistics of Carthage' got its genesis, even though the story itself takes place four years later in AD 1457.

In AD 1477, Burgundy vanished.

This is straightforward textbook history. The country that had been Burgundy – a principality of France, according to France, an independent country, according to the princely dukes of Burgundy – vanishes out of history in January of 1477 – 1476 in the pre-Gregorian calendar. Duke Charles the Bold (or 'Rash', as 20:20 hindsight has it) lost a battle to the Swiss, was inconveniently found dead without leaving a male heir, and, to cut a short story shorter, France swallowed Burgundy with one gulp.

And rich and splendid and *powerful* Burgundy vanishes instantly from the history books. You would never know that for large periods of medieval history, Western Europe was not solely divided between the power blocs of Germany, Spain, and France. I'm not the only writer to be fascinated by this phenomenon. M. John Harrison's splendid and non-alternate-universe novel *The Course of the Heart*, for example, revolves around it in an entirely different way. Tropes of history and the past and memory are endlessly valid. But it was my starting point for *Ash: A Secret History*, which is, of course, the *real* story of why Burgundy vanished out of history in AD 1477, and what took its place.

Of course it's the real story: would I lie to you?

I am shocked – *shocked!* – that you think I would . . .

And then there's AD 429. In history as we know it, this is the start of Gothic North Africa. A Vandal fleet sails over from mainland Europe under Gaiseric, who kicks the ass of the Roman inhabitants and – becoming pretty much Roman himself in the process – establishes the rich and powerful kingdom of Vandal North Africa, with its capital established in Carthage by AD 439. In AD 455, Gaiseric sails east and sacks great Rome itself.

For *Ash*, I thought it would be neat if it hadn't been the Vandals who invaded North Africa.

I preferred the Visigoths – a rather different Gothic people who had ended up conquering the Iberians and running Spain, and whose elective-monarchy system by the early medieval period is, as one of the characters in *Ash* says, 'election by assassination'. I decided I'd have a Visigoth North Africa instead.

Then, while wandering through a book on post-Roman North

Africa, I discovered there had indeed been a vast Visigoth invasion fleet that set off towards North Africa. Thirteen years before the Vandals.

It was sunk by a storm.

So I had AD 416, a concrete and inarguable point of departure for an alternate universe that I would have been perfectly happy to set up as a hypothetical what-if. History plays these wonderful tricks, always. I love it.

And then we come to AD 711, when in our timeline the Muslims decided, quite reasonably, as they thought, to invade Visigoth Spain. This resulted in a long occupation of chunks of Spanish kingdoms, a number of *taifa* buffer states that were part-Christian and part-Muslim, and a self-defined 'entirely beleaguered and all-Christian' north. It's a story that doesn't end until AD 1492, when the last of the Moors leave Granada, and one of the most fascinating mixed cultures of Western Europe goes belly-up.

However, for *Ash*, having had my earlier point of departure set up as a non-Arabic North Africa, I ended up with a Visigoth Arian Christian invasion of a Spain that was part of the Church of the Green Christ. That rumbled along nicely from AD 711 until the 1470s, with the North African Visigoths largely taking the place of the Byzantines in our history. It may say in the KJV that nations have bowels of brass, but we know that history is endlessly mutable . . .

And then there's 'The Logistics of Carthage'. Which I had not intended to write, after *Ash*. No way! When a 500,000-word epic is over and done, trust me, you do not want to see any more of it. Two walk-on characters tugging at one's elbow and remarking that they, too, have their story that they would like to tell, is something guaranteed to have the writer running off gibbering.

So I gibbered, and I decided I wouldn't write it, because the story of *Ash* is over. *Over* over, not here-is-a-sequel over. Not nearly over, but really sincerely over.

Ah yes, they said to me: but this isn't a sequel. For one thing, it's set twenty years before the main action of the book. For another, one of the people whose story it is was a minor character, and the other appears solely for a half sentence in one place in the book. And it's set somewhere we didn't get to in *Ash*. And, and . . .

And there's the Fall of Constantinople, you see.

AD 1453, and one of the defining points of Western European history. The great capital of the Byzantine empire, Constantinople, falls to the Turks and becomes Istanbul. Among the things that come out of the city with the flood of refugees are all the Hermetic writings of Pico and Ficino, who themselves have what amounts to an alternate-universe history of what the world is *really* like. The fall of Constantinople (in some theories) turbo-charges the Italian Renaissance, which kicks off the Renaissance in the rest of Europe and leads to the Scientific Revolution, the Industrial Revolution, and hello modern world.

But 'The Logistics of Carthage' isn't about that.

It's about the war *after* AD 1453, when the Turks move on the next obvious enemy in the *Ash* history: the Gothic capital of Carthage, under the Visigoth king-caliphs. A war taking place on the coast of North Africa, where a troop of European mercenaries heading toward Carthage in the pay of the Turks find themselves with a corpse they cannot bury because of a religious dispute, and we start to get a look at a love story – and pigs – and the mechanisms of atrocity.

Carthage, you will note, is another entity that vanishes out of history. Frequently. There isn't anything particularly mysterious about it. The Punic city of Carthage gets flattened by the Romans in 146 BC, in a very marked manner, and sown with salt. Roman Carthage gets sacked, in turn; Gothic Carthage is taken by the Arabs in AD 698. Tunis grows up in the same area, and has its own troubles. History has a way of happening to cities.

But, mystery or not, Carthage has fascinated me for rather the same reasons as Burgundy does. Here is something completely gone, its people do not remain, and how do we *know* that the history we hear is anything like what really happened?

In 'The Logistics of Carthage,' one of the soldiers has what she takes to be dream visions, sent by God. It wasn't possible to bring on stage, in a novella, the reasons why they're not dreams – they are glimpses of the real future, five hundred years ahead from where she is – but the rationale is present in *Ash*, and for the purposes of these people, it doesn't matter whether what Yolande sees is scientific or theological. What she *feels* about it is real.

And I get to push the history that runs from these points of departure on a stage further, which I naturally couldn't do in *Ash*, and am therefore glad to have the chance. Yolande sees future-Carthage, future-North Africa, and they are not our twenty-first-century Carthage and North Africa, just the up-to-date version of what the history would become, if it was to become our time.

But the alternate-universe story isn't always about 'Cool, a POD!' Stories of people's experience are only rarely about seeing history turn. This story, which wouldn't let me go until I wrote it, is about a woman who followed her son to the wars, and how it feels to her then to be working for the worshippers of the child-eater goddess Astarte (which is where, in this history, the Turks get their red Crescent Moon flag). Military history gives short shrift to mothers – but then, Guillaume, finding himself with a reluctant appreciation of a woman's usual role in history, is as much a mother as Yolande.

And pigs. Never forget the pigs.

They don't know a damn thing about history, pigs.

They just become its victims – as people without power tend to.

And for those readers who have read *Ash* . . . yes, you do recognise a few names. And, yes, this is the early life of those particular people. I didn't know it either, until I came to write the story.

Oh, and the baby is precisely who you think she is. But she isn't important to this narrative. For these people, it could have been any nameless baby at all.

For most of us, after all, names are the first thing lost by history.

Kitsune

'It's not the end of the world; it's just bad sex.'

Tamiko said that to me towards the end, when she had learned to speak pretty good English.

For a fox spirit.

I blame Greg for it, myself. He's an odd type; late twenties, still lives with his mother. It's far too complicated to tell you how he became a cook, from being a qualified painter and decorator; but he did, and his first real job (when he got it) was in a Japanese restaurant in London. I used to call it NipponHut; what it really sold was *okunomiyaki*, omelettes, with bits in, which seems to be the Japanese equivalent of fast-food pizza.

His boss had wanted an English cook; the rest of the staff were Japanese; by default – and evening classes – Greg ended up learning some conversational Japanese. If you consider '*Sumimasen ga*, pass me the *netto* beans,' to be conversation. So I think he understood Tamiko better.

Greg is one of those people who you can never trust to be one thing or the other. He'll be abrasive as hell for ninety per cent of the time. He makes a habit of asking me why I have hair that changes colour every three weeks, knowing that I'm just trying to keep the grey concealed and not hitting any solution that satisfies me. He makes remarks about us both fancying the same type of women that are offensive rather than buddy-buddy. He treats me like a guy when it suits him, like a woman when it doesn't. But, one time he made me a *saki* cup, without asking, and glazed and painted it himself, and gave it to me without a word.

I think he knew what she was like from the beginning.

He brought her into class one Sunday morning. I'd been training for a while, gone through warm-up, used a *bokkan* first to loosen up muscles and tendons while I found my *hara* centre, and was performing *kata* with a steel sword in the bright sunlight that comes down from the gym's clerestory windows.

If either one of the two of them had come into blade-range I would have registered them immediately. Lifting, cutting, blocking, slicing; people remain wallpaper around the sides of the gym, faces with whom I do not make eye-contact. My body thinks, not my mind.

I stopped, breathing deeply but not fast, and I heard a stifled little giggle, and turned around to see Tamiko with her hand over her mouth.

'Samurai,' she said, in her as-yet accented English. 'You are a girl samurai.'

Greg, beside her, said something quick in Japanese. I recognised the syllables, couldn't remember what it meant (all I have is a small technical vocabulary covering the finer points of sword manufacture). I turned away from him, and fell in love the second that I looked her in the face.

The first thing you notice about Japanese girls is that they're tiny. With short legs. I have a friend who lends me girlie magazines from Tokyo; all the models avoid the classic stockings-and-suspenders, because on them it looks wrong. Disproportionate. (The Japanese have a thing about women in nylon pantyhose; perhaps this is why.) Tamiko had little fat-thighed legs, and her black hair cut in a short crop around her little plump face, and she stood about five-foot-nothing, and *none of it mattered.* I loved her instantly.

And she was straight.

I know, now, why I thought this so decidedly. She had her hands wrapped around Greg's arm, and her chin tipped up as she whispered to him, and one foot off the ground, trailing a little slippered toe across the gym flooring, all the signals that any teenage bimbo would use to say, 'this one's *mine*' .

'This is Tamiko,' Greg introduced her. About nineteen: could be older. She was being very touchy-feely for a Japanese girl. I've seen enough Japanese female students who never do go back home to Osaka or Tokyo or wherever to recognise her immediacy of freedom.

Tamiko giggled again. They really do do that. Her accent was slightly American. 'Lady samurai. This friend, you?'

Greg said, 'Tamiko, this is Rowena.'

I had about ten seconds of excoriating jealousy of Greg; the real why-was-I-ever-born variety. Not because Tamiko was holding his arm, and that meant he was probably poking his dick into her on a regular basis, but because she *could* hold his arm, and if it had been me, we couldn't have. Even long ago, when I was what I cheerfully designated a baby butch, I couldn't get away with that one – you'd think they'd take us for teenage heteros, clutching each other's arms and squealing and giggling, but they always know.

None of this stopped me doing big-cute-sports-dyke. Or perhaps it ought to be cute-martial-arts-dyke. Bow to *sensei*, to excuse myself. Slide the curved *katana* blade back into its black lacquered scabbard. All of which will, if you do it right, show off the lines of hips, spine, shoulders, biceps, and pray she doesn't notice the very slight double chin that passing thirty-five is giving me.

'So: did Greg bring you down here to see the *iaido* class? You must get enough of this at home.'

'No. I have never seen martial arts, except in the movies. Is difficult to do, perhaps?'

She raised her eyes to my face. I loved her even more. At that time, I didn't know that I didn't have a choice.

'It's not difficult to start off with. Come over here, I'll show you.' I took her over to one side of the gym, and brought out my lightest blade and wrapped her tiny fingers around the grip.

She had a warm body in a short black dress, and she smelled of something floral. I made a mental note to buy her musk, she would suit musk far better than light-and-flowery scent.

'You hold it like this. No, this. One hand here. And the other here. Now your arms. No: let me show you.'

I wondered dizzily if she could tell. I used my hands to move her arms, placing her elbows closer in to her body, and I straightened her wrists, and moved her palms apart on the braid-and-rayskin grip of the sword, and all the time *I* could feel myself shaking. She just looked down the back of the bright steel blade with an expression that was part-giggle, part bloody-minded determination.

It seems ironic, now, that I touched her with a desire so strong that I could taste it, dry, in my mouth. That my hands did shake, and the pads of my fingertips left sweat-dots on the sleeves of her dress. I was turned on to that point where your clothes feel uncomfortably tight. There was no way I was going to turn round and look at Greg.

At the same time that I heard him talking to two or three of the other students, I realised that the class had broken up, that I was very likely in trouble for being disrespectful to *sensei*, and that Tamiko had a natural stance. She carried her body erect, her feet about eighteen inches apart, one foot pointed forward and the other pointing slightly to the side. She could move, lightly, in any direction; her balance almost perfect.

'Where did you learn that? You *must've* done *iaido*.'

'No. I know a man who—' Tamiko frowned. Her loss of words was apparent on her face; her black eyes like oil in sunlight.

She brought the blade up above her head and cut down, arresting the stroke some twelve inches above the floor, and her hands wrung out the grip of the hilt as you might twist a washcloth dry, and the edge of the sword *whicked*! as it cut cleanly through the air.

'A man who,' she completed, satisfied.

I wanted, more than anything on earth, to step behind her and put one of my hands flat on her belly, and the other across her tiny, rounded breasts, and hug her body back into mine, push her plump buttocks into my groin. Well, wanted it more than anything on earth except not to be *seen* doing it, in public.

I wonder if it would have made a difference if I'd given way to the impulse? I would have left the class – but I've left other places. Or stayed, when I felt bloody-minded. I leave when there's not enough prejudice to make a fight pleasurable, only a faint miasma of difference that can't really be combated.

'That was amazing!' Michael said. Michael is another regular at the *iaido* class; an asthmatic whose stoop has almost vanished in the years that he's been doing this. I knew him, he'd move in on her; and Greg knew it too, it was arm-around-shoulder time. In the confusion and conversation I put my sword away.

Tamiko appeared at my side as I was clearing up.

'This also is a tradition of the samurai,' she said, 'when same loves same.'

My ears burned; I knew they'd be bright red. Without moving

my body, I flicked my gaze sideways, saw no one – Greg, Michael, Simon, Jean – no one looking this way, or listening; some dumb argument going on about where would we go for lunch? And could it be non-smoking? And cater for a dairy-products allergy?

I managed the all-purpose English *what*-the-fuck-did-you-just-say. 'Sorry?'

'A man with a man.'

'Tamiko . . . you don't *say* things like that!'

'But you are—'

I didn't know how she was going to phrase it. Some impulse of devilment made me almost wait to find out; but dark, crew-cut Michael was turning around to see where the newcomer was, Greg tracking his movements like a radar-dish. I spoke over her voice:

'You could be good at sword work, if you wanted to put in the practice hours. How long are you over here for?'

Greg, at my elbow, said in quick slurred English, 'She doesn't know what you're asking her to do.'

If it had been anyone else but Greg, I would have assumed that he referred to *iaido*.

Tamiko looked puzzled.

I repeated slowly, 'I would like to help you to learn this. If you want to, Tamiko.'

'Yes.' She nodded her head many times, enthusiastic. 'Yes. I will learn what you have to teach.'

Tamiko learned *iaido* from our *sensei*, and English from Greg, and from me – what? How to walk down a summer street, sweaty arms just touching, brushing skin, and to smile at our reflections in shop windows? How to kiss briefly, as if we were friends? Where to find the cafés and clubs, and sink into the atmosphere of women-ness; never knowing, until you relax into that exclusivity, how tense you are everywhere else?

'I was so sure you were straight,' I told her, in a café around the back of Centre Point.

Tamiko smiled her amazing dimply smile.

'I am fox spirit,' she said; and corrected herself, with the careful pronunciation Greg was teaching her: 'I am *a* fox spirit. *I'm* a fox spirit. Better, yes?'

' "*Fox* spirit"?'

'So I'm able to love who I wish. Not who you say I must. Or must not. Is not the same for me. I can make love with whatever I want to.'

The June sun came through the glass of the café's big window, picking out posters, copies of *The Pink Paper*, women seated in pairs and foursomes; one dyke talking into her cellphone. The smell of coffee drifted up from my half-empty cup of cappuccino.

'Tamiko . . . what's a fox spirit?' I thought it might be a college sorority, a girl-gang: who knows what exotic social arrangements they have in Tokyo?

'Fox-spirit, *kitsune*, she is a woman-demon.'

'A *demon?* What do you mean? What are you really saying, here?'

The Japanese woman linked her fingers under her chin. She gazed up at me. The lustre on her flesh is youth, rounding out the plumpness of her sallow face until it does not seem like fat, but like some bursting ripeness. Her eyes, with their folded skin, defy my attempts to read her expression. That would take far longer than learning her language.

'A demon, a bad ghost,' she said.

'Tamiko . . .' the oh-come-*on* tone. I still thought we had some difference of translation to overcome.

'I am the spirit of a white fox with nine tails. I have the body, no, the *shape*, of a girl. Rowena, you are on the outside, too. I can tell you.'

It – she – made me laugh, ruefully.

'Come on then, demon. Little demon. Demonette. Let's go home and fuck.'

'I'm a true fox-spirit, Rowena.'

'And I'm a . . .' I could think of no stichomythia to match her. The light from outside shone plainly on her face, with a white foam of coffee froth dabbed on her slim lips, and nothing at all – in our language of the body, or in what I had been able to piece together of hers – nothing I could see indicated humour, satire, pretence, or confusion.

'Come on.' The chair scraped back as I stood up to leave.

That night I made love to her.

If you're one of the 'but what do lesbians *do* in bed?' variety, I suggest you find a tolerant dyke friend and ask her. We do what you do, we just do it more enthusiastically. Let's face it, if one of us just lies there, nothing's going to happen.

'I am a fox-spirit,' she insisted.

Real delusion is frightening.

I couldn't come.

I couldn't make her come.

At the moments when I should have been worshipping flesh with my mouth, some voice in the back of my head started saying *this woman is a fantasiser, a psycho, she's got problems, you've had far too much of women with problems; she's probably some Japanese therapy-dyke playing the innocent student*.

'Rowena?'

One fantasy drives out another. Or is it that fantasy, always, can drive out the reality? Fantasy, unreality, psychosis, suspicion: they're all stronger than reality. I lay in curdled sheets, looking at the smooth skin of this woman that I really do not know.

'I can't,' I said. 'I don't want to.'

'So where's Tamiko, then?' Greg asked, with unerring accuracy for pain.

I sat with my legs curled under me, alone on his old red vinyl sofa, sweat sticking my skin to the surface of the cushion. His house's open window let in the sound of bored adolescent boys yawping and bragging. Someone on one of the other roads, further into the estate, had a Ford engine being tuned; a rhythmic, predatory roaring. He still lives there because his mother does. He's no more gay than I am straight.

I asked question for question. 'Where'd you meet Tamiko? First?'

'She came into the restaurant.' Businesslike and brusque, as if nothing could be more ordinary. 'Matthew says she's Ainu.'

'What's that?'

In his usual staccato, Greg said, 'Yeah, I asked Matthew. He told me. The originals. The people that were there before the Japanese. Well, what we call Japanese. Matthew says there's still some of them up on the north island.'

I suspected the word Greg was looking for was *aboriginal*, and

I also suspected the word that Matthew, the restaurant's man-
ager, had used was something else entirely.

'How long's she been here?'

'She hasn't told you?'

'I still don't understand her English that good.'

Greg gave a barking laugh. It had all the male drive-cars-
watch-football-poke-women in it that I could stand. I left. The
best you can say about Greg is that, being unaware of social
amenities, he doesn't demand them from his friends.

Saturday: twenty-four hours until I might meet her, at the
iaido class. If she came. If I went. Twenty-four hours until she
would come up and ask me, probably out loud and in front of
whoever, 'Why haven't I seen you? Why are you angry with
me? Why don't you want to make love any more?'

I lengthened my stride, crossing the estate's bald grass-patch
in front of the shop, remembering that the library closes early on
a Saturday, and one of the throng of boys mis-kicked a football
so that it landed at my feet.

I flipped it up and kicked it solidly back.

'Thanks, mate!' He waved a short acknowledgement. The
name and the acknowledgement that you give to guys: his
contemporaries.

In broad daylight, too. It wouldn't be dusk for hours yet.

I found that I was grinning to myself as I walked into town.

The newtown county library had a bit of stuff on Japanese
legends. All of it had the authenticity of folk-legends from
foreign cultures, in that none of the stories seemed to have a
definable closure, or a point.

As for fox spirits, there was the kind of crap you might see on
some kiddies' morning power-fantasy cartoon. I was sure Tamiko
could tell it all to me: *kitsune* are spirits, ghosts, immortal in their
fox form; they take on human form and seduce men, and then
leave them after various events lead to disclosure and tragedy.

They don't sit beside you in a dyke café and say *Hey, I'm a fox
spirit, how about that!*

I sat with my chin cupped in my hands and stared out of
the library window. The study area was empty, the staff moving about purposefully downstairs with a definite air of *we're
closing*.

'So . . . when Tamiko comes up to me, I'm going to say, "You're a nutter, go away!" Yeah. Right . . .'

I skimmed the paragraph I'd been staring at as I stood up to put the book back on the shelf. In his pedestrian, mediocre prose, the writer on folklore had finished his chapter with this sentence:

'Notably, the treacherous kitsune or "fox-spirit" also has the power to make any human mortal fall in love with her.'

It was easy enough to dismiss the folklore. Something real intervened, wrenching at my gut. That is what I would like to tell you: that it hurts, it hurts, it hurts enough to make you breathless, when you realise:

'I still love her. Whatever kind of an airhead she is, I haven't stopped loving her. Not for a minute. Maybe I never will.'

That feeling that you *never will* went away, of course. It does. I've loved before, and now I can barely remember the cauterising pain of leaving or being left. I won't say I forget their names, but I can no longer remember in my gut how it felt to be connected to them by love.

You can't say that you'll never stop loving somebody. 'Never' is a very short time, these days.

I stood on the library steps and wondered what I was going to do with myself for the next – *timecheck* – eighteen hours.

There's a ravine left over from when they bulldozed in the park on the town planners' map.

Black shapes trotted in the half-light.

Urban foxes use the ravine now, for their run down to the backs of the kebab houses in the town centre. Long, low bodies loping; led by their pointed noses.

I sat until dusk turned to night. I got close enough for one orange-furred young vixen to stare at me, for an animal half-second, before turning and sliding off into the undergrowth. Her cry sounded like a baby being eviscerated.

These are foxes.

Feeling grounded, I called in at Greg's house on my walk back, to see if he'd got back from evening shift.

'You'll have to go. I've got to sleep.' Greg rubbed at his eyes, at his front door. 'Trouble with you, Rowena, is, you need to move out of this town. Go to London. Somewhere like that. This place is a dump. And get yourself a job!'

He spoke as if he thought I might be genuinely interested to hear his opinion, and not as if I might want to hit him.

'Oh well.' Greg ignored my silence with a tired, cheerful laugh. 'See you down the class tomorrow. Maybe.'

The weight of the sword becomes an extension of your arms, wrists, hands, until you can feel its balance as much as your own. A true cut *feels* right. You know it from the inside.

Sensei had not suggested that I go for a grading this summer. I know him and respect him better than to think this is pique on his part, for disrespect. It's just an accurate reflection of what I've been doing: literally screwing around. Wasting training time. My mind is not in my blade.

The *hamon* of the sword catches the sun: the edge's satin wavy finish, comparatively dark against the mirror-brightness of the flat of the blade. Step, move, cut. Step, move, cut. Nothing I can do, despite the smooth sliding of tendons and muscles under sweating skin, to make my cuts even adequate this morning.

The bells from the nearby Anglican church broke my concentration, and Tamiko walked into the *iaido* practice hall on the sound of them, her high-heeled tapping footsteps hidden. Skimpy blue dress; sandals – looking nothing like a fright-haired, white-faced, spike-fingernailed Japanese fox-ghost. I lowered my blade, sheathed it, bowed.

'Well,' I said, when I got to her, 'any more new stories? What's it going to be this time? You learned your stance and balance from a genuine live samurai warrior, five hundred years ago? I know: you're immortal.'

'Yes.'

Her flat reply frightened me. Not because she might believe that she was telling the truth, but because I had no way that I could trust of judging whether she believed it or not.

'Come for a walk outside,' Tamiko said.

I tied the *katana* into its purple satin bag and followed her out into the sun; into the village tail now wagged by the newtown dog. She walked across the road, and I couldn't tell whether she was aimless or determined. She went through the lych-gate and stood under the yew tree in the churchyard; leaning against a pollution-eaten gravestone and listening to the hymns, barely audible through stained-glass windows. The traffic on the by-pass sounded louder.

I followed. Heat reddened the back of my neck.

'Tamiko.' I squinted at her, and rested the sword across my body. She was in the tree's shadow, and I moved to join her, excusing myself to myself that it was only because of the heat. 'Tamiko . . .'

Fear kills sexual desire. Only the remnants of wanting her shivered across my skin. Here in the tree's dankness, she was rubbing her hands over her upper arms. I wanted, for one second, to kiss the alert skin of her shoulder, her throat, her little breasts with the big brown nipples; wake the stab of pleasure between my legs.

'It's not the end of the world; it's only bad sex.' Tamiko's black eyes moved to my face. 'It wouldn't be like that for ever.'

Desire goes sour like music going flat. 'Yes. It would. I don't want you any more . . . shit! Look. I don't know who you are, Tamiko.'

I refused to play her game and say *I don't know* what *you are*.

'Put the *katana* down,' she said.

Through the slippery silk, I could feel the slick scabbard and rough grip of the weapon, which I didn't realise I had been cradling across my body. I put it down. I leaned it carefully across a guano-spotted marble surround, under *Susan Neville, beloved wife of the above*. Inside the church, a few old ladies quavered about the swift close of life's little day.

'Now what?'

'Hold my hands,' Tamiko said. 'Kiss me. Here, now, Rowena. Kiss me on my lips.'

Across the road, I saw Greg and Michael standing with their heads together outside the practice hall.

'You're joking!'

'No. I am not. What can you show them that they will not know?'

I saw Greg stealing a quick cigarette, Michael saying something and glancing across at the churchyard. I couldn't hear what he said but I could guess the sense of it: *another one of Rowena's fuck-ups*.

Both of them would be kind to me later.

It was something to look forward to.

'I can't.' It sounded like a whine. I attempted controlled, deprecating humour. 'Any more than you can stop telling me you're a spirit, a ghost, whatever. Fox-woman.'

'Kiss me!'

Anger came fast-forwarding up out of me as I looked at her shadow-dappled, sallow features. 'It's too easy for you! You can go back and play straight! What am *I* supposed to do when you've gone? Too many things would have changed . . . I wouldn't know how to talk to any of them. They wouldn't know what to say to me.'

'I would never leave you. For ever.' Tamiko hugged her arms across her plump body. She smelled of musk-scent: a gift. Her black eyes searched my face, and I couldn't read her expression. Her voice sounded like despair. '*Touch* me. You love me. Where is your courage? I know that you love me, Rowena. You must!'

'Why "must" I love you?' I asked.

Tamiko looked up into the shafts of light between the yew's branches. I wanted, more than anything, for her to say something I could understand without the need to filter it through a translation. Something that would feel as clear and right and immediate as a good cut.

'Because I chose you,' she said.

This time I used it against her deliberately. 'Yeah. Right. Because, if you chose me, I *have* to love you. Because you're a "fox spirit". Tamiko, come *on*!'

She wouldn't look into my face. She put her hands up so that her fingertips just covered her lips. 'I thought that you were outside. Different. A foreigner, like me. You have no – guts. Honour. Not should carry *katana*!'

Tamiko walked away, quickly, into the sunshine; across the graveyard and into the street. I lifted and cradled the sword in its bag and watched her go.

In the end, difference is too hard. Or I'm too stupid.

I dream about her. Constantly. I really do.

It's such a dumb thing that I don't tell Greg about it, and I certainly don't tell Michael, who was in bed with her about five minutes after she crossed the road and hung onto his arm and giggled up at him.

'Slut,' Greg said after class, brief and businesslike as ever. 'Funny, if she'd've been English, I'd've spotted it right away.'

And then at the end of the summer she went home, wherever home was; maybe on one of the north islands, like Greg said. Maybe to some condo in Tokyo, with her parents.

I don't practise any sword *kata* now.

Sometimes, when I dream of Tamiko, she *is* a white fox.

This all happened about six years ago. There hasn't been anyone else since. No one. I still love her. 'Never' is turning out to be a longer time than I thought it would.

But – since I don't believe in fox spirits – I will stop loving her, in the end.

Afterword

There's a sort of hang-over from the Victorian Romantic idea of the writer, whereby he – and it usually is 'he' – reclines gracefully on a couch like the dying Chatterton, awaiting dictation from the Muse. The story is inspiration; it doesn't require anything so mundane as work.

On the whole, sprawling around like a dying duck in a thunderstorm and waiting for the Muse to deliver doesn't result in much but blank paper. It's banging your head against the keyboard, and learning your art and your craft, that produces stories.

So it's slightly embarrassing that 'Kitsune' turned up out of nowhere, over forty-eight hours, pretty much as it stands, and only required a bit of tidying up. It's not perfect, but it's itself.

Since my usual style of inspiration is more along the lines of 'stare at the blank page (or the computer monitor) until your ears bleed', this was a surprise.

Maybe it's a matter of emphasis.

There was a lot of Japanese stuff going on around me at the time – Japanese language students; English friends studying martial arts and Japanese cookery and Sengoku period arms and armour. If someone who's going to write is around something like that, osmosis comes into play. The subconscious is primed for a story.

It's less easy to see where the people and their situation come from. A different level, perhaps; you dig down into yourself and find cognate experiences. Except that it *feels* more like being told a story by another person. I had Rowena's voice in my head.

I guess the Victorians – and the Ancient Greeks – had to get the idea of a Muse from some observable phenomenon. As far as I can see, writing isn't, in fact, a God-derived gift channelled by superior people from the superior social classes. It's just that, sometimes, it feels like being ridden by a Vodoun *loa*.

Emphasis . . . on those bits of the writing process that are available via conscious manipulation, and those that come from the subconscious.

Then again, maybe I only conceptualise it as a subconscious mind because that's the name this culture gives to the Muses.

'Kitsune' can be General Fiction or Weird Stuff entirely according to how you prefer to read it, which is also not what I usually do. *Is* there a nine-tailed fox spirit there?

Either way: it doesn't make any difference to Rowena.

The Road to Jerusalem

Banners cracked in the wind and the hot grass smelled of summer. Sweat stung Tadmartin's eyes. Long habit taught her the uselessness of clashing mail gauntlet against barrel-helm in an attempt to wipe her forehead. She blinked agitatedly.

Sun flashed off her opponent's flat-topped helm; that brilliance that gives mirror-finish plate the name of white harness. A momentary breeze blew through her visor. Unseen, she grinned. She cut the single-handed sword down sharply, grounding her opponent's blade under it in the dirt.

She slammed her shield against the opposing helm. 'Concede?'

'Eat that, motherfucker!'

Knowing Tysoe, Tadmartin's unseen grin widened. She slipped back into fighting-perception, apprehending with the limited peripheries of her vision all the tourney field (empty now, the formal contests down to this one duel), the ranked faces of the audience, the glitter of light from lenses. A soughing sound reached her, muffled through arming-cap and helm. Tournament cheers.

Tysoe launched an attack. Tadmartin panted. Both moving slow now after long combat.

Strung out so tight, nothing real but the slide of sun down the blade, the whip of the wind coming in on her left side; foot sliding across the glass-slippery turf, heat pounding in her head. The body remembering at muscular level all the drills of training. Tadmartin moved without thought, without intention.

She felt her hand slide on the grip, the blade's weight cut the air – Tysoe's two-handed sword smashed down, parried through with her shield, her own blade cutting back; Tysoe's wild leap to avoid the belly cut – all slowed by her perceptions so that she watched it rather than willed it. Felt her body twist, rise; bring the thirty-inch blade back up and round and over in a high cut. Metal slammed down between Tysoe's neck and shoulder. The impact stung her hand.

'Shit!'

Tysoe dropped to one knee. Now only one hand held the greatsword; the other arm hung motionless. Tadmartin stepped in on the instant, footwork perfect, sword up:

'Yield or die, sucker!'

'Aw, shit, man! Okay, okay. I yield. I yield!'

Tadmartin held the position, shield out, sword back in a high single-handed grip, poised for the smash that – rebated blade or not – would shatter Tysoe's skull. Through the narrow visor she caught the lift of the marshal's flag. A sharp drum sounded. Instantly she stepped back, put down the shield, slipped the sword behind her belt, and reached up to unfasten the straps of the barrel-helm.

'Fuck, man, you broke my fuckin' arm!'

'Collarbone.' Tadmartin pulled off the helm, shaking free her bobbed yellow hair. Sound washed in on her: the shouting and cheering from the stands, the shrill trumpets. A surgeon's team doubled across the arena towards them.

'Collarbone,' Tadmartin repeated. 'Hey, you want to use an out-of-period weapon, that's your problem. That two-hander's slow.'

'It's got reach. Aw, fuck you, man.'

Tadmartin held the barrel-helm reversed under her arm. Casually she stripped the mail gauntlets off and dropped them into the helm. She shook her head, corn-hair blazing against the blue sky. Conscious now of the weight of belted mail, hugging her body from neck to knee; and the heat of the arming doublet under it, despite the white surcoat reflecting back the sun.

'Tysoe, babe.' She knelt, and put her helm down; awkward with the blunt sword shoved through her belt; reached in and undid the straps and buckles holding Tysoe's barrel-helm on. The steel burned her bare fingers. Gently she pulled the helm loose. Tysoe's arming-cap came away with it, and her brown hair, ratted into clumps by sweat, spiked up in a ragged crest. The woman's bony face was bright scarlet.

'Shit, why don't it never rain on Unification Day?'

'That'd be too easy.' She loosened the taller woman's surcoat. Tysoe swore as the belt released the weight of the mail coat, and leaned back on the turf. 'They're going to have to cut that mail off you, girl. No way else to get to that fracture.'

Disgusted, Tysoe said, 'Aw, fuck it. That's my *hauberk*, man. Shit.'

'Gotta go. See you after.'

The drum cut out. Music swelled from the speakers: deliberate Military Romantic. Tadmartin, not needing the marshals' guidance, walked across the worn turf of the stadium towards the main box. Breath caught hot in her throat. The weariness not of one fight, but of a day's skirmishing in the heat, knotted her chest. The muscles of her legs twinged. Bruises ached; and one sharp pain in a finger she now identified as a possible fracture. She walked head high, trying to catch what breeze the July day might have to offer.

The PA blared: '—the tournament winner, Knight-lieutenant Hyacinthe Tadmartin—'

It's PR, she reminded herself. The Unification Day tournament; blunt weapons; a show; that's all. Aw, but fuck it, I don't care.

The applause lifted, choking her. She walked alone; a compact woman with bright hair, looking up at the main box. A few of the commanders' faces were identifiable; and her own Knight-captain with the white surcoat over black-and-brown DPMs. Tadmartin saluted with all the accuracy left to her. The steel mail hauberk robbed her of breath in the suffocating heat. She plodded up the steps to the platform.

Spy-eyes and bio-reporters crowded close as Marshal Philippe de Molay, in white combat fatigues with the red cross on the breast, stood and saluted her. He spoke less to her than to the media:

'Knight-lieutenant Tadmartin. Again, congratulations. You stand for the highest Templar ideal: the protection of the weak and innocent by force of arms. The ideal that sustained our grand founder Jacques de Molay, when the Unholy Church's Inquisition subjected him to torture, and would have given him a traitor's death at the stake. The ideal that enabled us to reform the Church from within, so that now our relationship with the Reformed Pope at Avignon is one of the pillars upon which the Order of the Knights Templar stands. While there are women and men like you, we stand upon a secure foundation. And while we stand upon the past, we can reach out and claim the future.'

Tadmartin at last gave in to a long desire: she smeared her hand across her red and sweating face, then wiped it down her surcoat. The grin wouldn't stay off her face. 'Thank you, sieur.'

'And how long have you been in the Order, lieutenant?'

'Seven years, sieur.'

Questions came from the spy-eyes then, released to seek whatever sightbites might be useful for the news networks. Tadmartin's grin faded. She answered with a deliberate slowness, wary in front of camcorders and Virtual recorders. Yes, from a family in Lesser Burgundy, all her possessions signed over to the Order; yes, trained at the academy in Paris; no, she didn't watch the Net much, so her favourite programmes—

A blonde woman, one eye masked by a head-up Virtual Display, shoved her way between Tadmartin and the Marshal of the Templar Order. Philippe de Molay's long face never changed but his body-language radiated annoyance.

'Knight-lieutenant Tadmartin,' the young woman said, with a precise Greater Burgundian accent. 'Louise de Keroac: I have you on realtime for Channel Nine. Knight-lieutenant Tadmartin, will you confirm that you were in charge of the company responsible for the Roanoke massacre?'

5 July 1991

One estate over, the houses and the cars are newer and there's more space between everything. Here the cars are old, knocked about, and parked bumper-to-bumper. Heat shimmers off pavements. Terraces and semis shoulder each other. Pavement trees droop, roots covered in dog-shit.

'Hey, Tad!'

Both Hook and Norton wear old Disruptive Pattern Material combat trousers, the camouflage light brown on dark brown;

and Para boots. Hook's hair is shaved down to brown fuzz. Norton grinds out a cigarette against the wall.

'So what about the Heckler & Koch G11.'

Tad ruffles Norton's hair; he catches her arm; she breaks the grip. Time was when bunking off school left them conspicuous in the empty day. Now there are enough anomalies – unemployed, sick, retired, re-training – that they merge. Tad with braided hair, jeans; pockets always full.

'Caseless ammo. Eleven millimetre. This one really works. Low penetration, high stopping power – they want to use it for terrorist sieges.'

Tad knows. She can remember the excitement of knowing the litany of technology. The skill in knowing all measurements, all details; all the results of firing trials. She can remember when it was all new.

Tad and Hook end up in Norton's house, watching films on the old VCR. The living-room smells of milk and sick, and there are dog-hairs on the couch. Someone – Norton's older sister, probably – has left a clutch of empty and part-empty lager cans on the floor, along with stubbed-out cigarettes.

'So what's he say?'

'About training camp?'

Tad snorts. 'Of course about training camp.' Norton's brother is in the forces, and sent somewhere we don't talk about. Not if we want Norton's brother to remain the healthy, brutal, nineteen-year-old that they remember him.

'He says he nearly couldn't hack it.'

There is an awed pause: Norton's brother transformed from the squaddie in uniform to the sixteen-year-old that Tad remembers from summers ago. Word came back to Tad that Norton's brother and his mate done a runner from basic training; later she will know this is not true. Not and stay in the forces. Which Norton's brother does for five years – until, in fact, some New Amsterdam paramilitary unit fires a rocket launcher at a garrison. The rocket goes literally between the two squaddies on Norton's brother's truck, giving both of them a bad case of sunburn: injuries from the rocket-motor. Norton's brother is inside talking to the on-duty watch, and there isn't anything of him left to find.

Tad, two years from knowing this, says, 'But did you ask him?'

'Yeah. He says you'll get in. They'll take you.'

Norton goes quiet after this. Hook prods him with one of the endless arguments about the stunts in the aerial sequences of *Top Gun*. Tad sprawls against the broken sofa. She is among clutter: a folded pushchair, someone's filthy work jacket, Tonka toys. She makes three separate efforts to join the argument and they exclude her. She feels bewilderment and hurt.

Remembering that hurt, it comes to her that they shut her out because they can see what she, at that moment, still cannot. That she will be the one to do what they never will – follow Norton's brother.

And more, that she has always meant to do this.

'I have nothing to say.'

The blonde woman spy-eye persisted. 'You were at Roanoke, Knight-lieutenant? You were at Roanoke at the time when the incident took place?'

Tadmartin let her face go blank. 'Nothing to say. You can talk to my company commander, Demzelle Keroac. I have no comment.'

'Will you admit to being on service in the New World at that time?'

'You can't expect a junior officer to comment on troop movements,' Philippe de Molay said smoothly. 'Thank you, Lieutenant Tadmartin.'

She saluted smartly. Shoulder and arm muscles shrieked protest, stiffening after exercise. She about-faced, trod smartly down the steps; heard the woman's voice raised in protest behind her as the security detail closed in.

Lights and camcorders crowded her face as she stepped off the platform into a crowd of reporters.

'Just a few words, Knight-lieutenant—'

'—you think of the European Unification—'

'—opinion on the story breaking in New Amsterdam; please, Demzelle Tadmartin?'

She knew better than to react. Still, New Amsterdam in that colonial accent made her blink momentarily. She looked between jostling bodies – and memorised the face of a tall man, wispy-haired, with a tan skin that argued long Western service or Indo-Saracen blood.

'And your view of the Order's investment holdings in the New World—?'

She wiped her wrist across her nose and grinned at him, sweaty, breath eased from the long combat. 'It isn't my business to have financial or political opinions, sieur. If you'll excuse me, I have duties to attend to.'

Voices broke out, trying for a final question, but her patience and control ran on thin threads now.

'Yo, Tysoe!' She broke free and jogged across the field to the surgeon's van. The large, gawky woman waved her uninjured arm, beaming groggily through pain-suppressants.

'Wow, man. You look pissed off. What did they give you, six months' hard labour?'

Tadmartin heaved the buckle of her belt tighter, gaining more support for the mail hauberk. Disentangling herself from mail was an undignified operation – arse-skyward and wriggling – that mostly required help, and she was damned if she'd do it for an audience on the network. She swung herself up to sit on the van's hard bench seats. The orderlies snapped Tysoe's stretcher in place. Tadmartin saw they were ordinary grunts.

'I'll go back to base with you,' she stated, and pointed at one of the orderlies. 'You! Get my squad leader on the radio. I want him to supervise the clearup detail here. I said now, soldier.'

'Yessir, ma'am!' Tysoe said, in a broad Lesser Burgundian accent. 'Boy, are you pissed off. What happened?'

'I'll tell you what happened, Knight-lieutenant Tysoe.'

Tadmartin leaned back against the rail as the van coughed into gear. The sun slanted into the stadium, ranked faces still awaiting the final speeches that she need not sit through; and a granular gold light informed the air. She wiped the sweat-darkened hair back from her face.

'Someone wanted to interview me about Roanoke.'

Tysoe grunted. Pain-suppressants allowed a shadow of old grief or guilt to change her expression.

'That was settled. That was accounted for.'

'No,' Tadmartin said. 'No.'

5 July 1992

Tad hits cover at the side of the track, body pressed into the bank. Her body runs with sweat. She stinks of woodsmoke survival fires. Listening so hard she can hear the hum of air in the canals of her ears. She risks a glance back. She can't see the four men in her squad who are down the track behind her – which is how it should be. They can see her. Their responsibility to watch for silent signals.

Looking up the track, she can see Tysoe, Shule, and Warner flattened into bushes and behind trees. On ceaseless watch, Tysoe catches her eye: taps hand to shoulder in the sign for *officer* and pats the top of her head, *come to me*. Tad immediately slips up to join her.

'We've got to move up. What's the problem?'

Tysoe: all knees and elbows, face plump with puppy-fat. She shrugs. 'Warner and Shule. You put them on point. They keep going into cover.'

'Jesu Sophia!' Tad, bent double, dodges tree-to-tree as far as Shule, who's belly-down behind soft cover. 'For fuck's sake move!'

'The scouts—'

'Just fucking move!'

She picks up Shule bodily by the collar, throwing him forward. He opens his mouth to protest. She slams her rifle-butt against the back of his helmet. His head hits the ground. He and Warner move off. She signals the squad forward in file, settling in behind point, shoving Shule on every ten or fifteen yards. Too late to change point now: Tysoe would have been better, but she needs Tysoe as her other team leader, so – command decision.

At low volume she thumbs the RT. Out-of-date equipment, like so much else here. 'Sierra Zero Eight, this is Oscar Foxtrot Nine. Give sit-rep, repeat, sit-rep. Over.'

No voice acknowledges. The waveband crackles.

'Sierra Zero Eight, do you copy?'

White noise.

'Fuck.' She looks back to catch Tysoe's eye, signals *close up* and *move faster*; slides the rifle down into her hands and jogs off at Shule's heels. The kevlar jacket weighs her down; her feet throb in her boots; and the assault rifle could be made from lead for all she knows.

Running, she can hear nothing.

The forest is a mess of brushwood, high trees, spatter-sunlight that's a gift to camouflage; noisy leaves, her own harsh breath in her ears; sweat, anxiety, frustration. Her eight-man squad moves tactically from cover to cover, but all of it soft cover. No time to check her watch but she knows they've exhausted all the time allowed for this flanking attack and then some.

'Fuck it!' She skids to a halt, signals cover and beckons Tysoe. The young woman spits as she hits cover beside Tad.

'What?'

There should be silent signals for all of this: she's forgotten them.

'We haven't got time for this! We're leaving the track. I'm taking them down through the wood; we'll come out above the camp and take them from there. Pass it back.'

She hears Tysoe go back as she moves forward to Warner and Shule. The woods are still. Not a crack of branch. And no firing from down by the base-camp. Nothing. A hundred square miles and there could be no one else there . . .

'Move!' she repeats, throwing Warner forward bodily. He stumbles into the brush. Giving up, she takes point; ducking to avoid snagging her pack on branches. One look behind assures her Tysoe – thank God for Tysoe! – is taking the back door and moving the squad up between them by sheer will.

Sacrificing tactics for speed, she cuts down a steep pine slope, over needles and broken branches; pauses once to thumb the RT and hear nothing but white noise; hits a remembered gully and slides down into it, feeding Warner and Shule and Ragald on and past her.

Just turned sixteen, Tad is not yet grown; a young woman with her hair under the too-large helmet shaved down to bootcamp fuzz. She hooks her neckerchief up to cover her mouth and nose and crawls down the gully, placing each of the eight-man squad at intervals.

Now she can hear voices, or is the fool-the-ear silence of the Burgundian woods? Let it ride, let it ride . . . and yes: a voice. The crackle of a voice over an RT, muted, a good twenty-five yards over the far rim of the gully. She gives the thumbs-down for *enemy seen or suspected*, points direction, holds up three fingers for distance. Looking down the line, she sees Tysoe grinning. All of them acknowledge. Even Shule's smartened up.

Eight sixteen-year-aids in soaked and muddy combats, weighed down with packs and helmets, assault rifles ready.

She signals stealth approach.

Up to the edge of the gully, assault rifle cradled across her forearms, moving in the leopard-crawl. One hand lifting twigs out of her way; not resting a knee until she knows the ground is clear underneath.

Concussive explosion shatters the air. The rapid stutter of fire: still so noisy that she hardly believes it. She flattens down to the turf, the camp spread out below her, anyone who so much as glances up from the APCs and tents can see her—

The basecamp grunts are hitting dirt and hitting cover behind the gate barrier. Tad grins. There goes the diversionary attack, in on the gate. Blanks, loud and stinking.

She jerks her arm forward, and the dummy grenades go in; then the squad, charging, yelling, running as if they carried no weight at all. Firing on automatic.

Tad never sees the end of it.

A stray paint-pellet rips open across her stomach, splattering her scarlet. It is assumed the attacking grunts' blanks mostly miss. It is established that the training sergeants' pellet guns rarely do. The impact bruises. Tad goes down.

The wilderness training range echoes with gunfire, shouts, radio communications, orders, pyrotechnic explosions. She lies on her back. Men and women run past her. A smoke grenade goes off. Orange smoke drifts between the trees. Tad, with what she assumes for convenience's sake to be her last conscious effort, puts on her respirator. The choking smoke rolls over her. The firing continues.

An hour later, exhausted, dirty, hungry; Tad calculates that, within the confines of this exercise, the medivac team failed to reach her before she became a fatality. She resigns herself to latrine duties.

'Sieur Tadmartin.'

She grins. 'Sarge.'

The sergeant kicks the foodpack out of her hands; she's up, outraged; he hits her fist-then-elbow across the face. 'You're a dead grunt – *sieur*. Why? I'll tell you why. Because you're a shit-stupid, dumbass excuse for a soldier. What are you?'

'A shit-stupid dumbass excuse for a soldier.' Sergeants run armies; she is not, even at sixteen and in officer training, stupid enough to answer back the company sergeant.

'And just why are you a shit-stupid dumbass excuse for a soldier, Tadmartin? Speak up! These people want to hear you.'

'Don't know, sergeant.'

This time she sees it coming. When his fist cracks across her face her nose begins to leak dark blood.

'Because you set up an opportunity and you blew it. You took your people in like fucking cowboys. Next time you start a stealth attack you keep it up until you're in charge distance, you don't fucking waste it, you pathetic bitch, do I make myself clear?'

'Yes, sergeant.'

'Coming in from the gully was good. You weren't spotted at all until you broke cover. Not,' he raised his voice to include the trainees guarding the base, 'that that should particularly surprise me, since none of you hick-stupid officers can see your arses without a map and searchlight. Now you're going to clean up the area and then you might eat. Move it, fuck-heads!'

The next day they repeat the exercise.

And the next.

The mess hall still had the smell of new buildings about it. Pre-stressed concrete beams, plastic benches, tables bolted to the floor; all new. Only the silence was old. Tadmartin, changed back into the white fatigues of a Knight-lieutenant, ate with the Sergeant Preceptors in the familiar silence. She fell into it as she fell into combat-perception: easily, as a body slides into deep water.

The bell for meal's end sounded.

'Knight Brothers and Sergeants of the Convent. Every perfect gift comes from above, coming down from the Father of Lights and the Mother of Wisdom, Christ and Sophia, with whom there is no change nor shadow of alteration.'

The frère at the lectern cleared his throat, addressing the grunts in the main body of the room.

'The reading today is from the bull of Pope Innocent-Fidelia. "For by nature you were children of wrath, given up to the pleasures of the flesh, but now through grace you have left behind worldly shows and your own possessions; you have humbly walked the hard road that leadeth to life; and to prove it you have most conscientiously taken up the sword and sworn on your breasts the sign of the living cross, because you are especially reckoned to be members of the Knighthood of God." '

Tadmartin sat easily erect on the hard bench. Sunlight slanted down from the clerestory windows on shaven heads, DPM fatigues. The smell of baking bread drifted out from the kitchens: the esquires and confreres working in silence except for the clatter of pans.

The words slid over her and she busied herself remembering equipment maintenance and duty rosters; found herself looking down at her hands in her lap: short-nailed, callused, and with a perceptible tremor.

The bell took her by surprise. She rose, saluting with the rest, about-faced and marched out.

'Tad.' Tysoe, arm strapped, fell into step beside her. 'You know where the rest of the company are now?'

'They were split up.' She didn't break stride.

'We should talk.'

'No.' She walked off without looking back at the taller woman.

Once in her quarters, she ripped the top off a can of lager, drank, and vocalised the code for network access. The cell's viewscreen lit up with the public channel logo.

'Search Tadmartin,' she said morosely. 'Then search Roanoke. Backtime forty-eight hours.'

The small viewscreen beeped and signalled a recorded sequence. Green leaves. Shells: the flat thud of one-oh-fives. A soundtrack:

'Here in Cabotsland, in the Indo-Saracen states, gunfire is an everyday sound. Terrorist explosions mingle with the artillery barrages of brushfire wars between settlements. For generations there has been no peace.'

The shot pulled back to show a spy-eye reporter standing below the walls of Raleighstown. Sun, swamp, forest, and mosquitoes. Tadmartin smiled crookedly. The reporter was a blonde woman in her twenties, eye masked by head-up Virtual Display.

'This is Louise de Keroac on Channel Nine, at Raleighstown. Centuries of settlement – our reformed Gnostic Saracen settlements imposed on the indigenous Indian population – have brought about not the hoped-for melting-pot of civilisation, but a constant boil of war for land and hunting rights. The Crusades suppress this temporarily. But, as we all know, even if governments are reluctant to admit it, after the troops are withdrawn, the fighting breaks out again.'

The woman's visible eye was a penetrating blue. She spoke with a breathy, cynical competence. Tadmartin raised the can to her mouth and drank, the alcohol pricking its way down her throat. She raised a thoughtful eyebrow. The alcohol combated the cell's official 55 degrees F.

De Keroac's voice sharpened:

'But Roanoke is different. Roanoke: our oldest successful settlement in the New World. Five years after the unexplained deaths of fifty-three civilians, as well as fourteen Knights Templar and thirty-three Knights Hospitaller, here in Roanoke, rumours continue to grow of a quasi-official shoot-on-sight policy. None of the soldiers wounded in that battle have ever been available for interview. Official sources have always spoken of "surprise heathen attacks". But now, finally, New Amsterdam is demanding an official enquiry.'

A shot of the shitty end of the settlement; Tadmartin recognised it instantly. In the arms of a great forest, dwarfed by trees, the wooden buildings hug the ground by the river. The palisade fence winds off out of shot. The stone crenellations of the Templar castle came into shot as de Keroac's spy eye panned.

Tadmartin rested her chin on her chest as she slumped back, watching Raleighstown. Bustling, full of men and women in short flowing robes and buckskin leggings, veils drawn up over their mouths against the mosquitoes and the White Fever. Crowded market stalls, with old petrol-engine taxis hooting against herded buffalo in the streets; women with children on their hips; the glitter of sun off low-rise office blocks. The camera caught *Franks go home!* and *To Eblis with Burgundy!* graffited on one wooden wall.

'This is the garrison. The locals call it the garrison of the Burgundian Empire—'

Tadmartin groaned.

'—rather than that of United Europe. Whether partisan attack, terrorist bombs, or one lunatic with a grudge was responsible for the destruction of half its troops has never been known. Now, however, new evidence has appeared.'

'It's the sakkies.' A man leaned up against the door of Tadmartin's cell. Tall, young, broad-shouldered; and with the Turcoplier's star on his collar.

'Yo, Vitry.'

'Yo.' He stubbed out a thin black cigarette against the concrete wall and walked in. 'That one's all bullshit. You want Channel Eight real-time.'

'Eight,' Tadmartin said. The video channel flicked obediently.

'—ever-present knowledge that the European governments could bomb them back into the Stone Age.' A bio-reporter looked to camera: the man with the faded skin, Indo-Saracen blood. 'Talk to the Templar grunts and sergeants. They call them sakkies. Their word for Saracen. No one I've spoken to will believe that a small paramilitary group of sakkies could destroy a trained Knightly garrison—'

'Bollocks.' Vitry squatted beside Tadmartin's armchair and reached for her can of lager. 'Every damn local regime gets lucky some time or another. We all know that. And that's the answer he'll have got. Lying bastard.'

'—attempted to talk to the winner of this year's Unification Tourney; the lieutenant who, as a junior officer, found herself in charge of this Burgundian frontier outpost; Knight-lieutenant Hyacinthe Tadmartin.'

She regarded the screen morosely, watching the stadium from a different angle than the combatants saw. Dust covered the melee in the main field. Vitry peered closely at the screen.

'There's you – and there's me, look!' He lifted his voice without looking away from the screen. 'Yo! You guys! We're on the network!'

'Jesu Sophia!'

She watched herself walk down the steps from the main box. The mail hauberk glittered and the stained surcoat's red cross blazed. The camera zoomed in and held the image of her face: oval, youthful until the eyes. The Knighthood of God. She thought that she looked both older and younger than twenty-six: fitter in body than most, but with weathered crows-feet around her eyes.

She snapped her fingers to mute audio, not being able to stand the sound of her own voice; bringing it up again only when the camera cut back to the bio-reporter.

'Hiding within the strict rules of the Templars – a Templar frère may never "disclose the House", that is, give out information on Templar activities, on penalty of losing their place within the Knighthood – hiding under this cover, no one can cross-examine this member of Burgundy's most elite force—'

'Yo!' Vitry roared. 'That's one for the Hospitallers. We're the most elite force!'

The rest of the mess, crowding Tadmartin's narrow cell, swore at or yelled with Vitry according to temperament.

'—no one can even establish who did command at Roanoke; even less what happened there, and why. Moves are being made to take this to the High Council of Burgundy when it meets with Pope Stephen-Maria V in Avignon later today. But will the truth, even then, be brought to light?

'This is James de Craon, for Channel Eight—'

Talk broke out, the Templars dispersing back to the mess.

'Ah well. Bullshit baffles brains.' Vitry shrugged. 'You never had an overseas posting as far north as Roanoke, did you.'

Since it was not a question Tadmartin felt no obligation to give an answer. She snapped her fingers to kill audio and video. As the crowd moved away from her door, a grunt anxiously saluted her. She returned it.

'Yes?'

'Message from Commander St Omer, sieur. He'll see you in his office at oh-six-hundred hours tomorrow morning.'

5 July 1994

'Fine brother knights.' The Preceptor Philippe de Molay clears his throat and continues to read. 'Biaus seignors frères, you see that the majority have agreed that this woman should be made a frère. If there be someone amongst you who knows reason why she should not be, then speak.'

The dawn sun hits the mirror-windows of Greater Burgundian office blocks and reflects back, slanting down through ogee arches into the chapel, failing to warm the biscuit-coloured stone. Tad, at attention, can just see her instructors – in formal black or brown surcoats – to either side of her. The stone is bitter cold under her bare feet. The Preceptor's voice echoes flatly.

'You who would be knightly, you see us with fine harness, you see us eat well and drink well, and it therefore appears your comfort with us will be great.'

And so it does appear to Tadmartin, used now to being provided with combat fatigues, formal uniforms, assault rifle, all the technology of communication and destruction.

'But it is a hard thing that you, who are your self's master, should become the serf of another, and this is what will be. If you wish to be on land this side of the ocean, you will be sent to the other; if you wish to be in New Amsterdam, you will be sent to Londres . . . Now search your heart to discover whether you are ready to suffer for God.'

One does not go through the specialist training – *the suffering for man?* Tad wonders – to refuse at this late stage. But some have. When it comes to it, some have refused in this very ceremony.

Outside, the deep blue sky shines. She can hear them drilling, down on the square. Voices, boots. Here in the cold chapel, the commander and turcopliers in their robes stand side-by-side with the medic and psychologist – to certify her fitness – and the solicitor.

'. . . Now I have told you the things that you should do, and those you should not; those that cause loss of the House, and those that cause loss of the habit; and if I have not told you all, then you may ask it, and may God grant you to speak well and do well.'

'God wills it,' Tadmartin says soberly, 'that I hear and understand.'

'Now your instructors may speak.'

De Payens is first. A short, dark-haired woman; worn into service; a sergeant who will do nothing else but train now, although Tad knows she has been offered command of her own House.

De Payens' warm voice says: 'She passed basic training at 89 per cent and advanced training at 93 per cent. We consider this acceptable.'

Six o'clock mornings, runs, workouts, assault courses; field-stripping weapons and field-stripping your opponent's psychology; all of this in her memory as de Payens smiles.

'Advanced strategic and tactical studies,' St Omer concedes, '85 per cent, which we accept.'

'Combat experience,' de Charney's voice comes from behind her. 'No more errors than one might expect with a green lieutenant. I don't give percentages. Christ and Sophia! She's here, isn't she? And so are her squad.'

The Preceptor frowns at that, but Tad doesn't notice. The cold of the chapel becomes the cold of fear. Brown-adrenaline fear, and the boredom and the routine; and the training that takes over and takes her through rough southern days fighting mercenaries on the Gold Coast.

The Preceptor commands, 'Appear naked before God.'

Her fingers are cold, fiddling with the combat fatigues, and it is a long moment before she strips them off and stands naked. The chill of the stone reverberates back from walls and weapon-racks and the altar crowned with the image of St Baphomet. Her skin goosepimples. She has learned to ignore it, resting easy in her body, unselfconscious with their eyes on her.

The Preceptor, de Molay, searches her face as if there is something he could discover. Waiting long minutes until the other Templars stir impatiently.

At last he asks, 'Do you wish to be, all the days of your life, servant and slave of the house?'

She meets his gaze. 'Yes, if God wills, sieur.'

'Then be it so.'

He doesn't look away. She takes the white livery with the red cross from de Payens, who helps her rapidly dress; she signs the document the solicitor gives her, assigning all possessions now and for her lifetime to the Order; she takes the congratulations of the officers relaxing into informal talk. All the time, de Molay's eyes are on hers.

She does not – cannot – ask him what he sees. Woman, frère,

special forces soldier; none seem quite to account for that look. As if, before the altar of God, he sees in her what God does not.

'Roanoke was Border country, sieur.'

'You might as well say bandit country and be done with it.' St Omer spoke quietly and rationally, not looking at her. 'It's still a devil of a long way from being an explanation.'

'I know that, sieur.'

A truck rumbled past outside the window. The dew was still on the tarmac of the camp; grunts doubling across wide avenues to kitchen and latrine duties. Tadmartin ignored her griping stomach. The commander's office smelled of photocopier fluid. Three of the six telephones on his desk blinked for attention.

'Emirate Cabotsland . . .' Knight-Commander St Omer sighed. 'I'm formally warning you, Knight-lieutenant, that it may become necessary for an enquiry to be held.'

'Permission to speak, sieur.'

The middle-aged man responded tiredly. 'Speak as God bids you.'

'The Roanoke House already held such an inquiry, sieur. Report dated 10 July 1997. You can access it above rank of captain, sieur.'

Tadmartin stared at a middle-distance spot six inches to the left of the commander's eyes, wondering what particular circumstances had left him manning a desk while other, younger knights gained field promotions . . . She steered herself away from seeing her image mirrored in him.

'You misunderstand me,' St Omer corrected. 'It may become necessary to hold a public enquiry. I suspect that that's what Avignon will come to, ultimately. You're to hold yourself in readiness for that event, and, if it should come about, act in all things in accordance with your vows of obedience to us.'

Tadmartin stared. Caught, for the first time in five years, unprepared. She dropped her usual pretence of just-another-grunt-sieur and responded as Templars do. 'They can't ask me to disclose the house!'

'Normally, no, but his Holiness Stephen-Maria may release you from that vow. Publicly.'

'That – sieur, excuse me, even his Holiness can't reverse a vow made before God and the chapter!'

St Omer stood and walked to the window. He remained facing it, a black silhouette against brightness. Tadmartin returned to staring rigidly ahead.

'The Magister Templi requires me to inform you, Knight-lieutenant, that – if necessary – you will answer questions on the secret history. Is that clear? Of course,' the level voice added, 'what you perceive as a necessity will prove of interest to us all.'

Maps of Cabotsland's settled east coast on the walls, satellite photos of its Shogunate west coast; network terminals, old mugs half-full of coffee: the commander's office is one Tadmartin has often stood in, on many different bases. And there are the insignia on the walls, of course. Banners of campaigns. Some traditions do not die.

'You'll leave at oh-nine-hundred for Avignon; you will be accompanied at all times by a security detail; you will report to me immediately on your return. Go with God. Dismissed.'

5 July 1995

Tadmartin hefts the sword in her hand. It's lighter than she expects, no more than two or three pounds. A yard-long blade, a short cross-guard, a brazil-nut-shaped pommel.

This is a live blade. Bright, it nonetheless has the patina of age on its silver. But a live blade, with a razor edge, and it slides through the air as slick as oil. It flies, it dives. The weight of it moves her wrist in the motions for attack, parry and block.

'And that's the difference.' The combat instructor takes it back from her reluctant hand. He replaces it in the weapons rack. The sun from the gymnasium window lights his sand-coloured, whitening hair.

She wants to hold it, to wield it again. She has the height and strength now of adulthood; a woman of slightly less than medium height, with strong shoulders. She wears new white combats, with the Templar red cross above the breast pocket.

'You, however, are going to use this for today.'

He hands her, single-handed, a greatsword.

Two-handed grip, wide cross, forty-four inch blade. Tadmartin takes it, coming into guard position: the balance is good. But it weighs as much again as the single-hander.

Probably her body-language broadcasts impatience: she would rather be out on the ranges. Possibly he has had to deal with other recruits to the House of Solomon. The instructor, Sevrey, shifts into combat speed; and she is left defenceless, holding the grip in sweating hands, as his blade swings to cut at face, belly, groin: the blunt edge barely touching the cloth of her combats each time as he stops it. Ten, twenty blows.

'It's a discipline. The Templar discipline.'

A yard of steel, rebated or not, is an iron bar that can break and crush. She freezes – after all her training, freezes, like any green conscript or civilian – and the blade flashes back brilliance.

'We've never broken this tradition. From the first Holy Land until now.' He stops, sudden but smooth; he is not breathing any more strenuously. When he wields the sword he becomes something other than a forgettable-faced sergeant. The sword and the body are one.

'It's what we are.'

She has seen him fight. Nothing of grace in it, unless it is the grace of chopping wood or driving stakes; the whole body weighing into the movement.

'I'll teach you,' Sevrey says. 'At the moment you're thinking about it. Where's the blade coming from, how do I move to parry, can I block that, where shall I attack? Train. Train and practise.'

'And then?'

As he speaks she moves out onto the mat, gripping the sword, swinging it through the drill movements of parry and blow. Sometimes the blade is inert. Sometimes it moves like running water.

'Sword and intention.'

She will understand intellectually but not in her gut. That comes later. With some it never comes at all.

'The sword is not part of you. You have an intention to use it.' Sevrey moves out onto the mat with her. They circle. She watches, watches his eyes, the blade. Later she will learn not to watch any particular point in her field of vision, but to see it all, central and peripheral, simultaneously.

'First comes no-sword,' Sevrey says. His blade comes out of nowhere, feints; she pulls back from a parry and his sword connects firmly across her stomach. An inch and a half behind the peritoneal wall coil thirty yards of intestine, and how much pressure does it take on a razor-edge to split muscle?

'No-sword: when the sword becomes an extension of yourself. You don't move the sword. You and the sword move.'

She flips the blade back, lets the weight carry it over; and he cuts behind her cut and parries her through, the steel clashing in the echoing gymnasium.

'And then—' the first break in his stream of words as he almost follows her feint; gets back in time to block '—if you're good, then no-intention. You'll have done so much fighting that in combat you don't even think, you don't even see an opening. You just watch the sword come down and cut home – it'll seem slow to you. No-sword, no-intention. But for that you're going to have to spend a lot of time at it, or be naturally good, or both.'

If he says more, she doesn't hear, the fight speeds up now. Combat speed.

In three months she will find herself fighting in this same gym, in a multiple melee; she will – and she only realises it after the moment, and stands still in mid-combat and is cut down easily – strike down one opponent to her right and, in a reverse movement, block a stroke coming at her from behind with a perfect glissade. Nothing of it conscious. Nothing. But to the end of her days she will hear that back attack connect with her blocking blade, and hear Sevrey's profane astonishment at her getting it there.

Air-conditioning hummed in the room without windows.

His Holiness Stephen-Maria V sat at the centre of the horseshoe-shaped table. He intently watched a small monitor, resting his chin on his gloved hand. Two priests stood in readiness behind his chair. Incense drifted from their censers, whitening the corners of the room and smelling of sandalwood.

Tadmartin came to attention the prescribed three yards in front of the table and knelt, bowing her head. The heavy material of her white surcoat draped the floor. She noted with detachment the shoes of the others seated at the horseshoe-table: officers' boots, politicians' shoes, and the fashionably impractical footwear of the media. Everything impinges itself on the detachment of combat-vision.

'Rise, demzelle.'

She rose easily. Only her eyes moved, checking the faces. Civil servants. Priests. Mostly unknown: these would be the power-brokers, and not the men put there for show. Military: the heads of the Templar and Hospitaller Orders. And two other known faces – Channel Eight and Channel Nine seated side by side, all rivalry gone; James de Craon bending his ruddy countenance on her blind side as Louise de Keroac murmured some comment.

Outwardly calm, Tadmartin waited.

'I think we may offer the demzelle a chair, don't you?' His Holiness Stephen-Maria glanced at one of the dark-suited men on his right.

'I prefer to stand, sieur.'

Outside the claustrophobic secure room, Avignon's baroque avenues and domed cathedrals shone with rain, the last of it dampening Tadmartin's red-crossed surcoat and white combats.

The Pontiff leaned back in his chair. Fluorescent lighting glittered from his white and golden robes, stiff with embroidery. He shone against the beige walls like an icon. His small owl-face creased with thought.

'Knight-lieutenant, will you summarise for the board of inquiry the purpose of the Order of Knights Templar, please.'

At this moment and in this place, a minefield of a question. Tadmartin responded instantly. 'We're a trained elite force, sieurs. Founded in 1130 AD, in the first Holy Land. We do undertake Burgundian missions where necessary, but we see action primarily overseas in Cabotsland. We operate out of the Templar fortresses down the east coast. Our main objective is to keep the pilgrim roads clear from the coast to New Jerusalem. It's therefore necessary for us to keep civil order.'

The bio-reporter De Craon raised his hand. The priest at Stephen-Maria's side signalled assent.

'Lieutenant Tadmartin.' De Craon turned to her, the room's fluorescent lights shining in his wispy hair. 'These fortresses are garrisoned with Templars?'

'Yes, and with lay-brothers.'

De Craon smiled. Skin creased lizard-like around his mouth. 'There is another Order, am I right, who assists you in this?'

She kept her eyes from the Knight-Brigadier of St John. 'The Hospitallers provide auxiliary services, yes, sieur.'

'But they also see action?'

'After a fashion, sieur, yes.'

An almost imperceptible lifting of Stephen-Maria's hand and the bio-reporter became silent. The Pontiff, amiably smiling, said, 'Demzelle de Keroac, do you also have a question?'

'Sure I do.' The woman planted her elbows on the table. Her curled hair glittered yellow in that suffocating light. She fixed Tadmartin with a brilliant blue eye. 'You know your Templar organisation also provides a banking service for the United governments?'

'I know that one exists.' Tadmartin paused. 'I don't know how it functions, demzelle. It never occurred to me that it was my concern.'

The woman twitched a muscle in her cheek. The spy-eye whirred into zoom, closing on Tadmartin's face. 'Do you know just how rich the Templars are, Knight-lieutenant? Do you realise why that makes them close advisors to presidents?'

'I don't know anything about banking, demzelle. I don't have any money of my own.' Momentarily amused at the disbelief on the woman's face, she added, 'The Order provides my housing, uniform, food, and equipment. Anything I own was signed over to them when I joined the Order. I never handle money unless I'm getting supplies from the locals round a garrison.'

Louise de Keroac snorted. 'You're telling me soldiers never go out drinking, or to the local brothels?'

'We are the Knights of God.' Tadmartin, not able to hear the tone in which she quietly said that, was surprised to find the room silent. 'Some backslide, yes; if they do it repeatedly they lose the house.'

A movement snagged peripheral vision. Tadmartin turned her head. Not the Templar Marshal de Molay, sitting still and expressionless. The stout man next to him in black-and-red DPMs and Knight-Brigadier's insignia.

'Harrison, Order of St John,' he introduced himself briskly to the media. 'What is your view of the Knights Hospitaller, Demzelle Tadmartin?'

Dangerous. She refrained from saluting, which was some

return for the *demzelle*. A coldness touched her which was not the air-conditioning. Thoughtfully, she said, 'I suppose there's a competitive spirit between all the knightly Orders, sieur.'

'But between Hospitallers and Templars? Wouldn't you call it more than "competitive"?'

She looked towards Stephen-Maria's small, bland face. 'Competition is strong, yes, sieur. The Hospitallers being under worldly jurisdiction.'

Abruptly Stephen-Maria snatched off his gold-rimmed spectacles, leaning forward and pointing at Tadmartin with a gloved finger. 'Knight-lieutenant, do you ever think of the young Indo-Saracen women and men whom you fight? Although they are terrorists and heretics, do you think of them as people, with souls? Human feelings?'

Tadmartin gave that due consideration, relieved at the change of subject. 'Not really, sieur. I don't think you can afford to. I tend to think in terms of target-areas.'

'But you are aware of it.'

'Yes, sieur.'

'One should thank God for it. Since there is wheat among the chaff – innocent civilians among the terrorists.'

His eyes were an exact faded blue. It was not possible to tell his age. Tadmartin remained easily at attention. The security detail at the entrance to the building had relieved her of her automatic.

'Under what circumstances is it permissible to kill, lieutenant?'

'I do my job, sieur. It's a professional job, and I've been trained to do it very well. Yes, it says in the holy texts Thou shalt not kill. It also says Suffer not the enemies of God to live. Sometimes that has to be done, and it's better left to trained personnel.'

'Pariahs for the Lord.' Stephen-Maria smiled. It was not, despite his creased face, a gentle expression. 'Who are the enemies of God in Cabotsland, lieutenant?'

Knowing he must know all, Tadmartin nevertheless blinked uneasily at that question. 'Indo-Saracen terrorists, sieur. Natives. Tokugawa-backed paramilitary groups.'

'Yes . . . and only those. Lieutenant, remember one thing.

Your Order answers to no president or government on this earth. It answers to us. We think it would be as well if you answer us truthfully.'

'Yes, sieur.'

How much for the media? How much for the anonymous suited men and women around the table? And who is to be the scapegoat? Tadmartin relaxed imperceptible muscles so that she still stood effortlessly to attention under their scrutiny.

'Lieutenant Tadmartin, you know what is meant by the secret history.'

'Yes, sieur.'

'Will you give us your understanding of the term, please? For the benefit of these people here.'

Tadmartin cleared her throat. 'It's a traditional term for the Cartulary of a knightly monastic order. It contains the full details of campaigns.'

'Full details?' Louise de Keroac pounced. 'So what's given to the outside world is censored?'

Tadmartin politely took the offensive. 'Not censored, demzelle, no. Condensed. Would you want all the details of how many water-bowsers were sent to which port and when; how many aerial refuellings took place on any given mission; how many sergeant-brothers were treated for blisters or heat exhaustion—?'

'Just how condensed is the history for public consumption?'

Stephen-Maria V said, 'Demzelles, sieurs, you can judge for yourselves. Knight-lieutenant Tadmartin, we're going to ask you to answer according to the secret history. We want your own account of the Roanoke incident. You were there. You were, however temporarily, the officer in charge of that company. Regrettably, innocent people died. The reports the public can access through this—' Stephen-Maria tapped the computer console '—are official. You now have our order to speak without reservation.'

For whom does one tell the truth? Tadmartin let her gaze go around the table, seeing bankers and politicians and the media; and she did not let her gaze stop at the Templar knight Philippe de Molay in his white and red. No question. Finally, there is no question at all.

Tadmartin said, 'No, sieur.'

'We,' Stephen-Maria V said, with a deliberate gravitas, 'are granting you absolution from your vow.'

Unspoken, his gaze tells her this is enough of the obligatory refusals.

'You can't absolve me from the vows of secrecy, sieur, no one can. I'd lose the House and the habit.'

He scowled at her stone-wall morality. 'My daughter, there have been public accusations made, that the Order of the Knights Templar operates a shoot-on-sight policy in the emirate lands. These talks are to give an equally public refutation of that accusation.'

But truth is a seamless whole. Part told, all will be told. Tadmartin shrugged. 'Sieur. You don't understand. If I speak, I'll have to leave the Order; I couldn't stay – I couldn't face them.'

The Supreme Pontiff remained silent, but the priest at his left hand said quietly, 'For refusing to obey the supreme head of your Order you will lose the House, demzelle. I remind you of this.'

'Yes.' Tadmartin did not say *I know*. She let the media frustration wash over her, standing steady, her gaze fixed just slightly to the left of the Pontiff's head.

James de Craon interjected, 'What have you got to hide, lieutenant?'

'Nothing. This isn't about me. It's about the Rule of the Knights Templar.'

Pope Stephen-Maria V said, 'Will you speak?'

Tadmartin shook her head. 'No.'

'You must.'

She allowed herself the luxury of showing, in full, what she felt in part. 'Sieur, I can't!'

For the first time her voice varied from its reasonable calm. A soldier's voice, roughened with shouting over the noise of firefights; a woman's voice thinned by the heat of bandit country. Now she heard her voice shake.

'We're Templars. We are what we are because of how we behave. You don't break vows. You don't. We're not just any body of fighting men. Sieur, you must understand, you're the Pontiff. I can't obey the order you're giving me.'

The priest leaned forward and murmured in the Pontiff's ear.

'I warned you, your Holiness. The men won't speak, the officers won't speak; it was most unlikely you could persuade a junior officer of the Templars to speak out in open court.'

'We are the head of the Order!'

Tadmartin made as if to say something, opening her mouth, but her throat constricted and she was silent. All muscles tense, as if her body urged her *speak out!*, but she literally could say nothing.

Am I really going to do this? she thought. Am I going to let them – no, am I going to *make* them throw me out of the Order? Jesu Sophia! I'm too old to go back to the regular army – and they won't take me anyway.

'For God's sake, sieur.' She at last appealed to the Templar Marshal seated midway down the right-hand side of the table. She spoke doubly: in her role as stolid knight, and with her own secret knowledge. 'I've got nowhere to go if I leave the Order. I couldn't even buy civilian clothes! Don't let them force me out. Sieur, please!'

'There's nothing I can do, lieutenant.'

De Molay's tone let her know he was aware of duplicity. The man's face was flushing a dull red: anger at her display of emotion, anger at his own embarrassment. Not until he looked away from her to the Knight of St John, and then back, did she catch his expression properly. Seen once before, in a chapel, one cold dawn.

'Get rid of these people!'

The Pontiff swore at his attendant priests and shoved his chair back, rising. The chair clattered over. The swirl of his robes as he turned caught a censer, tipping out burning sandalwood coals. One black-suited man stamped furiously on the sparks. Stephen-Maria stalked out.

The men and women at the table rose, caught by surprise. Talk broke out; the media people checking recordings; the rest debating uncertainties.

Tadmartin stood, undismissed. Even now, hoping against knowledge for a reprieve. Praise, even, for her steadfastness. Nothing came.

A quartet of military police officers filed in to escort her out.

5 July 1997

When it comes to a question, which do you choose?

There is no question.

The truck jolts and her ribs slam against the rim of the cab-window. The road to New Jerusalem winds up into the high lands, white under the moon. An exposed road, here.

The Hospitaller APCs judder past, tracks grinding white dust that falls wet and heavy from their passing.

'What's the intelligence report on hostiles?'

'They're saying up to sixty hostiles, heavily-armed. Fucking sakkies.' Tysoe spits.

Tadmartin has never seen that trail's end. Has never been posted to that tiny Vinland settlement where, one millennium since, Sophie Christos came to preach her gnostic gospel and reap the reward commonly given to reformers. But Tadmartin has, on the same chain as her dog-tag, a tiny fragment of the Second True Cross embedded in clear plastic.

'Give the Hospitallers sixty minutes dead,' she directs Tysoe. 'If they can't get their half of the ambush set up by then, fuck 'em.'

'Bastards.'

Brown cam-cream distorts the angles of moonlight on Tysoe's face. She's leaner than she was in training, five years ago; a long-jawed, bony woman.

'Something you should have reported to me, girl?'

'Pfcs Johannes Louis and Gilles Barker aren't on duty.'

The captain absent, Tadmartin is senior of the four lieutenants at the garrison. Tysoe has Squad One, Cohen Two, and Ragald has Three; sergeants are keeping the fort secure. Close on a hundred men, a company-size operation. Needless to say she has not commanded at this level before, or not officially, and not under combat conditions. It tends to blur the minutiae.

She notes now that Squad One has a replacement man on heavy-weapons support, and a woman Tadmartin recognises from the garrison taking the RT. She misses Gilles Barker's snap-on laconic radio technique. Johannes Louis will be missed by no one, realistically, but that's not the point; he was part of the squad.

'Brawling, wasn't it? They're both on the medic register.'

The exigencies of ambush take her away from the vehicle for a minute, sending Two Squad and Three Squad up into position to approach the valley. Trees sway and creak. The night is uneasy, and the full moon an annoyance. And all the time that white, white road runs east away from her, dusty with the feet of a million pilgrims, trudging or riding broken-down trucks from Templar fort to Templar fort, all the way to the end of the trail.

She hauls herself up into the back of the truck.

'We'll move out in five.'

Tension. Final checks of equipment – grenade launchers, heavy machine-guns, flamers, assault rifles – and the mutters of *shit* and *fuck* and *Jesu Sophia!*, and the churning gut that always comes with action; the fear that stops the breath in your lungs. Tadmartin puts her head down for a second, inhaling deeply, and straightens with some electric excitement replacing breath.

'Barker and Louis,' Tysoe says, joining her. 'Hospitallers jumped 'em last night.'

'Sophie Christos,' Tadmartin says, disgusted.

Raleighstown, a spring night, Tadmartin new in the outremer territories; she and the other Knight-lieutenants gone drinking. In downtown bars where the whisky is rough and cheap, and there are the young men and women who naturally congregate around military bases: who know what to offer and what to expect in payment. But Tadmartin tells herself she is only there for the drink. And Tadmartin, leaning out of a bar door and throwing up in the street, is hit in the kidneys from behind, sprawls face down in her own vomit, white DPMs stained yellow and brown.

'Fuckin' Templar cunt!'

Tadmartin does nothing but come easily up onto her feet. Head clearing, the night slipping past in freeze-frames: herself on hands and knees, herself standing, three Hospitaller squaddies grinning – a red-haired man and two sharp-uniformed women.

'Yo,' she says softly. Turns smartly, unsteadily, on her heel and walks back into the bar, back where Tysoe and – names? – names forgotten, but the company lieutenants are there, and two sergeant preceptors, so there are six of them; and out into the night, where one of the Hospitaller women is still visible down the road, and off and running into the downtown quarter. Following her down the road at a sprint, streetlights failing, and swinging down one alley and across into the next—

Where there are thirty Hospitaller squaddies waiting. Her buddies. Tadmartin finds out that they even call it Templar-bashing.

Arrests and enquiries do not follow, not even for a shit-stupid dumbass excuse for a lieutenant. Templars and Hospitallers have to police the same territory, after all. There are nominal noises of disapproval on both sides. She is out of hospital in a matter of months and feels pain in her hands for two winters after.

'Stupid cunts. Aw, shit, Tysoe, girl!'

Warnings go out from the company captain's desk, strict warnings with penalties attached. Leave the Hospitallers alone. There will always be grunts who regard them as challenges, or a matter of pride.

'Louis'll be back.' The woman puts on her helmet, clips the strap, checks the internal RT. 'They blinded Gilles Barker. Left eye. Going to be invalided out.'

'Christ.'

Implications flick through her head. For a shared op.

'Where's the report on this?'

'It's on your desk.'

'Shit. Okay—' Too late to change the plan now. All she can do is keep a closer eye on Squad One. 'Okay, I'll come in with you guys; Ragald can take Three up the road. That's time – let's roll.'

Out of the truck and into the forests. Maybe a mile to cover, but a mile in silence. They melt into night and quiet, each one; going down into a silent crawl, shifting twigs and branches as they move, falling into the rhythm of clear ground, move elbow, clear ground, move knee . . .

Fifty minutes.

The terrain changes. Leaving the forest for wet heather, and then up along drained hill-slopes and into pine. Tadmartin moves in the night, combats soaked, warm with the weight she carries. Slow, slow. Cold breath drifts from her mouth; camo-cream is cold on her skin. She crawls past a fox. Unspooked, it watches her go. The night wind moves the creaking pines.

'Delta Alpha, sit-rep, over?'

'This is Delta Alpha, in position, out.'

'Hotel Oscar, sit-rep, over.'

'Hotel Oscar to Romeo Victor, say again, over?'

'Romeo Victor to Hotel Oscar, sit-rep, say again, sit-rep, over.'

'. . . Victor, in position, do you copy?'

'Hotel Oscar, I copy, out. Sierra Foxtrot, sit-rep, over.'

'In position, Romeo Victor. Out.'

She curses the moon. Too much light. It blotches the ground under the gnarled pines, splashes the jutting rocks at the edges of the deep valley. Low-voiced zip-squirts over the RT assure her Tysoe's got Squad One in position along the cliff-top, Three's further up; Two covering flank and rear.

Tadmartin moves up, assault rifle cradled, crawling silently from cover to cover. She edges on her belly into the brushwood that overhangs one jutting rock.

The night wind is cold against her eyes. At least the noise will screen movement – but that's a two-edged weapon. She stares down into the valley.

A bright flicker of light is moonlight on the stream, thrashing in its rock-strewn bed. The road winds along the valley floor, sometimes beside the river, sometimes crossing it. The overhang she lies on is fifty yards upstream of a bridge. Nothing moving down there yet. No sound of engines. She merges into the stripes of moonlight and brushwood, thinking tree.

And across the other side of the gorge a glint of light shows her someone using night glasses. She sub-vocalises for the helmet RT and zipsquirts:

'Romeo Force to Juliet, repeat Romeo Force to Juliet, do you copy? Tell your men to lay off the night scopes, they can see 'em back in town, for fuck's sake! Over.'

There is the split-second time-delay of zipsquirt transmission, then:

'Juliet Force to Romeo, wilco, out.'

Curt to the point of abruptness. Tadmartin grins but it stiffens, becomes a rictus on her face. Thinking of Johannes Louis and Gilles Barker.

She lies on her belly and stares across the gorge, idly pinpointing the more unwary of the Hospitaller troops. The ambush will lay fire down into the valley and nothing will walk out of it. Assuming that the hostiles come down the valley and not around it. Assuming that intelligence is right and an arms-shipment is due. Assuming.

Always assuming.

'Romeo Victor, this is Sierra Foxtrot. We have a possible contact, repeat, possible contact at Falcon Station. Advise, over.'

'Sierra Foxtrot, this is Romeo Victor. Confirm sighting and advise numbers. Let them come past you. Out. Romeo Force to Juliet—' She swallows, continues with a level voice. 'Possible contact at Falcon Station. Over.'

'Juliet to Romeo, I copy, out.'

Each of the valley bends has been assigned a name. She listens to the zipsquirt transmissions: Falcon, Eagle, Duck, and Crow all passed, and then the sound of engines is clear to her. She blinks up visual enhancement, closing one eye and staring down the valley. Patches of moonlight blot and blind. She blinks enhancement off and relies on one eye's night vision.

There.

Nosing around the corner of the gorge, one . . . two . . . three closed trucks, rolling with the movements of heavily-loaded vehicles. An artic, straining at the gradient. Three more trucks, and a battered old limo. The engines shatter the silence of the woods.

'Romeo Victor to all units, confirmed sighting at Bluejay Station.' Sliding the assault rifle up the length of her chilled body so that it will not catch on the rock. The way behind her is clear for retreat. The gorge in front of her is one killing zone. 'Hold your fire until I give the signal—'

Silence shatters. The night coughs a throat of flame. The abrupt noise stutters her heart. The limo at the rear of the line swerves in a pall of fire, hits the edge of the stream and rolls half-over. Shouts and screams come from the valley, the advance trucks gun their motors.

'—fuck!' Tadmartin rolls over on her side.

Muzzle flashes burst down the whole other side of the valley: the Hospitaller troops opening fire.

'Okay. Okay. Take out the front vehicle!'

Two of the rear trucks accelerate into the shadows of over-hangs. Inside seconds there is the rattle and crack of small-arms fire. The flares blaze in. Tadmartin hears the *whumph!* of a grenade launcher and ducks her head into her arms, comes up and looses off suppressive fire down towards the rear of the column. There is the amputating roar of claymore mines as hostiles abandon the trucks.

Explosions deafen her. Hot air hits her cheek, splinters of wood spatter the rock-face. The grenade explosion takes out a chunk of the bank and starts fire in the brushwood.

'Heavy weapon! Tysoe, take that truck out!'

Tysoe's yell from ten yards away: 'Assault team move up!'

'Romeo Victor to Sierra Foxtrot, close up the back door, repeat, close up the back door. Out. Romeo Victor to Hotel Oscar, Cohen, cover our fucking arses, we've got an illegal firefight going on up here, watch our backs, out; Tysoe, do you copy? Repeat, do you copy, over?'

Now there is no answer.

'Romeo Victor to all squads. Bottle the bastards up. Out!'

Two rounds clip the branches above her head and she swears, sprayed with exploded fragments of pine wood. The stink of resin fills the air, sickly-sweet with cordite and woodsmoke. She glances over her shoulder at the brushfire.

'Move 'em down!' She falls into cover, finding Tysoe a few yards ahead. In the valley, one of the trucks swings around in an impossible turning-circle and accelerates back towards the bridge. Someone screams. 'Medic! Squad One Medic – through there.'

She pushes the medic on down through the trees and leaves him squatting over a grunt with a shattered face. Hair blown black, face glistening red, eye and jaw mincemeat. There is blood on her combats to the elbow, she doesn't remember touching him.

'Where's it coming from?' Tysoe and the assault team hit cover beside her. 'It ought to be a fucking turkey-shoot, where's it coming from?'

'You!' Tadmartin grabs the woman with the heavy weapon: a shoulder-fired rocket launcher. 'Take that bridge out – *now*.'

The grunt belts past her, kneels. Two successive blasts shake the air. Flame shoots from the rear of the rocket launcher as the shell projects. Line of sight into the valley is obscured by flare-lit shifting smoke. Muzzle flashes gleam through it, and the roar of brushfire whipped up by the night wind. Tadmartin hears voices screaming – on the banks? in the valley? – and the *whoomph!* of a truck going up. Hot air blows against her face. She smells the charred stink of cooking meat. Rounds whistle through the pine trees. Belly-down, crawling; and then there is a hollow concussive sound from the end of the valley and a cheer from the assault team.

'Bridge is down, L.T. We cut off the retreat.'

'Good. Lay down fire into the valley—'

There is a *crump!* and the night lights up like Christmas. That one landed behind: a cut-off shot. The pine trees burn like pitch torches and the night is hot; she is sweating and covered with black ash and her hands are blistered.

'L.T., that came across the valley!'

'Give me a range and direction!'

'Fifty metres, two o'clock.'

'Lay down suppressive fire. Tysoe, take 'em down the south side of the valley. *Now.*' Tadmartin falls into cover behind a rock outcrop. The stuttering cough of a heavy machine-gun vibrates through the earth. Flashes of light strobe the night: give her lightning-strike views of branches against the night sky, grunts running, a casevac team with a bodybag. Her face bleeds. 'Romeo Force to Juliet, do you c—'

'They're firing on us. The fucking Hospitallers!' Tysoe, camocream smeared with blood, stands up waving the assault rifle. 'For Christ's sake tell them to cease fire!'

'Romeo Force to Juliet, repeat, Romeo Force to Juliet. Cease firing on friendly targets. Repeat cease fire on valley wall. Juliet Force, do you copy? You're firing on us! Do you copy? *For fuck's sake answer me.*'

Her dry throat croaks. She is aware of her split lip, bleeding in the night's chill. The helmet RT has insufficient power in this atmospheric muck; the woman with the RT was the casevac case; and Tadmartin pushes up from her cover and leans round the outcrop, spraying the far valley wall with undirected fire. 'Cease fire! Cease fire! We're in a fucking killing zone here!'

The rifle is hot, magazine almost exhausted; she with swift precision removes it and snicks another one home. She feels the slick, greasy heat of shit down her thighs.

'Squad One reform and move up!' Tysoe bawls. She dips for a split second beside Tadmartin. 'They're asking for it – they're asking for it! We're going to take them out! It's the only way!'

Another shell lands behind, up the valley wall. Rock splinters shrapnel the woods. Pull out? The way's blocked. Back to basic procedure: fight through.

Tadmartin yells, 'Take the fuckers out. Go!'

Squad One are gone, pounding through the brushwood. Tadmartin goes a step or two after them and then falls into cover. The situation's sliding out of control, and she's got two other squads to contend with and the hostiles in the valley: let Squad One go do it. Cut losses.

'Romeo Victor calling Delta Alpha, move up into position at the valley wall above Bluejay Station, I repeat, move up into position at valley wall above Bluejay Station. Fire at will. Out. Romeo Victor to Hotel Oscar – get your asses up the south side and give Squad One covering fire. Move it!'

At daybreak she will walk through the floor of the valley, past burst and burnt-out trucks, when dawn glitters through the trees and off the stream. The track is puddled with red mud for two hundred yards. There are bodies and bits of bodies in the vehicles, charred and black. There is meat hanging from the trees.

She will walk the far side of the valley wall and watch the casevac of Hospitaller troops. Flying out to the same field hospitals as her own troops. She will hear the Hospitaller captain's oddly apologetic offer of help; an offer that vanishes when it emerges his troops are chewed up twice as bad as the Templars.

What will she feel? Satisfaction, mostly. Righteous satisfaction.

Daybreak, and things become visible.

There aren't half a dozen rifles together in the column. Of course, it wasn't a shipment of arms. Nothing for a stealth ambush to make an example of. It was, it later transpires, thirty families of paramilitary terrorists being shifted out from an up-trail district (in secrecy) into Indian territory. For their own safety.

Families with a small guard. Civilians.

Anything more than a quite minor investigation and it is unlikely Templar and Hospitaller troops will be tenable in the same territory. When it comes to a question, truth or something you can live with, which do you choose?

5 July 2002

'Did you hear? They want to cancel the Unification Day parade next year.' Knight-lieutenant Tysoe leans morosely against the door-frame of the cell. 'Because the ordnance damages the streets, for Chrissakes! Fucking government shit. When they start worrying about tanks chewing up a few roads, then you know you've lost it.'

Tadmartin ignores her. The cell containing only a small mirror, she is studying her full-length reflection in the metal door.

'Shit . . .'

A woman something under medium height, shoulders stretching the cloth of her demob tunic. Blonde hair far too short for a civilian. A young woman with a sunburned face; moving uneasily in the heeled shoes, smoothing down the plain cloth skirt.

'Who'd be a fucking Templar? You ain't missing nothing,' Tysoe assures her uncomfortably.

Tadmartin looks.

'Well, fuck, man . . .'

'It's all right,' Tadmartin says. 'It's all right.'

'We know what you did.'

Tadmartin hefts her small shoulder-bag. Gifts, mostly. Face-cloth, toothbrush, underwear, sanitary towels. 'Write or something, will you?'

It is a momentary lapse. Some lies are easier than others. Tysoe says 'Sure!' and ducks her head uncomfortably, waits a moment in the face of Tadmartin's calm, then shrugs and leaves.

Little now to do. Tadmartin reaches up to the weapons rack on the cell wall and takes down the rebated eleventh century sword.

The TV snaps on, on autotimer: she ignores the whispering voices.

Tadmartin sits on her bed, her back against the wall, the rebated sword resting with its hilt against her shoulder and the blade across her body. She rubs microcrystalline wax into the metal with a soft cloth, the movements rhythmically smooth.

It is the last piece of equipment she will return to the armoury.

She finishes with maintenance, stands; holding the hilt and letting the blade flip up into first guard position. The sun shines into the monastic cell. There is just space enough to lose herself in the drill of cut, parry, block . . .

The blade moves smoothly in the air. The solidity of the grip, the heft of the blade; moving in a balance that makes it all – edge, guard, grip, pommel – a singularity of weapon.

She loses herself in it.

Becoming no-sword, one culminates in total resignation, abandoned to the skill of the blade. Nothing matters. One cannot care about winning, losing, survival, dying. One cannot care, and act right. She enters the complete, balanced resignation of the fighter: dead, alive, alive, dead. No matter. No difference.

The face on the TV screen focuses in her combat-widened peripheral vision. The fair-haired woman, de Keroac; capable and triumphant. Tadmartin hears her speak.

'The government's denial of accusations that they are operating a shoot-on-sight policy in emirate Cabotsland was further complicated yesterday by the breakdown of the Avignon talks.

'Talks broke down when a Templar officer, Demzelle Hyacinthe Tadmartin, refused to give any eye-witness evidence whatsoever about her command at Roanoke. Claims will now continue to be levelled at the government that the civilians killed at Roanoke were innocent casualties of what is, in all but name, a war in the New Holy Land. It is five years to the day since the Roanoke massacre claimed fifty-three civilian lives. This is Louise de Keroac, for Channel Nine.'

The words are heard but they do not matter.

She is a sword, a sword now out of service. But held in the balance of that resignation she knows, no-intention will carry her far abroad. Alone. Away from bystanders who she may, instinctively, hurt.

Tadmartin walks out of the cell, putting the first foot on the pilgrim road – unrecognised as yet – that will take her, solitary and one day in the far future, to the New Jerusalem.

Afterword

It's probably not any surprise if I tell you that 'The Road to Jerusalem' was written when the 'Desert Storm' Gulf War was in progress, and the situation in Ireland was different from today.

Which is not to say that Tadmartin's career in New Cabotsland is a one-to-one analogue of troops in Northern Ireland, or that the blue-on-blue incidents in that Gulf War (the first in which people killed by their own side exceeded people killed by the enemy) are reflected directly in the story. Some incidents in Tad's training are borrowed from life, true; and there's precedent for all of what she does, but it's more like ink in water – what happens in the world dissolves into, and informs, what comes out as story.

Too, this story is where I took a first stab at something that's always fascinated me about the medieval kingdom (or 'province', if you happened to be the French king) of Burgundy. These days Burgundy is the name of a wine. Then, it was a more powerful country than France or Germany. It doesn't take much of a nudge to history to produce an AU timeline in which Europe's culture becomes primarily Burgundian, instead of – as actually happened – Burgundy losing a major battle in 1477 and vanishing off the face of history . . .

(It takes rather more than a nudge to have the Tokugawa shoguns become rulers of an expansionist Japan, but, it being a short story, I quietly fudge over the background to that one, whistling innocently. Assuming that it *could* be made to work, however, a Shogunate West Coast is reasonably probable.)

The next time I came to try conclusions with vanished Burgundy, it would lead to a half-million words of *Ash: A Secret History*. The military tactics and the 'up-to-your-knees-in-muck' feel of 'The Road to Jerusalem' also took me towards *Ash*, and towards *Grunts!*, too, although the short story doesn't have the black humour that *Grunts!* does.

Oh, and it wasn't until I'd finished writing that I realised *why* the scenes in Tad's memory are told in present tense, and the current events in past tense, when you might expect it logically to be the other way around. Her memories exist in a permanent vivid 'now' – they haven't ever stopped happening for her – and the story has to be structured the way she sees it.

Orc's Drift

by Mary Gentle and Dean Wayland

This story concerns a little-known incident of military history which took place some months before the Last Battle of Dark against Light . . .

'I don't like it, Sergeant,' orc Major Bugruk remarked, 'it's too quiet . . .'

FOOM! *'Arrggh!'* DAKKA-DAKKA-*FOOM*! 'Urk?!' BOOM! *Screeeeee*!

Beside him, on the walls, orc Sergeant Krag looked down from the lonely fortress at the Halflingsbane Desert. In the fort compound, the sound of musket fire echoed back from the massive stone walls, together with orcish shrieks, growls, the shouted orders of Corporal Sprak drilling his elite Troll troops, and the loud explosions from the Weapons Research & Development Division.

Sergeant Krag nodded sagely. 'You're right, sir. It's much too quiet.'

Orc Major Bugruk tugged his smart pillar-box red military tunic down over his humped, muscled shoulders. He polished one of his tusks, listlessly. An air of dejection hung about him.

'We don't see any action,' he complained. 'What is the point, Sergeant, of us orc soldiers having wonderful new weapons, highly-trained troops, and *no enemy*?'

'Her Darkness must know what She's doing, sir, stationing us out here.'

Krag reflected that *out here*, three hundred miles north-east of the Blasted Wasteland, nothing very much ever happened – mainly because Her Darkness had obliterated the happy singing halflings of the country twelve generations back, and no one had wanted the territory since.

And no wonder, Krag thought, surveying the desolate sandy wasteland that stretched away from the fort in all directions.

Major Bugruk remarked, 'Hardly a strategic posting, Sergeant Krag.'

'Not so's you'd notice, sir, no.'

'Very few opportunities for bringing the Peace of Darkness to the local inhabitants.'

'That's because there aren't any, sir.'

'Why, the indigenous race won't even communicate with us, their local garrison!'

Krag sighed. 'Being dead will do that for you, sir.'

Major Bugruk tugged down the cuffs of his brass-buttoned tunic. 'If it weren't for the Orc Marine battalion inspection, Sergeant, I'd think we were undervalued. By the way . . . when *was* the last Orc Marine battalion inspection we had here?'

'Thirteen years, ten months, seventeen days ago, *sah*!'

'No losses of military equipment since then, eh, Sergeant?'

'They're away for maintenance,' Krag protested automatically. She coughed. 'Er, I mean, no, sir. No losses. Nowhere to lose it *to* . . .'

Beyond the walls of the fort, a desolate and hilly landscape sweltered under the noon sun. Some scrub, a few bushes, nothing else visible. Sergeant Krag narrowed her eyes under her heavy brows, and squinted towards a ridge a kilometre away. *'Corporal Sprak, turn out the guard!'*

Krag's deafening bellow echoed back from the fort's walls. Turning to Major Bugruk – who was fingering one pointed ear, with a pained expression – she saluted smartly.

'Beg to report, sir, hostile troops in view!'

'*Really*? Where?' Major Bugruk whipped out a brass telescope and, after some thought, put it to the eye which did not have a patch over it.

'I distinctly saw *movement*, sir!' Krag reported, her bass voice bellowing over the noise of four hundred orc and troll troops scrambling to man (or perhaps 'creature') the crenellated walls and portcullised gate of the fort.

A small panting orc with spindly ears, a scarlet tunic, and white webbing, trotted up onto the parapet and saluted. 'Beg to report, Sarge, the troops is in a "ready" posture!'

'Thank you, Sprak.' Krag turned back to looking out from the walls. She halted. Quietly, but distinctly, she swallowed; a very small gulp.

'*That* . . .' Major Bugruk pointed. 'That is an *enemy*?'

'Take your point, sah!' Krag could see that Major Bugruk's desire to cover himself in military glory was hardly likely to be satisfied by the small figure moving down from the ridge.

'What exactly *is* that, Sergeant Krag?'

'I, ah, I think it's a fairy, sir.'

'A fairy . . .'

'Yes, sir. Positive, sir. That's what it is, all right . . .'

The approaching figure was all of twelve inches tall. As it came closer, Krag saw that it – or rather, *she* – was flying. No, fluttering. Definitely fluttering. Krag could clearly see now the pointed ears, the blonde curls, and the shimmer of the desert sun on dragonfly-coloured gossamer wings.

The fairy was wearing a scanty pink costume and seemed to be entirely without weapons.

Some fifty feet from the walls, the fairy halted, hovering in mid-air.

'I don't *like* orcs!' her voice piped. It was shrill, and accompanied by the ethereal sound of bells. 'You're nasty, and you're noisy, and you *smell*. And you're in *my* desert. I've had enough. Go away! Leave, now! Or *else*!'

Major Bugruk gazed down from the walls of the fort.

'You're telling me that's a fairy, Sergeant.'

'Sir. Sand Fairy, sir.'

'Calling on us to surrender.'

'Sir.'

'*Duhhh* . . .'

'Yes, sir.'

The walls of the fort were now lined with four hundred orcs in red tunics and white webbing. Their tusked jaws gaped open.

Major Bugruk leaned out from the crenellations, frothing at the mouth, and Krag took a firm grip on the back of his belt to prevent him pitching head-first off the wall.

'Who does she think we *are*? Send in the orcs, Sergeant! Flatten her!'

Deep-throated cheers roared out. Several hundred orcs beat their musket-butts against the walls.

The small figure of Corporal Sprak lined up a unit of heavy-shouldered, bow-legged, razor-tusked orcs. He gestured at the portcullis. 'Open up – *urk*!'

A large mob of orcs, each struggling to be first through the gate, thundered over the small corporal, trampling him into the dirt.

Sprak sat up, rubbing his head, and recovered his pith helmet from where it lay, rocking gently in the dust. 'Fifty troops set out on patrol, Sergeant,' he quavered. 'Approximately.'

Sergeant Krag put her taloned hand over her eyes. 'Uh huh.'

She opened her eyes again and watched the mob of scarlet-uniformed orcs charge over the ridge in the wake of the fleeing Sand Fairy.

'KILL KILL KILL!' the orc soldiers chanted.

Major Bugruk followed his troops' progress with the help of his brass telescope. They vanished from sight over a rocky ridge. The sound of rapid musket fire crackled.

Silence resumed.

The landscape remained empty.

Major Bugruk lowered his spy-glass. 'They did have orders to return, did they not?'

'Yessir!' Corporal Sprak saluted frantically.

Sergeant Krag gazed out at the empty desert. Her yellow eyes narrowed.

The sun sank down the sky.

And down.

At last, Krag said, 'I don't think they're coming back, sir.'

When the shadows of sunset were long, a small winged figure fluttered over the ridge, and flew to hover below the walls of the fort.

'*Naughty* orcs!' she squeaked. 'I won't tell you again. Take your nasty guns, and leave my beautiful desert!'

'Bugger off!' Sergeant Krag roared. She coughed, apologetically. 'Sorry, Major Bugruk, sir. Overcome by feelings, sir.'

'Understandable, Sergeant.' Major Bugruk's orcishly handsome face twisted into a scowl. 'We're not scared of a Sand Fairy! Send the elite Troll unit in, Sergeant. Our specialists in night stealth attacks. That Fairy will be orcsmeat before morning!'

'Sir, yes *sir*!' Krag saluted.

'Kill! Kill! Kill!' whispered the hulking figures that tiptoed out of the gate. A hundred Trolls. Some of them, Sergeant Krag noticed with satisfaction, carried the new-issue Gatling Gun, which they would fire from the hip.

The Troll company vanished over the rocky ridge.

BOOM! *Screeee*! FOOM! *'Arrggh*!' DAKKA-DAKKA-*FOOM*!

The moonlit night was split by the sound of rapid rattling gunfire. The darkness lit up in strobe-flashes. Distant screams and orders echoed across the desert.

Silence.

Lots of silence.

Eventually, the sun rose. A lonely bird flew across the yellow fiery disc as the world became illuminated with morning light. It tweedled a lonely song.

Corporal Sprak saluted his sergeant. 'Sarge, I don't think *they're* coming back either, Sarge – ow!'

'Let that be a lesson to you about morale, corporal,' Krag growled.

Corporal Sprak moved down the parapet to where Major Bugruk leaned on the crenellations, gazing out into the silent and empty desert morning.

'Sand Fairy,' Bugruk gritted.

Corporal Sprak nodded helpfully. ' "Snot fair, sir. All the other orc battalions get *dragons* to fight, and elf-knights, and—'

'Balrogs.'

'No, it's *true*, sir, honestly! An' what do *we* get?'

'We get *that*,' Sergeant Krag said, taking it upon herself to answer her corporal's rhetorical question.

She pointed.

The Sand Fairy's diaphanous wings fluttered in the rising sun.

'Maybe violence isn't the answer,' Sergeant Krag began thoughtfully.

Major Bugruk clouted her firmly across the back of the head. 'Don't be ridiculous, Sergeant! Violence is *always* the answer! Damn it, we're *orcs*!'

'Yes, sir. Sorry, sir! Don't know what came over me, sir.'

The Sand Fairy fluttered closer to the walls of the fort.

'Why won't you live together with me in *harmony*?' she piped exasperatedly.

'Never!' Major Bugruk roared. 'Never! My troops would sooner *die*, than surrender to the tiny heel of the oppressor!'

'Er,' Corporal Sprak said. 'Er. Have you, er, *asked* them, sir?'

'I don't *need* to ask! It's a matter of orcish military honour. Right, lads?'

The rather less than three hundred orc soldiers lining the walls of the fort shuffled, whistled, and stared absent-mindedly off into the distance.

Orc Major Bugruk drew his service revolver and fired.

FOOM!

Thud.

'I *said*, isn't that *right*, lads?'

'SIR YES *SIR*!'

The Sand Fairy departed in a flurry of pink chiffon, fluttering away, and vanishing back over the rocky ridge.

'That does it,' Major Bugruk snarled. 'That's it. No more Mister Nice Orc! I'm sending in our Special Forces Unit. And if *that* doesn't work, then it's an all-out attack by everyone! Corporal Sprak – see to it!'

'Yessir!' The small orc corporal shot down the steps into the fort's central compound.

Sergeant Krag asked quietly, 'Are you sure, sir? I mean, our Special Forces mob – they're hard bastards, even for orcs! It don't seem fair, sir, somehow.'

'This is war, Sergeant! You've seen what that fairy fiend can do. I'm taking no chances. But . . .' Major Bugruk frowned. 'I will send Corporal Sprak with them. He'll restrain them. Stop them getting too far out of hand.'

'Sir.'

Krag looked down from the parapet at the gate beneath. Marching out of it, into the sunny morning, went a mob of the nastiest orcs she could ever wish to see. Their smart red uniforms did not entirely cover the ritual scars and tattoos on their hides. Some had filed the tusks jutting from their heavy jaws to a razor-sharpness. And in addition to their issue muskets, most of the orcs had adorned their webbing with a variety of close-combat weapons – machetes, hand-saws, knuckle-dusters, and sharpened entrenching tools.

One orc glanced up and saluted Sergeant Krag, with a taloned hand that held something closely resembling the haunch of a small orc, much chewed.

At their rear, white pith helmet firmly buckled down over his spindly ears, and his musket on his shoulder, Corporal Sprak proudly marched.

'Good luck, lads!' Major Bugruk's voice quavered with emotion.

'I want her fairy wings nailed up over the drawbridge before noon!' Sergeant Krag growled. 'See to it, Sprak!'

'Yes, Sarge!'

The band of orcs, over a hundred strong, marched across the empty desert. They crushed the small bushes and scrub under-boot, kicking up clouds of dust that hid them before they ever crossed over the rocky ridge.

The dust settled.

FOOM!

TAKA-TAKA-TAKA-*BOOM*!

Screeeee—

KER-*FOOOM*!

Silence.

Major Bugruk and Sergeant Krag gazed out from the walls of their fort. Behind them, the sound of shuffling orcish combat boots announced that the rest of the battalion were giving up all pretence of going about their duties, and were lining the walls to stare across the empty desert.

A tweetling bird flew back across the sky.

FOOM!

Splat.

Major Bugruk blew smoke away from the muzzle of his revolver, and watched dispiritedly as the bird plummeted to earth.

Waiting.

Waiting . . .

Major Bugruk turned to Sergeant Krag. 'That's it, sergeant. Ready the whole garrison for an all-out attack on that Fairy's position!'

'Yes, sir. *Sir*!' Krag pointed a talon excitedly towards the ridge. 'Look, sir! What's that?'

A tiny figure came into view. It was running back down the track towards the fort. Dust partly hid the figure. Sergeant Krag shaded her eyes with her hand.

The figure frantically threw aside what looked like a long-barrelled musket, and a pith helmet.

'It's Corporal Sprak!' Krag bellowed.

The orcs on the walls leaped up and down, cheering wildly. Major Bugruk climbed up onto the crenellated wall and leaned forward, peering out.

'He's alone,' the Major muttered.

The small orc corporal sprinted down the slope towards them. His red uniform tunic was unbuttoned, his boots missing, and he was pointing behind himself as he ran. Sergeant Krag cupped a hand around her pointed hairy ear, but could not make out what Sprak was shouting.

'Come on, lad!' Major Bugruk roared.

The small orc ran like a mad thing. He was sweating, and panting, and still pointing behind himself, back towards the rocky ridge.

Sergeant Krag could not make out any other orcs with him. The rest of the attacking force were nowhere to be seen.

'What's that, Sprak?' she roared at him. 'Speak up! Report!'

The orc corporal staggered, and collapsed on hands and knees outside the gate. He stared up through the dust, at the walls lined with worried orc soldiers.

His tough orcish hide was scarred and bloody.

'What is it, Sprak?' Sergeant Krag demanded. 'What *happened*?'

Without any orders being given, the gates of the fort slammed deafeningly shut. Frightened orc guards peered over the spiky top of the portcullis. Muskets protruded from every slot-window in the walls, and between every crenellation on the parapet, pointing in all directions. The remaining orc soldiers of the garrison fearfully scrutinised every inch of the desert outside, with expressions of acute paranoia.

Orc Corporal Sprak, panting, shouted up to Major Bugruk. 'Don't launch the all-out attack, sir! Don't do it! Please, sir – think of the orcs – don't do it!'

Major Bugruk and Sergeant Krag leaned over the wall, staring down at the wide-eyed corporal.

'Why not, son?' Sergeant Krag asked gently.

Orc Corporal Sprak, sobbing, pointed back towards the rocky ridge. 'It's a *trap*, Sarge – there's TWO of them!'

Afterword

'Orc's Drift' is probably best summed up in the words of my partner-in-crime and co-writer, Dean Wayland – 'We got *paid* for this?'

And so we did. But it was peanuts – well, *a* very small peanut, in fact – so the karmic balance of the universe wasn't too greatly disturbed. And the editor who bought it is almost better now.

I blame the *Grunts!* orcs entirely. Having written the book, the characters showed no signs of upping and leaving our heads – and, when Dean inflicted the world's shaggiest joke on me, and I felt we had to share, the orcs just looked at each other and said *We'll do that*. And shortly thereafter, they were away with the fairies . . .

The Tarot Dice

It begins with a rose. A white rose, its embroidery old and stained so that it is closer to yellow, to the colour of old bone. That rose-badge has been on the breast of his jacket for years now. He has caught his reflection in the glass window that faces the night, stands for a moment transfixed – face almost as worn and old as the badge – and then he takes up shoulder-slung gun and descends through the Levels. Others acknowledge him as he passes by, with the genuflection of the White Rose, of whose orders and degrees he is (with but one exception) the highest.

Walking down towards the river-dock: the naphtha flares bleach all colour from his lined face, from the hair like frayed hemp-rope and pale, sparse beard. Now that you can see him, he seems younger than his thoughts or his walk; he could be under forty-five, even under forty.

Mist coils in the silver gloom.

Between the buildings runs the river.

Flat mud stretches out, bubbling and stinking, to the rotten brickwork on one side and the black moss-covered masonry on the other. Acres of mud, but here the deep channel of the river runs close by the dock; the water glinting with blue, platignum, purple, green. The colours of poison. It runs, both visibly and by underground sewers, towards the Edge.

He walks along the dock, keeping to the shadows. The White Rose is used to concealment: like the iceberg, only a tenth of his Church is visible at any one time.

There, in the circle of light, a flare of white naphtha, men are crouched on the cobbles of the quay. See now what they are doing:

Playing dice – but these dice have no number-spots. Each

die on its six faces carries one image of the Thirty Cards of the Major Arcana. These Tarot images are enamelled, small and very precise; and in the light they tumble like icons spilt on the pavement. The men who play dice are squatting in a circle, sheltered from the night wind by boxes and piled crates; and shadows fall on their faces, black in eyes that seem only sockets now, so that they sit in a circle of skulls.

He sees a boat nearing the river-steps, the dip and plop of each oar, the scattering trail of metallic water-drops. There is a figure, so still, in the prow. Again, all kinds of premonitions touch him: all legends of chosen ones that will come to this city by way of the river . . .

The river is never silent, the river flows: the bank a constant and the waters always new. He has spat in this river, passing over the city's many bridges, is there (he wonders) some small part of him now that is part of the sea?

The boat docks, the passenger steps ashore. The men look up as a woman enters the light. A thin young woman in man's clothing: dark jacket and trousers and boots; and with startling hair. She nods a greeting, speaks one in a thick, almost-unintelligible accent. They make a place for her. She squats down on her haunches, and as she reaches out to take the five dice – there are Minor Arcana dice, but few can afford the whole set – he steps from the cover of a warehouse entrance.

'Sanzia?' he says.

Look at her now: she gives us such a penetrating look. Her eyes in that pale, sharp face (malnourished, certainly, and for some time by the look of it) are a brilliant pale blue. Her hair is silver-white, thick and coarse and long; not an old woman's hair that is yellowed because she is no more than nineteen – or is that a trick of shadow? Is she twenty-five? Thirty-five?

As he moves forward, she looks up; that pale gaze is something he cannot easily look away from. He sees it register the badge of the Rose, and his fingers stray automatically to feel the bulk of ancient embroidery: the nine-petalled rose, the rose whose serrated petals could so easily be teeth.

She (as if hours and yards separated them, not years and continents) says 'Hainzell.' And throws the dice that she has gathered:

The Phoenix. The Weaver. The Rose. Death. Flight.

These are well-made dice. Though the space for the image is no larger than a thumbnail, they are there and clear:

The eagle that burns and is not consumed, forked white fire issuing from its own body: *The Phoenix*,

The spider whose back, looked at carefully, becomes the image of an old woman's face: *The Weaver*,

A skull in whose eye-sockets are set tiny periwinkle-blue flowers: *Death*,

And then *The Rose*, whose petals are toothed and cogged, are interlocking clockwork. And *Flight*, sky-blue, with one Icarus-feather falling . . . or is it rising?

One of the men, reading casually as Tarot gamblers do, says 'Intrigue, well-made plans. Immortality and re-birth. Death and great change: the fall of a mighty house . . .'

'Content,' Sanzia observes, her accent more obtrusive than ever. She reaches out a hand, rests one finger on a die. There is a callous on that middle finger of her left hand, which only comes from long use of a pen. She touches *The Weaver*:

'Read me that one.'

Hainzell steps forward, bends and scoops up the dice in one rough movement. He meets her startled gaze.

'Empty the pouch – show me!'

The men playing dice are dock-workers, soldiers, a smith, a boy who has the look of an armourer's apprentice. While they mutter and stare, they as yet make no move.

The rage that creeps into his voice is response to her stillness: 'Show me!'

She takes her pouch from her shoulder. It is large, thick, full; from it she draws sheets of paper. All are inked. All are in large ill-set type, all are identical. He snatches one, reads it, sneers.

'Pamphlets! Heresy and revelation – is that why you've come here?'

And in disgust or anger he throws down the handful of dice, that rattle on the cobblestones, gleam in the spitting naphtha glare:

The Rose. Flight. Death. The Phoenix. The Weaver.

An indrawn breath, in that circle. There are thirty faces that can fall – too many for the fall of these same five to be coincidence.

It is, surprisingly, the apprentice who reads: fingers touching the Icarus-feather of *Flight*, not quite daring to touch *The Rose*:

'Knowledge through suffering; intrigue and death; the passing away of a great power.'

Hainzell stares down at the dice, then turns and strides away; confusion and anger in him contending with something else.

Sanzia stands up, looking after him; takes a pace or two after him, and then pauses indecisively. The group of men remain squatting in a circle, the Tarot dice spilling onto the flat cobbles. The armourer's boy suddenly picks them up, seizes her hand in his cold fingers, and presses the bone-and-enamel dice into her left hand:

'Take them!'

She might have said much, but Hainzell is gone, the sound of his footsteps diminishing, so with only a nod (thanks, or merely acknowledgement?) she tightens her fist round the dice and hurries off after the man.

'Why?' This from an elderly dock-worker.

'Oh, she might – need?' The boy hesitates. 'She's a stranger, a foreigner, she might . . . things are bad in the city now.'

The men rise and stand looking into the dark.

'We can't trust her,' one of the older soldiers says.

The apprentice nods. 'She can't betray what she doesn't know. She's not from here. She knows the Church of the White Rose, but not as we do. But it's the man of the Rose that I'm sorry for.'

'Well, I am sorry for all of them,' another dock-worker says. He flicks a match from his fingers into the river, and the red spark arcs down. 'Sorry for all of them who take no notice of us because they can't see us. Well, they will see us soon enough.'

A fifth man (they are all men here, you will notice – or perhaps you will not notice – although some of them have wives, and some have children; the former not a necessity for the latter; and I don't know where the women are), he says 'They don't matter to us at all.'

The armourer's apprentice says, 'What about the Bridge-builder? What about the Visconti?'

The group remains together for some few minutes, talking, but with the dice gone, some of the spirit is gone from them, and

they soon disperse, each going separately back into the alleys
that open onto the dock.

Hainzell is passing shells of buildings so tall that clouds can float
in through the broken windows. And cellars where fungus
grows tall as a man: inkcaps and puffballs, stinkworts, creeping
veined mats of white fungus-flesh, slatted layers and shelves of
it, spores like a fine mist in the air.

He walks quickly to begin with. Then, aware of the inevitable,
slows his steps; not quite willing to admit he is waiting for her to
catch up. He has reached the river-bridge before a footstep
behind him makes him turn.

'You shouldn't run,' Sanzia says.

'You shouldn't be here—!'

Sanzia wants to touch him, the way that the hair is rough just
at the nape of his neck is too much for her, she puts the flat of
her hand against the skin of his neck, soft, sweet-smelling; and
he knocks her hand aside and turns to face her, his back to the
parapet of the bridge.

Her voice, somewhere between resignation and anger:

'You are *not* my brother!'

As if it were the continuation of a long dialogue (and it is, over
some years) Hainzell says, 'I feel my blood in you sometimes.
I've washed you, seen you naked, sung you to sleep, bandaged
your cuts and scrapes, listened to the first words you could
speak—'

'I am not your sister!'

'I raised you so.' Hainzell, a little ironically, adds 'The White
Rose would have you now, if that wasn't so. I knew of your
arrival.'

'I want you,' Sanzia tells him. 'I want no one else.'

They stand on the bridge, unobserved, but for how long?

'Do you still wear that?' She touches the raised embroidery of
the Rose. 'I don't understand you. We began together. You
came here to bring them down, not join them!'

When Hainzell speaks again, there is the trace of an accent
that he lost years ago: her accent. 'Go home. The Church will
take you into the Levels. They would do it now if not for the
death—' And then he hesitates.

'The Rose made a promise. People have forgotten, or fear to

remember. There was a promise to lead us into the Heartland,' Sanzia says, as if thinking of something quite other; and her hand reaches out to his, as if the desire moved it and not her; the same desire that makes the fingers tremble, and he steps back.

Hainzell, touching the Rose again, thinks: Has it been the sweet rose for so long, and is it now to be the devourer? Instantly, as my flesh answers to hers when it should not: sister, sister . . .

He at last looks her in the face, that thin, malnourished face that is framed by coarse silver hair. 'I have had to settle for the possible,' he says, 'and I won't help you, except in this one thing: if you leave the city tonight you will be able to leave, because of what is happening now, but if you stay until tomorrow you will not be able to leave. And that,' he finishes, 'I would tell to my sister but not to my lover, Sanzia.'

She watches him leave, and still she carries the two words that have been together in his mouth: *Sanzia, lover.*

The snow falls on the great square, and on the stone mausoleum, and on the open coffin and the exposed face of the dead man where he lies in state.

Oddly, there is only one thought in the old woman's mind: *Now there is no one left to call me Luce . . .*

You're cold, Visconti, Luce thinks. And has an impulse, surprisingly strong, to reach forward and wipe away the snow congealing on dead flesh. She suppresses the impulse with a too-easy facility.

She is alone and moving painfully, she who in her youth was a fighter, Luce; could run fast enough to throw molotov-cocktails into the cabins of tanks (not fast enough to escape the screaming) and now she moves achingly slow, arms bound in the metal grips of crutches. She has been tall and is now stooped, has been fat but is now worn down, like sea-polished wood, to sparse flesh on spare bone. They have slowed the cortège so she can follow it these last few steps to the mausoleum.

Hainzell, beside her, is troubled.

The yellow sky is flecked with falling blackness. Below the city's roofline the snow turns white, softening cornices and cupolas, whitening the shoulders of men (and some women) who stand in drab coats, motionless, their heads for the most part bowed, as the loudspeakers play funeral marches and a requiem mass.

Luce looks down at the coffin, that seems too small to contain that body – too narrow a space for the Visconti, the Bridge-builder, that they have called 'a living force of history', and were well-advised to call him (while he lived and heard).

The cortège stops. The music ceases. A kind of concerted movement goes through the crowd in the square, like wind across a cornfield. The white discs of their faces dip in and out of vision, as they turn and speak with each other.

Luce brought a microphone on the mausoleum steps, and leaning heavily on her crutches, says:

'Brethren and citizens, I speak with you in sorrow. The father of our Church has been taken from us, the Heartland has him, and we are left alone. We know how great a debt we owe to him, through all those years of poverty. There is not a man among you who cannot say: life in the city would be different today had the Bridge-builder not lived.'

A sudden disturbance in the crowd resolves itself into an eddy of movement, and protesting figures with banners and pamphlets: against squalor, want, disease, hardship. Luce signals to Hainzell and he to his men: voices are silenced with a quiet and brutal efficiency.

'The whole city will mourn our father Visconti's death,' Luce concludes. Her gaze falls on the embalmed body as officers of the Church lift the coffin, to place it in the mausoleum, upon a glass panel of which are engraved the words of the philosopher-magicians of the White Rose: *Between the Heartland and the Edge is only the space of a breath.* Luce looks at that dead white face.

Now you bastard – now we're rid of you, and your stultifying grip on us; now there's only me, and maybe we can turn this Church into what we meant it to be, in the revolution – and I hope you can watch what I'm going to do!

To Hainzell, she says, 'That's the old bastard buried at last.'

Hainzell glances at his superior of the White Rose. 'You wouldn't have dared to say that while he was living.'

'There wouldn't have been the necessity.' Luce is acidic, but his words shake her, in the way that truth does. She thinks: One day we may know why we were so afraid of Visconti—

Or is it: Why we loved him for doing what we couldn't and dared not?

Hainzell says, 'Sanzia is in the city.'

This shabby man, who knows (who better) exactly what sedition and heresy pass under the eyes of the White Rose.

'What do you want to do about it?' Luce says. 'If I send her away, she'll return. Shall I have her killed?'

'*No.*'.

There is an expression on his face that she cannot identify, and that – after some fifty years' experience of the human race – worries her.

'She's dangerous.'

Hainzell, with a cynical humour, says, 'I think she won't give us time to reform. Seeing no further than the Visconti, and expecting us to be the same. And—'

'And who's to say we won't be?' Luce completes his thought for him, seeing his startled look. 'I know. Believe that I know. I have lived fifty years doing what's possible. With these people and this city, the Heartland is a dream and a prayer and a vision, and nothing more. What action will she take?'

Because he is who he is and what he is, he asks, 'Do we *wait* for her to act?'

'No,' Luce says at last. 'When this flummery's done with and the bastard buried, find me a way to speak with this Sanzia of yours.'

Hainzell, much too quickly (and even he can tell that) protests, 'Not *my* Sanzia.'

Later they will say, or she will claim, that Sanzia brought these instruments of heresy, but the truth is that they were in the city and in use long before she arrived. Gamblers' dice, children's toys – that use closer to their nature than the use she found for them.

'They are not unknown to the Church of the White Rose,' says a man one night, a little later, when there are many of them gathered in the Tunnels below the city. The tunnel is an iron pipe a dozen yards in diameter. Rivets as big as a child's head weep rust, fanning down in orange-gold runnels. Icicles hang down, two yards long. Light from braziers glows orange on the walls.

Sanzia sits on her outspread jacket. Her head is bowed. The Tarot dice lay before her, unstable on the cloth, and she turns them almost absently in her fingers, laying die-faces upright:

Plague, whose tiny illustration is the knot with which, in this city, they tie the head of a corpse's shroud—

Twig and leaf of *The World-Tree*, a star caught in it; no room on it for the larger images of the Card, the Tree and what rests under its roots and branches—

The Triune Goddess, which is here depicted as a drop of blood upon a surface of stone—

The man interrupts her, indicating the last die-face, protesting, 'That is an old heresy, the White Rose would burn you for bringing it here, what use is it to us?'

Sanzia continues to turn the dice so that in time they will have seen all. The dance of their succession: *Hermit, Lovers, Chariot, Weaver* . . .

As one grows old, one grows careless with the flesh; but still, she thinks, to be burned—!

. . . *The Lightning-Struck Tower, The Fool, The Star, Justice* . . .

'I bring you keys,' she says, 'and you ask me what use it is to go through an opened door.'

It is the kind of saying that may well be recalled and requoted – to really fix it in people's minds she should die a martyr's death. And that comment wouldn't have occurred to me, she thinks, if I hadn't met and spoken with him again. Hainzell, brother and not-brother. What do I care about these belly-brained citizens?

There are two or three dozen gathered round her now, hugging close to the warmth of the brazier. They may be waiting for morning to come, and they may be working towards some realisation of their own: who can say?

The same man asks, '*Is* there a Heartland?'

Thinking of the Heartland, the light grows brighter, one dreams of older buildings, small and homely, and white court-yards under an everlasting noon.

A child no more than ten says, 'There are houses there full of gold and diamonds, and food, and you can fly.'

'Lovers,' says an old man, 'and children and those we have long forgotten who knew us once, they are waiting for us in the Heartland.'

'No,' says a third voice, lost in crowd and shadow, 'for each of us there is one thing we can do best, one thing we must become. Heartland is where we find out what we are for.'

The dice turn: *Wheel of Fortune, Phoenix, The Players, Fortitude* . . .

- Sanzia says, 'The White Rose tells you what you must do. These show you what you might do. The White Rose tells you what was in the past and what is in the future; these show you Now. I don't know if there's a Heartland or not, or if it's an inner or an outer place. These . . . are a guide but you don't know where they will take you, or when you have reached it, or if the journey continues. There is always a part of us that we don't know, and it speaks to us here.'

They are only words, she thinks, and frail against the grey high walls of the Church of the Rose, and the Rose's servants, and the unreachable Bridge-builder, who was called Visconti and is now named Luce. What use a handful of bright images that are only children's and gamblers' toys?

A young man as palely fanatical as she says, 'There are ways. We can bring them down. There are ways, but put the dice away now and help us.'

She has pamphlets of heresy and sedition and doubt, but it comes to her now, she has more trust (with these child-brained people) in the toys of children. If used properly . . . (Does she hear that she now says *must* instead of *might*?)

Sanzia says, 'I know what we must do.'

It begins now with rusted rails, between which the grass grows tall and brown. To pick a way across these is difficult, to cross them hindered with crutches almost impossible, and it is Hainzell who at the last, diffidently, offers to have her carried; and for his trouble gets what he expects, a vicious refusal.

The sun is a white disc behind mist. Pale blue and milky sky, and the shadows cast by the rails are fuzzy-edged. Luce pauses, wipes her forehead that is running with salt sweat. The quilted black tabard is too hot, she wears it only because, sewn into the quilting, are hard thin plates of metal.

'Here?'

A rusty brazier stands by a broken wall, that may once have been part of a shed. The skeleton of a steam-engine hulks in the background. She is aware of movement as they approach, of how people slide away into distant dips and hollows of the ground, into distant buildings, as a school of fish disperse when water is disturbed. One person remains. A young woman – or is she older? the misty light is kind to her skin – with firewhite hair, who squats on her haunches by the brazier, throwing dice left hand against right.

Hainzell stops a short distance away, gun settled easily under his arm, enough protection here in the Yards. And Luce inches her way forward, weight on metal crutches, not on wasted muscle; until she can stand over the young woman who must be

'Sanzia.'

The young woman ignores her, speaks to Hainzell:

'Brother. I'll call you brother, if it helps. Why are you here with her? Why have you brought so many of your own people?'

Luce looks around. There is no apparent sign of any guard, and that is as it should be: the White Rose are trained well. Luce doesn't speak, and this prompts Sanzia to ask, 'What do you want?'

Luce thinks of the Visconti, buried now, the snow freezing on that mausoleum; how many ages of death now he has to think of the years of power, how many long ages to grow sick of the taste of them.

'I can't do it differently,' she says, 'I must act with what I have, with people as they are and not as they ought to be.'

There is a look in Sanzia's eyes, pale and brilliant and feral, the look of those who search for the Heartland – or the Edge.

Luce says, 'I want you to help me be seated, child. And then I wish to see you throw and read the dice, as I hear so many now in my city see you throw and read dice.'

The old woman is helped to sit on the warm earth, her metal crutches laid down beside her. Hainzell stands at her back. His eyes are not on her, they move from Sanzia to the Yards and back again: there is sweat clear on his upper lip.

The woman who is white-haired and may be young gathers up her handful of five dice, upon which are the faces of the Thirty Major Trumps: which can be thrown in sequence to ensure all faces have a chance of coming up in combination with all others – or who can, as now, be merely cast once.

Sanzia kneels down on the earth, facing the old woman. She is in shabby black, still, in trousers and shirt; and wears a necklace half-hidden by the cloth, that may be made out of yellow bone. The dice rattle in her hand. Her fingers are long, sallow, supple. Luce stares at the earth-stained fingers, at the dice that are clotted with dust. Then the casual flick:

The Weaver. The Rose. Death. The Phoenix. Flight.

And Luce, before Sanzia can act, reaches down and turns over a die: the image of enamel bright, as clearly limned as dreams of fire and silver, as images reflected in black water:

'These are the dice *I* will read for *you*—'

She has turned *The Players* instead of *The Phoenix*: an androgynous mask, half-comic and half-tragic, across which is laid a flute.

Luce says, '*Flight* is your presumption in coming here; you would aspire to my role – *The Players. The Rose* is your nemesis, and that's linked with *Death*; and *The Weaver*, that old spider, entoils you deeper and deeper, girl . . . Now cast again.'

Sanzia kneels for a minute, feeling the warm earth under the palms of her hands, and the sun on her head.

'Madam, you hold the city in your grip, but I will lead them to the Heartland . . . The dice *I* cast were clear. *The Rose* is closest to you—'

Set into the die-face is a rosette of petals that are toothed cogwheels. Above the two women, Hainzell moves one hand to touch that yellow badge, the serrated petals.

'—you trust him and he will betray you; there are those who work righteously for your downfall, that's I; and the Church will fall and you be forced into flight—'

Hainzell interrupts, 'We're not puppets for these!' and in sudden anger flicks the Tarot dice with the toe of his boot and sends them spinning. None of the three of them can help bending forward to see what faces show now:

The Rose. The Phoenix. Flight. Death. The Weaver.

Luce's hand reaches out, quicker than Sanzia's to grab the five dice and cast them a third time:

The Weaver. The Phoenix. Flight. Death. The Rose.

At this the old woman laughs, laughs and cannot be stopped for long minutes, until she coughs herself into silence. The sunlight falls silently on the old deserted sidings of the Yards.

'Now that I admire,' Luce says. 'That I *do* admire – loaded dice! What intelligence. Child, you do him credit.'

Sanzia, prompted, must ask, 'Who?'

'Your lover-brother who would like to see me excommunicated,' Luce says, 'but I am not so easily taken, not after so many years of working at the right hand of the Visconti. *Guards!*'

Luce is still seated, cannot rise without help. She sees the White Rose emerge from nearby shelter, from distant buildings. Hainzell turns his head to gaze at them. And even as she wonders how he feels now, having been their commander for so long, to know they no longer move at his bidding; even as she commands 'Arrest them,' Luce feels for a moment as if she moves in a stylised puppet-masque of Judas-betrayals, almost knows what will come next.

Hainzell and Sanzia exchange glances of complicity.

'Arrest the Bridge-builder,' Hainzell gives a pre-arranged signal. 'We cannot, any of us, take the chance of having a Visconti back; Madam, you were with him for too long.'

But:

'And you've been with her for too long,' says one of the guards. As it happens, this guard has a brother who works down on the docks. Among the crowd now are the armourer's apprentice, the armourer, the smith (you will notice there are still no wives or unmarried women with them, or perhaps you will not notice), and all, citizen-brethren and White Rose both, wear ragged white cloth tied about their arms as a badge of identification: white that is the colour of the Heartland.

'You are a priest-tyrant, and you her chief of police, and you a fanatic,' says this anonymous guard (to whom, in the traditional manner of dealing with the proletariat in fiction, we will not award a name): 'The city doesn't need any of you and is a dangerous place with you here – go!'

One moment of their unity: then Luce calls to her old supporters, Hainzell to the men he has commanded, Sanzia to the people who have heard her read the dice—

The dice, scattered in uproar and fighting, after all their tumbling fall again to show *The Weaver, The Phoenix, The Rose, Flight,* and *Death.*

*

There is a great square in the city, and a mausoleum, and on its steps is set a heavy iron cage.

'Do what your predecessor would have done, execute me!' Sanzia insists. Her face is all eyes, brilliant with light. And then that fades. 'Where is my brother?'

Luce says, 'You love him.'

Sanzia grips the bars of the cage. She looks out at the old woman. There is dirt ingrained into Sanzia's skin, and her hair hangs down in grey strings.

'If I could get him away from you—'

'That isn't what you came to the city to do.'

'No,' Sanzia says, 'I came to do what you claimed once that you would do, lead the brethren into the Heartland. He came here with that in his heart, and you took him away from that, and you broke him; but if he was with me I'd heal him.'

Luce says, 'You're free. And I give you a choice. Stay here, use your dice, show these people the Heartland inside or outside of them; try and take them there. You won't do it. They're lazy, and won't think or feel, and if their bellies are full they don't care about anything else. But I give you free leave to try.'

Sanzia tries to stand but the cage is too small. All she can do is hunch over and grip the bars and keep herself in this simian-upright position. The snow beats across the square, and feathers the collar of Luce, and of those brethren still curious enough to gaze on this captive heretic.

'And the other choice?' Sanzia is insistent.

'I set your lover-brother free,' Luce says. 'He could have stayed here with me, the Church of the Rose is merciful. He could have stayed here with you. Instead, he has gone where he always longed to go, and from which journey the Visconti and I only delayed him. He has gone towards the Edge.'

Luce, reaching for the great iron key, adds, 'I have been called cruel, and perhaps I am. I don't give you the third choice – martyrs are a nuisance, and we not strong enough now to suffer one – the third chance: to stay here in the cage.'

Sanzia, hearing the lock click and slide, says, 'If you had given me that choice I would have taken it.'

It is never a long journey, although the distance is far.

Down at the Edge, the Feral infest the sewers. Down at the

Edge there are loners, toilers at solitary machines. This is how it is, where you can look out of filthy half-paned windows and, beyond spiderwebs and dirt, look down upon the stars. The deeps are full with light. The cliffs go down forever.

This is how it is: the morning makes a gold glory of the windows dazzling from the depths. Frost snaps in the dawn. No birds fly on that high wind. Do not let yourself be tricked into thinking it an illusion: this is the Edge.

And time passes.

Sanzia learns as the light grows brighter to draw her strength from it, hardly needing to eat. There is a cold wind that all the time now blows into her face. When she speaks to herself, or calls ahead to him, the sound echoes off glittering ice curtains, in white vapour on frozen air.

Up on either side now rise walls, acres of blackening brick-work that diminishes up to a thread of sky. The crepuscular light shows a metal-floored alley that she can span with out-stretched hands. Frost gleams on the walls. A high, almost-inaudible thrumming rings in the ears. She touches her palm to the metal paving, it is faintly warm.

Ahead, the alley widens.

When fog sweeps in and douses the light she feels weakened, having so long taken nourishment from its radiance.

'You!' she calls, not loudly.

And for the first time is answered: 'Leave me to go on.'

'I need you,' Sanzia says.

'No.'

'I came to find you.'

'No.'

'*Yes—*'

He walks out of the mist, a man to all appearances human; the same Hainzell, with frayed-hemp hair and beard, in a worn, patched jacket and trousers; still (she is determined to think) the same Hainzell.

Perhaps it is the force of her will that snaps the world back into focus for him, the Edge drawn a way back off. Hainzell sees that she is shivering.

'Are you cold?'

'*No.*'

Now the mist has encircled them, cut them off from city and Heartland and Edge: a sea-fog, bone-chilling, that blurs the edges of reality.

Hainzell sits down beside her in the shelter of the wall. Her hair gleams, the lashes fringing her eyes are pale, and are those lines, crows'-feet, at the corners of her eyes? The thought of that is strange: Sanzia to show the signs of age . . .

He puts his arm round those thin shoulders, amazed at how clearly he can feel the bone. She is shivering. He reaches down to unfasten her jacket and – as she lies limp and unresisting – fumbles to put his arms round her body. Her skin is warm: her heart beats.

'No harm in it,' he says.

'No harm?'

'I've done this often, when you were a child, when we were travelling and you were cold. It means nothing more.'

Sanzia, bitterly, says, 'And you call that "no harm"?'

So close, the bones of her ribs distinguishable under his hands. He feels her own hand move to his, raise it, and put it to her breast—

'I am not a child!'

—as he pulls his hand away; there is a minute's undignified tumble, rolling on hard, gritty metal; and then she gets her hand to where she intended:

'Is *that* how you respond to a sister?'

Hainzell, now reaching to her, is astonished: she rolls away and stands up, hair tangling across her face; stands and backs away, as he (with some physical difficulty) moves towards her.

'I thought you wanted—' He, almost laughing, almost crying: 'Just when I began to think of you as a woman, not seeing you for years, you're different, not a child—'

Sanzia kneels down, a few yards away; her legs are shaking. One of her own rough-skinned hands moves to lie on her breast, feeling the erect nipple through the cloth; and then moves down to rest at the junction of her thighs, as if unconsciously protect- ing the ache that is there.

'I don't want – it would be like bribery; as if I tried to make you stay here—'

'Don't whine!' He is breathless with anger: anger at being made ridiculous, at being rejected, at having his – charity? –

despised. And resentful, as a boy is resentful; and turns aside to arrange himself in his clothes, swearing in frustration. 'And isn't this the same – I can't have you unless I stay, isn't that it?'

'No!' A whine of despair. And then Sanzia takes a breath, looking at him clearly and coldly for a time, while the sea-fog condenses and pearls in her hair. At last she sighs and her taut shoulders relax; she sits back, laying her hands flat on her thighs.

'It shouldn't be something for bargains or contracts,' she says, 'or staying or leaving . . . You're not who *I* remember you to be, either. Does it matter? I want you, I want no other; that doesn't mean on no terms—'

Hainzell, more sulkily than seems possible for a man of his age, says, 'I'm cold.'

She grins at that. He, hearing himself, smiles reluctantly. Not long after that, they sit together again in the shelter of the wall.

Moved with no thought of the future, it is Sanzia who reaches across to take his hand, and clasp it in both of hers. She sits with her knees raised, resting her arms on them; resting her mouth against the skin of his hand, that is fine-textured and cool. Thinking *This moment, now, no future and no past, only now.*

He reaches across her with his free hand, fumbling in her pocket so that she (surprised) giggles; it is when she realises that he is trying to get the Tarot dice that she snorts, breaks into giggles that would have been controllable had Hainzell not, in a voice of completely bewildered irritation, said 'What's the matter *now*?' and then she laughs so long and so violently that she breaks off in a fit of coughing; takes one look at his lined and puzzled face, tries to say something, and laughs again until she has to hug her ribs against the pain of it.

Hainzell, looking down at the dice in his hand (seeing *The World-Tree, Plague,* and *The Triune Goddess*), shakes his head. And then grins like a boy.

'Sorry,' he says.

'What did you – think you—'

Seeing her threaten laughter again, Hainzell says, 'Some kind of guidance, a reading, a. . . . I wanted something else to make up my mind for me. I've had too many years of making my own decisions. I'm tired.'

Sanzia lets go of his hand and moves to embrace him: sisterly.

And, her eyes fixed on his, reaches down to unfasten the buckle of his clothing where he is (still, or again) hard; trying to read in his face his reaction, his flesh warm in her palm, her muscles loosening with want.

He pulls her to him, reaching to her; there is a confused few minutes of cold hands and squeals and helpless laughter (he who has not laughed for so many years); a few minutes in which she can think of the ridiculousness of elbows and knees and one convulsive moment that is never passion but always a cramp in the hip-joint (laughter again) and then they are unshelled, hot flesh in the fog-ridden air, joined and co-joined and half-controlled – pulling clothes round them in a warm nest – and most uncontrolled: Tarot dice forgotten except as small and sharp obstructions under incestuous bodies.

She wakes alone.

Before dawn, she comes to the Edge, and waits while the Heartland's radiance makes the east grow bright.

Pale snow-light illumines the city. The towers, gables, cup-olas, battlements, arches and spires are limned with white. Shadows fall towards her: cobalt-blue. She leans her bare arms on the roof-rail and feels the iron bite. Below her, myriad rows of windows set into the building's cliff-face burn orange-gold. A chill wind blows out of the east. Her bare feet are too numb now to feel the cold. She grins, sniffing back tears, and beats her blue-purple fingers together. They clap loud in the silence.

She leaves off looking at the city (all its filth and poverty hidden from this height) and crosses the snow on the flat roof, where other feet have trodden before her, while she slept. And comes to the rust-orange rail that is all the barrier now between herself and the Edge.

The sheer side of the building falls away at her feet, red bricks blackened with aeons of neglect, windowless, obscure, spidered across with great vines and creepers.

Below the building – she must strain to see down so far – the brick ends and the solid rock begins. Rock as black as iron, faceted, terraced, creviced, split. Some ledges are grown over with what she at first takes to be moss, but then as her sight lengthens sees to be giant pines, firs, sequoias.

Down in the dark gold-dusted air, clouds gather and thicken.

Then a rift appears in the clouds far below her, and she sees down through it the fingernail-patches of green, the bright thread of a river that becomes spray and a last rainbow where it pours over the farthest Edge . . .

Down to the darkness where stars shine.

Just once, she thinks of following him; of letting her snow-tracks end here, as his do. She lifts her head. She sees the light behind the sky and hears the depths singing, tastes snow and fire in her mouth – and grips the rail tightly enough to dapple her hands with rust and blood.

Defeat is bitter in her mouth.

Time passes.

Travelling, she is aware at one point that her hands, stiff in the cold air, are liver-spotted, the skin pinched with age.

Sanzia returns from the Edge, alone, limping because the soles of her feet are blackened and swollen with cold-bite, the pain just on this side of what she can bear.

Midwinter lies on the city now, with more than a vengeance, with a black-ice hatred that matches her heart and mind.

I had him, I held him; his breath was warm and moist on my skin; I felt his heart beating in the circle of my arms that I could barely make enclose him, and now that warmth is gone forever, and this is selfish pain: *I don't care, I hurt!*

In her mind, the voice of Luce (long dead now) asks her 'Where is the comfort that you had from the ordered patterns of the universe, that dance of symbols, that endlessly-returning spiral: the Thirty Faces of the Arcana Dice?'

She walks across a great square. The paving-stones are vast, and between their irregular joints creep up small tendrils of black weed. Frost is stark on the stone. Somewhere there are voices, somewhere there are people doing whatever it is warm breathing people do in this black-ice stasis of the heart.

Sanzia walks across the paving-stones and the sky above her head is that colour between milk-white and blue that comes with midwinter. She stops then, and quite deliberately kneels down on the frost-cracked stone. The melting ice touches the flesh of her shins, cold through cloth; darkens the hem of her jacket. It is not difficult then for her to feel through her pockets for the dice. She must hold all five of them cupped in both her hands or they will spill.

Sanzia's hands are brown, with snow-burns from the Edge; and on them blue veins stand up like worms and serpents. Dirt is grimed into the skin so deeply that now they will never be washed clean, and they are (are they?) an old woman's hands, though her face framed in that metallic hair still seems young.

She casts the dice, or lets them fall.

The Weaver. Flight. The Rose. Death. And – *The Triune Goddess.*

Sanzia turns her face up to the sky. It is noon, and the sun is a white disc, no more brilliant (or no less) than her hair. *The Sun* is also a card. And the dice are a weight in her hand, an irregular weight: *These are loaded dice, they cannot fall differently—*

Her breath is white in the air, the stone a bitter cold under her flesh. She casts again:

The Weaver. Death. The Phoenix. The Phoenix – again; and again *The Phoenix.*

Thirty die-faces, thirty Arcana cards, no way for double and triune images to fall.

Her eyes fill with water that is momentarily hot on her cheeks, and then as it runs becomes ice cold and burning. *The Rose* gone, gone with *Flight*: that Icarus-love of the Edge that is stronger than whatever they had between them, not-brother and not-sister.

And the stone is numbingly cold now, and the voices louder, approaching. In the middle of the square is a mausoleum, and steps, and on them stumps of rusted metal that might have been bars, a lock, a cage. There are no high walls of the White Rose's Church, the name of the Bridge-builder is forgotten.

She casts again those heavy cubes of bone that she, long ago, so carefully drilled and weighted with lead:

The Phoenix. The Weaver. The Phoenix. The Phoenix. The Phoenix.

And now that finely-etched skull is gone, with the peri-winkle-blue flowers inset into its empty eye-sockets, as blue as the eyes of Luce in the long-ago. Sanzia is afraid to cast again, cast with loaded single-image dice that should not be able to fall against the grain of this world. Afraid that the spider-*Weaver* should go and all five dice show a white bird consumed in the fire of its own making.

She casts again, bent in concentration over the flagstones,

idly brushing away fronds of black weed that the frost had killed . . .

And it is there that they find her.

There is a man wheeling a cart that steams with its load of hot food, small coins scattered in his tin; with him is a boy. After them comes a woman dressed in blue, and after her a woman who cradles a bundle of her work-clothes under her arm (you will notice that things have changed in the time that has passed, a change that has very little to do with Sanzia or Hainzell or Luce; though it has not changed as much as either the men or the women think. And if the time has come for that, perhaps the time has also come to award the crowd names):

Foxfield, resting the cart on its supports for a moment, looks uncertainly at the woman who kneels (it is an unfamiliar posture these days). He turns to the small crowd that has gathered, hoping for some kind of support:

'Is she ill, do you think?'

The woman with work-clothes, Gilfrin, says, 'An old woman like her out in this cold, it's shameful!' at the same time as Foxfield's boy Veitch (who will grow up to have one of the finest minds in the city, but that is much later) exclaims, 'She's too young to be out, she's only a girl—'

After that they stand and watch her for a while, and the wind blows colder, and she sits, nameless, staring at five Tarot dice (but do they show what you expect to see?).

If the dice show *The Phoenix*, one of the citizens of this city, probably the other woman, Tallis, will take her home; take her into warm shelter in the iron tunnels, where braziers glow, where there is food, where she can sleep, where they can watch her to see what she will become

If the image is *Death* they will remember who she is or was, and see in her face what was once seen on the face of Luce, and I think they will kill her—

If what shows is *The Weaver*, they will abandon her as a politic madwoman or mystic, and the bitter black winter cold will kill her—

The dice cannot show *The Rose* or *Flight*, these two are not hers to have, they belong with whatever bloody death or lightborn apotheosis he now owns—

But then, there are Thirty cards in the Major Arcana, and

once loaded dice have gone wild and random, any of the
symbols may fall in that scatter to the frost-bitten stone. As the
eyes of these people see an old woman and a girl in the one face
(who knows how differently they see each other? Allow them
their different vision) so who can tell which may fall: *The Hanged
Man* or *The Magus* or *The High Priestess* or *Last Judgement*, cards of
sacrifice, of magic, of occult knowledge, and resolution; or
perhaps, it may be, that dancing figure that is both Woman and
Man, surrounded by symbols of beasts and apotheoses, the card
The World.

Throw the dice and see.

Ask: you will be answered. Between destruction and transformation is only the space of a breath. I am only bone and
inlaid enamel, I can only tell you what story you think I will
tell—

And she, rising, looks at the faces that surround her; takes
Veitch's hand, with a nod to Foxfield, and – as she begins
to speak with Tallis and Gilfrin – they walk away, across the
weed-studded square, leaving the dice where they have fallen.

Afterword

This one arrived as pictures.

I think fictions can end up telling the writer a personal story, irrespective of what they are for anyone else. Like a Tarot card, with interpretable symbols and archetypes – and if someone else had precisely the same card, it wouldn't give the same reading at all.

So while my aim was for the reader to find enjoyment, I can nevertheless tell now that the 'pictures' of the world where physical laws don't work right, and the Earth has an edge to it, are try-outs for 'Beggars in Satin' and 'The Knot Garden' and *Rats & Gargoyles*. I didn't know that at the time. It's at least a semi-answer to that perennial question: 'Where do you get your ideas from?'

'The Tarot Dice' turned out to be a try-out for characters, too; people that I wouldn't understand until another fifteen years had gone by. Hainzell and Sanzia are pretty much unrecognisable – I was wrong about almost everything, including their relationship to each other – but I got them nailed down, these last couple of years, for a book called *1610: A Sundial in a Grave*, which is set in a remarkably ordinary seventeenth-century Europe where there are only the standard four directions on the compass, and no dice except the normal sort.

Maybe that's the thing about being a writer: you're always stumbling along at the back of the tapestry, catching up all the lost threads in the dark – and hoping against hope that the picture on the *other* side actually makes sense . . .

And in this case I'm not as sure as I'd like to be that the front of the tapestry is explicit. It seemed reasonable to me that the conscious viewpoint of inanimate objects, imbued by human beings with the qualities of Fate and archetype, should be . . .

odd. The Tarot dice see history in freeze-frame crucial moments. I've always liked the concept of visual images that you can use to explore subconscious associations – and the thought of gambling with them, and cheating, seemed screwy enough (given the initial concept) to be pleasing. But if the reader is primarily audio- or kinaesthesia-focused, rather than primarily visual, I suspect this won't be an easily accessible story.

Maybe those readers will get on better with the political sub-plot. I can always hope.

The Harvest of Wolves

Flix sat in the old sagging armchair, leaning forward, and tore another page from the *Encyclopaedia Brittanica*. The fire took it, flickering in the grate.

'What the—' the boy, closing the door as he entered, strode across the room and slapped the book out of her hand. 'What's the matter with you? You could *sell* that for—'

'For money to buy fuel?' Flix suggested. Adrenaline made her dizzy. She looked down at her liver-spotted hands, where the veins stood up with age; they were shaking. 'Thank you, I prefer to cut out the middle man. Self-sufficiency.'

He glared; she doubted he recognised irony.

'You're crazy, you know that?'

'If you know it, that ought to be enough. Have you put in your report yet?' She shot the question at him.

He was still young enough to blush. Angry because of it, he snarled, 'You keep your mouth shut, citizen. You hear me?'

'I hear you.' Age makes you afraid, Flix thought. Pacifying him, she said, 'Well, what have you brought me?'

'Bread. Milk's out. Can't deliver, there's no transport. I got you some water, though. It's clean.'

You wouldn't know clean water if it bit you, Flix thought bitterly. She watched the boy unpacking the plastic bag he carried, throwing the goods into the nearest cupboard. He was growing taller by the week, this one; broad-shouldered with close-cropped black hair, and the changing voice of adolescence.

'Marlow,' she said, 'what makes you choose community service?'

'Didn't choose it, did I? Got given it, didn't I?'

He straightened, stuffed the bag in the pocket of his uniform jacket, and came over to squat beside the open fire. Though he never admitted it, it attracted him. Probably because he'd never before been in a house old enough to have a grate, she thought.

' "Community service", ' she repeated, unable to keep the edge out of her voice. 'Snooping under cover of charity; you call that service? Bringing Welfare rations, weighing me up . . . and all the time new laws, and cutting it closer every time, eh? If they've got as far as these slums, Marlow boy, then pretty soon we'll all be gone.'

Resentment glared out of him. 'Think I want to come here? Crazy old house, crazy old bitch—'

'That's "citizen" to you, if you can't manage "Flix".' She offered him a crumpled pack of cigarettes, forcing a smile. 'Only tobacco, I'm afraid.'

The Pavlovian response: 'Filthy things'll give you cancer.'

'Ah, who'll get me first, then: lung cancer, hypothermia, starvation – or you and your bloody Youth Corps?'

'You got no room to talk – it was your lot got us in this mess in the first place.' He stood up. 'You think we want to live like this, no jobs, nothing? You got no idea. If it weren't for the Corps I'd be—'

'You'd be waiting out your time on Welfare,' Flix said, very carefully. 'Seeing the deadline come up. You'd be being tested – like I am now – to see how fit you are to survive. To qualify for government food. To get government water, so you don't die of cholera. Government housing, so you don't die of cold. Instead you're here, waiting for me to—'

'That's the way it is,' Marlow said. He lowered his head, glaring at her from dark, hollowed eyes. (Why, she thought, he's been losing sleep.) 'You got to produce. You got to work. You got to be worth keeping on Welfare. Or else – and don't tell me it ain't fair. I know it ain't fair, but that's the way it is.'

'Ah,' she said, on a rising inflection, 'is that the way it is.'

'*Look* at you!' He swung his arm round, taking in the single-room flat. The wallpaper was covered by old posters, garish with the slogans of the halcyon '90s (that final, brief economic flowering) when protest was easy. Planks propped up on bricks served as shelves for old books and pamphlets and magazines. Some had sat so long in the same place that the damp had made of them an inseparable mass. A long-disconnected computer terminal gathered dust, ancient access codes scratched on the casing. Cracking china lay side by side on the drainer with incongruously new plastic dishes, and a saucepan full of something brown and long-burned sat on the stove. A thin film of plaster from the ceiling had drifted down onto the expanse of worn linoleum, left empty by the clustering of table, chair, and bed round the open fire.

Flix poked the ashes with a burnt slat, and glanced up at the windows. Beyond the wire-mesh, the sky was grey.

'You could fix those boards,' she said. 'There's a wind whips through there that could take the barnacles off a ship's hull, since your friends left me with no glass in the windows . . . What, no reaction?'

'You can't blame them.' The boy sounded tired, and very adult. 'Thinking of you in here. Eating, sleeping. Doing nothing to earn it.'

'Christ!' Flix exploded, and saw him flinch at the word as he always did. But now she wasn't goading him for her amusement. 'There was a time you didn't have to *earn* the right to live! You had it – as a human being!'

'Yeah,' he said wearily. 'I know. I heard about that. I hear about it all the time from my old man. Free this, free that, free the other; holidays in the sun, cars for everybody, everybody working – yeah, I heard. And what happens? What do you leave for *us*? You let the niggers come here and steal your jobs, you let the Yanks put their missiles here! You let kids grow up wild 'cause their mothers were never home; you sell us out to the Reds—'

'Oh, spare me. If you're going to be bigoted, at least be original!'

'Citizen,' Marlow said, 'shut up.'

Not quite under her breath she said, 'Ignorant pig.'

He yelled. 'Why don't you clean this place up? *You* live like a pig!'

'I was never one for housework – and besides, I've got you to do it for me, haven't I? Courtesy of the Welfare state. Until such time as the state decides I'm not worth keeping alive.'

His would not be the first report made on her (though the first under this name), but time and purges had culled the number of officials willing to turn a blind eye on changes of code, name, and location.

I am, Flix thought, too old for this fugitive life.

'Pig,' Marlow repeated absently. He rummaged around in the toolbox by the window, and began nailing the slats back over the lower windowsill.

'There's coffee in the cupboard.' Flix made a peace-offering of it. 'Have some if you want it. You'll have to boil the kettle. I think the power's still on.'

'Where'd you get *coffee*?'

'I still have friends,' Flix observed sententiously. 'They can't do much, being as they're old like me; but what they can do, they will. The old network's still there.'

'Subversive,' he accused.

Lord Brahma! I can't seem to keep off it today, Flix thought. What is it with me – do I *want* to die? Well, maybe. But not to suit their convenience.

'Do you ever listen to anything except what they tell you?'

Marlow whacked the last nail in viciously, threw down the hammer, and stalked over to the sink. Filling the kettle, his back to her, he said, 'I know what's right. I know what's true.'

'I am sick to death of people who *know*. I want people who aren't sure. I want people who're willing to admit there's another side to the argument – or even that there is an argument, for Christ's sake! Marlow, will you bloody look at me!'

He plugged the kettle in. Turning, and leaning back against the chipped unit: 'What?'

'You don't believe all that bullshit.' Again, he flinched. They are abnormally sensitive, she thought. 'You can't believe it, you're not the age. Sixteen's when you go round questioning everything.'

'Maybe in your day. It's different now. We got to grow up quick or not at all.' He shrugged. 'Listen, I'm looking back at it, what it was like – I can see what you can't. While you sat round talking, the commies were taking over the unions; and if it hadn't been for Foster we'd be a satellite state today—'

Flix groaned. 'Jesus. Marlow, tell me all the shit you like, tell me we were all commie pinko perverts, tell me we were capitalist running dogs who brought the world to ruin—' she was laughing, an old woman's high cackle '—but in the name of God, don't tell me about your precious Foster! I knew all I needed to know about dictators before you were born!'

His mouth twisted. She could see him lose patience with her.

'You don't know what it's like,' Marlow said. 'Five of us in a two-room flat, and the power not on, and never enough food, and for why? Because there's no work, and if there was, there's nothing to buy with the money! At least he's making it better. At least there's less of that!'

'Where do you go when there's nowhere to go?' Flix asked rhetorically. 'I'd OD if you could get the stuff, but that's another thing banned in your bloody utopia. Fetch us the coffee, Marlow, and hand me that half-bottle in the top cupboard.'

He was as disapproving as any Youth Cadet, but he did what she asked. Whiskey, and coffee (the last now, the very last) bit into her gut. I am fighting, she reminded herself sourly, I am fighting – God knows why – for my life.

'I suppose it's no good offering you a drink? No, I thought not. Hell, Marlow, loosen up, will you?'

She had, over the weeks, gained some small amusement from tormenting him. Like all of Foster's New Puritans, the Corps strongly disapproved of drugs, blasphemy, lechery – and there, she thought, is a fine old-fashioned word. Not that I've quite got round to that . . . but wouldn't he react beautifully! Or is it that I'm afraid of him laughing? Or afraid of him? For all his 'community service', he's still a thug.

She tore a few more pages from the thick book, crumpled them, and poked them into the fire where they flared briefly. 'What about coal, Marlow?'

'Reconstituted.'

'Christ, that stuff doesn't burn. Still, what the hell. Come and sit down.' She watched him kneel by the flames. In the dim cold room, the light made lines on his face, he looked older.

'In the nineties,' she said speculatively, 'there were, for example, parties without supervisors – supervisors! – and music without propaganda—'

'Without whose propaganda?'

'Bravo, Marlow!' She clapped gently. 'Without theirs, of course. With ours. Now it's the other way round. Do you realise, I wouldn't *mind* if he had the grace to be original? But it's the same old thing; no free press, no free speech, no unions; food shortages, rabid patriotic nationalism—'

'You were traitors! Was that any better?'

No way out, she thought, no way in; God preserve us from the voice of invincible ignorance.

'One thing we didn't do,' she said. 'We didn't weigh people up as to how useful they were to the state – and let them die when they got sick and old.'

He was quiet. 'Didn't you?'

'We didn't *plan* it.'

'There's less poverty now. Less misery. It's a hard world,' he said. 'They're starving in Asia. Dying. That's not going to happen here. You used it up, this world. So you got yourselves to blame if you don't like what's happening now.'

'Marlow,' Flix said, 'what are you going to say in your report?'

Now there was no evading the question. He looked up with clear puzzled eyes. 'I don't want to do it.'

'I know, or it wouldn't be nearly a month overdue, would it? No, don't ask me how I know. Like I said, the old grapevine's still there. When are they going to start wondering, Marlow? When are they going to start making reports on *you*?'

He stared into the fire. She got up slowly, taking her weight on her wrists, and went across to pull on her old (now much cracked) leather jacket. The cold got into her bones. Now would I be so weak if there was proper food? she thought. Christ, my mother lived to be eighty, and I'm not within twenty years of that!

'I've got family,' Marlow said. 'The old man, Macy and the baby. We got to eat.'

She could see herself reflected in the speckled wall mirror, lost in sepia depths. An old woman, lean and straight, with spiky cropped hair that needed washing from grey to silver. Marlow, out of focus, was a dark uniform and the glint of insignia.

Flix looked straight at him, solemnly; and when his eyes were fixed on her, she smiled. She had always had one of those faces, naturally sombre and sardonic, that are transformed when they smile. Vanity doesn't go with age, she thought, savouring the boy's unwilling responsive grin.

'I could have shown you so much – so much. You haven't got the guts to run wild,' she said, 'you haven't got the guts to *question*.'

The implication of promise was there. He watched her. The

light dimmed, scummy and cold; and the fire glowed down to red embers. The ever-present smell of the room, overlain for a while by coffee and spirits, reasserted itself.

'You're a drunk,' Marlow said. 'D'you think I haven't seen the bottles you throw out – and the ones you hide? Yeah, your friends keep you supplied, all right! I've come in here when you were dead drunk on the bed, place stinking of shit; I've listened to you maundering on about the old days – I don't want to know! If this is where it leaves you, I don't want to know!'

'Is that right?' Tears stung behind her eyes, her voice thinned. 'You'll never live the life I lived, and you'll never know how I regret its passing – ah, Jesus, it tears you up, to know it's gone and gone for good. *You* were the people we wanted to help. I mean you, Marlow! And when it came to actually thinking – God knows how difficult that is – you don't want to know. You'd sooner march with your mobs. You'd sooner smash places up on your witch-hunts. You'd sooner cheer the tanks when they roll by. And God help you, that's not enough, you've got to think you're *right*!'

The boy crossed the room and pushed her. She fell back on the bed with an ugly sound. He stamped back and forth, sweeping the cracked cups crashing to the floor. Violently he kicked at the piles of old books and pamphlets. They scattered in soggy lumps.

'This!' he shouted. 'You preach about your precious books and you burn them to keep warm! You talk about your "subversive network" but what is it really? Old men and women hoarding food and drink, keeping it from us who need it!'

She, breathing heavily and conscious of pain, didn't answer. His first energy spent, he came back and helped her into the chair; and made up the fire until it blazed. The cold wind blew belches of grey smoke back into the room.

Flix felt down into the side of the chair for the hidden bottle there; fist knotted about it, letting the alcohol sting her back to life. When she looked up again he was putting on his coat.

As if nothing had happened, she said, 'Books aren't sacred. Ideas are, and I've got those up here.' She touched her lank hair. 'Whatever else we are, we subversives, I'll tell you this – we care about each other. That's more than your Corps will do for you when you're old.'

'I'll come in again tomorrow.' He was all boy now, gangling, uncertain, sullen.

'I don't care if you don't agree with me! Just think about what you're doing – for once, *think* about it!'

At the door he turned back and said, '*Will* they look after you?'

After she heard the door slam, she plugged the power outlet into the antique stereo equipment, and played old and much-mended '90s revival-rock cassettes, blasting the small room full of sound. It served to stop the treadmill-turning of her mind.

'You've got a letter!' Taz yelled down the stairs after her the next morning. She grunted, not taking any notice; the old man (occupier of the building's only other inhabitable room) was given to delusions, to happenings that were years after their time.

But when she crossed the hallway it lay there in the crepuscular light: a thin rough-paper envelope folded and addressed to Citizen Felicity Vance. Flix picked it up, wincing at the pain in her back. An immature hand, the letters mostly printed. So she knew.

She took it into her room, closing the door and resting her old bones on the bed.

Where is there anyone I can tell? she thought. That's another one of the boy's taunts – 'if you had a husband, citizen.' Ah, but I could never live in anyone's company but my own.

Now it came to it she was afraid. Shaking, sweating; the old cold symptoms. She opened the letter.

'Citizen—

'I have to tell the truth. They check up on me too. It is the truth. You drink too much and your alone and cant take care. I have to live. If your friends are good friends you better tell them I sent my report in. Its not your fault things are like this. Im sorry I said it was. Sometimes I wisht I lived in the old days it might have been good. But I dont think so not for most of us.

'Peter Marlow'

She dressed slowly; fashions once adopted from a mythical past and previous revolutions: old jeans and sweater and the ancient leather jacket – the smell took her back, with the abruptness of illusion, to boys and bikes and books; to bright libraries, computer networks; to Xerox and duplicators, to faxsheets in brilliant colours that had been going to change the world.

He believes I'm a drunken old woman, alone, friends no more than geriatrics; he has to report me or be reported himself – and does he hope that it's more than an illusion, that some secret subversive organisation still exists to whisk me off to – what? Safety? Where?

Things are bad all over, kid.

But at least he's sent in the report.

She left, locking the door behind her. It was a long time and a long walk to where she could borrow a working telephone. When she called the number, it was a while before it was answered; and a while before he remembered her name.

'Well,' Flix said, 'you'll have had the report by now.'

'You're a fool,' the man said. 'You won't last a week in the Welfare camps! Flix—'

'I'll last long enough to tell what I know,' Flix said. 'About you – and who your father was – and what "societies" you used to belong to. I'll do it, Simon. Maybe it won't make much difference, maybe it won't even lose you your job. But you won't have much of a career afterwards.'

After a pause he said, 'What do you want?'

'I want somewhere decent to live. I want to be warm. I want enough to eat, I want to play my music and read my books in peace. That's all. I'm tired of living like a pig! I want a place like the one you've got put by for yourself when *you* get old. No Welfare camps for Foster's boys, right? Now they'll put me in one – they can't ignore that report – and when they do, you know what I'm going to say!'

She could feel his uncertainty over the line, knew she had to weight things in her favour.

'Would it help,' she said, 'if you could turn in a few of the old subversive cells, by way of a sweetener? Those that didn't know you, those that can't give us away?'

' "Us." ' His tone reluctantly agreed complicity, barely masked contempt. 'Names?'

'Names after, not before.'

And he agreed.

Flix grinned to herself, a fox-grin full of teeth and no humour. You and me both, Marlow, she thought; you and me both . . .

'Like someone once told me,' she said, 'I have to live.'

Afterword

Really, this one's a play. Not that it was written as one, but that's what it is – two people in one room, and the action comes solely through their dialogue. Nothing in the way of SFX but a thrown cup and a telephone call . . .

I don't do stuff like this.

Maybe there was a little hitch at Muse Central – or else it was my personal Muse exercising her evil sense of humour, and sending me things she thinks I *ought* to learn how to do. Many people who write fiction get wary of saying 'But I can't *do* things with no sword-fights/special effects,' or whatever their particular *bête noire* is, since that tends to be an open invitation to the subconscious mind to promptly hand up an idea of that very nature. And then it's bang-head-against-keyboard time again.

I enjoyed doing an unashamedly political story. There's stuff that looks dated in it, after twenty years. (It *cannot* be twenty years. I demand a recount!) But you can pretty much rely on stories about UK governments messing around with the Welfare State being periodically relevant. Unfortunately.

I enjoyed spending time with Flix and Marlow, too. He's not intelligent in a sense that lets him easily gain from poor schooling; she's so smart she'll cut herself. He still has compassion; she's hoping, I think, that the alcohol will kill her before she finally loses all of hers. I find myself still hoping it turned out okay for them.

Oh, and as an SF writer, I managed (amongst other things) to dismally miss the opportunity to predict the mobile phone. But you can't win 'em all.

Anukazi's Daughter

'Our information was correct,' Ukurri said, pointing. The ship was just visible now, its prow appeared out of the dawn haze, already in the calm water of the bay. 'Let them come ashore. Attack as soon as the light's good.'

'Prisoners?' Rax asked.

He grinned at her. 'Try to keep one or two alive. They might have things to tell us. These Islanders are weak-willed.'

Low chuckles came from the mounted company that formed Bazuruk's first Order of the Axe.

'Ready yourselves,' he ordered.

Rax knotted the war-horse's reins on the saddle. She breathed deeply, excitement cold in her gut. Her palms were damp. She wiped them on the black surcoat, feeling cold links of mail underneath, and adjusted the buckles on her leg and arm greaves. The shaft of the war-axe was familiar under her hand. The shield hung ready at her side.

The ship nosed close inshore. Sea foam went from grey to white. A cold wind blew. Here great shelves of rock jutted out into the sea, channels worn between them by the waves, so that at low tide a ship could put into what was a natural quay.

There were thirty men – no more – she estimated. Our numbers are equal, then.

'There!' She saw the flash of light from the cliffs at the far end of the bay: a signal-mirror in the hands of the Third Axe, telling them that the other half of the company was in position.

'*Now!*' Ukurri shouted.

Her heels dug into the horse's flanks. For a few strides she was out in the open, ahead of them all. The rocks echoed. Sparks struck from flying hooves. Rax, cold clear through, hefted the great axe. Ukurri and Azu-anuk and Lilazu rode with her, and

the rest of the Order behind, but she spurred forward and out-
distanced them all.

The war-mount cleared a channel where crimson weed hung
delicate and fragile in clear water. She heard cries, shouts; she
saw the men half ashore from the ship and heard the thunder of
the riders from the far end of the bay. She rose up in the saddle –
sweating, cold as death under her mail, excitement drying her
lips – and caught a spear-thrust on her shield. She struck. The
great blade sheared up under the man's helmet. The jaw, ear,
half the skull ripping away.

Another struck at her, jabbing with a barbed spear. Her blow,
which seemed only to brush him, spilled a crimson trail.

On the backstroke she put the axe's spike through another
man's eye socket and left him screaming. The horse reared, came
down, crushing with iron hooves. Smooth rock became treacherous, slick with blood. The sun hit her eyes. Her face was wet,
and her black surcoat had turned rust-coloured with blood – not
hers. An Islander fled. She leaned dangerously far out of the
saddle to slice through his leather jerkin and left him face down
on the rock. She smelled burning and heard flames crackle. A
dozen of the Order were at the ship. The pitch that caulked its
seams burned fiercely. A man screamed. She saw Ukurri strike,
hurling the man back into the blaze. Flames were invisible in the
sunlight; only the shimmering air betrayed them.

'Bazuruk!' She heard the war call behind her.

She wheeled, lifted the axe – it was heavy, and her arm was
stiff – and saw Lilazu fighting on one of the narrow rock spurs.
His horse shifted uneasily. It was no help now to be mounted.
Two Islanders had him pinned against the water's edge.

Her thrown hand-axe took one in the back. Rax struck with
the flat of the axe, sending the other man full-length into the
shallow pool. Lilazu acknowledged Rax's aid with a raised hand,
guiding his horse delicately onto solid rock, then galloping off
toward the last knot of fighting.

Rax leaned down from the saddle, using the spike of the axe
to hook the stunned man ashore.

The crackling of the flames was loud. Surf beat on the rocks.
Gulls cried. The air smelled of dank weed, of burning, of blood.
Rax's hands were red, her arms streaked with blood that dried
and cracked. She hauled the Islander over her saddle, clicking to

the weary horse, and rode over to where Ukurri watched the burning ship. The early sun was already hot. A warming relaxation spread through her. If she had not been exhausted, she would have sung.

'Rax Keshanu!' Ukurri slapped her leg and pulled the Islander down from her saddle. 'A live one . . . and not half-killed. Good! That's four.'

She was grinning amiably at nothing in particular: she recognised the after-battle euphoria. 'Shall I bring him with me?' she asked.

Ukurri hesitated. Rax's light mood faded.

'Do you think I'm stupid enough to let him escape?'

'Women have soft hearts,' Ukurri said and then laughed as Rax held up her bloody hands. 'But not in the Order of the Axe, no – though we've only you to judge by. Bring him with us to the Tower, then.'

The others were rifling the dead, leaving the bodies unburied on the rocks. If the stink offended any of the nearby settlements, they'd send a burial party. If not, enemy bones would bleach in the cove, and the storm tides would carry them home to Shabelit and the Hundred Isles.

At their first camp, she tended the unconscious Islander's head wound. He was young, no more than twenty, she judged: Ukurri's age, ten summers younger than Rax. He had pale skin, red-brown hair, and green eyes in a face marred by plague-scars.

She felt an indefinable pang: not of desire or pity, but somehow familiar. If I'd seen him, I couldn't have killed him, she realised. Anukazi! What's the matter with me?

She had fought before, taken prisoners for ransom; none had ever disturbed her the way this Islander boy did.

The Order headed north, resting in the heat of noon, crossing the humid, insect-ridden flats of the Shantar marshes. Rax guarded the Islander closely. After the first day his rage and grief – displayed beyond what a Bazuruki considered proper – subsided into quiet. She thought that meant loss of spirit until she caught him cutting himself and the other survivors free with a stolen knife. After that she watched him constantly.

'I didn't think he had the wits to try it,' she admitted to Ukurri, as they rode on north.

'You served on the barbarian frontier, the Crystal Mountains. They're cunning in the cold south,' he said. 'The Islanders are the worst of all. That one's a Vanathri – you can tell by the cropped hair. The others are mercenaries, from the Cold Lands, I'd guess.'

Rax shrugged. 'It's not our concern. They'll discover the truth in the Tower.'

That night she took a water flask for the Islander. He regarded her with disgust.

'Bazuruki killer,' he said.

She pulled off her helmet, letting the coarse black hair fall free. She grinned, feral, content.

'Yes,' she said, 'I am a woman and a warrior.'

She realised that he wasn't shocked or even surprised. That sent her back to Ukurri with oblique questions, and he told her that in the Hundred Isles a woman was barred from no profession, not even that of warrior.

On the third day they rode through rice fields to the river estuary and came to the city.

'That's Anukazi?' The Islander rode beside her on a remount, bound securely. 'A great city, Rax . . .'

'Wherever you heard my name, keep it out of your mouth.' She almost regretted her harshness. Her curiosity was stirred. 'Why did you come here – one ship's company against all Bazuruk?'

'You have my freemate there.' His voice was rough. 'I would have fought my way to the city – but I used mercenaries. It is no surprise that I was betrayed.'

The Order rode down the brick-paved way that led to the South Gate. Ox-carts drew aside. Insects whirred in the dust-clouds. The heat made Rax thirsty. As the shadow of Anukazi's squat square buildings fell across her, she became aware that her joy at returning was less than usual.

'You have women-warriors in your islands, then, Vanathri?'

'If you can recognise a Vanathri, you know we don't bind ourselves with useless laws.' His body tensed as they rode down the wide streets. 'Though it seems your laws aren't as strict as I'd heard.'

'You don't think so?' Her bitterness was never far below the surface. Her long fight to be accepted in an Order had been successful, but the struggle robbed her of half her satisfaction. At last she said, 'I've spent most of my life in the northern mountains. All I know of the Archipelago is rumours.'

'That can be remedied.'

He was talking to keep his fears at bay, she guessed. He didn't look at her. She studied his familiar features. What does he see when he looks at me? Rax wondered.

She listened while he spoke of the Shabelit Archipelago, which began in the sandbars off Bazuruk's coast and ended as far south as the Cold Lands. He talked about the Hundred Isles, where life was trade and where half a hundred petty lordlings engaged their private quarrels, with no Tower to bind them into one nation . . .

'Rax,' Ukurri called, as they entered the Tower walls, 'take that one down to the cells with the mercenaries before you go off duty.'

She acknowledged his order curtly. While the rest of the Order dismounted at the stables, she made her way with the prisoners to the dungeons. The underground shadow was cool.

'You've got another Islander in here,' she told the jailer, keeping charge of the Vanathri man. 'Put them in together. They might talk.'

Brick walls were scarred with nitre. Pitch-torches flared, blackening the ceiling. The jailer searched down the entry scroll.

'Three-five-six,' he announced. 'Let him sweat. They won't get to him for a while.'

'Why not?'

'A conspiracy was discovered against the Firsts of the Orders.' He glanced fearfully at her. 'The guards are interrogating everyone in the Tower and executing traitors.'

'Anukazi save the Tower from harm,' Rax said, and the man echoed her fervently. 'Give me the keys, I'll take this one down for you.'

Shadows leapt as they descended the long stairways. Rax held the torch high, searching for the right cell.

'I'll send a physician to look at you.'

'No.' He was hostile.

'You're young,' she said, 'but you're not stupid. If you've no friends, you won't live long here, Vanathri. These cells are plague-pits.'

'I'll do without Bazuruk's help.'

She fitted the key in the lock, thrust the torch in a wall-socket, and pulled the heavy door open. There was only one other Islander listed – a Shabelitan – so this must be his freemate. It would be interesting to see a warrior-woman, Rax thought.

The Islander came into the torchlight, dragging his chain. Rax was disappointed. It was a man: stocky, in his forties, with a lined face and mocking smile. This is the wrong cell, she thought, or the Islander woman's already dead—

'Devenil,' Vanathri said, holding out his bound hands. The other man stepped forward and kissed him on the mouth with a lover's kiss.

'So here you are to rescue me. Again.' The older man smiled tightly. Behind his mockery there was pain. 'Vanathri are impetuous, I know, Kel. But this is stupidity.'

'Did you think I wouldn't come?' Kel Vanathri asked, looking younger than ever.

'Did you come for me or for Shabelit's heir? Vanathri's not a rich island, and if ever I inherit Shabelit – though lord knows my mother may outlive us all – then I can see why you'd want to be Shabelit's freemate.'

'I'd stay with you even if I thought you'd never inherit – or if you weren't heir at all. You should know that by now.'

Cynicism marked Devenil's face, but his voice was tired and uncertain. 'Would you? Yes, I think you would.'

'I should have managed this better.' Anger darkened Kel's eyes. 'I'm a fool, and I've paid for it. I've lost a mercenary company and my freedom. But a chance will come. We're not dead yet.'

Rax crept away from the spy-hole, leaving the torch to burn itself out.

I should report it.

Lost in thought, Rax made her way to the Axe Order's building in the Tower complex. Devenil, that was the name: heir of Shabelit of the Hundred Isles. They can't know, or they'd be asking a ransom for him. But they'll know as soon as they start interrogating him, as soon as this purge is over.

Anukazi keep them from me!

She reached her own chambers, a bare brick-walled room divided by rice-paper screens. Through the window she could see across the flat roofs and ziggurats of the city. She pulled the thin linen shutters closed in order to keep flies and a degree of heat out. Then she shed her mail, bathed, and donned a silk robe.

She sat on the pallet. A brush and paper lay on the low table, unfinished calligraphy spidering across the page. She wasn't yet calm enough to write. She called the house slave and ordered rice and herb tea.

The Islanders had reeked of dead meat. So they eat animal flesh, Rax thought with revulsion. The men couple with one another, and the women too, I suppose; and women are warriors, and men – but he's a fighter, that Kel Vanathri.

Seated cross-legged before the carved Keshanu mask that hung on the wall, she gazed at the abstract face and tried to achieve harmony. Patterns of light and shade entered her eyes. Her breathing slowed.

She was free, then, of Rax. She could stand outside herself and see the tall strong-limbed woman whose skin was lined with exposure to wind and sun. With black hair, green eyes, red-brown skin, she was born of hot Keshanu in the Crystal Mountains . . .

But then she thought of Kel Vanathri and Devenil, Shabelit's heir.

She tried to consider them dispassionately. The image that came to her was not Vanathri's but Ukurri's. Of an age with the young Islander, Ukurri was already First Axe of this Order, her commander and sometime bedfriend. And she, a decade older, with experience gained on the barbarian frontier . . .

You'll never be First Axe, a voice said in her mind. No matter how good you are, how many successes you have, they won't give you an Order because the men wouldn't accept you as commander. You're good, better than Ukurri, but you're a woman.

In Vanathri, Kel said, there are women-warriors; and in Zu and Orindol and Shamur, and all the Hundred Isles . . .

She cursed Kel for disturbing her peace of mind.

He's young to end in the Tower. He, she thought, has courage, too; he crossed the sea, which is more than I'd do.

Outside, the gongs sounded for evening prayer. She belted her hand-axe over her robe and put on her sandals, preparing to go down to the main hall.

Keep low, Rax thought. There have been conspiracies and interrogations before. I'm loyal to the Tower. They'll take Anukazi's sons but I don't think they'll take Anukazi's only daughter.

She followed the disciplines of the Tower, attended weapons practice and theory classes and services for the preservation of Anukazi's priests. She knew better than to ask about missing faces or empty places. Finally the atmosphere of tension eased: the purge was – for this time at least – finished.

The dice were kind. Rax found herself on a winning streak for the first time in a long while. She was able to bribe extra rations for the Islanders without touching her own pay. When she heard that the Guard had begun interrogating the mercenaries, she went back to the Tower and paid for an undisturbed time in the cells.

The torch burned bright. Kel had fallen against Devenil while he slept, and the older man sat with his back to the wall, supporting Kel. All the mockery was gone from his worn face.

Rax was noisy with the lock, and when she had the door open, hostile stares greeted her.

'What do you want?' Kel Vanathri demanded.

Rax shook her head. The calmness that was a discipline of the Order deserted her. She couldn't name the influence the Islanders had over her.

'They're starting the questioning soon,' she said.

'Bring me a knife,' Kel said, 'I won't ask more, Bazuruki.'

It was pointless to tell them that one day their rations would be drugged, that they would wake in the upper chambers – in the hands of the Anukazi Guard.

'Say you're only mercenaries, pirates, whatever,' she pleaded. 'As for freemates, for the love of Anukazi himself, keep that quiet!'

'There's no love in your Orders?' Devenil asked sceptically.

'I—' The Order denied love fanatically and practised it covertly. Every Order had its pretty boys, vying for favour and carrying rumours. Looking now at Kel and Devenil, she thought no, it's not the same thing at all.

'What they forgive themselves, they hate in others.'

'Take advice,' Kel Vanathri said, 'stay out of here.'

She knew they had plans to escape, or to invite a quick death. The thought bothered her more than it should. She slammed the door and walked away. In a little while they'd be dead.

They'd be good companions in an Order, she thought. It's a senseless waste . . .

To kill Bazuruk's enemies?

No!

What am I thinking? We're caught between the northern barbarians and these damned islands, which, if they could ever unite, could crush Bazuruk. We can't afford mercy, not even for those two. Ah, Anukazi! Why should *I* care?

Rax couldn't sleep that night. She rose and dressed – in mail, with her war-axe – and went down to the main hall. But even dice-games couldn't ease her spirit.

All the city slept. There were no lights in the squat buildings, no noise from the beast markets, no carts in the street. She went by way of the river wall and entered the Tower as the guards changed shift.

Torches burned low in the guardroom.

'Jailer – ' Some instinct held her hand, when she reached to shake him awake. A thin thread of blood ran out from under his head, bowed on the table.

Movement caught her eye, where the torch guttered. The axe slid into her hands. A scuffed noise came from down the passage. She tensed. The jailer had no knife or sword. They would be armed, then.

Softly she said 'Vanathri?'

'Be silent.'

'Devenil.' The strength of her relief was alarming. 'Where's Kel?'

'Put down your axe!'

She rested the spike on the floor, hands clasping the shaft. 'Now I'll tell you something. You're not the first to kill a jailer and come this far. But can you fight your way out past every guard in Anukazi's Tower?'

'If we have to.' It was Kel Vanathri's voice.

'Wait.' She sensed movement. 'Suppose you were taken out
of here by a guard? There are river boats. You might cross the
sea to the Hundred Isles.'

'And let you sound the alarm?' Kel said. 'Put down the axe. I
can throw a knife as well as any Bazuruki.'

'You're not listening to me, Islander. Take the jailer's uniform.'

They stepped forward into the light. Devenil nodded, watching her with a curious expression. 'We'll lock you in one of the
cells, unless you prefer a glorious death – as Bazuruki do, I've
heard.'

'And how will you get past the gates? I'll have to speak for
you. Trust me,' Rax said. 'Only be quick!'

It was only then that she knew her long career with the Order
of the Axe had ended in betrayal.

A fishing boat was moored with sails still raised. The man aboard
answered Rax's hail from the dock.

'Stay back,' she said to the Islanders. The man's head came
above the rail, and she drove her knife up under the soft part of
his jaw. Blood spilled over her hands. She wrenched the blade
loose, feeling it grate against bone, and shoved the body off the
side. It sank quickly. She led the Islanders down the stone steps.

'Now, Devenil, Shabelit's heir,' she said, 'take this young fool
with you and get out of Bazuruk. The alarm's out, I expect, but
the tide's in your favour. Go!'

'They know who brought us out,' Kel Vanathri said. 'You
can't stay.'

'But my Order—'

'You should have thought of that.' Devenil gave a sardonic
grin. The early sun showed dirt, blood, the traces of long
confinement; he looked a good ten years older than his age. His
mocking face disturbed and attracted her. She felt he understood motives she herself didn't recognise.

'We owe a debt we'll never pay you,' said Vanathri. His young
face looked vulnerable. 'But if you come with us to the Hundred
Isles, we'll try.'

From the first moment I saw you, she thought. That lover's
kiss between you and Devenil . . . how could I leave you two
innocents in the Tower? You remind me of—

Yes. Is it that simple? He'd have been very like you, if he'd lived: my son Tarik.

'I'll come,' Rax said.

The sun burned, and the sea shimmered. The stars hung like a mist of diamonds, and the night wind cut to the bone. Cottonwool fog hugged the coast. The deep swells rolled like hills. They headed south, into ever-colder seas.

Rax lay moaning in the coffin-sized cabin, sweating, heaving with every lurch and dip of the sea. Days passed. Kel and Devenil sailed, fished, fed her fresh water. Once she woke to see them lying together, Kel's pale arm across Devenil's scarred body.

Solitude and loss and sickness frightened her. She slept with the war-axe tight in her grip. No Tower discipline, no skill learned in battle helped her now.

On the tenth day, when they sighted the coast of Dhared, she barely stirred, and at noon, when they passed it and came to Vanathri itself, she was too weak to do more than stare. She saw a green land, chill under a grey sky and lashing rain, where slant-roofed buildings hugged a narrow harbour. They sailed into it and were recognised.

Rax stood on the quay, swaying, seeing Kel and Devenil in each other's arms – in broad daylight, she thought dizzily. Then they pulled her into their embrace. The gathering crowd of Vanathri Islanders cheered, and every bell in the town rang out.

When she was well, they crossed the straits to Shabelit, and there Devenil took her before the Island lords and the head of the Council.

'Lady Sephir,' he said to her, 'here is our rescuer, Rax Keshanu of Bazuruk, axe-warrior of Anukazi's Tower.'

The chamber was full of brightly dressed men and women – and children, she saw, appalled. The air stank of old cooking, new perfumes, and the sea. Rax pulled her stained surcoat over her mail and kept the axe close to her hand. Shabelitans jabbered and pointed while Kel Vanathri told what had happened in Bazuruk.

'We do not welcome Bazuruki,' Sephir said, when she had heard his story, 'but you have brought my son back to me and restored Kel to Vanathri. You are welcome, Rax Keshanu, in all the Hundred Isles!'

The woman, white-haired, had Devenil's face with more delicate lines. She stood as Rax bowed – the formal acknowledgement of a Bazuruki warrior – and embraced and kissed her. Rax froze, smelling the scent of a meat-eater.

Amid the general applause, the Lady Sephir pronounced her an honorary captain of Shabelit. It was then, identifying the white scars on the old woman's arms as ancient sword-cuts, that Rax realised she had met her first Shabelit woman-warrior.

Cold spring turned to cool summer. Rax moved into rooms in Shabelit, a city founded on trade and almost as big as Anukazi. She lived with Islander customs as much as was possible for her but followed her version of Bazuruk's discipline. One midsummer day Devenil found her in the practice courts using the war-axe.

'Come up and talk,' he said, and she joined him on the seafort's wall.

'I see too little of you both lately,' Rax said as she pulled on a tunic against the Archipelago's cold wind. 'I suppose Kel's back on Vanathri or another of your damned rocks.'

'Kel offered you a place on his ship,' Devenil said. 'Why don't you take it?'

'The sea, with that sickness?' she scowled.

A brisk wind blew across the sea-fort, spattering her face with dampness. She watched the light on the straits.

'If you wanted to come, sickness wouldn't stop you.'

'I'm a soldier,' she said at last. 'You people . . . I didn't expect anything like the Orders, but you've no standing army at all. You don't understand. I'm a warrior. It's what I do, and I do it better than most. You're asking me to drop it and ship out as some kind of deck hand—'

'A guard. You'd work on the ship, but so do Kel and I. Even Bazuruki aren't killed by honest work.'

'Damned Islanders,' she said.

Devenil smiled. 'You're not the first person to perform a generous act and regret the consequences.'

'I don't regret what I did!'

In her mind's eye, Rax saw her chambers in the Tower of

Anukazi. The cool light, the shade, the fine carving of the Keshanu mask. Ever since I came to the islands, she thought, my mind's been in a fog.

'Let us pay our debt to you,' Devenil said. 'Come with us on the *Luck of Vanathri*, if not for our sake, then for your own.'

'You love him, don't you?' The thought still amazed her.

'I'll do anything I can for him, including ordering you aboard the *Luck* if it eases his mind. I'm still Shabelit's heir. I can do that.'

I got you out of the Tower, she thought. How much more must I give?

'You don't order me. I'm Bazuruki.'

'Not any more! You have to see that.'

She sighed. Eventually she asked, 'When do you sail? I'll come if I can, Devenil, but don't wait for me.'

They waited anyway, but she never came.

'You've got company,' Garad said. 'At least I'd swear it's you he's looking at.'

Rax glanced up from the dice. Sun and windburned from his months at sea, brown hair grown untidy, wrapped against the cold of a Shabelit winter night – Kel Vanathri.

'Stay here,' she said, 'we'll continue our discussion later.'

Garad smiled, shuttling the dice from hand to hand. 'Don't leave. I have your debt-slips—'

She gave him a look that stopped his voice in his throat, then crossed to the doorway.

'Rax!' Kel gripped her hands, then let them fall, puzzled by her lack of response. 'The time it's taken me to find you—'

'Did I ask you to come looking?'

'I came anyway. It's a strange place to find a Bazuruk warrior. With mercenaries.'

'Mercenaries and gamblers are no worse company than traders' sons and lords' heirs with nothing better on their minds than piracy.'

Her message hit home. She sensed that he was on the edge of violence, and she grinned. He studied her closely.

'You're drunk,' he said, amazed.

'Am I? It's a custom we could do with in Bazuruk.'

He frowned. 'Devenil said you'd end in a place like this. I'm sorry he was right.'

'Listen.' Rax laid one long finger on the centre of his chest, leaning closer. The spirit-fumes blocked his meat-eater scent. 'I'm a soldier by profession and choice. I had no quarrel with Bazuruk, except they wouldn't make me First Axe, which I earned. I'll practise my skills where I please. You were glad enough of them in Anukazi.'

'You can't live on old debts.' His anger was under tight control. 'I see you have new ones. I'll leave you to settle them, if you can.'

She waited until he'd left the smoke-filled inn before she went back to the table.

'That's a rich trading house,' Garad said. 'The Vanathri.'

'Shut your lying mouth.' She fell into the seat, draining the mug of spirits.

'Gratitude doesn't last.'

I'm trapped, Rax thought foggily. Money doesn't last, honorary captaincy carries no pay – and I won't beg from Kel or Devenil! How else, in Anukazi's name, can I live? And to sneer at me for being with mercenaries . . .

She missed the act of violence, the revulsion that, in the cold moment before battle, transmuted to recklessness; the empathy that made her imagine each blow, each wound. It was not skill nor craft, but art – an ache and an addiction.

'I can find the people you need.' Garad interrupted her thoughts. 'There are lords in the Cold Lands who'll pay well for a mercenary company, but first you need money to equip them.'

'And pay off my debts,' Rax said, grinning. 'We'll talk. Call to mind three or four men you can trust, and a good lockpick. I've a plan to pay off my debts and get all the gold I need to go to war.'

The house was dark. Rax led them cautiously. Her hand clamped over the mouth of a guard, and her long knife cut his throat. She wiped her hands. Garad came forward with the lockpick. Their breath was white in the icy air. Rax took another drink from the flask to warm herself.

'It's open.' The lockpick stood back.

Her heel skidded in blood. She cursed and regained her balance. Darkness cloaked them. She led the way to the cellars. Above, the house slept. Rax hummed under her breath.

'It's a fine revenge on Vanathri,' Garad said as his men searched the stacked chests. Silver glinted in the lantern's light.

'It's only a joke,' Rax corrected him. 'Try that one there – yes, and there. Good.'

After a few skirmishes in the Cold Lands, I'll come and pay back what I've taken. I wonder if he'll see the joke? she thought.

The flare of the lanterns took her totally by surprise.

The war-axe slid into her right hand, the throwing-axe into her left. One man yelled. Dazzled, she struck by instinct. Garad heaved up a chest and threw it at the advancing men. She let fly with the throwing-axe, heard a scream as it found a target. Garad screeched—

New lights from five or six bright lanterns blinded her. Something struck a paralysing blow to her arm. The men, out of her striking reach, held crossbows. Fear sobered her. Even mail could not stop the crossbow bolts pointing at her breast.

A familiar voice shouted, and no one fired.

Garad bubbled out his life at her feet. The lockpick breathed harshly in the sudden silence. Her other men, and several guards, lay dead. Kel Vanathri stood at the head of the steps, in night robes, carrying an unsheathed sword.

He cried out.

Devenil slumped against the wall. Blood matted his hair and soaked his shirt; his flesh was laid open, and white bone showed in the redness. The throwing axe's blade was buried under his ribs. He was dead.

'He was always a light sleeper.' Kel sounded stunned. 'He said he'd see what the disturbance was. By the time I could follow—'

'I'm sorry,' Rax said. 'I liked Devenil.'

'I loved him!' Kel's agony flared. 'He was the best. The Island will never see another like him. That you could kill him . . .'

'His rescuer in Bazuruk is his killer in Shabelit,' Rax said, rubbing her face wearily. Chains clinked. 'He'd appreciate the irony.'

It was less complex in Bazuruk, she thought. That is what

comes of charity. I'd never have hurt him if I'd seen who it was – Devenil.

'You're nothing more than a butcher. I thought you were different because of what you did in Anukazi, but you're just another Bazuruki killer.'

'Of course I'm Bazuruki.' She was bewildered. 'I was born in Keshanu. I spent ten years defending the borders of the Crystal Mountains. What else would I be?'

It took time for the anger to leave him. Almost to himself, he said, 'That's the tragedy. I know you have compassion, but it doesn't matter, does it? The Bazuruki training is what matters.'

'I am what I am,' Rax said, 'and so are you. And so was he. We can't change.'

'I can't believe that.' He stood, pacing the cell. The guard looked in and went away again. They wouldn't stop him from visiting his own justice on her, she guessed. Not on Shabelit, Sephir's island. She knew how a mother felt for a dead son.

'What will you do?'

'Nothing. You will answer to the law for theft, murder, Devenil.'

'Not a cell. Not caged. You owe me that.'

'I owe you nothing!' Leaving, he stopped. 'He – loved you, Devenil did, for fighting to be what you were. He would have given you a lord's inheritance if you'd asked. You were his friend.'

She watched him with Bazuruki eyes, Rax Keshanu, Anuka-zi's daughter.

'Tarik – Kel, I mean—'

'Better we'd died in Bazuruk.'

'I'm a long way from home,' Rax said. 'I'm tired, Kel.'

'I won't cage you,' he said from the doorway. 'But I won't let them free you, not after what you've done. If you leave, there's only one other way from here.'

'Yes,' she agreed.

After a time, she knew he had left.

She stood looking down through fine rain into the prison courtyard, where soon they would raise a block, and Rax Keshanu would for the last time behold the clean stroke of an axe.

Afterword

Here she is, for her first real appearance in a story I managed to make work: the swordswoman. She fascinates me. Still did, back in 1984, when I wanted to know what it would be like for a 'fantasy warrior' facing pretty much the same worldview as the one we have here.

It was becoming clear then, and has become clearer since, that genre fantasy would rectify a perceived omission from Tolkien and produce, not just the one-female-warrior, but the woman who is a warrior or a soldier in the world where that's a recognised career choice.

I like both tropes.

When I wanted to get the woman-as-recognised-soldier into *Golden Witchbreed* and *Ancient Light*, I needed to do two things – to tinker about with the biology of the sword-using alien race of Orthe/Carrick V, so that gender isn't apparent until long after career-training starts; and to assume that the humans will have had women in the military long enough that it isn't an issue. There's something comfortable about it not having to be an issue.

And then again, there's a lot of interest when it is. Rax Keshanu in a patriarchal fantasy world leads me to Knight-lieutenant Hyacinthe Tadmartin, and Tysoe, in 'The Road to Jerusalem', and to *Ash*, in a historical Europe where they use swords. It's all the same question: How can you want to do this? As a person; as a woman?

Why?

Rax is good at what she does. She's better than most. In the end, she's fit for nothing else. And though the particular way that shows itself happens because she's a woman, in the end it demonstrates what non-fiction research indicates: that on the battlefield, differences erode.

What God Abandoned

What God abandoned, these defended,
And saved the sum of things for pay.
Epitaph on an Army of Mercenaries,
A. E. Housman

There had been no rain for a month and the ground was hot iron under Miles's bare feet. Running, his bones pounded the earth. He bled. Dust rose, choking.

'*—take him!*'

The camp stretched away, apprehended in a single moment of time smaller than sundial or chronometer could measure. All its white tents, pennons, smoke from the cooking fires in the sutlers' quarters, shouts of muleteers, bellows of drill and counter-march, sun, dust and heat blanked out, narrowing down to just two things: two yards behind him the ratcheting-cogwheel snarl of one hound; the other four dogs running silent, without breath to waste, jaws dripping white foam on to the dust.

Half a world away (half the camp away) there was the glint of sun on metal: great-barrelled cannon and ranked organ guns. Men played cards on an upturned drum in the meagre midday shadow of the artillery field. The provost's voice shouted again:

'Seize *hold* of him, rot your guts!'

Miles threw himself forward, legs pumping; healing muscular changes going on at cell level, fibre level . . . To think, now, in the heat of panic; to change anatomies without meditation or preparation – predator's instincts cut in. His muscles hardened, swelled, and drove him surging forward. A dog snarled, heart-stoppingly close, and then swerved, its bay rising a register into distressed yelps at the changed flesh. It doesn't like my smell, Miles Godric thought, smiling despite everything. The baring of teeth became a snarl and he held back the instinct to turn and rip the animal's throat out.

The hounds' smell was sharp in his nostrils, like vinegar or

stale wine. Below lay the slow burn of anger, his pursuers'
pheromones on the still air. And below that the stench of the
camp: sweat, undercooked food, bloody cloth bandages, gan-
grene and lice, wine, dung from the herds of sheep and cattle
and somewhere the smell of women, camp-followers with their
scrawny arms deep in washtubs, the tang of menstrual blood so
at odds with the blood shed in battle.

He loped, now, in a pace that ate up distance like a wolf's
sprint, the tents and the open ground flashing by. His chest
heaved deeply. The hounds fell back, out-distanced.

'Sanctuary!' He pitched on to his knees on the rutted earth,
throwing his arms round the carriage of the nearest cannon.

'You're my countrymen – sanctuary!'

Sun-hot metal burned his cheek. He made his chest heave as
if panting, dizzy with effort, releasing the sudden changes of
flesh. As his body subtly altered, he clung to the culverin.

'Hand him over!' The provost, shouting. And the baying of his
accusers:

'The witch! Give us the he-witch!'

'—demand the justice of the camp, and execution—'

'—I'll gut him like a rotten fish and leave him stinking!'

'Sorcerer – man-lover!'

'Who do you want?' That would be the artillery master. John
Hammet: the English mercenary and a stickler for camp law.

'He,' the provost said thickly.

'The big Englishman there. Godric.'

'He has right of three days' sanctuary, he has claimed it.'

Miles lowered his head, resting it against the barrel of the
cannon, not looking round. The earth under his body breathed
heat out, and dust whitened his shabby clothes, and a thirst
began to rasp in the back of his throat.

The provost's voice sounded, close at hand.

'Very well. Three days only. I know the sanctuary of the
artillery fields – he must move no further than twenty-four
paces from the gun, or he is mine for the high justice.'

The master of the artillery train chuckled down in his throat.
He removed his pipe from his mouth and spat. The spittle hit the
earth a yard from Miles's sprawled body, darkening the dust.

'Take him now and I'll take my guns out of the camp, I swear
it on God's bones and the Virgin's heart. And then you may

fight your next battle with your pike and shot, and may all the saints help you to a victory without us! Sweet Lord, ten weeks since Maximillian's paid us, and now you come sniffing about to maintain justice in my own camp—'

Miles rolled over and sat with his back against the culverin. A blazing blue sky shone, as it had shone for most of the summer. Bad campaign weather. Plague ran through the camp on little feet, taking more men to God than ever the King of Bohemia's muskets and pikes had. He wiped at his sweating forehead. The card-players had turned away and had their heads bent over their gambling again. He raised his head and looked up past John Hammet at his accusers.

The provost with his staff of office, a burly man with the veins on his cheeks broken into a mass of red threads, and warts on his hands. A dozen other men, mostly from his own pike unit. Familiar faces blank with a fear not shown in battle.

'I will station a man here to watch. Three days, you. Then broken on the wheel, before the camp drawn up to watch you.'

The provost spoke in a slightly stilted English: a version of the camp patois that was part a myriad German dialects, part French, Spanish, Walloon, Pole and Irish.

'May God damn your soul, and may the little devils of Hell play pincushion with your balls.'

Miles had the satisfaction of seeing the provost snarl.

The men turned away, muttering. Miles Godric could not help but look for those he would not see – the little French boy, beardless, hardly out of swaddling bands; his friend, who dressed as a southern German should but whose accent was never quite in one country for more than a day, and the big man that he had first seen after the battle a fortnight ago.

'Succubus!' a departing voice yelled. Miles suddenly felt chill sweat down his back. *Sarnac's* voice?

John Hammet hacked at the dirt with the heel of his boot. His face was red, either from wearing good English woollen breeches and doublet in this hellish heat or else from anger.

'Is it true? Have you turned witch? God knows, the priests are burning enough of them now.'

Miles stared after the men walking away across the camp. The provost's leashed dogs bayed. His scent came to them still on this still air. His lip lifted a little over a sharp white tooth.

'Give me a drink,' he said, 'good John, and I'll tell you the truth, I swear.'

A week ago . . .

. . . A warm night. Stars shone thick above the makeshift tent. They lazed half in the shelter of its canvas, protected from a myriad biting insects attracted by the warmth of their flesh, and passed bottles of sour wine back and forth as they drank.

'But how will I believe you?' the French boy said. 'When Master Copernicus *proves* that the great world hath the sun at its centre, and we and all the lesser stars move about it, and all this without necessity of star deities to guide the planets in their courses.'

Miles rolled over and took the bottle from him. A young man – face spoiled from handsome by pox-scars – with lively eyes and magnetic, sharp gestures. Miles was a little in awe of him: the admiration of the Weerde for a creative mind.

The third, older man said lazily, 'Was not what I showed you today sufficient?'

'I have seen instruments for searching out the stars, that's true, but I have seen nothing of what makes the stars move.'

The older man, who spoke slightly imperfect French (as he spoke slightly imperfect Spanish and Walloon, to Miles's certain hearing) took a deep draught from the bottle. He appeared to be fifty or so; broad-shouldered, strong, and sunburned. Miles noted with half his attention that the man, Maier, did not grow drunk.

'Love moves the stars, as the Italian wrote.' Maier wiped wine from his thick, spade-cut beard. 'Look you, Master Descartes, you asked me for such wisdom as I can give, and it is this: there are correspondences between the earth and the heavens, such that all living things are subject to influence from the stars, and it is with the help of star talismans that I draw down influences and perform healings.'

'And with such powers that you perform your alchemical experiments? You note I have studied your own *Arcana arcanissima* and *Atalanta fugiens*, Master Michael Maier. And for all this,' the boy Descartes said drunkenly, 'you ask no pay. A sad thing in a mercenary army. Much more and I shall truly believe you one of that Brotherhood that travels the world secretly, apparelled in each country as that country dresses, cognisant of secret signs, and practising the occult arts. But we are not—'

Descartes' beardless face screwed up in concentration, and he brought out:

'—we are not in an inn, neither are we under a rose.'

An interrupting voice took Miles by surprise so that his heart thudded into his mouth. The fourth man, Sarnac, said: 'Rosicrucians, is it, now? And will you have our Maier a member of that secret Order?'

He bellowed a big, relaxed laugh. A look went between Maier and Descartes that escaped him. He has the intelligence of a bullock, Miles reflected. How can it be that I . . .

The big man's smell dominated the tent, blotting out all others. Miles lay on his pallet, picking at ends of straw; the breath shallow in his chest, breathing in, breathing in the male smell that dizzied him. He watched, in the campfire's shifting illumination, the curl of a lock of hair, the fall of loose wide shirtsleeves and buttock-hugging breeches, the knotted bare calves, the shape of broad shoulders and belly and balls. Wanting to bury his face in soft and solid flesh. He reached across Sarnac. His hand brushed the man's yellow-stubbled cheek as he grabbed a wine bottle, and the man swatted absently as if at an insect. Sitting up to drink, Miles shifted so that they sat hip to hip.

'Give me room, can't you?' Good-natured, Sarnac elbowed him a yard aside with one hefty shove. Miles spilled wine, swore, and slammed the bottle down to cover the sight of his hands: shaking so that they could hold nothing. Sarnac stood, took a pace or two to the other side of the fire, and hitched down the front of his breeches. One unsteady hand grabbed his cock. A stream of urine arced away into the darkness, shining in the fireglow.

O wine it makes you merry, Sarnac sang, *O wine, the enemy of women;*

It gives you to them, it makes you useless to them . . .

Michael Maier lay with his upper body in the rough shelter of two sticks and a length of canvas, so that his face was in shadow. His voice sounded from the darkness:

'Come into Prague with me, master Descartes.'

Miles Godric belched. 'What is there in a sacked city that we haven't had already? The gold's gone to the officers, and there isn't a woman left virgin between here and the White Hill.'

Descartes ignored him. 'And see what, Master Maier?'

The bearded man pointed a stubby finger. 'You came searching for that Brotherhood in which you profess not to believe. If I tell you what is old news, that the city of Prague has been the heart of Hermetic magic since the days of Doctor Dee, then will you believe me when I say there is enough yet remaining that you would wish to view it?'

'Bollocks!' Miles snorted. 'There's nothing left. The fornicating Hapsburg Emperor's fornicating army's had it all.'

He settled back on his loot-stuffed pallet. The burghers of Prague had shown little inclination, last month, to stand a siege for their king after the battle of the White Hill. They threw open their gates to welcome the invading troops with indecent haste, but it did them no good: Maximillian of Bavaria and Tilly and the Imperial general Bucquoy ordered the city closed and gave the mercenaries a week to loot it bare. Truly, the troops should have robbed only the followers of the King of Bohemia, sparing those loyal to Hapsburg Ferdinand; but questions are not asked in the heat of plunder, and Miles Godric had little German and the complexities of the German Princes' wars defeated him in any case, and Prague as it now was – burned, stripped, slaughtered and deserted – lacked only the scars of artillery fire to make it seem as if it had been taken after a six months' siege.

'Will you come?' Maier demanded of the boy.

Sarnac prowled back into the circle of firelight, his feet unsteady. He elbowed Descartes aside and went down on to his knees and fell into the makeshift tent beside Miles, face down, breathing thickly. The light shone on his white-blond hair.

Descartes said, 'Yes.'

'Don't leave without us,' Miles said. He studied the finger he had waved accusingly in the air with owlish curiosity. 'We'll come into the city with you. We'll come into . . . what was I saying?'

He let himself slip back down on to his elbows, then rolled slowly sideways off his pallet, so that his back and buttocks rested snugly against Sarnac's chest, belly, prick and thighs. Somewhere on the border of sleep, he smelled Sarnac's flesh tense. The big man grunted, asleep and instinctive, throwing one arm across him, then rolled and kicked until Miles could only sit up, dazed, and say, 'You're a plague-take-it unquiet bedfellow, Sarnac!'

He lay awake and aching the rest of the night, not daring even to relieve himself in dreams.

Morning came welcome cold, the hour before dawn.

Miles stood with feet planted squarely apart, lacing the unfastened front points of his breeches to his sleeveless doublet. Between his feet, scabbarded, lay an arming sword and a foot-and-a-half dagger. The sixteen-foot pike that was most of the rest of his equipment still rested across two notched sticks, supporting the tent canvas. He absently picked at a rust spot on its blade with a pared fingernail. The fingernails he had not pared with a dagger grew white and hard and more pointed than might be expected. Momentarily he covered his face with his hands to hide the change of stubble vanishing and leaving him clean-shaven.

He buckled on sword-belt and sword. Dew damped down the dust. He squinted across the waking camp, seeing the French boy on his way back from the sutlers with his arms full of bread and raw meat. Miles turned to build the fire in the fire-pit hotter, sanded out the inside of his helm, and filled it with water to boil.

'Beef?'

'Beef,' the boy agreed, kneeling down and spilling his load on to the earth. 'Out of Prague. We didn't eat like this before White Hill.'

Experienced, Miles said, 'We won't eat like it in a month, so eat while you can. Did you hear aught?'

'The usual rumours. We're to strike and move towards Brandenburg, to catch Frederick's Queen who's there with child; or else march on Mansfeld's mercenaries – but he'll turn his coat if we offer him pay, they say – or else we're to sit here and wait while the German Princes decide which one of them'll rebel against Hapsburg Ferdinand *this* time.'

Miles grunted. The morning had brought no sign of the woman and two boys he'd hired as servants to carry his plunder. He suspected the company captain had added them to his growing entourage. 'I'd happily winter here.'

Prompt on that, Sarnac groaned inside the tent and crawled out with his fair hair all clotted up in tufts and sleep grit in his eyes. Miles reached down and, with the hand that would have thumbed clean those eyes and lashes, handed the big man a pot of mulled wine.

'Urrghm.'

'And God give you a good morning, also.' Amused, suddenly warmed and confident, Miles chuckled. He ruffled Sarnac's long hair roughly enough for it to count as horseplay, and walked a good distance from the tent to piss, standing for long moments cock in hand and squinting his eyes against the lemon-white blaze of sunrise. On his return (the smell of boiling beef rank on the air) he found Maier about, dressed, armed, and neat as ever.

He remembered, with one of the flashes of memory which come in the dawn hour, Maier elbow-to-elbow with him in the thick of the line-fight, his pike raised up to shoulder level, a yard of sharpened metal slamming into enemy eyes, cheeks, throats, ribs. Not neat then. Splashed red from chest to thigh, doublet and breeches soaking. A bad war, White Hill. The boy Descartes had vomited most of the following day, and Miles had also – but he could smell the gangrenous wounded two leagues away, and hear them too; and to excuse his reaction had drunk himself into a stupor and woken – yes, woken to find himself beside the big drunken Frenchman from another pike unit, a man in his thirties, smelling of sweat and grass and blood: Sarnac. Sarnac.

He rescued some of the beef from the boiling helm and gulped it down hot, ripping the fresh bread apart with his strong teeth. Preference would have given him raw fresh beef, too; but the teaching held that such habits were unsafe. He chuckled under his breath. As for what the Kin might say about this appetite . . .

'God's teeth, man! You're not going looting without your comrades, are you?' Sarnac put his arm across Maier's shoulder. The bearded man (Swiss, could he be?) smiled. Young master Descartes sulked.

'Loot for the wit, Master Sarnac, not the belly or the purse.'

'What difference? We'll come.' His gaze fell on Miles, and his brow creased.

'God save us,' Miles Godric crossed himself, 'let's go to the city while we may. Tilly's thieving bastards have been there again, but they may have left something for thieving bastards like us.'

Dawn began to send white light across the camp. Pennants flickered into life on the officers' tents. The harsh bray of mules sounded. The four of them threaded a way through the rest of the pike unit with its drudges, wives and servants; through musketeers, grooms, hawkers, children and quacks; past two sutleresses coming to blows over a stray sheep (Sarnac stopped to watch and Miles hung back with him, until the big man suddenly realised that neither Descartes nor Maier had stopped for the entertainment), and out through the ranked wagons that formed the military camp's walls.

Midmorning found them in Prague, picking a way over blackened timbers, across squares and alleys choked with debris. Miles found a chipped dagger and shoved it under his belt. The rest of the ground was picked clean. Only the stench and the bodies heaped up for the common grave remained in the city. Refugees dotted the countryside for leagues around. It seemed to Miles that wherever he stepped, flocks of crows rose up from the streets. He watched them wheel, wide-fingered wings black against the sun, and drop down, and stab their carrion beaks into sprawled limbs. Maggots, disturbed, rippled away like sour milk. The only things more numerous than the crows were the flies. He wiped his mouth clear of them.

'This . . .' The French boy waved a hand vaguely, as if he had lost his sight. '*This*.'

Sarnac plodded back from the open door of an unburned house, empty-handed. 'Nothing! This quarter's been done over – I'll wager ten thalers it was that bastard Hammet's gun crews. I wonder they left food for the crows. Or if I heard they'd been selling this to the sutlers, and we eating it, it wouldn't surprise me.'

The boy retched and bent over, a thin trail of slime swinging from his mouth.

'This way,' Maier directed.

Miles, hot in brigandine and morion helmet but not about to go even into a sacked enemy city unarmoured, followed the older pikeman down between two stone mansions and out into an open space.

The gardens of Prague had not been deliberately sacked, but

fire had raged down from the slum quarter and made a scorched earth of the Palace grounds. Miles shaded his eyes, staring out across lines of blackened hedges at stumps of trees.

'There is enough left yet. Master Descartes! Here.' Maier turned and walked to where a terrace stood, the stone blackened, and stood staring out across the ruins. Miles followed him. Descartes and Sarnac came some distance behind, walking out into the gardens, the boy with his hand on Sarnac's arm. Miles felt his chest tighten. He stripped off and threw down his mailed gloves, and swore.

'The Order of which that boy speaks,' Michael Maier said softly, 'has its rules, which are these. That each Brother of the Order travel, alone, through what countries of the world he may visit. That he in all things dress and speak as a citizen of the country he is in, whatever it may be, so that each man shall take him for one of his own. And also that he shall teach, as he goes, and not take life; but that last—'

Maier frowned, dreamily.

'—that last rule is not so strictly adhered to as is said.'

Miles Godric flared his nostrils, catching no scent even of a feral line, and smiled, showing clean and undecayed teeth. Cattle sometimes imitate their masters, all unknowing.

'Are you a Brother of the Rosy Cross then, Master Maier? I'd heard Rosicrucians infested Prague and are half the reason the King and Queen fell into exile. Not a safe thing to be if concealment is your rule. In this country they burn sorcerers.'

Maier grinned. 'And in this country, Master Miles, they burn sodomites. I think your big man there will not consent to your desires. I think him a woman-lover only – well, they have their peculiar superstitions, these men.'

'Yes,' Miles said. He watched Descartes and Sarnac climb up on to the ruined terrace. The big man wiped his sleeve across his face, mopping sweat; Miles's teeth nipped his tongue.

'You may yet see the patterns of the knot gardens,' Michael Maier said, expansively gesturing. The sun flashed from his breastplate and morion helmet, 'Master Descartes, allow me to instruct you: *that* was the astrological garden, whose hedges grew in the shapes of the zodiac, and within the hedges the plants and herbs pertaining to each sign. *That* was the garden of automata, and *that* of necromancy—'

'Necromancy!'

'You cannot stand in a sacked city and balk at the dead, young master.'

'But necromancy! But there,' the boy said, all his vitality momentarily gone, 'it is superstition, as my friend Father Mersenne tells me; and the Holy Church would not allow its practice, even were it a real danger.'

Maier asked acidly, 'And does your Father Mersenne instruct you in logic?'

Miles left them quarrelling. Sarnac, idly wandering, hooked a bottle out of his half-laced brigandine and swigged at it, his back to the garden. Miles moved cautiously towards him.

Trails of soot blackened the masonry surrounding the garden. Something that might have been a rose-vine straggled up the wall, a dead bird crucified in amongst its thorns. Sarnac sat down with his back to the sun-hot wall. The harsh calls of crows drowned Miles's footsteps. The big man sat with his head thrown back, eyes closed. Dust grimed his corded throat. The bright curls of his hair showed under the battered morion he wore, the straps dangling loose; and sun shone through the golden hair on his chin and arms and bare shins, gleaming. A pulse beat in the hollow of his neck. Wine dried on his mouth and chin.

Cold to the belly, Miles sat down on his heels. Sarnac opened his eyes. Light shone in them, as in brandy: brown and gold. He half frowned.

'Sarnac.' Miles swallowed. The cold hollow under his ribs remained, and the smell of the man made him feel as if the earth dissolved. He said, 'You must know I would lie with you.'

The briefest joy in gold-brown eyes; then Sarnac's face went blank, went white and then red. His voice came thick with disgust. '*You?* The Italian vice? Sweet saint's bones, you mean it for truth.'

Miles held up his hands in protest. He looked at his rough, callused skin speculatively. 'Please . . . please. Listen. I'm not as men are.'

The big man burst out into a laugh that began in scorn and ended in revulsion. 'So I've heard many say.'

'Sarnac, have you ever seen me unclothed?' He held the man's gaze. 'Or bathing in a river, or pissing?'

'No.' Puzzlement on Sarnac's face.

No, because you have been with the unit no more than a week. Miles bent forward, intense; he used the Frenchman's own language. 'Because of my great desire for you, and because you should not think me capable of an unclean sin, I tell you my secret. I am no man, because I am a woman.'

The big man's mouth opened, and stayed open. His coarse brows dipped, frowning. A look began to come into his face: something between pity and lust and condescension.

'A woman soldier? One of the baggage train, tricked out in breeches – no, but I've seen you fight as no woman can! Are you one of the mankind sort, then, aping us?'

Behind him, Miles heard Maier's impatient raised voice: 'But I cannot prove it to you *here and now*! You *must* wait. Whether you will or no.'

Softening his voice, Miles held Sarnac's gaze. 'No, I wish for the privileges of no man: I would not have manhood if it were to buy. It is an old tale. I have seen such played on the public stage in London – a woman in boy's guise following her sweetheart to the wars. I dressed in male garments for safety and preservation of virtue and, when I learned he had died upon the field, stayed, and grew used to weaponry, since what else is left to me but to serve my Prince?'

A *very* old tale, Miles reflected sardonically. Sworn virgin warrior-maids are acceptable to him; this man had for country-woman three centuries gone that Jehanne, who fought the English. Were I to say: I am a woman who loves fighting, who loves not the lordship of men, who will not wear petticoats – well then, Sarnac, would you lie with me? No, you would not.

Sarnac, still frowning, began to smile. 'Are you truly a she?'

Miles let out a breath he had not been aware of holding.

'Ay, ay, God's truth, and I'll prove it to you. Will you lie with me, and love me? Nay, not now, we're observed. Secretly. Tonight.'

Maier's voice sounded closer behind him, quarrelling with Descartes' importunate questions; but Miles did not move, still sitting forward on his haunches, the cloth of his breeches hiding his erection.

'Yes. Tonight,' Sarnac said.

*

Habit kept Miles outside the camp, in concealment. He lay up in a burned-out cellar near the walls of the city, eating crow-meat and less palatable offal and at last sleeping the thick, heavy sleep of the change. Shifting subcutaneous layers of body fat, retracting testicles and penis, moving cartilage and hollowing muscle. Knowing what he would be when he woke.

The dark-lantern, its shutter half closed, made a golden glow in the cellar. Sarnac grunted. Straw dug sharply into Miles's back. She rubbed the slick length of her body against his, her breasts against the rough hair of his chest; shifted so that his hips and elbows were more to her liking and wound her legs about his hips. He thrust, his penis finding obstruction (she had not, after all, forgotten the hymen) and then pierced her.

'Ah-h . . .'

Miles Godric made deep noises in her throat. She buried her face against his shoulder, smelling the sweetness of his skin: sweat and dirt and woodsmoke. She bit at the bulge of muscle with her teeth.

'Wildcat!'

He pinned her. She shoved her hips up, taking him deep inside her; the tightness of a new vagina not wholly according to her plan, but still she held him and thrust against his thrusts, and rolled over still holding so that she straddled him.

'Damn, but you're lively!' Sarnac, sweating, leaned up to nuzzle and suck at her breasts. 'Miles – no, what do I call you? What's your name?'

'Jehanne.'

The word came out unplanned; Sarnac, his eyes bright and heavy, never noticed. He mumbled the name into her belly and pulled her down, one hand flat on the small of her back, pumping up into her.

'Woman!' he groaned.

She rode him as he climaxed, expecting nothing for herself, but the smell of him and days of wanting surprised her: she raked fingernails down his chest and bit his shoulder, drawing blood, with her own orgasm.

That day and the following she came back sweating and grinning from training fights, stepping lively and whistling, not

caring who saw. For those who questioned she told tales of a
rare treasure looted out of Prague.

'You should have something for this,' she said expansively to
Descartes on the third day, sitting outside the tents. 'Didn't you
fight at White Hill with the best of us? What will you take home
to your sweetheart?'

The boy looked up from where he sprawled outside the tent.
His deft fingers shaved a pen-nib, and a notebook lay open
beside him. 'Pox, if I'm unlucky!'

'You're too young,' she teased.

'I was twenty-two when I left Paris,' Descartes said, naming an
age precisely one-third her own, 'when I joined with Maurice of
Nassau's men. It being my thought that, were I to be with an
army, I would as soon be with confirmed victors.'

Miles rubbed more carefully with oiled cloth at the blade of
her pike until it shone. She laid it down on the earth and
stretched, and lodged one ankle over the other and leaned back
on her elbows, surveying the evening.

'Nassau's bastards win,' she confirmed idly. 'So what are you
doing with Hapsburg Ferdinand instead of the Protestants?'

'I belong to Holy Mother Church. It's Maier who's the
Lutheran. He's the one you should question, or—' he quoted a
prevalent maxim, ' "So we serve our master honestly, it is no
matter what master we serve".'

She squinted at the horizon, seeing thick pine forests darkening the mountains and, below them, white harvest fields burned
black in the army's passing. 'You had that out of Sarnac's
mouth.'

'Ay. Along with "In war there is no law and order, it is the
same for master and man", and "He who wages war fishes with
a golden net".'

The boy rubbed at his scarred face and rolled on to his side to
look up at her. His small body had a kind of electric vitality to
it; some spiritual equivalent of the wiry strength that made him
train for the pike instead of (as he more properly ought) the
musket.

'Master Maier showed me Tycho Brahe's famous astro-
nomical apparatus, in the city, before the – before it was taken
away.'

Miles snorted. 'Before the Rosy-Cross brethren had it?'

'You don't believe in them.'

She shrugged, looking down a longer perspective of history than the human. 'I don't know what I *do* believe in, boy. I doubt, therefore I must think: and if I think, I cannot doubt that I am; what else is there?'

His eyes glowed. 'Much! Master Maier is instructing me. I write it all down here. Listen.'

In a sudden expansive affection for the boy and all the world, Miles Godric sat and sharpened the blade of her dagger, and listened to him declaim on analytical geometry, alchemical marriages, and other subjects not worth a penny beside the colour of the hair on Sarnac's belly.

On the fourth night Miles stayed in the cellar after Sarnac departed. The big man kissed her, left the lantern, and at the doorway turned with one last puzzled look.

'You should let me guard you back to camp . . .' His voice trailed off. She could see in his face how he could not take in the idea of a woman who was neither to be raped nor protected against rape. 'Are you content, lass?'

Miles nodded. 'I'll return later, as I have before.'

She listened to him go, hearing his footsteps halfway across the ruined city. Owls shrieked and rats scuttled; and she curled up with her chin on her forearms, eyes dazzling in the lantern's yellow glare. She reached out and extinguished it.

And for tomorrow's drill? she thought. Sword and falchion I can use in this shape, and have; but for the pike should I change and be a man? The weight may be too much to bear . . . And if not, still, there's risk of discovery. Not as Family, but as woman, and then what? The baggage train, washing and whoring. I might stay concealed a woman soldier, as I have seen many do, with only a few of her comrades knowing and keeping secret. But too many of *my* comrades have already seen me male.

She was not a small thing, lying there in the starlight; only her skin was a little smoother for the layer of fat beneath it, cushioning the muscles. Her eyes gleamed flat silver like pennies. One hand stroked her breast, and she closed her eyes and slid down into the sleep of change. And so did not wake when they came.

*

'But *when* will you show me? *When?*'

'Soon! Be patient. You had patience enough to spend two years searching us out. Have a little more.'

The voices finally woke him. Miles shifted uneasily, rolled over, grabbed breeches and brigandine and – old habit of many night alarms – stood dressed and armed before he properly woke.

The cellar was dark, the door outlined with silver.

On silent feet he slid out into the ruined moonlit alleys, shaking his head against sleepiness and chill. Voices, familiar voices, but where? And he – Miles grabbed inelegantly, discovering himself awake and male. And the voices . . . he slid the morion briefly from his head and cocked an ear. The voices were not as near as night-bemusement had made him think. But they were none the less familiar voices. Maier and Descartes.

He glanced at the constellations. Two hours to dawn. The way to the camp would be clear, and the dead-watch not prone to querying brother soldiers (if, indeed, they were not risking execution by dozing on duty). But then there was curiosity, and the question of what the French boy and Maier might be doing here, now, of all times.

Miles padded through rubble-choked alleys, silently climbing shifting, burned beams, avoiding pits, the pupils of his eyes wide and dark. The small winds of night brought him little but the stench of decaying flesh. For that reason he didn't realise Maier and Descartes were not alone until he heard boots scratching at stone. Half an hour's solitary backing and tracking brought him to where he could observe. He eased into the shadow of a fire-blackened tree stump. Dry ferns brushed his face. He eased up a little, looking over the bank, and blinked momentarily at the space opened up before him.

Far below, the river shone silver. The town ran up in steep banks to either side. No lanterns, no movement; the darkness shrouded destruction. Directly ahead, the towers of a palace rose up, almost untouched. The Emperor Ferdinand's banners now draggled from its spires, and men were quartered in its far chambers; but this part, overlooking the formal gardens, had no occupants that his hearing could detect. The only living beings – four of them – moved in the gardens below.

Miles slid on his belly over the bank and down, moving

soundlessly despite armour, his dagger drawn and carried in his left hand, ready. He moved silently through burned gardens, past a hundred blackened and overturned marble statues, into what had been the centre of a maze.

'I had such dreams, last winter.' The boy, Descartes, stood with his arms wrapped in his cloak, hugging it around his body. His sharp, uncomely face caught the full moon's brilliance. Miles saw the moon's reflected twin in his eyes.

'Dreams. Nothing to do but winter over in Bavaria with the rest of Nassau's soldiers, get drunk and have women. I wondered, why did I ever leave Paris? Why did I ever join the God-forsaken Protestant cause?'

Softly, so that even Miles could hardly hear him, Maier prompted: 'But the dreams?'

'Of the black art which is called mathematics.'

Enthusiasm in the boy's voice, that faded with his next words. 'I dreamed that mathematics answered all, accounted for all, was all. That nothing moved on this breathing earth but mathematics could account for it, down to the final atom . . . They were dreams of terror. They had no God in them, or if they did, removed far off and become watchmaker to the world: winding it up and leaving it until the end should strike. There was no magic.'

Unguarded, his French was of better quality than heard in the camp, and Miles with difficulty adjusted his ear to it.

'And then I began to read pamphlets published out of Amsterdam and Prague. The *Chymische Hochzeit Christiani Rosenkreutz*, the *Fama Fraternitatis*. And broadsheet appeals to the Brotherhood of the Rosy Cross to come out into the open, to share their secret knowledge of how the world works – how everything that is, is living and magical. Everything. How rocks, gems, trees and stars share souls, as men do. How the alchemical transformation can change all our spirits to gold, and bring again the Golden Age of which the ancients wrote! And how a great instauration of magical science will come on the earth, and the bond be knitted again between the Lutheran Churches and the Roman Church into one great Christendom.'

Someone sighed behind the half-burned hedges. A woman, Miles realised. He felt bare-handed to see what cover he lay on, detecting no twigs to snap; and slid up on to one knee and then on to his feet. He reached down and loosened his sword, thumbing it an inch out of the mouth of the scabbard.

'And all this is words!' Descartes' voice snagged on pain. 'I must have proof. *Is* there such a Brotherhood? Do you have such magical knowledge? And is it truth, or charlatan tricks?'

Miles flared his nostrils. The sweet stink of rotting flesh covered all other scents. He could hear heartbeats, indrawn breath; but the four of them so close blurred his senses, so that he could not tell where the last one stood, or how near he was to the woman. The moonlight blinded his night vision. Using a habitual trick he searched the shadows with only peripheral sight. There?

Michael Maier put his hand on Descartes' shoulder. He carried his cloak bundled over his left arm, leaving free the hilt of his military rapier, hood covering the glint of his helmet.

'That is a poor world you have in your dreams.' Maier's voice softened uncharacteristically. His French was adequate, not as good as the boy's, but as good as his Italian, or Spanish, or (if it came to it, Miles knew) English. 'I will give you *magia* for your mechanical universe, if you will.'

'*Magia?*'

'Platonist magic, sometimes called the Egyptian or Hermetic Art. It is easier explained if you have first seen. Hold in your mind the thought that all you have read is true. I have stood in these gardens on the day when statues spoke with human voices and moved, inspired by the spirits in them; when the sick came and left healthy, and the dead with them – believe it – and the sacred marriage of the rose and the dew made bud, blossom and fruit grow upon these same trees all in one hour.'

Miles heard the rustle of cloth. He stepped easily between sharp twigs and pressed his hand over the woman's mouth, his dagger-point denting her skin. He pitched his voice to carry no further than her ear. 'Cry out and I'll rip out your throat. What do you here?'

This close to her he smelled satin, sour flesh, dirty hair, but no fear whatsoever. Maier's voice sounded again and Miles could feel the woman strain to hear what came so clearly to him.

Michael Maier said, 'All this through *magia*. All this because our souls and our flesh are one, and at one with the living universe. We are demiurges upon this earth, and all of it from stone to sea will obey us, if a man but know the prayers, words, actions and sacrifices necessary for it. We of the Brotherhood may speak to each other across vast distances, travel the sky and sea unhindered, heal, create gold and pray down the wrath of the Divine upon the Divine's enemies.'

Miles Godric showed teeth, amused: one of the Weerde hearing – despite the searing belief in the man's voice – the old lie from a human mouth.

Descartes coughed. 'You may say so.'

Miles heard the fourth heart beat now, not so close as he had feared. A dozen yards away in the wrecked maze.

'I say so!' Maier shouted. The empty gardens echoed and Miles saw him look about, startled. More quietly, the burly man repeated, 'I say so.'

'But your true Alchemical Marriage, your Rosicrucian Kingdom to be founded here in Prague where all this is to come about, where is that now – now that the city is sacked and the King and Queen exiled or dead?'

'That hope is not ended.'

The woman breathed hard against his body. Her hands hung limp in the massive folds of her gown. Stiff, starched lace rasped against Miles's face and he felt the small coldnesses of gems in her hair. Listening hard, he momentarily ignored the sensations of his skin.

A soundless blast lifted Miles and threw him.

Stone and gravel scarred his palms. The world dissolved. Miles shook, his mouth full of blood, head ringing, hands and face afire. Mortar fire or cannon? His left hand hung bloody and empty; he did not recall drawing his sword but the fingers of his right hand locked about the hilt.

Neither sword nor shot, but the suddenly loosened power of a human mind seared the marrow in his bones.

'Maier!'

The voice he did not recognise as his: a bewildered and outraged child's shriek. He cowered, one hand over his head, sword thrusting aimlessly into the dark. Voices screamed and shattered around him; he stood up, and the sky laughed as his sight cleared. The night glowed blue.

Rich blue and gold. and the stars above were gone. The night sky over Prague shone with figures: planetary gods and zodiacal beasts, figures with swords and flaming hair, balances and spears, winged feet and bright eyes that shone no colour of the earth. The tides of power rocked the sky and Miles fell down on his knees. He stared at the spade-bearded man. He heard the French boy cry out, and could not tell whether it was in joy or terror.

'Maier!'

The older man laughed.

'What, Miles, you here? Well, then. See. See with clear eyes. Master Descartes, the Rosicrucian Kingdom is not ended, albeit the city has fallen. Look with clear eyes upon the Marriage of the Thames and the Rhine, the Winter King and Queen. Strength and Wisdom, *sophia* and *scientia*. Look upon the true Alchemical Union: Frederick the heir of the Germanies, Charlemagne's heir, Barbarossa's son; with Elizabeth the Phoenix Reborn, the daughter of Jacobus and heir of Gloriana, England's Virgin.'

The oldest of Weerde fears pierced him.

'Oh God I am most heartily sorry that I have offended Thee!' Miles buried his head down against his knees, mumbling. The hot stench of urine made his eyes water. He rocked, holding his bloody hand to his gut, gripping the hard hilt of his sword; even in this extremity giving to his fear the name humanity in this age knew. 'I am most heartily sorry; preserve me from the Devil; preserve me from Him who walks up and down among men; dear God, most holy Lord . . .'

Maier's hands gripped his shoulder, shaking him. 'Miles!'

Miles Godric at last lifted his head. 'Is it you who are doing all of this? Don't you know you'll call him, you'll call the Devil down on us? On *all* of us?'

Maier, kneeling behind him, put his warm arms around Miles's shoulders. 'Is *that* anything to fear? Look.'

Miles whimpered.

The two figures walked out into the centre of the maze. A woman and a man. Now the sound of their hearts beat against his ears, deafening him. A man with a plump face, dark hair and soft dark eyes; dressed in cloth-of-silver doublet and breeches, the Order of the Garter at his knee, but crowned in nothing save rose-coloured light. And a woman in cloth-of-gold farthingale and stomacher and ruff, a fashion two generations out of date: her sharp-featured face the living image of a greater Queen. Frederick and Elizabeth: Winter King and Queen of Bohemia.

Not being human, Miles had only to gather his wits – thinking *Yes, they escaped the battle*! – to see the truth of it: a shabby man, a woman in a torn kirtle, their faces the pinched faces of refugees. The power that beat about them was not theirs. But a power none the less, that brought the beasts of the night – foxes, wolves, wild boar – creeping to their feet, eyes shining. The rose light gleamed with images of lion and stag, and pelican piercing her own breast. Fireflies darted across the suddenly hot air.

In the false, living tapestry of the night sky the Lords of Power bowed from Their thrones. Roses seemed to bud and blossom from the garden's blackened twigs. A petal brushed Miles and he shuddered uncontrollably, feeling it against his skin.

'How can they . . .' The French boy knelt beside Maier, his face wide and wondering. 'How can they still be here, and their armies defeated and the city taken?'

'Because they are not defeated. Because they only await their time. Which I, and you, will help to bring about. Nay, speak to them, question them. I will be your warrant for it.' Maier stood and pulled Descartes to his feet. 'Come.'

The boy wiped his hair off his face, with the gesture seeming to take on years. He stepped forward. Something in his expression commanded: not the wonder, but the confirmation of knowledge.

'Is it so?' he said softly. 'And is it true, this union and this harmony?'

The woman spoke. '*Witness. We would have you witness, for you are the child of Our marriage. You are herald to the ages to come of what We proclaim: the union of man and beast, spirit and matter, soul and substance.*'

The man spoke. '*Witness Us as We are. Yours is a great soul, such a pivot as the world turns on, and We have called you these two years that you should witness Us, and proclaim the Rose and the Cross openly to the world. So all men may be as We are.*'

To Miles's ears they mouthed rote-learned words badly. But the boy grinned, sucking at his still ink-stained fingers, and opened his mouth with the light of debate in his eyes.

'No!' Miles shielded his face with his arm. Shaded from that illusory light he could stagger to his feet, gain; balance in the shifting world.

Time split now into clock-ticks, each one for ever, as time

changes on the field of battle into a thousand non-sequential *nows*. He saw Their lips move, and Descartes' face shining. He saw Maier with arms folded, standing; as a man stands who controls all circumstance. He saw the maze now blossoming with a hundred thousand red and white roses, their scent choking him with sweetness. And he heard, on the edge of consciousness, something else: the metallic clash of legions marching, lost legions, led by the Devil, and coming here to feed – he sobbed laughter – attracted like moths to a campfire. Attracted to the Light. Small whirling bodies crisped in flame . . .

Miles Godric beat at his clothes with bloody hands. His sword fell, discarded, and stuck point-down and quivering, a bar of silver fire. The French boy took another step forward, holding out his hands. Miles strode forward and grabbed him around the body, lifting the boy and making to throw them both backwards away from Maier and his illusion of a mystical Marriage. Descartes struggled. The boy's head jerked around. Miles stared into his eyes: eyes as dark blue and wide as a child's. It seared into him, the origin of this force. Not Maier.

Not Maier, no more creative than a Weerde, but one of the human minds that is bound to change an age, whatever age it is born into; a mind only requiring, like a sun's beam, to be focused for it to burn. This boy's mind, tapped all unknowing, so that he spoke to the figures of his own desires – his own, and Michael Maier's. Miles staggered, this close to the boy; all barriers permeable now, even the barrier between soul and soul.

Memory filled Miles Godric: memory not his own. The Kin's memory. A vast coldness seared him, and a vast dark; and then the darkness blazed into a light more unbearable because in that light he saw one speck of dirt, himself, standing upon another speck of dirt which is the turning world; all circling a match-flame sun, one more in a swarm of firefly-stars. And between earth and suns, between stars and stars, such an infinite predatory emptiness and appetite that he whimpered again, eyes shut, himself and the boy curled foetally together on the garden earth, choking back tears in case they should be heard.

'*No!*' Maier screamed. His hands pried at Miles. 'No! Give him back to me! I want him for this—'

In a kind of battlefield calm, Miles knelt up and supported the boy across his thighs. He pried back one eyelid to study the boy's dilated pupil. 'Want must be your master.'

The approaching tread of the Devil's legions beat on his ears. Miles lay the boy down and stood up, grasping and recovering his sword.

'Well, I will have him for this in any case, and damn you,' the older man said. His voice held all the blindness of human belief. He knelt down, efficiently scooping the boy up, the thin body slumping forward, and drew his knife. 'I've waited for this conjunction of stars – and They have waited also, my King and Queen there – and now I shall give Them what They need to make Them actual, in this world, for ever.'

The irregular tread rasped in Miles's ears. He rubbed one sweat-sticky hand across his eyes. Movement in the Rose Garden, now. The tread of legions . . .

The moon, distorted by the boy's mind, made a false *magia*-light in the Garden. A white figure seemed to come into the centre of the maze, moving jerkily and swiftly towards Miles. The light shone on stone armour, full Gothic harness and stone sword, stone features; shone upon limbs where white marble flushed now with the rose-and-gold of incipient life.

Reacting instantaneously Miles feinted and slashed, backed two steps and then came forward, his blade swooping under the marble statue's sword and hitting with two-handed force where the armour gaped vulnerably under the arm.

His sword broke against the motionless statue.

His fingers fell open, numb. Metal shards shrieked and whirred past his face. He shouted, his voice ringing across the broken city gardens. Other white things appeared to move in the moonlight: all the stone warriors of the Garden, bleeding like Cadmus's dragon's teeth.

Miles stumbled back, no longer sure what illusion might become truth, given such an outpouring of the mind's power. He caught a heel against Maier's outstretched leg and staggered.

The older man bent over Descartes, his dagger carefully bleeding a vein in the boy's left wrist. With the blood and his fingers, he drew sigils on the hard earth. The spirals of psychic force tightened, tightened, building higher. Miles saw the boy's eyelids move and finally open, saw him look up into Maier's face; saw him realise the open conduit, his soul drained to power visions, illusions, that Maier demanded become reality. The boy shrieked.

'Put an end to this.' Miles kicked Maier accurately and hard on the side of the head. The older man's dagger stabbed up and pierced his thigh. He sat down heavy, staring at the bleeding. Maier groped around for the boy's arm, and Descartes crawled crab-wise away from him on the burned earth.

'Stop it. *While we yet can.*' Miles hoisted himself up and sat down again heavily, one leg no more use to stand on than water. He began to drag himself towards Maier.

Roses seemed to grow up from the ground and twine around his legs and arms. Their thorns bit deep into his flesh. He threw back his head, teeth gritted, straining. The vines held. Twisting, for one second he found himself staring into what he had avoided seeing.

In the heart of a rose-and-gold light, two naked and winged figures are embracing. Man and Woman, they are becoming more: draining the power of a human mind to become Lion and Phoenix. Their faces are radiant. They are a beacon of joy.

A beacon that can be seen for how great a distance?

Miles Godric lifts himself up again, as the rose-brambles bind him to the earth. The ground shakes with the approaching tread of legions. A yard or two away, Michael Maier picks up his dagger and positions it under the French boy's ear; lifts his elbow to thrust.

The night explodes.

Nose and mouth bleeding, head ringing, eyes dazzled with the vanishing of a Light beyond all lights, Miles Godric lies amongst tangled dead briars and watches the moonlight shine on battered helms, scruffy brigandines, one smoking musket, halberds, and the excited faces and shouts of Maximillian of Bavaria's army.

'What was it, a quarrel over loot?' Sarnac shifted his body, pulling Miles's arm further over his shoulder. Miles slumped against the big man. 'Christ's bones, I didn't think there was enough left in the city to burn! You could see that fire clear from the camp.'

'Fire?'

'It's gone now. Odd.'

Miles felt the cold night air sting his face. He glanced down. The moon's light showed him dark patches on his breeches and hands, and his leg was still numb. He groped at his head. Something sticky matted his hair. 'I don't . . .'

Only moonlight. Grey matter and dark liquid spattered his doublet. The memory of a musket-ball taking off one side of Michael Maier's head came back to him and he tried with a dry mouth to spit into the road, knowing how inaccurate muskets are.

There was a bustle of soldiery around him and someone somewhere shouting orders. The road to the camp shone white and dusty.

'Where's the boy?'

'Vanringham has him. Living, I think. God's death, what were they quarrelling for?'

'I . . . forget.'

Sarnac's body heat warmed him, and Miles conscientiously tried to stop shivering but without success. He would have sent men to search out the man and woman, if he could have spoken – or if he could have been certain they had survived the illusions.

The march back to the camp seemed at the same time long and over in a heartbeat. Prague's ruined walls gave way to dawn and the ranked wagons of the camp, the provost and one of the company commanders, all of it happening somewhere far away. An hour passed in a minute.

Straw rasped against his back. An early light shone in under the makeshift canvas tent. Weakness pressed him down. He could not focus his eyes on what lay beyond the immediate circle of earth, fire-pit and scattered equipment. He tried to moisten his dry mouth, swallowing. Sarnac, his back to Miles, boiled soup in someone else's upturned helmet.

'I . . . need a surgeon.'

'Do you, lass?'

Miles tried to make himself wake, move, protest. He saw Sarnac turn, face beaming with good intention.

'Think I'd let 'em treat you and discover you for a woman?'

'*No*—' He managed to raise his arms and grab Sarnac's hands. He knew himself safe with surgeons, the surgeon's tents a cover for the many-partner marriages of the Weerde, and besides a

necessary means for taking dead Weerde bodies from a battlefield.

'No, that's right.' The big man frowned down at him. 'I'm
going to treat these wounds. Christ's little bones, woman, you're
bleeding like a pig with its throat cut!'

The effort brought sweat out on Miles's face. His hands shook
with the effort of holding Sarnac away. At some level of cell
and blood he called on strength, knowing it was no use to call
on change, but the big man deftly slipped his grip away, strip-
ping off Miles's doublet and breeches together and pulling at his
shirt.

'Damn but you women always have some vapouring quibble.
Haven't I seen you naked bef—'

Miles giggled faintly. The sheer bald shock on Sarnac's face
made him splutter, not wishing it; robbing him of any words. He
thought muddily, What words could there be? The man bent
over him, freckled shoulder close to his face, and Miles breathed
in the smell of him through swollen and blood-choked nostrils;
felt the big hands slide down the skin of his chest and belly and
move as if stung from his cock and balls.

'But you *can't* be—'

The hot morning slipped a cogwheel, reassembled itself into
an absence of Sarnac and somewhere a voice shouting.

'*Succubus! Witchcraft!*'

With an effort that brought blood streaming from his thigh
Miles Godric crawled out of the shelter, pulled up breeches and
doublet, and staggered away from the tent. The voice shouted. A
dog bayed. His head came up and he searched the stirring camp,
forcing his body to walk; to run . . .

. . . John Hammet sat beside him, back resting against the gun
carriage.

'And thus I thought of you,' Miles finished, 'being a country-
man of mine. And Family.'

Swallows and bats flew against the darkening evening sky,
snapping at gnats.

'Pox take it, it's the world we live in that gives such schemes
life.' The artillery man spat tobacco into the dew-dampened
grass. 'I would the Kin might change it. But witness our attempt
to rid these lands of their superstitions – now half of the German

principalities are burning witches, and half of their inquisitors are Protestant Lutherans. Such was never our intent.'

Miles hunched his shoulders against the dust-clotted wood of the carriage. Heat stung his hands and face, blood now scabbing on their flayed skin. He tightened the bandage around his thigh.

'Will they burn me, think you?'

Hammet ignored the question. 'I talked to your French youth when they brought him in last night. I've seen men regain their rightful sense and speech, with less courage and spirit than he. Yet if I mistake not, he will fear "magic" all the days of his life. Do you know, Kinsman, I think I would much like to live in his mathematical world. I would like a world where there are no devils and spirits in men, to risk calling down the Dark on our heads. It would be a peaceful one, I think, Descartes' world.'

Miles Godric shivered in the summer heat. Crows called.

The artillery man said, 'They will either burn you or break you on the wheel for a man-witch. So the provost orders. You had best shift your shape this night and join another unit.'

Remnants of fear chilled Miles Godric's bones. A vision came before his eyes of Sarnac's face loose in the concentration of pleasure. 'And leave Sarnac?'

Desire moves in his body for the man Sarnac, will move in it no matter what shape he wears; as if his mind were merely carried in this fleshly machine, a passenger subject to its will.

'How we love these mayflies,' he said ironically. 'Well, and in a while I may change flesh again, and find him again.'

'If he lives,' Hammet said. 'What is it draws us to wars?'

Miles Godric leaned his head against the metal of the culverin. Thinking of the heat of metal, firing case-shot; of pike and musket and the long sharp blades of daggers, watching the evening dusk come on. 'We don't begin them. We only follow the drum.'

He got slowly to his feet, adding, 'We have few enough pleasures that we can afford to miss that one.'

In months to come he will hear rumours of Frederick the Garterless King – the royal boy having mislaid that English Order in his flight from Prague – and see him represented on satirical broadsheets with his stocking falling to his ankle. The drawings will show a plump young man and a hard-faced woman tramping the countryside in old clothes, trying to whip up support for their lost Bohemian kingdom. But support never comes.

In years to come Miles Godric will think of the taking of Prague, first bloodshed in thirty years of grinding war, and hear of Elizabeth's son Rupert fighting bloody battles in England that civil war also engulfs. Word will come to him that Elizabeth, in exile, has the no longer young Descartes at her court at The Hague, and that he has dedicated his *Principia philosophiae* to her. He will wonder if the man remembers what the boy once experienced in Prague, in a garden, among roses.

And, being of the Kin of the Weerde, he will live long enough to fight in most of the wars of the Age of Reason that Cartesian dualism will usher in.

But for now it is a summer evening and Miles Godric is earning his reprieve; forgetting all else to stand, wounds stinging in the surface change of stature and feature, and laugh, and anticipate the next battle.

Afterword

HISTORICAL NOTE

The young Rene Descartes shared a common preoccupation of the European scholars of his time – contacting the hypothetical organisation known as the Rosicrucians. His desire did not outlive his period of service in Maurice of Nassau's army in 1619, however, during the winter of which his diary records singular dreams.

It seems probable that he was in Prague after the capture and sacking of that city, after the Battle of the White Hill in 1620. Michael Maier's connections with that centre of neo-Platonic experiment are longer and better documented. The mysterious vanishing of this European scholar and author is reported to have taken place in Prague in 1622.

Upon Descartes' return to Paris at the height of the Rosicrucian scare, he was himself widely assumed to be a member of that invisible college, and could only counteract this by making himself available to the public and therefore, after a manner of speaking, visible. In his later writings he continues, to say the least, to distance himself from the hermetic world-view.

The Pits Beneath the World

A wind stirs the blue grass of the Great Plains. The flat land stretches out to the perfect circle of the horizon. There is not a rock or tree to break the monotony. Seventeen moons burn in a lilac sky. A blue-giant sun is setting, its white dwarf companion star hangs in the evening sky.

The small figure stands waist-deep in the grass. She aches from running bent over in a crouch. Now she straightens, biting back a gasp at the pain.

Shrill chittering and whistling noises come from the distance. Seen!

Up until today she's been sorry that she's small for her age. Now she's glad. Only a small human could lie concealed in the Plains grass. She edges away and crawls on, hands and knees stained blue by the grass sap.

Behind her, the whistling of the Talinorian hunting party begins again.

There is no doubt: she is their quarry.

When did it go wrong? Pel Graham wondered. The Talinorians are our friends. What happened?

She was hurt and bewildered as well as afraid.

It had all been fine until two days ago . . .

There! – the Talinorian whistled – The *chelanthi!*—

Pel peered ahead between its sheaf of stalked eyes. Far out across the Great Plain, grass rippled where no wind blew.

'Hold on!' called Pel's mother, riding high astride the glittering carapace of another Talinorian, Baltenezeril-lashamara.

With a clatter of shell the Talinorian hunting party edged down the side of the cliff. Pel clung as Dalasurieth-rissanihil lurched under her, body-suckers clutching the rock as they moved down the almost vertical surface. The long segmented body rippled.

'Faster!' she yelled, and then remembering that the human voice had too low a frequency for the Talinorian's sensors, tapped the message out on the alien's eye-carapace. The stalked eyes retreated briefly under the hard shell. Pel had learned to interpret this as amusement.

Now they went more slowly. The Talinorians were better suited to rocky cliffs and scarps. Only for the traditional *chelanthi* hunts did they venture down onto grassland.

Pel waved to her mother, and to the other members of the Earth scientific expedition honoured to ride in the Talinorian hunt. It was a time of relaxation. They must have finished negotiating, Pel thought, not very interested. She didn't want to leave Talinor yet.

The wind blew her hair in her eyes. She turned her head, seeing the rocky 'coast' behind them. Clusters of rock rose starkly out of the flat grassland. It was impossible to think of them as anything but islands, jutting out of a grass ocean. On the rocking-gaited Talinorian, Pel felt like a ship at sea. Hunting the beasts of the ocean, the *chelanthi*.

—We're falling behind—

The other unburdened Talinorians were faster. Dalasurieth-rissanihil slowed still further.

The 'islands' they had left were small, and in a natural condition. They were covered with bush-berry-trees, the purple fruit hanging down in long strings; and with the *cureuk* flowers that folded up when touched. Mothbirds flew only in this hour between the blue sun's rising and the white sun's following, when they again roosted. A multitude of singing insects nested in the crevices of the rock, and the nights were bright with luminous starflies. It was different from Talinor-Prime, Pel thought, where the expedition had set down the shuttle.

—They have made a kill—

—Where?—

Pel stared ahead over Dalasurieth-rissanihil's carapace, but saw nothing in detail. If she admitted the truth she preferred riding to hunting, and wasn't sorry to miss the end.

A wisp of smoke coiled up ahead.

—Dala', look!—

—Stray laser-beam. Don't they realise what a grass fire might do?—

Dalasurieth-rissanihil sounded, so far as she could tell, furious.

—I thought you had to use spears?—

—Tradition demands it. The leader will have something to say to them back at Prime!—

Pel saw the Talinorians put the fire out before it could spread. Others carried the scaly *chelanthi* slung across their patterned carapaces, held in place by their forked scorpion-tails. Clusters of thin jointed arms waved excitedly.

—Will you stay for the hunt tomorrow?—

—I have to go home. It's my— The click and whistle language failed her.— It's a party. The northern team should be back. And besides, it's my . . .—

She couldn't find a word for 'birthday', and struggled to make it clear. Dalasurieth-rissanihil rattled its forked tail.

—So you will have been alive eleven seasons of your home world? That is a long time to be adult. I had thought you younger—

Privately she laughed. Aliens were often stupid about the most obvious things. Except, she thought, I don't suppose it *is* obvious to them; not even an eleventh birthday . . .

—How old are you, Dala'?—

—I have been adult three seasons—

Pel couldn't be bothered to translate that into Earth-standard years. She knew it wasn't long.

—Yes, but how long ago were you born? I mean, I'm not adult. Not exactly. I don't come of age until I'm fourteen—

—You are not adult?—

—No, not yet; I told you. Oh, you don't understand—

They were turning back towards the islands and Talinor-Prime. Dalasurieth-rissanihil was unusually silent on the way back across the plain, and she wondered if she had offended him.

Talinor-Prime. An 'island' in a grassland 'ocean', but this island was a continent. Big enough to take a flyer three days to cross it. A rock plateau a few metres higher than the surrounding plain, and with a totally different ecology – as Pel's xenobiologist

mother was very prone to telling her. More important from
Pel's point of view, Talinor-Prime held the city and the starship
landing-field.

It was noon before they arrived. The two suns – blue Alpha
and white Beta – blazed together in the sky. Pel had a black
and a purple shadow following her on the carved rock walkway.

'Ready for the party tomorrow?' her mother asked.

'You bet. Are the others back yet?'

'Not yet. I'm expecting them to call in soon.'

The long arthropod bodies of the Talinorians glided past them
on low trollies. Some preferred the powered walkways that
riddled the rock of Prime. They were too low for an adult
human to enter without stooping, but Pel was small enough to
stand upright in them.

They turned down another walkway and saw the starfield
between the wasp-nest dwellings of the Talinorians. Pel looked
through the view-grills as they walked. She liked the inside of
the 'nests', with their powered valve-doors and beam-operated
equipment. Talinorian manipulative limbs weren't strong, but
they were good at delicate work. Their great love was glass,
which their formulae made stronger than anywhere else in the
galaxy. Sculptured, woven in filaments, blown into spheres and
cubes and octagons, the ornaments glittered in the light of the
two suns; and Talinor-Prime chimed as the wind blew.

'Pel!'

Pel ran on from staring through a view-grill. She caught up as
they began to walk across the vast expanse of the starfield. The
blue-grey rock was hot underfoot.

'Tell me,' her mother said, 'what do you and Dala' talk
about?'

'Oh . . . things.' Pel shrugged.

'I'm sorry in a way that there are no other kids with this
expedition. I always wonder if it's fair to bring you on these
trips. But since there are just the two of us . . .'

Pel made a rude noise. 'Try and stop me coming with you,'
she invited. 'Anyway, it's training – for the future.'

Her mother laughed.

The starfield was on a long spit of 'island' jutting out into the
grassland. At that time there were no other ships there. Pel

looked at the squat dirty shuttle with affection. It would be great to have the other half of the team back with the ship.

I wonder if they brought me any presents? she thought; and didn't answer when her mother asked her what she was grinning at.

Blue Alpha's dawn light stretched her shadow far behind her on the rocks. The morning smelled clean, spicy. A cool wind blew out of the south. Pel scrambled down the long spit towards the edge of the grassland. Mothbirds beat their fragile wings round her, bright against the amethyst sky.

She could just have waited on the shuttle. But Pel preferred to keep watch in the open, and wait for the ship's return.

Something whirred past her ear.

She swatted at it automatically. Glancing round, she saw some Talinorians on the slope above her, and recognised one of them as Dalasurieth-rissanihil.

A shadow flicked her face.

The spear clattered on the rock beside her.

Pel sprang up. The red line of a laser kicked the rock into molten steam. While she watched, Dalasurieth-rissanihil raised the gun and took aim again.

She took a flying leap off the rocks, running as fast as she could through the grass. It slowed her, but she managed to reach the cover of a rock overhang.

Another party of Talinorians waited beyond it.

She swerved out into the open, running like a hare. Arms and legs pumping, lungs burning; she fell into a stride that took her far out into the blue grassland.

It dawned on her as she fell into the scant cover that the grass afforded, far from Talinor-Prime, that those first shots had not been meant to kill. Only to start her running. Only to force her out into the grass ocean, where killing might take place honourably with glass-tipped hunting spears.

She put her head down, gripped her knees, and tried to stop shaking. When the first panic subsided, bewilderment remained. Then it hardened into a cold determination.

Pel Graham looked back to the distant cliffs of Prime. She thought, Somehow I'll get back. I'll make them pay. Somehow I'll find out . . . Dalasurieth-rissanihil – *why?*

She heard the hunting party in the distance.

Evening found her still further away, driven out of sight of Prime. The islands were specks on the horizon. If it had not been for the gentle ridges and undulations of the ground here, she would have been spotted long ago. Now she clung to cover under an alien sky. The grassland went from aquamarine to azure to indigo as Beta set.

The expedition will come looking, Pel thought. I only have to stay free until the shuttle flies over and finds me. I bet they're already on their way—

The grass rustled.

Pel flopped down on her stomach. A blunt muzzle pushed along through the reed-bladed grass. A *chelanthi*. Its low flexible body was covered in mirror-scales, camouflaging it. She saw tiny eye-clusters almost hidden under the muzzle. The actual mouth was further back, between the front pairs of legs. As she watched, it began to crop the grass.

Aren't they meat-eaters? Pel wondered.

A scaly hide brushed her arm. She shot back, biting off a yell. The *chelanthi* raised its muzzle, eye-stalks wavering reproachfully. Pel stifled laughter. It scuttled off past the first *chelanthi*. She followed it.

The ridge concealed a dip beyond. The hollow was pitted with holes, among which many *chelanthi* were grazing. They seemed harmless. They probably were . . .

Another *chelanthi* emerged from one of the pits. They must burrow deep, Pel thought. How else would they hide from the Talinorians?

A long whistle sounded through the gathering twilight. She thought, What if the hunters have heat-seeking equipment? That'll show up human body-heat miles off when it's dark . . .

Pel Graham grinned. It was a crazy idea she had. Good, but crazy; still, she might be a little crazy herself by now. There was every excuse for it.

The *chelanthi* did not object when Pel crept into one of the pits beside them. It was dry, earth trodden down hard, and surprisingly roomy. She lay sheltered among their warm scaly bodies, hidden from anything on the grassland above.

The blue sun set in an ocean-coloured sky. The few stars of

the galaxy's rim burned in lonely splendour. The moons rose, all seventeen of Talinor's satellites. Sometimes their varying orbits made them appear in clusters, but now they hung in a string of crescents. Pel Graham slept fitfully in the warm night. The Talinorian hunting party passed five miles to the west.

Morning came chill. Disturbed out of one pit when the *chelanthi* went to graze, Pel crawled into another. It had only one occupant. This *chelanthi* made a racheting noise like a broken clock and nipped at her hand. Pel backed out in an undignified scramble.

She watched. The *chelanthi* was busy at the mouth of that pit. It appeared to be stringing a substance from glands under its body. The stubby forepaws gripped the pit's mouth, and Pel saw that it was beginning to weave a web over it.

She listened, but heard no sound of the hunt.

I'm safe here. At least I'm hidden. But I have to get back to Prime. I have to warn them!

The day wore on. Pel was extremely bored by the *chelanthi*. True, they did her no harm. They did nothing except crop the grass. The webbed pit remained closed, and she was not sure if the *chelanthi* inside were sleeping, hibernating, or dead. Hourly the mass of its hidden body became more shapeless.

Unless the Talinorians stumbled across her, the *chelanthi* would hide her. They camouflaged her against long-distance night sensors, and in the day radiation from the two suns made long-distance sensing impossible.

It was not until then that it occured to her; if she was hidden from Talinorian sensors, she must also be hidden from those of the Earth expedition.

The second evening came. The blue giant Alpha eclipsed the white dwarf Beta as the suns set. Pel was hungrier than she had ever thought it possible to be. Thirst made her drink the water that collected on the flat-bladed grass, and hope that it didn't carry infection.

She was even more determined to get back to Talinor-Prime. It was think of that, or panic, and she didn't dare panic.

The *chelanthi* gave up grazing and headed for the pits.

Pel thought about the webbed pit, she hadn't looked at it in a while. She walked over to it.

As she watched, the webbing over the pit's entrance twitched. It bulged as if something beneath it were trying to get out. Pel stepped back rapidly.

The webbing reared up and split. Something sharp, grey, and glistening protruded. It twitched again, slitting the web still further. A multitude of thin many-jointed and hard-shelled limbs followed, gripping the sides of the pit. A carapace emerged. Under it, clustered eye-stalks waved. The body heaved itself up onto the grass, segment by armoured segment, disclosing the suckers on the underside. The patterned shell gleamed. Last to leave the pit was the forked scorpion-tail.

Pel stared.

The young Talinorian looked round at the grass-eating *chelanthi*, at Pel Graham who stood frozen with astonishment, and clicked and whistled softly. As it scuttled off it said— Don't you know that there are some things it's better for you not to see?—

It changes everything! Pel thought.

The grass was harsh under her hands and knees. She followed the line of a low ridge. The pits and the broken web were far behind her. She knew that the new-born Talinorian would betray her to the hunting party as soon as it found them.

White Beta rose, and the plains flooded with colour. A little warmth came back to Pel as she moved.

It spoke. It was a *chelanthi*, and it – changed.

It had looked very like Dalasurieth-rissanihil, who was only three seasons 'adult' .

Shrilly in the distance came the whistle of the hunters. Abandoning the *chelanthi*, she had abandoned safety.

I will get back to Prime! she told herself.

She saw something flash in the morning sky like a thrown coin.

'Hey! Hey, shuttle!'

They'll never hear me, never see me, never sense me . . . If there was any way I could mark myself out . . .

Fire would have been best, but she had no way to set the grass lands on fire. And then she remembered the *chelanthi* hunt.

Deliberately Pel stood up and ran to the crown of the ridge. She waved both arms over her head, semaphoring wildly.

The shrilling of the hunters was louder, much louder.

As fleet as fear could make her, she ran. A laser-beam licked redly out to her left, and even through her exhaustion she had time for a grin of triumph.

A line of grass burst into crackling fire. The shuttle's course veered wildly. It began to descend.

Pel could hardly breathe. The world was going red and black round her. But she staggered over the ramp a hundred yards ahead of her pursuers and fell into her mother's arms.

The Talinorian hunting party dwindled below.

'*That* took some sorting out. You mustn't blame them,' Pel's mother turned away from the computer console. 'It's not uncommon in nature to have a larval stage, after all. Even on Earth, moths and butterflies . . . And until they change they're quite unintelligent. Just animals, really.'

'Did you tell them?' Pel asked. 'About – children?'

Outside the shuttle's viewport, Talinor-Prime sparkled in the light of two suns. The wind ruffled the grasslands.

'It's a great step forward in understanding each other.' She put her hand on Pel's shoulder. 'You see, when you said you weren't adult—'

'They thought it was all right to hunt me down?'

'Don't be bitter. Worlds are different places.' She turned her back. 'If they'd hurt *you* . . .'

Pel knew what that note in her mother's voice meant. Lightly she said, 'I'm all right.'

'I know you are, love.'

But you don't understand, she thought. Dalasurieth-rissanihil was my friend . . .

'Were you afraid? Oh, that's a stupid question . . . it was a brave thing you did, Pel.'

'Will they stop the hunting?'

'You don't have to be afraid. Not now it's been made clear to everyone.'

'No.' Pel shook her head impatiently. 'The *chelanthi* hunting. Will you stop that?'

'You know we can't interfere on alien worlds.' Her mother sat down at the console. 'You get some rest. I'm going to pilot us in.'

The door irised shut. Back in the main body of the shuttle, Pel stared out of the port. Hunger, exhaustion; she has been told that these will pass.

Two suns cast the descending shuttle's double shadow on the landing-field. She remembers the endless grassland like a great sea. She remembers Talinor-Prime jutting up in headlands and cliffs and peaks. And she remembers the pits beneath the world, and the *chelanthi* as they nuzzled at her in their sleep.

She sits down and hides her face in her hands.

Pel Graham is thinking of the other children.

Afterword

The first time I was ever asked to contribute a story to an anthology, it was shortly after *Golden Witchbreed* had been published, in 1983, and it was *Peter Davison's Book of Alien Planets*.

Peter Davison was the then Dr Who – although there was not supposed to be anything Whovian in the collected stories themselves – and, being one of the generation that grew up on *Dr Who*, I jumped at the chance.

The idea of being actually asked to write something left me glowing, too, I have to admit – although that may have come from spending the two years before I wrote *Golden Witchbreed* in writing short stories, and not being able to get arrested as far as selling them was concerned.

You know that idea that people who want to write novels should learn to do it by writing short stories first? I mean, they're *shorter*, right? They don't take as much time. You can do more of them . . .

Turns out, that rather depends on what you find you have an instinctive head-start on, when you begin to write.

Pacing, characterisation, dialogue, focus – they're all different depending on whether the story's a short or a novel. As a natural long fiction writer, it turned out that the idea of learning to write novels by writing short stories made about as much sense as learning to scale mountains by practising ski jumps. And with a rather similar tangle of skis at the bottom of the cliff, usually.

Occasionally, I'd manage to hit the right note for a short story; and the concept in 'The Pits Beneath the World' is a short-story-sized one, and I still rather like it. It's hard science (well, as hard as I get), and it has a Lovecraftian title; what more can you ask for?

Then I had to carry on learning how to write novels. *And* learning how to write short stories. To which learning (as it says somewhere in *Ecclesiastes*) there is no end . . . But that's okay, because apart from the odd *crump!* at the foot of the ski-jump, it's still immense fun.

Cast a Long Shadow

E very night, now, Suze's lover shouts herself awake from dreaming.

In her mind, Suze tries to excuse her inadequate concern. *This is the first time I've had a female lover: for all I know, this is normal.* To be white-faced, unreachable, blank-eyed, every 4 a.m. . . .

Late afternoon, now. Suze's old Ford Escort drives along the seaside promenade of the English coastal town. Hotel roofs spike the sky to her right. On the left, the passenger side, is the pavement: long shadows spreading across it from the promenade's lamp-posts. One or two late-season tourists, walking. The sea. She loves to smell the sea.

In the front passenger seat, Natalie also inhales – her eyes are shut. Her head is cocked as if she is listening. Her yellow-stained fingers shake.

The nails of her bitten fingers are painted a clashing cherry red, and the pads stained nicotine-yellow. Nats smokes. Suze would have said she'd find that an utter turn-off.

'I hate—' Suze stops herself.

'What, love?' Nats looks seedy and preoccupied for a woman in a holiday resort. One arm rests on the open car windowsill. The forearm of someone who works out in the gym. Smoking, though. Contradictions.

I hate the way cigarette smoke makes the car smell. And my clothes. And Barry's. And what it must be doing to your lungs.

Suze doesn't complain about the early-morning nightmares. The woman – *the lover* – she came out of nowhere. A gift.

'Nothing,' Suze says. 'Let's not spoil the day, right?'

Natalie's body appears to relax, as if – Suze thinks, hiding a frown – the woman expected a different answer.

Or a different question.

The shadows of the lamp-posts flick under the car like the bars of a cattle-grid. Suze drives slowly, looking to park. She approaches the Marina funfair. Roundabouts, a Ferris wheel, a helter-skelter slide. The beep of arcade games comes in through the open window. The shadow of the Ferris wheel falls across the road.

This was meant to be a treat. A family treat. In so far as two women and a child can be a family, she thinks.

Suze checks the rear-view mirror. Slumped in the back seat, Barry has his head buried in a Manga comic, refusing to look out of the car. He looks younger than twelve, she notices with a pang, seeing his chainstore denim jacket and T-shirt, his shaven hair.

Nats is a gift that came out of nowhere: on holiday down from the Smoke. Dodgy, charming – usually. A lover who can laugh her out of her black moods. Distant, though? Oh yes. Distant, from time to time.

The boy hates Natalie. Hates 'mummy's friend'.

Suze returns her attention to road and gear-shift; sneaks a look at her front passenger. Would anyone see she's more than a friend?

Natalie inhales quietly but intensely; self-possessed, like the cat she sometimes resembles, with her sharp little features. She wears an ivory-coloured cotton dress, with a print of rich, curved burgundy-coloured plums. A black bum-bag encircles her narrow waist.

Around her neck – startlingly frivolous for such a cynical woman – she wears many pendants on thin chains and cords: pentagrams, bear-totems, Stars of David; Thor's Hammers, crucifixes, a sheila-na-gig; the Kanji character for Rat and two different icons with Sekhmet's lion face. Beautiful Arabic script is tattooed in black around her pale upper arms. Nat is nothing if not eclectic.

Suze can see herself through the other woman's eyes as clearly as she can see Barry in the rear-view mirror. Suze Parker – ratty blonde. Early-looking-like-late thirties. Chainstore light summer dress; south coast accent. Her one lifeline a medium-expensive perfume from three Christmases ago, before her last lover walked out.

Suze doesn't complain if Nats is sometimes distant. Yeah. So? Not too many *men* would want to take on a divorced woman on Income Support, with her twelve-year-old son, never mind a street-smart London lesbian.

Barry is not interested in hearing that mummy's friend and mummy might want to be a family.

Suze tries to ignore that. It's just a tiny shadow on the horizon. Just jealousy. On which her now less-conventional dream of family life may be wrecked, but—

'*Shit!*' she yells out loud, amazing herself.

The car tilts over. Jerks. *Falls.*

In the slow-down of crisis she sees how they veer towards a whitewashed plank wall, pasted with faded publicity posters.

She glimpses Natalie leaning back, grabbing the outside of the chassis-frame with one hand, bracing herself against the dashboard with the other. *She's done this before?*

Suze wrenches the wheel, stands on the brakes in an attempt to regain control of the car as it plummets forward.

It goes through her mind in a simultaneous split second: *subsidence? sewer collapse? coastline erosion?*

One minute there is a road, the next – a black gaping hole.

Barry sprawls forward from the rear seat, seat-belt digging into his belly, the comic gone flying. Natalie's head impacts smartly with the windscreen – Suze's heart is suddenly sour in her mouth – but not hard enough to fracture the glass into a star.

Suze, sprawled forward over the steering column, sees only tarmac ahead, crossed by a widening sharp edge of blackness. The car squeals, lists; stops.

Natalie scrambles out of the passenger side with the rapid focus one only sees in emergency services personnel and the military.

Suze, in shock, focuses on the smooth length of the younger woman's leg as the thigh and calf-muscles extend. Tanned, bare, no stockings under her flowing dress. A delicate hint of perspiration.

Suze sits up in her seat, dizzy, and hits the catch to open her door.

It swings open fast, gravity pulling it forward out of her hand.

The Ford Escort's front wing, wheel, and part of the open door are overhanging a blackness.

It ought to be a hole.

There is no visible earth or rubble-filling where the tarmac ends. The road just stops. If the car weren't stuck, axle and undercarriage jammed down, grating on the impossible edge—

She looks out of the car as if under anaesthetic.

People are just beginning to turn and stare, on the paved promenade. She smells sea, holiday crowds and fast food. Mechanical music blares.

The bottom of the stationary Ferris wheel casts a shadow. It stretches long and black across the perimeter fence of the Marina, out across the road.

And where the shadow lies on the tarmac, the Ford Escort has crashed nose-down into it. Is *teetering* – her stomach tells her – doors open, headlights cracked, on the edge of a completely black . . . nothing.

Not a pit. *Nothing.*

'Mummy!' Barry squeals like a much-younger child.

The next she knows, Suze is kneeling in the road by the passenger doors and hugging Barry, ignoring how pissed-off he now seems by this display of maternal concern. Natalie stands at her side, looking at the car, in the process of lighting another cigarette.

In Suze's mind, her voice whispers, Stronger dreams than mine have been . . .

'. . . Wrecked?' Suze completes her thought, wonderingly. *On a shadow?*

'Know what?' Natalie gives a delicate snort. 'Never did trust bloody cars.'

Nats is the only woman Suze knows who doesn't drive.

Suze grapples her son to her. 'Barry!'

The boy wrenches himself out of her hug. Twelve-year-old boys are strong, if you're a not-very-tall, not-very-fit, mother. He glares at her, not babyish now. The crowd also stares. The reserve of the English around strangers holds them back – who wants to get involved? – but Suze can see one man with a kind expression who is evidently about to ask if he can help. And his eyes go blank every time he looks at the shadow-pit.

'*Time to go.*' Natalie puts one arm around Suze's shoulders and one arm around Barry's, hustling them bodily away from the car. 'Always think I'm gonna spot the moment – and it always takes me by surprise . . .'

Barry stumbles, being dragged unwillingly from a scene of confusion and consequent interest, but he goes. The nothingness in the road must be terrifying him, Suze thinks, if he'd only admit it.

Her vision registers, unseeing, a sign amongst the posters on the whitewashed wall: FUNFAIR. Behind her, voices are raised around the wrecked Ford. She hears a siren; glimpses the flashing blue light of a police patrol vehicle.

'The *car*!' She actually stops. One heeled sandal turns over as they come to the Marina gateway, the surface changing from paving stones to hard-packed earth. She winces. 'The damn car. It isn't taxed. It isn't even insured!'

'Some things you just can't insure against.' Natalie's dark hair has fallen over her red-rimmed eyes. She pushes Suze on. 'Walk, Suze. Let's not hang about, eh?'

Suze resists, stubborn; reaches her hand up to the younger woman's forehead. Her fingers come away bloody.

Partly occluded by the woman's proto-anorexic body, the sign on the fence now appears to read UNFAIR.

'You're hurt!'

'Dun't matter.' Nats is casual, but her eyes are glassily bright. Her gaze flicks all around. 'Got to tell you something.'

Shock and the smell of the seaside hits Suze. She feels nauseous. Sea-salt, old weed left behind at high tide, sickly candyfloss . . . salt and vinegar chips, hot fat, and perspiration. Suze shakes her head, wondering if she really hears Nats over the mundane banging noise of arcade games and rides.

'I said, I've got to *tell* you something, Suze, love. Let the kid go on the rides for a bit.'

'But . . . *Rides*? The car . . . ! *That*—' Suze's protest fails.

It took so long for Natalie to get Suze to trust her. To believe that, yes, this is something she has always wanted. And that Nats – loving, funny, haunted Nats – is her introduction to a newer kind of life. How can Suze not obey her now?

The fair is shabby, dusty at the end of a three-month season. Weary vendors and tourists cast long evening shadows. Ferris wheel, helter-skelter, shooting stalls; video arcades, carousel roundabout, swings . . . This is the hour when the afternoon population of children is just changing over to evening customers. Teenage boys with adrenaline and impressionable girlfriends. Barry's too old and too young to be here.

She reaches across Natalie to squeeze Barry's hand, not glancing back over her shoulder at the abandoned car. The crowd hides them from whatever is happening out there.

'Go on the stalls.' Suze feels in her purse for pound coins. 'Barry, love, be careful—'

'Place's *stupid*. Came out of the *ark . . .*' He doesn't look behind them either. His mother's son.

Natalie's voice drops to mock-grim gravel. 'Run along, kid; I want to talk to your mum.'

Barry gives her a look that, for once, isn't pure hatred. The unbelievability of what just happened to them is knocked out of Suze's head by hope. If Barry can like – no, just *tolerate* – Nats . . .

The boy sprints off between an elderly man and woman in identical cardigans, who tut. Suze spares them a hard stare. Her son runs amongst the boys in leather jackets, the girls in floral print skirts, the three-year-olds who are cleaner than Barry could ever be kept.

'Loves his old mum, that boy.' Natalie sounds philosophical. 'Takes after his dad, too.'

Suze stops, deep in the funfair crowds. She can hear the siren again, behind her. 'Alan never sees him now!'

'Twice in the last month.'

'*You what?*'

Nats says, 'You going to tell me you really didn't know?'

Suze feels herself flush hot as a girl. 'You can't meet a twelve-year-old at the school gates every day! And . . . okay, Alan still lives over on the next estate. I thought he might help out financially if he remembered his damned son *existed*. Maybe I turned a blind eye. So sue me!'

The look on Natalie's face is strange. More serious than you'd expect.

Dread twists her stomach into pain. Suze begins, 'Is what just happened to the car—'

'Down to Alan? My money's on it. Quite famous in certain circles, your Alan. He—' Natalie screams. '*Shit!*'

Nats is down on her hands and knees, suddenly; down on the

hard earth with its trodden-on gum. Suze stares at the black-haired woman – at the toes of the shoes of people who stop, stare, mutter in shocked whispers.

Natalie's left leg is impaled through the muscular part of the calf by a very thin black spear or spike.

It has the same absolute blackness as the nothingness into which the car crashed.

Blood wells, staining the hem of Natalie's dress. She lifts her head, grinning with pain. As if to herself, she says, 'Wasting time, I know. OK. I get the *point* . . .'

Suze kneels by the taut guy-ropes of the fairground tent. The shadows of those ropes are thin, straight, and sharply defined on the earth beside her.

One rope is missing its shadow.

'It's not possible. It's crazy.' Suze is amazed, afraid. But – she knows, with dread congealing inside her – not as surprised as maybe she should be.

She stares at the impaling void. Stuck *through* Nats. 'It's . . . solid.'

'It hurts, damn it!'

Recklessly, copying the way that she has taken fishing hooks out of Barry's thumb, Suze grips the shadow-spear and pushes, then pulls it out of Natalie's calf.

It feels flat and not particularly like anything else, and it leaves a hot red line across her palm.

'Alan . . . He used to threaten me. Not now, surely? Not after five years!'

The carousel is between her and the setting sun. The shadow of a galloping horse is elongated on the canvas wall of the tent beside her where she kneels.

'Alan—That bastard *swore* to me he'd never hurt Barry!'

'Maybe he doesn't think he is. These arrangements have . . . benefits. Or maybe he lied, Suze. But you wouldn't think of th—Jesus!' Natalie abandons the makeshift handkerchief bandage on her calf and staggers to her feet, still bleeding.

Suze jumps up to see where she's staring.

A running crowd of people. Running towards them.

Parents, young kiddies, teenagers. All running between the crossbow-shooting stalls and the games arcade, towards Suze. Voices screaming in panic.

She registers that the canvas wall beside her is blank. And then she sees the shadow-horses with their curling manes, rearing through the crowd.

An old man holds up his arm as he falls, calling for his equally-old wife.

A mother throws herself across her child.

Suze sits down hard on the packed earth. She hadn't known she was going to.

'*Barry!*' She grabs for Natalie's hand, hauling herself up again; slips, bangs her knee, sways up onto her feet. 'My God! Where's *Barry*?'

Bleeding, Nats holds herself up on Suze as Suze holds herself up on her.

There's no sympathy in her face.

'Stupid cow.' Natalie's grip bites into her shoulder. 'No time to explain. I better wrap this one up fast now.'

The sun glares into Suze's eyes through the steam carousel. The shadow of its canopy and brass poles falls on the ground. Painted horses with crimson nostrils are frozen on the candy-stick-poles.

There is nothing on the earth but the shadows of the poles.

Seagulls scream in a darkening blue sky. The crowd streams past Suze, sprinting for the Marina gates. Dazzled, sun-motes in her vision, she sees a man lying face down on the ground a few yards ahead of her. His jeans are soiled. She sees the deep black imprint of a horse's hoof in the back of his white T-shirt. The hole is still oozing lung-tissue.

Natalie lets go of Suze's shoulder, standing shakily. She glances at her bleeding leg. Wry, she remarks, 'Suze – believe me. This hurts me more than it hurts you.'

Suze turns on her. '*Where's my baby?*'

Nats still has her ratty leather bum-bag around her thin waist. The woman reaches into it and takes out a thin school exercise book, rolled up tight.

'See,' Nats says. She doesn't seem surprised that Suze isn't hurling herself against the flow of the panicking crowd to find her son. 'See, I didn't find this until yesterday. I knew he had to have it well-hidden. All these weeks – months – Turns out he kept moving it. At school, at a friend's house. Hoping I'd be a step behind all the time, I guess.'

'Nats—'

'I finally found it in our – in your spare room. With a couple of girlie mags. Surprisingly well hidden.' Natalie holds the unrolled exercise book towards Suze. 'Surprisingly accurate.'

The late sun casts the shadows of the open pages across Natalie's hands. All the hand-writing is Barry's – that of a much younger child than he actually is, Suze always fears. Letters scrawly, not joined up. The ink is brown.

She recognises things he has obviously copied out of the astrology columns in the tabloid newspapers, unknown but familiar symbols. Other diagrams remind her of Alan's collection of hand-written books.

The page is headed *To Call Up Shaddoes*.

'Not bad work,' Nats says caustically, 'for "Daddy's little bargain" . . .'

Suze starts, *'What?'* – but her son's voice interrupts her.

'That's *mine*! Mum, that's mine!' Barry's voice holds rage. 'Don't let *her* muck about with it!'

He stands a few yards away, between a shooting gallery and a darts-throwing stall. Men and women lay on the ground around him, not moving.

He keeps his gaze firmly above ground-level, she sees.

There is no one conscious. The wail of an ambulance sounds, out on the promenade.

There are two other kids with Barry. A boy with black skin and a rainbow knitted woolly hat. A white girl with hair dyed indigo, and a nose-stud. Both about twelve, both in leather jackets.

Suze sees that they have pointed fingernails, pointed ears; eyes with the vertical pupils of cats.

They are brat-cute, in a pre-pubertal way. They and Barry share the same shit-eating grin.

Suze takes one step forward, her hand raised, her voice hard. Reflex is a profound comfort. 'Barry Parker, you get over here *right now* or I'll clout your bloody head off!'

His 'friends' change in the blink of her eye.

Each is now a head taller than Barry, and tougher-looking. Each puts a hand on one of Barry's shoulders, claws gripping his denim jacket. They are older, nastier, considerably less cute. One kicks aside a dropped baby's bottle.

As if he doesn't notice the change, Barry calls, 'Mu-um! C'mere. *Quick*. Over here. Leave her alone. We don't need *her*.'

Worse: he *might* have noticed the change.

She knows her son, can spot his reactions. He may notice and not care.

'Barry – I said *get over here*. NOW.'

She hears Natalie grunt behind her. Until then, she hadn't realised she'd started to walk away from the woman, towards Barry.

The metal frame of the space-pod ride casts a cage of shadows around the black-haired woman, her lover.

Nats grips the shadow bars that have suddenly turnéd solid on her – and bends to step through the just-wide-enough gap.

'Have to do better than that, won't you?' Nats limps as she approaches Suze, her gaze fixed on Barry's companions. 'Much better . . .'

The thought of Alan is in Suze's mind, and she will not – *will not* – look at it. She stares at Barry. 'You little sod, what have you done?'

Natalie takes hold of her elbows from behind, holding her.

Suze whispers, 'Barry . . .'

It is so quiet without the crowds that she can hear the sea-waves landing on the beach, a hundred yards away.

She repeats aloud the words that Natalie used. ' "Daddy's little bargain" . . . Nats, *what*—?'

Nats says, 'Walk over there and I'm dead.'

Suze smells the skinny woman's perspiration. Not the same as the smell of sweat when they've been making love, or the outdoor odour when Natalie has been digging their tiny patch of garden, showing off her fitness and her lean, toned muscles. Fear-stench.

The things that are with her son have adult-sized shadows now. They are difficult to look at directly.

Natalie's breath is warm at her ear. 'Walk over there and *I'm dead*. You'll be dead too, of course, if you do it, but who do you expect me to worry about, me or you?'

The cynicism is a slap in the face. Suze quivers. 'Nats, you don't mean that.'

'You're his mother. He's protecting *you*. Maybe not for long, but long enough—'

The hands are gone from her elbows.

Suze turns.

Two black shadows grip Natalie's throat, shadow-fingers elongating up into her hair, shadow-thumbs digging into her trachea. Natalie pulls at them. Her head twists painfully back.

Shadow arms inhumanly elongated . . . and, as Suze looks, she sees the lower part still a shadow on the earth, attached to Natalie's shoes. It is Natalie's own shadow strangling her.

Suze's heart thumps hard enough to make her dizzy.

She thought it would be hers.

Suze plunges her fingers into the substance of shadow, that still does not feel like anything much, trying to claw it off Natalie's skin.

It tightens like rubber bands.

'Barry, you *stop* that! You hear me? *Now!*'

Abruptly, only her human hands are on Natalie's throat.

Nats' shadow is gone – lies flat on the earth. Who can trust it now? Suze shivers, appalled.

Natalie spits, rubs her throat. 'Always known it. I'm my own worst enemy.'

'How can you *joke*—'

'I always reckon it helps me.' She turns towards Barry, moving as swiftly as Suze has come to expect from this gaunt, not-quite-thirty, not-quite-cohabitee lover.

And did Suze only pick a woman because it's easier to fool Social Services that way? A woman visiting, even overnight, is only a friend . . .

Suze grabs Nats' arm. '*Help him.*'

'We're standing in a bloodbath here, Suzy-girl. *He* did it. How far past redemption do you think he is?'

Natalie holds the school exercise book. She wears a cynical, terrified smile: a smile Suze has only seen on her face after Nats wakes from nightmares.

Barry looks furious, terrified, jealous. He steps forward from between his two companions. They are mid-twenties, now; the sort of drug-dealing, car-stealing, new-town unemployed thugs that Suze is used to.

'He knows me,' she whispers. 'What else could he do that would worry me more? Running around the estate in bad company, older company—'

'*Much* older company.' Nats grins painfully.

The larger female manifestation is drooling. The male one kneels down beside Barry, embracing his waist, glaring not at Suze but at this woman with her.

'Help him . . .' Suze whispers. 'He's my son and – I'm scared to touch him.'

The male voice hisses, speaking to Natalie, not her. 'He wished for us. He desires us used against you. We will not be denied your flesh, your soul, your shadow and self.'

The female voice picks it up: 'He is not of sound mind. A child. He is not of rational age. A mere child. Do we allow ourselves to be his plaything, and then see you escape us?'

The female's skin is now a suppurating yellow mass, and gobbets of phlegm drip from her mouth. Her hands are chitinous hairy spider-claws.

'It's . . . *absurd*,' Suze proclaims, as if this will make them go away. 'They look like things I've seen in his comic-books!'

Nats doesn't take her eyes off Barry. 'Of course they do, he's fucking twelve years old!'

Barry leans his head back against the female's shoulder and stares past Suze, at Natalie. 'You leave my mum alone!'

Suze sees the female thing with her son smile. For the first time, it looks directly at her. Her stomach folds inside her. Suze feels an abrupt trickle of hot liquid down her smooth inner thigh. It splashes over her ankle, spatters her open-toe sandals. Fear numbs fear itself, sometimes. It takes her a second to realise that she has urinated over herself in terror.

The female thing says, 'His father gave him to us. A bargain, for our help. But the child agreed. Willingly. He is our price and our prize. When he fails, he is ours by right.'

The female edges forward, as if she would come closer to Suze. Barry swats at her – *it* – as if it were a large, ill-tempered, but intimidatable dog. His fists clench, his face screwed up in concentration. 'Stay away from my mum, or else!'

Suze could weep, seeing how all the qualities of determination and persistence that she has eulogised to him have come to this. She makes a noise that is neither giggle nor sob. 'What a time to stop being a lay-about . . .'

Behind him the sun is red on the sea, and the shadows of the funfair stretch out long and threatening.

Suze takes one step back.

It puts her beside Natalie.

Suze looks at Nat. Nats' expression is weary and disgusted and afraid. The blood on her forehead is dry now. Suze would like to touch that black hair. To have pressed it to her lips one more time.

'He's just a little *boy*!' she protests. 'He *idolised* Alan.'

Natalie, with a quirk of her mouth, nods.

'Nats, this . . . you and me . . . was it *all* so you could get near Barry?'

There are brown shadows under the younger woman's hollow eyes.

'Of course it was. Alan's always known someone would come looking through the kid's things. He even knew they'd have to get to Barry through you. He probably enjoyed thinking about that part. Don't suppose he expected a dyke. He should have been more broad-minded. But if he had, I'd've been dead before this . . .'

'You could have told me!'

'I don't make the rules.' There is a lighter in Natalie's hand now, from her bag. She flicks, and the flint sparks a blue flame. 'Some of 'em I can't even bend, never mind break.'

Nats holds up her son's exercise book and the cigarette lighter.

'You won't!' Barry yells, absurdly confident. 'Nobody'll burn that! Everybody wants it too much. Dad told me!'

'Yeah, well. People lie, kid.' Natalie holds the cheap school exercise book by one corner, the pages opening fan-wise.

She touches the lighter's flame to one corner. The paper suddenly burns – curls, rapidly, and turns black. Smoke in unreasonable quantities starts to flood up into the darkening sky.

'He isn't a bad boy . . .' Suze sounds dreamy. She notes this with an amount of dissociation that – under other circumstances – would frighten her.

Her son. *Her son*.

Barry crouches, one hand reaching up towards the drifting smoke. She can't let herself look at the expression on his face. 'Mum!'

His shadow falls towards Suze.

Over him fall two other shadows.

Neither is now in the least human. There are aspects of insect and rodent and octopus about them. They would grace the pages of any comic book, any heavy metal or B movie poster.

Suze swallows, mouth dry. 'I'm – I'm the bad one. I thought Alan . . . I thought it was just New Age woo-woo stuff, you know? Except I *knew*—'

Her son screams, 'You don't need *her*! What about *me*?'

Natalie drops the charred fragment of the exercise book from one hand.

With the other she grabs Suze's arm as Suze tries to run forward, gripping her hard enough to leave immediate blue bruises.

Suze's son rises and races towards her, sprinting as young boys can.

Whatever is the real nature of what is behind him, it looks now to be composed of equal parts tarantula, muscleman, horned devil and pus.

Suze puts her hand over her mouth to stifle horrified laughter. This isn't going to happen. This can't happen like this!

Remnants of the leather jackets are still embedded in the being's multiple limbs. One misshapen arm casts a shadow over the boy. *'The compact is broken! The contract burned! By his father's terms he is ours!'*

'Mum! *Mummy!*'

Suze's voice is almost normal. 'I never dared ask for help.'

She lets Natalie's hand restrain her.

Not that Nats could hold her, if she wanted to move. The skinny woman is light enough for Suze to break her in two, if she really wants to walk forward.

Suze doesn't shift her gaze from what is happening in front of her.

'They would have taken him into Care. They would have taken him away. I know about people who go away . . .'

She finally hides her face. Her nails dig bloody crescents in her forehead.

A sickly green light leaks in between her fingers.

There is a smell of cinnamon.

'*Mum—!*' The word is only recognisable by courtesy.

She snatches her hands away from her face, desperate to have a last sight of him.

She shouldn't have done it: she knows that. His expression

sears into her memory, blasts her; a retinal after-image she will for ever see between her and the visible world.

His face is a Greek mask of terror, so far beyond normal human expressions that she almost blurts out laughter.

But the most comical extremes of terror are, finally, real.

Silence.

A deserted funfair, at sunset.

A wailing fire engine joins the other emergency services, out beyond the gates.

The sky is dark blue above; gold in the west.

All the shadows are still.

Natalie stares down at the burnt fragments of the exercise book on the ground. Carefully, she grinds each fragment under her sandal until it is broken ash.

'Don't beat yourself up.' Nats shrugs, cups her hands to her mouth, lighting a cigarette; inhales. Cynical. That cynicism that so attracted Suze. 'All you coulda done was die with him. Although he ain't exactly dead. Not as such . . .'

Suze can't take in the sheer size of the absence. The permanence of this gap in her life.

I know about people who go away. I know about . . . 'Hell?' she says.

Natalie gives a brief confirming nod.

Suze turns her back on the setting sun. Now – now, when it doesn't matter – her thoughts are moving as quickly as slipping on black ice. 'I never asked you where you came from.'

'No. You never did.'

'But I guess you . . . you people? . . . have – ways of dealing with men like Alan.' Suze unclenches her hand; looks down at the blood stigmatising her palms. 'You . . . hurt them, maybe. You see they don't do this to anyone again; ever, *ever* again—'

She looks back at Nats, who is drawing deep on her cigarette, and whose body has entirely and instantly ceased to yearn towards Suze's as a lover.

'I want to help,' Suze says. 'I want to help you stop Alan. Do . . . what I need to do to him.'

Nats shrugs, as casually as if she's never in her life orgasmed in Suze's arms. 'Why not? I can put you in touch with people who'll . . . interview you. Sure. Just so long as you don't think he's the only one responsible.'

Suze looks at her shadow. It streams away from her, away from the sunset – out towards the promenade, the hotels, the estates, the rest of the town.

Self-deception casts its own shadow over things.

'I know he's not the only one responsible,' Suze says. There is no *sorry* to be said. Not from either one of them.

She thinks she may have her own 4 a.m. wake-ups, now. But that's justice.

For the cowardice of not being willing to die with her son.

For the cowardice of not allowing herself to know what she always knew.

Suze and Nats walk back into the town. Side by side. But not together.

Afterword

A long while back, in the late 1980s, I was playing with ideas for graphic novel and comics stories, and I came up with the shadow-magic here – which seemed to me to be an essentially visual thing, and therefore good for that medium.

I story-boarded it out – whether or not that's still apparent in this version, I can't now tell – and I thought it *ought* to work okay. Story-boarding isn't that different from the way I normally work. Some writers get a feel for the sound of the words first; some get just the words themselves; some are kinaesthetic in the first instance. I tend to have an internal movie going (though it usefully comes in Sensurround and feelie-vision). And I'm used to ideas turning up as first-line-plus-picture.

But 'Cast A Long Shadow' sat around resolutely not working. I tried it on a few people; it remained a lemon; I put it back in the drawer.

It stayed out of sight a long time – which turned out to be what it needed in terms of gestation-period. When I took it out again last year, and read it without the script-form in my mind, I knew instantly what it was about.

And it's about things you can't see. Things you deliberately can't see. Which is ironic for something that started off with a visual key image.

So I rewrote it. If I were a good comics or graphic novel writer, I would have both seen the problem sooner, *and* made it work with words-and-pictures. But I remain resolutely word-bound, and so a short story is what you get.

It has a slightly erratic history, in that, unlike the other stories in this collection, it doesn't have a previous publication date. That's because there was one of those really odd hiccoughs that occasionally occur in publishing – an editor of a magazine (who can both remain anonymous, since they don't deserve jumping up and down on) bought the story. And then another member of the editorial staff overruled them. Sometimes, that's publishing as we know and love it . . .

As a writer, I'm never really a hundred per cent sure if any given story works; still less so when things like that happen. But, since I still like the shadow-pictures, and the dysfunctional family, I'm leaving this story in here, and hoping people enjoy it.

A Sun in the Attic

The Archivist sits in a high room, among preserved (and precisely disabled) relics; sorting through notes, depositions, eye-witness accounts, and memoirs.

Outside the window, the city of Tekne is bright under southern polar light. The room is not guarded. There is not the necessity.

In the somewhat archaic and formal style proper to history scrolls, the Archivist writes: In the Year of Our Lady, Seventeen Hundred and Ninety-Six—

Then she pauses, laying down the gull's-quill pen, staring out of the window.

Beyond the quiet waters of the harbour, the slanted sails of the barbarian fleets have drawn perceptibly nearer.

The Archivist turns back to her material.

Tell it as it happened, she thought. Even if it is not in a single voice, nor that voice your own. Tell it while there is still time for such things . . .

An airship nosed slowly down towards the port's flat-roofed buildings. Beyond the harbour arm, the distant sea was white and choppy. Tekne's pale streets sprawled under the brilliant Pacific sun.

'It *may* be a false alarm.' Roslin Mathury leaned on the rim of the airship-car, protesting defensively. 'You know what Del's like, once he's in his workshops.'

'That's why you've brought us back from the farm estates a month before harvest, I suppose?'

Roslin busied herself with straightening the lace ruffles at her cuffs and collar. Without meeting Gilvaris Mathury's gaze, she said, 'Very well, I admit it, I'm anxious.'

The airship sank down over the Mathury roofs, the sun

striking highlights from its dull silver bulk. The crew tossed mooring ropes, and house servants ran to secure them.

'I should have made him come to the country with us!' Roslin said.

'No one ever made Del do what he didn't want to,' Gilvaris observed. 'I should know. He's my brother.'

'He's my husband!'

'And mine, also.'

'When I married you, it wasn't to be told the obvious,' Roslin said, equally acidly; gaining some comfort from the familiarity of their bickering. 'Well, husband, shall we go down?'

The mooring gangway being secured, they disembarked onto the roof of the Mathury town house. The airship cast free, rising with slow deliberation. Its shadow fell across them as it went, and Roslin was momentarily chilled. She saw, as she looked past it, the crescent bulk of Daymoon, blotting out a vast arc in the western sky.

'*Se* Roslin, *Se* Gilvaris.' The housekeeper bowed. 'We're glad to have you back safely—'

Roslin cut the small elderly man off in mid-speech. 'Tell me, what's so bad that you couldn't put it in a message to us?'

'The *Se* Del Mathury worked while you were gone,' the shaven-headed servant said. 'He made some discovery, or thought that he did; he had us bring food to his workrooms, and never left. I think he slept there.'

Roslin nodded impatiently. 'And?'

'He saw visitors,' the housekeeper continued, 'admitting them privately; and received messages. Three weeks ago we brought his morning meal to the workrooms. He was gone, *Se* Roslin. We've seen and heard nothing from him since.'

Light sparkled from glass tubes and flasks and retorts, from coiled copper tubing and cogwheels. A half-assembled orrery gleamed.

Gilvaris turned, pacing the length of the workroom. Boards creaked under his tread. Sunlit dust drifted down from the glass dome-roof, and the swift shadows of seabirds darkened it with their passing. Their distant cries were mournful.

'He might have forgotten to leave word,' Roslin offered.

'Do you really think so?'

The caustic tone moved her to look closely at Gilvaris. Unlike his younger brother in almost everything: tall and dark where Del was fair, secretive where Del was open, slow where Del was erratically brilliant.

'No,' she said, 'I don't really think so. Where *is* he? Is he still in Tekne, even? He could be anywhere in Asaria!'

Gilvaris absently picked up a few bronze cogs and oddly-shaped smooth pieces of glass, shuffling them from hand to hand. 'I'll try Tekne Oldport. That's where he commonly gets his supplies. And I'll ask at the university. Also, it might be wise to discover who his visitors were.'

Roslin dug her hands deep into her greatcoat pockets, feeling the comforting solidness of her pistols. 'Damn, when I see him—'

'If he didn't go willingly? House Mathury has enemies.'

Her dark eyes widened. 'So we do . . .'

'Now wait. That's *not* what I meant. I know House Mathury and House Rooke are rivals in trade, but—'

Roslin came over to him, took his hand. 'Trust me.'

'You shouldn't see Arianne.' Gilvaris put an emphasis on the first word.

'Should I not?'

'You don't have the temperament for it.'

'And you do, I suppose?'

Gilvaris raised an eyebrow. 'I have been told that I resemble my aunt closely.'

Roslin bit back a sharp answer. 'Don't quarrel. You go to the Oldport, I'll ask questions elsewhere. We can't waste time. I'll never forgive myself if Del gets hurt because we weren't here when he needed us.'

A summer wind blew cold through the streets. Roslin walked down to the wider avenues of new Tekne, under the tree-ferns that lined the pavements. Sun gilded the white façades of the city houses. Daymoon was westering, its umber-and-white face blotting out a third of the sky.

She stopped to let a roadcar pass; the engine hissing steam, pulling its fuel car of kelp and a dozen trailers.

House Mathury has enemies, she thought grimly, approaching the wide steps that led up to one of the larger houses. She passed under the archway and entered the courtyard beyond. Servants showed her into the house. As she expected (but was none the less impatient) they kept her waiting for some time.

'*Se* Roslin.'

She turned from pacing the hall. '*Se* Arianne.'

Arianne Rooke, being a generation older than her, still affected the intricately braided wig, the face-powder and high-heeled boots of that fashion. Her eyes were bright, lively in her lined face; and they gave nothing away.

'It is a pleasure, *Se* Roslin. You should visit us more often.'

Her smile never faltered as she ushered Roslin through into a high narrow room. The walls were lined with bookshelves. It smelled faintly musty: the unmistakable scent of parchment and old bindings.

'House Mathury has, after all, connections here.'

'Connections? Yes,' Roslin said bluntly, refusing her offer of wine and a chair, 'you could almost say I'm here on a family visit.'

'I don't quite understand.'

She looked the woman up and down. Arianne was small and dark and, despite her age, agile. Roslin didn't trust her. She was head of House Rooke; she was also Del and Gilvaris's mother's sister.

'Where's Del?' Roslin demanded.

'*Se* Roslin, I don't—'

'Don't take me for a fool,' she said. 'Our houses have fought for . . . but he's one of your own blood! What have you done to him?'

Arianne Rooke seated herself somewhat carefully in a wing-armed chair. Resting her elbows on it, she steepled her fingers and regarded Roslin benignly over the top of them.

'Now let me see what I can gather from this. Your husband Del Mathury is missing? Not your husband Gilvaris too, I trust? No. It would never do to lose two of them.'

Roslin said something unpardonably vulgar under her breath.

'And for some reason,' Arianne continued, 'you imagine that *I* am responsible? Come, there are far more probable reasons; you as a wife should understand this.'

Such delicate insinuations did nothing for Roslin's temper. 'I'm not as stupid as you think!'

'That would be difficult,' Arianne agreed.

'I ought to call you out,' Roslin said, savagely, regretting that her pistols must be left with the servants.

'My dear, you're a notable duellist, and I have a regard for my own skin that only increases with age. So I fear I must decline.'

Roslin, aware of how much Rooke was enjoying herself, thought: Gil would have done this better.

'You're trying to tell me you don't know anything about what's happened to Del.'

'I can but try.' Arianne spread her hands deprecatingly. 'Would that I did. Would that I could help.'

That hypocrisy finished it.

'You listen to me, Arianne. I mean to find Del. And I will. And if you've had anything to do with this, I'll take my evidence before the Port Council, I'll bring House Rooke down about your ears, my friend. Or,' she finished, blustering, 'I may just kill you.'

'Isn't melodrama attractive?' Arianne Rooke observed. 'I'm sure you can find your own way out.'

She could not know that, when she had gone, Arianne Rooke chuckled a little. Then, sobering, took up pen and parchment to write an order for the immediate and secret meeting of the Port Tekne Council.

'Anything?' Gilvaris asked.

'No. She made me lose my temper, so naturally I didn't learn anything. Except that I shouldn't lose my temper. You have any better luck?'

'Not so far.' He sat back on one of the benches. They haunted the workrooms, he and Roslin. 'He could be held somewhere. Now we're back here, we may get a demand for money.'

Roslin looked round the darkening room. It was the short Asarian twilight: Daymoon had already set.

'Maybe . . . It doesn't look like there was a struggle here, does it?'

Gilvaris shook his head. 'It seems to me that there's equipment missing. I wouldn't know for sure – but it could be so.'

She knew he rarely admitted ignorance. Part of the reason for that was a life spent struggling in the effortless wake of a brilliant younger brother; if Del had not loved him so devotedly, Gilvaris's life might have been bitter.

Del, she thought. We're not whole without him.

'What I'm saying is, it's possible he packed and left. He's clever enough to do it without the servants knowing, if he thought it necessary.'

'You think he left us?' Roslin said, incredulous. 'Damn, you're as bad as Arianne Rooke.'

'I don't think he left *us*, specifically,' Gilvaris said, unruffled. 'I think he left. Those visitors he had: some were tradesmen, and some were from the harbour. But at least one was from the Port Council. They're no friends of Mathury. I think Del's in hiding.'

Roslin considered it. 'Why?'

Gil shrugged. 'Haven't I always said, one day he'll discover something that'll get him into trouble?'

'It's amazing,' Roslin said, as they dismounted from the roadcar on the Oldport quay. 'I always saw Del as a loner, shut away in those rooms. He knows more people than I do.'

'He kept in touch with a lot of colleagues from the university,' Gilvaris said.

The wet morning was closing to a rain-splattered noon. They had seen and spoken with, so far, a maker of airship frames, a glassblower, a metalsmith, a windvane repairer, a clockmaker (this being a woman Roslin disliked instantly, knowing that she had been a frequent visitor to House Rooke before Roslin had), as well as printers of news-sheets, and at least four sellers and importers of old books. All knew Del professionally and personally. None knew where he was now.

'He was on to something. When he shuts himself up and works like that . . .' Roslin shook her head. Gilvaris linked his arm in hers and they walked.

'Metal and glassware. His most recent orders.'

'Meaning?' Roslin queried.

'I wish I knew.'

A harbour ship chugged past, and the smell of steam and hot metal came to Roslin through the damp air. Viscid water slapped at the quay steps. Out in the deeper anchorages, up-coast ships spread flexible canvas shells. Steamships wouldn't risk leaving Asaria's canals for the cold storm-ridden seas. Downcoast krill-ships were arriving from the southern icefields.

'If he was that desperate, he wouldn't take one of our ships,'

Gilvaris forestalled her. 'I've made enquiries, there's one more chance. A barbarian ship.'

Roslin looked where it was moored by the quay, saw low sharp lines, great jutting triangular sails. And thought of Del: intense, impractical, obsessed.

'Would he go? Without a word to us?'

'He would, if he thought that staying would put us in danger.'

Roslin blinked. 'I – damn, I can't think like that!'

'There's plenty who can.'

After a moment Roslin put her free hand in her pocket, gripping the butt of the duelling pistol. They went forward to hail the barbarian ship.

'I have seen no one,' the barbarian insisted, in passable Asarian.

He was a tall man, taller even than Gilvaris, with pale yellow skin and bright, braided golden hair. His robes were silk, and from his belt were slung paired metal blades. Roslin recalled that rumour said barbarians fought with these long knives, like servants.

No one? she thought. He's lying.

'Perhaps I can speak to your captain. Will she see me?'

He said, 'I am captain here.'

'Oh.' Roslin sensed rather than saw Gil's amusement. Momentarily at a loss, she glanced round the bare cabin. Cushions surrounded low tables. The table from which the barbarian had risen was covered with parchments and thin ink-brushes. Seizing on this, she commented, 'Skilful work. What do you write?'

'Of my travels.'

Roslin studied the script. A scant number of repeated symbols were inscribed from right to left across the page, instead of from top to bottom.

Partly gaining time, partly curious, she asked, 'What do you say about us?'

He smiled. 'That the southern polar continent of our legends is no legend. That Asaria is a land in which women head the family; that women here take many husbands – where I come from, men take many wives. And that otherwise the strong oppress the weak, the rich oppress the poor; knaves and fools outnumber wise and honest men; and that the machines of peace are very apt to become the engines of war. In short, that Asaria differs very little from any other continent of the globe.'

' "Engines of war"?' Roslin queried.

'Why, ma'am, consider this: you have your cars not pulled by beasts of burden, what strong and tireless transport they might make for cannon! And your kite-gliders, they would let you know of the enemies' advance long before he sees you. You have ships that need not wait on wind or tide. You have ships of the air. Consider, there is not a city wall that could stand against you!'

Gilvaris Mathury, a little satirically, said, 'Ah, but you see, cities in Asaria have no walls.'

The barbarian inclined his head. 'Indeed, I have studied your Asarian philosophy: its alternative is to put walls around the mind.'

Roslin ignored that. 'In your history, sir, say also that in Asaria women love their husbands, and men love their brothers—'

'Man,' said Gilvaris, 'do you think *we'd* harm him?'

'Let us say,' the barbarian said carefully, 'that *if* there were such a man, and *if* he were due to arrive here, you would have but to wait until he came to the ship. But say also, that you may not be the only ones he is hiding from, and that – if you are seen waiting – you will not be the only ones to find him.'

Seabirds roosting under the eaves of the Oldport houses cried throughout the night. Roslin lay awake. Gil's arms round her were some comfort, but she missed the complementary warmth of Del.

Lovers: husbands: brothers. It was not in her nature, as it was not in Asarian custom, to compare. Two so different: Del with the obsessed disregard of the world that first attracted her, Gilvaris who had spoken of marriage with House Mathury (and only in that moment had it crystallised, to be without either of them was unendurable).

So she had spoken to her mother, head of House Mathury, and little help did she have from a woman whose three husbands had been acquired at different times from all over Asaria. Roslin, nevertheless, married the brothers. And a season later was, by virtue of the plague, left sole survivor and heir of Mathury, which served to bind them closer than was common.

Beside Gilvaris, aware of his quiet breathing, she knew he did not sleep. They lay awake and silent until Daymoon rose.

'Are we right to be here?' Roslin sat on the edge of the bed, lacing up her linen shirt. She could see from their high window the steps of Oldport South Hill, the fishing boats at the quay. 'Can we trust a barbarian?'

'It's all we can do. Can *he* trust us, that's what he'll ask,' Gilvaris's voice was muffled as he pulled on his coat. Adjusting the mirror until the polished basalt oval gave back his reflection, he flicked the lace ruffles into place. 'It could take time to get a message . . . *Quiet!*'

For once he moved faster than Roslin. She barely caught the sound of footsteps on the stairs, and he was by the door, pistol raised. There was a sharp repeated knock.

Roslin grinned, relaxing. 'That's the landlord. Breakfast, I'd guess, and not Arianne Rooke's cut-throats.'

Without releasing the pistol, Gilvaris pulled the door open, surprising the visitor with his hand raised again to knock.

It was Del Mathury.

'It's no good yelling at me!' Del protested. 'I didn't want to be found. I wouldn't be here now, if the barbarian hadn't said it was the only way to stop you turning all Tekne upside down.'

'What the—'

Roslin's temper cooled. She felt the sting of tears behind her eyes.

'What did you think we'd feel like?' she demanded. 'Damn, you might have been dead for all we knew!'

'You knew I'd be all right.' His open face clouded slightly. 'Didn't you? You didn't think I'd . . . it was a matter of staying out of sight until the ship sailed. I was going to send a message to you both then, so that you could join me on board.'

Roslin sighed, sat down on the chair-arm, and put her arm round him. Gilvaris positioned himself protectively behind Del.

It's like Del not to see the obvious. But you knew that when you married him, she reminded herself.

'Del, love, why would we want to go on a barbarian ship? And for that matter, go where?'

'Somewhere I can work without the Port Council bothering me.'

'You're the brilliant one,' Gil said. 'Tell us why we've got to leave, not Port Tekne, not the up-country farms, but all Asaria?'

'Don't be angry with me, Gil.'

'I'm not.'

Roslin had a sudden vision of them as children: the elder brother eternally trailed by, and eternally protective of, the younger. She wondered if either of them coveted the other's relationship with her as she coveted their brotherhood before they ever knew her.

'It was made very clear to me,' Del said, 'when I talked to people, that what I was doing wasn't liked. I don't know why. I don't expect it matters . . . Gil, Ros, I missed you when you weren't here. You'd better come and see what I've been working on.'

Del led them high up among the old deserted houses of the South Hill, below the derelict fort. Roslin was sweating long before they reached the ultimate flight of steps. She saw, across the five-mile span of Tekne, North Hill push out like a fist into the sea, and the kite-gliders and airships anchored on its crest. Inland from the Tekne the country went down into flat haze, broken only by the vanes of wind-and watermills.

'We should have stayed on the estate,' Roslin grumbled. 'You and your machines – Gil's conspiracies – I don't like any of it.'

Del, who was perfectly familiar with that complaint, only grinned. He took them up to the top floors of a derelict mansion that jutted out over the streets below. The walls ran with damp, and clusters of blue and purple fungi grew on the stairs. A continuous thin sound broke the quiet: the sifting of old plaster and stone dust in decay. Roslin smelt musty ages there. The sound of the wind died, and with it the shrieks of birds.

At the very top of the house, in an attic with a shattered dome-roof, Del had set up his makeshift workshop. Half of it was in crates, ready to go aboard the barbarian ship; but Roslin could only concentrate on the massive structure of metal and glass that all but filled the room.

'Look at this.' Del picked up a brass cylinder. Roslin turned it over in her hands, then gave it to an equally puzzled Gilvaris. Del snatched it back impatiently, and manipulated some of the wheels jutting from it. 'No. Like this.'

Dubious, Roslin copied him, holding it to her eye. The metal was cold against her skin. Her lashes brushed the polished surface of the glass. She felt Del take her shoulders and turn her towards the window. She saw a white blur, felt swoopingly dizzy; then as her long sight adjusted she made out houses, streets, tree-ferns . . . And lowered it, and the side of North Hill sprang back five miles into the distance.

Roslin turned the tube in her hands. It was blocked at both ends by glass, one piece of which slid up and down a track inside the tube, adjusted by cogwheels.

Del took it away from her and rubbed her fingermarks off the glass.

'It's a pretty toy,' Gilvaris observed, making the same test, 'but as to people's concern, I confess I don't understand that.'

'The principle can be applied to other things. It's producing the lenses that's most difficult; they have to be ground.'

Roslin, gazing at the arrangement of tubes, prisms, lenses and mirrors that towered over their heads, began to make sense of it.

'Hellfire! I bet you can see as far as the barbarian lands,' she said.

'Further than that—' Del stopped. Gilvaris held up a hand for silence. 'What is it?'

Roslin listened. There was something you couldn't mistake about the tread of armed troops. She moved to look down the stairwell.

She said, 'It's Arianne Rooke.'

'One would suppose we were followed.' Gilvaris leaned over her shoulder.

Roslin saw the first shadow of confusion on Del's face.

'You led them to me,' he said.

'Looks like we did.' There was movement below in the shadowed stairwell. Deliberately she drew the pistol from her greatcoat pocket, cocked it, aimed and fired.

The report half deafened her. A great mass of plaster flaked off the far wall and spattered down the stairs. The scramble of running feet came to an abrupt halt. Roslin handed the pistol back to Gilvaris to reload. She leaned her elbows cautiously on the rail and called down: 'Come up, Arianne. But come up alone – or I'll blow your damned head off.'

*

Arianne Rooke gazed up at the spidering mass of tubes and mirrors and lenses. The late-morning sun struck highlights and reflections from them. Roslin watched her lined, plump face. Her heels clicked as she walked across the floorboards, circling the scope; and she at last came to rest standing with hands clasped on her silver-topped cane. Her braided wig was slightly askew; exertion had left runnels in the dark powder that creased her skin.

'I have thirty men downstairs,' she said without turning to look at anyone there. 'This must be destroyed, of course.'

'You—'

Roslin gripped Del's arm, and he subsided.

Arianne Rooke turned, regarding Gilvaris with some distaste. There was a distinct resemblance between aunt and this one of her nephews. Roslin wondered if that meant Gil would, when he reached that age, be like Arianne. It was an unpleasant thought. And then she wondered if they would – any of them – live to reach Arianne Rooke's age.

'You,' Arianne said, 'I thought you, at least, had some intelligence, Gilvaris.'

'This rivalry between Rooke and Mathury is becoming a little . . .' Gilvaris reflected, '. . . excessive, isn't it?'

The older woman inclined her head. 'Think that, if you will.'

'This won't give you any trade advantage,' Del said, bemused. 'Or is it that you can't bear Mathury to have something Rooke doesn't?'

Roslin caught Gil's eye, and saw him nod.

'Arianne,' she said, 'do you know a woman called Carlin Orme? She's one of my husband's colleagues. She has a printing press. You may know her better as editor of the Port Tekne news-sheet.'

Rooke frowned, but didn't respond.

'I spoke with Carlin Orme last night,' Roslin said. 'And with a number of other news-sheet editors. I thought, in fact, that it would be a good idea if someone other than Arianne Rooke followed us here. They'll be interested to see what my husband Del has discovered. And to know that House Rooke is here with thirty armed men.'

'My dear,' Arianne said, 'never tell me that was your idea?'

'Well, no. Gil's the subtle one. I'd settle for something more straightforward. And permanent.'

The last chimes of noon died on the air.

'Call off your people,' Rooke said, 'and I'll do the same. Quick, now.'

Roslin said, 'I ought to give them something, *Se* Arianne, if I can't give them the treachery of House Rooke. Why shouldn't Tekne know about this?'

The woman looked round at all three of the Mathury. Roslin waited for the outcome of the gamble.

We have to win here, in Tekne, she thought, glancing fondly at Del. Because that ship's a dream – there's nowhere to go.

'Oh, you children!' Arianne Rooke swore explosively. 'You haven't the least idea of . . . Do you know that I can call on the Port Council to silence you? Yes, and silence Carlin Orme and her like, too, if I need. *Se* Roslin, I don't want to have to do that. Your husbands were Rooke before they were Mathury. But I will if I have to!'

'Port Council?' Gilvaris demanded.

For answer, Arianne Rooke drew from under her coat what even they must instantly recognise as being the Great Seal of the Port Tekne Council.

We underestimated you, Roslin thought.

'What *is* all this?' she demanded.

'Delay Carlin Orme.' Rooke reached out with her cane to tilt one of the great framed lenses. 'I'll tell you – no, I'll show you. I'll show you without any of us having to leave this room.'

Arianne Rooke stepped back from the scope, which she had most carefully adjusted. She handled it a sight too familiarly for Roslin Mathury's peace of mind.

'I want you to look through this – *without* upsetting it.' She arrested Roslin's hand. Her fingers were cool, almost chill. 'Each of you. And while you're doing that, I want you to listen to me.'

'So talk.' Roslin, hands clasped behind her back, bent to the eyepiece – and forgot all about listening to Arianne Rooke.

It took a moment for her eyes to focus. One side of her field of vision was starred with the sun's glare, and there was the deep purple-blue of Asaria's summer sky. And . . .

She gazed through the scope at the surface of Daymoon.

All her life it had been familiar, the sister-world that dwarfed the sun in the sky. Now she saw lands, seas, icecaps. The web-work of dry rivers, the arid ochre land; and white cotton that specked the world under it with the minute moving shadows of clouds.

A bright metallic spark travelled across her vision, high over the deserts of Daymoon, a sharp, unnatural shape that fell into shadow as it entered the crescent's darkside. Roslin went cold. Another speck followed. Now she became adept at picking them out, their mechanically perfect flight (and thought, without reason, of Del's workshop and the half-repaired orrery).

'But—' she straightened, blinking. 'Then it's true, the legends are *true*—'

'No,' Rooke said. 'Not now. Now there is nothing there. In all the archives of the Port Council, we have no record of any life. Look at what you do *not* see: patterns, lines, edges. No fields. No canals. No cities.'

'But I saw . . .'

'What you see are machines. Del Mathury, you will most readily comprehend that.'

'I thought as much,' Del admitted, unsurprised.

'Tell me country tales, servants' tales,' Arianne invited Roslin. 'What is there on Daymoon?'

Roslin recalled shadows and firelight, and how tall the world is to a small child.

'Daymoon's a fine world. The people live in crystal houses, and their lanterns burn for ever. They build towers as tall as the sky, and fly faster than any airship ever made. Their carriages outrun the speed of the sun. Each woman there is richer than a *ser* of the Port Council, each man also. They cross the seas and span the land, and no disease touches them.'

Abandoning the child's ritual, still bemused, she said, 'So I was told, when very young. Servants believe it still, and think to go there when they die.'

'Which is well, since few of us can be *ser* here in Asaria,' Gilvaris commented acidly, straightening from the scope. 'Is that what you'd hide, that they've no paradise waiting? That Day-moon is a lie?'

'Daymoon is true. *Was* true,' Rooke corrected herself. 'And you see what is left. To put it most simply: I wish to keep us from that road, the road they followed to destruction. Del Mathury, worlds have been destroyed by those like you.'

Roslin stared blankly. Gilvaris, glancing at Del, thought, No, you're not the first. How many years has the Port Council studied, to be so knowledgeable? And how many years have they kept it secret?

'I have often thought, in all of *that*—' Arianne Rooke's gesture took in light-years, infinity, '—that there must be worlds enough besides us and Daymoon. A million repeated worlds, differing only in small details. No sister-world, perhaps, or no southern Pacific continent, no Asaria, or perhaps a barbarian empire of the north, or – many things.'

Suddenly practical, she turned to Del. 'If you must work, then work *with* the Council.'

Del laughed. ' "Must" work? If no one made anything new, we'd never change.'

'I should not be ashamed to stay as we are now.'

'No, I dare say *you* wouldn't.' Del was caustic.

Roslin said, 'We'd better work out something to tell Carlin Orme.'

There was some argument, Roslin hardly attended. She was watching Arianne Rooke, who stood there with one hand on her cane, and the other tucked into her waistcoat pocket, for all the world like a Fairday shyster.

'I'll talk to Orme,' Gilvaris announced, cutting off further discussion. 'Del, you'd better send word to the barbarian ship.'

Roslin quietly moved aside, to stand near Rooke.

' "Machines"?' she said.

'On Daymoon, they mock the dead race that made them. Is that what you'd have over Asaria?'

She heard unaccustomed seriousness in Rooke's voice.

'Do you think you can undiscover things?' Roslin asked. 'Silence every Del Mathury yet unborn? You're mad!'

'I'm not mad. But I do have visions.' Arianne Rooke laid a dark hand on the scope. 'I believe there is a choice at some point. Perhaps now: an age of reason. And then an age of passionate unreason, ending as you have seen . . . There are scars of war on Daymoon. No, I don't seek to take away the machines, so much as the desire to use them so poorly.'

Roslin said, 'I don't understand you.'

Del, as he went past them, said, 'Arianne Rooke, who gave you the right to play God?'

As close to pain as Roslin had ever seen her, the woman said, 'Nobody.'

Silent for a moment, Roslin watched through the attic doorway as her younger husband went to speak with one of Rooke's armed men.

'How long have you been watching us?'

'Some years. The rivalry between Rooke and Mathury hasn't made it any easier, I'll admit. And for that reason – that you're less likely to believe me – I've taken the rather extraordinary measure of summoning the Port Council to full session. They can confirm what I say.'

After a perfectly-timed pause, she added, 'We shall have to do something for young Mathury.'

'For House Mathury,' Roslin corrected, at last on sure ground. 'Shall we say, a seat on the Council? Gil would be good at that. You see, if Del's going to work with the Council, I think he needs someone there to look out for his interests.'

Arianne Rooke chuckled. 'You bargain well.'

'And you flatter a little, bribe a lot, and hold force as a last card.'

'Which is only to say, my dear, that I'm a politician.'

Roslin squinted up through the broken roof at the sky. An airship glided soundlessly overhead.

'I don't understand what's been happening here.' She met Rooke's gaze. 'I'm missing something. Some chance I ought to take, some question I ought to ask.'

Motionless, watchful, Arianne Rooke gave the conversation more attention than an outsider might think it warranted, and thought to herself, Can this woman, who (let us be honest) is not altogether *bright*, can she come close to a Del Mathury's curiosity? Because if she can . . .

Rooke said, 'And shall I tell you more, *Se* Roslin?'

A silence fell. The sunlight sparked from brass, mirror, lens. And in the pause, it became apparent that Roslin Mathury could not summon so irresponsible a curiosity; did not desire, or see the need for it.

'No,' she said, smiling. 'Leave me to run the Mathury estates without your interference. That's all I want. Now do you think we should go and bring a little order out of this chaos?'

Rooke thought, I spoke with a barbarian once, what did he say? 'Putting a wall around the mind . . .'

The Archivist pauses.

That last sentence, true in its way, fails to suggest the whole truth. She carefully erases it.

Outside, bells ring gladly, and pennant ribbons uncoil on the breeze. She blinks away images three generations dead. Sees Tekne, now little changed. Fewer airships, fewer steamcars (but there are always servants to do the work). The only significant change is that there are barbarians in the streets.

But really, one shouldn't call them that. Not with the ser-Lords of all four continents here to celebrate the centennial of the Pax Asaria. And what better to encourage them in Asarian philosophy than a dramatic reading? She thinks, smiling at her own vanity.

Even if such turning points in history are largely guesswork . . .

In haste to join the carnival, the Archivist inscribes her final lines:

Arianne Rooke, alone and last to leave, adjusted one of the free lenses to catch the sunlight through the broken roof. She walked unhurriedly away. Where the sun focused, a thin wisp of smoke coiled acridly up from the wooden attic floor.

Afterword

Unusually for me, the title came first for this one – or rather, I had two titles and they cross-bred. 'Sun Magic' and 'A Clock in the Attic' sat in my notebook for a long time, until they mutated into an image I liked. So far, I never have got round to writing 'Clock Magic' . . .

For me, there's a lot of internal tension in this story.

Like most of us, I suppose, I'm always conscious of how fragile technological society is – not the machines so much as the shape of mind that makes them. Not long before I wrote 'A Sun in the Attic', I was reading Arthur Koestler's *The Sleepwalkers*, which – whatever holes you can pick in his theories – is fascinating on the double rise of science in history, first in Greece and mainland Asia, c. 600BC, and then in England and Western Europe, c. 1600-1770AD.

The gap between – the two thousand five hundred year gap between – has small tides of science that ebb and flow, but, until the swell starts to gather in the late Medieval West, nothing that matters. If it's not a dark age, it's still a period where most people, most of the time, stopped thinking in a particular way.

And I find that scary. So I ended up with the alternate-universe eighteenth century city of Tekne, and Daymoon, where the barbarians are not (I hope) who you first think they are. 'The room is not guarded. There is not the necessity.' The story came out of fear and irritation sparked by the view that, if something can be used badly, it should stop being used at all.

But I can see the other side of it.

I was writing about Daymoon's war-destroyed surface during the Cold War – ironically, four or five years before the Berlin Wall came down, and what had seemed a permanent state of societies melted like frost.

Asaria's change of society is low-key, but that's because it's a change back to stasis. The people are safe from dangers; closed to opportunities. It's impossible to disparage peace, and yet . . .

Tensions.

If I'd had more story-space, I would have liked to go deeper into the triune marriage of Roslin and Del and Gilvaris. And airships. But the story wouldn't let me: sometimes they do that.

A Shadow Under the Sea

'Look!' Ellis shouted. 'It's happening again – now!'

Spurlock took the ancient spyglass from her, training it on the sea. Light blinded her, images blurred: then she focused on the distant fishing boat.

'I see nothing.'

'Wait – there!'

The seawind whipped around them where they stood on the beacon hill. Under the cliffs, the tide beat against Orindol's coast. A calm summer day, nothing to trouble a ship's crew – particularly a crew from the Hundred Isles.

'There's nothing we can do, lady,' Ellis of Orindol said bitterly. 'Even if we had another ship out there, what could they do against *that* ?'

Distant, soundless: Spurlock saw the tragedy. The fishing boat (every minute detail clear, down to the nets spilling silver on her decks, the barefoot running sailors) heeled over and shipped water. Waves broke, spray flew. The boat was tangled in a great bed of floating weed . . .

'Clingweed?'

'I wouldn't bring you all the way from Shabelit for that, lady.'

The boat turned broadside to the wind, shipping water, foundering. Spurlock saw the crew running this way and that in panic, saw the soundless gouts of spray where they threw themselves overboard, and the weed-mass moved—

Moved lazily, opened a mouth of darkness.

Timbers floated on the water. Nothing else of the ship remained. The water swirled, then quietened, where the last man had been swimming desperately for the beach.

A great mass slid into the depths, out of sight of the spyglass, down into the hidden darkness. Spurlock lowered the glass, blinking at the suddenly-removed world. She was cold.

'That outsizes my largest ships,' she said.

'It's taken five boats in the last month,' Ellis said. 'Each time the crews were – killed. Only a coaster escaped – perhaps because the beast had fed, I don't know – to bring us the news. We didn't believe. Now it comes to our very shore. Lady, you must help us.'

Gulls cried, soaring in the middle air between beacon hill and the roofs of Orindol. Spurlock looked down on peaked roofs, tiled and slanting, bowed with age. The early light sent the gull's shadows darting across clapboard walls. Down on the beach, men and women were clustered round the net-drying sheds, talking in the shade of the tall tarred buildings. Fishing-boats were drawn up on the shingle. The fishmarket was closed for lack of business, and there too the Orindol islanders stood talking. The bright sea was empty.

You cannot have the Hundred Isles forbidden the sea, Spurlock thought, chilled. All the Shabelit Archipelago has trade for its life-blood.

'You're First in Council,' Ellis urged, 'you're lady of Shabelit itself. Help us!'

'That's nothing to send spears against. It would take a warship down as easily as a fishing boat. I won't send Shabelit's galleys.'

Ellis looked hopelessly at her. 'I know. I knew before I came to Shabelit. We can't kill it. But what am I to say to my people?'

What am I to say to mine? Spurlock thought, with a certain grim humour. How long will I be First in Council if I go away wringing my hands and crying defeat? More to the point, how long will the Peace of Shabelit last when the Hundred Isles hear of it?

The younger woman said, 'In the old time, they made sacrifices to the Kraken. That will begin again, now it has returned.'

'The Kraken is a myth. That's a sea-beast, nothing more. Listen to me,' Spurlock linked arms with the young islander, leading her down the track toward the village, 'the first thing you must do is leave poisoned bait. Float out a raft with rotten carcasses on it; let it take that for a guts-ache. If that doesn't discourage it, we'll think again.'

She left Ellis and the Orindol islanders working and went back aboard the warship. She dismissed all except her aide.

'Well, lady?' Dinu asked. 'Will you call the Council to Shabelit?'

'Too long a delay. They'd have to come from all the Hundred Isles. It's all stopgap measures! Sit down,' she said, knowing that his wound from the long-past Bazuruk campaign still troubled him. 'You're a south-islander. Tell me all the legends you know about the Kraken. I have to think quickly.'

'We've lived well under the Peace of Shabelit,' Ellis said. Rain had darkened her fair hair, her plain tunic and britches. The *Wind's Eye* rocked gently on the swell. 'But if we can't fish, or trade . . . that's when the fighting begins. Durinsir, Merari, Gileshta, Orindol; we're none of us wealthy islands. Lady, if your warships should be penned up in Shabelit—'

'Let's not anticipate. I've no wish to see the old days back. Island against island . . .' Spurlock shook her head. She wondered if Ellis were old enough to have fought in the last wars, the wars that Spurlock had led to bring about the Peace. 'The poison failed?'

'Perhaps it is no ordinary beast.'

In the silence, the summer rain was loud; and under it they heard – as you hear anywhere in the Shabelit Archipelago – the beating of the sea.

'Then it will take no ordinary means to defeat it. In my judgement, no other weapon but sorcery. I will leave you my Second, Dinu Vanathri; he will direct you to feed carcasses to the beast, so that it leaves your ships.'

'We haven't enough to feed a Kraken's hunger!'

'For a while,' Spurlock said. 'I am going south, to the Cold Lands.'

Ellis shivered. 'Lady, I do not know who has the greater peril; we who stay, or you who go to – that land.'

'They have powers. We must turn some weapon against the beast.'

The Orindol woman bowed respectfully. 'I wish you safe voyaging, lady. And I beg you; be as swift as you may. For all our sakes.'

The First in Council should have been received with great honour in the Cold Lands cities, anywhere from Sakashu to

Tulkys. Instead, Spurlock took the *Wind's Eye* down past Goldenrock and the Spice Isles, avoiding the populous regions of the Cold Lands, and came within the month to a narrow fiord far down the southern coast.

She left the ship moored there, taking none of her guards when she went ashore.

The valley grass was lush, rising to meet the blue-black forest that seamlessly covered each dip and hollow of the foothills. Above the tree-line, naked rock rose up to the snow. Sharp and cold, glittering white against a sky so dark a blue as to be almost purple: mountains. The wind blew damp.

How long since I went alone into wild country? Too long, she answered herself. A First in Council gains enemies.

She strode on, still a little uncertain of the solid ground after the shifting deck of the *Wind's Eye*. Herds grazed on the lower pastures, and the herders had pitched their skin tents by the river. They sent her on into the hills, towards the mountains and the pass that led eventually to great Tulkys. There, by a spring, she found a stone hut; beehive-shaped, a thin grey trail coiling from the smokehold. *Maresh-kuzor*: the shaman's house.

Spurlock hesitated. Many years had passed since she came to Tulkys, or crossed the pass, or visited the valley.

'Ash!' she called.

When the sound had died, the skin curtain of the hut was pulled back and a woman came out. She wore a skin tunic and leggings. Animal teeth hung on thongs round her neck and were bound into her braided grey hair. As she approached, Spurlock caught the smell of animal fat.

'You look well,' she said.

The shaman woman gazed at her. It was oddly disconcerting. Partly it was that her pale eyes, under the broad forehead, were set wide apart; she stared bird-like first from one eye, then the other. Partly it was her indefinable aura of power.

'I know why you are here,' she said. 'The far-sight brought me a vision of you. Come in, my sister. Talk if you will. I warn you now: I will not leave the mountains. I will not come to the islands.'

Spurlock nodded. 'Yes. We need to talk.'

The years were treating Ash well, Spurlock thought. Apart

from the grey hair, you wouldn't guess that she – a handful of years older than Spurlock – must be close on her fiftieth winter.

'I have an armed company on the ship,' Spurlock said confidently. 'I could have come here with them. Or, with a little more time, those in Tulkys would have commanded you to my aid. I won't tell you how Shabelit will reward you, because what would that mean to you? I can't bribe or force you. All I can do is come here and ask. Ash, the islands need your help.'

The high air was cold. Pale sun gleamed through the hut's entrance. They sat facing each other over the fire-pit. Spurlock leaned back against the rough wall, shifted her scabbarded blade.

'I can't help you. This beast—'

'This beast,' Spurlock said, 'is the Kraken.'

Ash was quiet. At last she said, 'Away from this land, my powers are small. If other shamans were with me . . . but none will leave; and they are too widely scattered to be found quickly.'

'If you need help, I'm of your blood.' Spurlock moved as the setting sun shone in her face. 'Will you have it known in Tulkys that you're half-islander?'

'Will you have it known in Shabelit that you are half blood of the Cold Lands?' Ash's gaze was steady. 'I cannot speak untruth. You know that.'

Spurlock scratched through her cropped hair and sighed. 'Ash, I don't like to say this, but . . . I looked after you when we were children, when we thought you were – before we knew it was the shaman-power.'

'And you will say I owe you a debt – you, First of Shabelit?'

Taken by surprise, Spurlock laughed. 'No. No, I don't think I'll try and persuade you of that.'

Ash smiled, losing twenty years. For the first time, there was the old warmth between them.

'Your way isn't my way,' Spurlock admitted, 'and I have to say I like most things that go with being First of Shabelit. I've earned them. But peace is a fragile thing. You're not stupid, you can see what will happen if I'm beaten here. Every minor lord between here and the Bazuruk coast will be grabbing whatever he or she can get. Then I've to fight all the last battles over again – and I'm not as young as I was.'

'And then,' Ash said softly, 'there is the beast.'

Spurlock nodded mutely.

'Wait,' Ash said. 'I'll see what I see.'

Spurlock settled herself in the smoky interior of the hut. Ash went out to the forest, returning some time later with her hands full of small scarlet fungi. She let the skin curtain fall, cutting them off from light and air. She fed the fire, chewing on the fungi, fed it until the stones in the fire-pit glowed white.

In the hot darkness, Spurlock edged back against the stone wall. She was sweating heavily; the palms of her hands were slick. She thought, What am I bringing back to Orindol?

Ash took up a wooden bucket and threw water on the stones. A sheet of steam hissed up. Spurlock's nails dug bloody imprints in her palms. Her lungs were seared, her eyes wept.

In the long darkness, Ash cried out.

Air was cold on her skin. She blinked, dazzled by early sunlight, and saw above treetops the floating crests of mountains. The stones under her were cold and hard.

My old bones don't like this, she thought as she stood and stiffly brushed herself down.

'Ah.' Ash came out of the hut. Briefly she laid her hand on Spurlock's forehead. 'You have returned, good. Do you remember anything of your time in the Otherworld?'

Spurlock adjusted the laces of her mail, and her sword-belt, before she answered.

'I'm a soldier, not a shaman.'

Ash nodded. 'I will remind you, as I was with you. This I learned from the Otherworld. Your Kraken is one of those elementals that cannot be killed – she is Water. You can no more slay her than you can prevent the tides.'

Spurlock was surprised by a sudden total and overwhelming terror. She gasped as if it was actual pain. When it ebbed, she saw Ash nod.

'Yes. That is the other thing. You islanders depend on the sea. Your children walk decks before they touch land. Yet you suffer foul winds, rocks, treacherous currents, storms . . . she is your special fear, the Kraken; the shadow-soul of the sea itself.'

More incredulous than offended, Spurlock said, 'You're calling me a coward.'

'You come from Shabelit and see the beast . . . you could

have sent word by your Second, I know Dinu Vanathri, but no; you board the *Wind's Eye* and sail from Orindol as fast as the winds will take you.'

'I had to speak with you,' Spurlock protested angrily.

'It will be the same for any islander. She is your fear.'

'If you're telling me you won't help us—'

'I didn't say that.' Ash regarded her sadly. 'I will need your help, sister; but even the sea can be contained. It will not be easy. It may fail. But I will come with you to Orindol.'

Spurlock studied the charts, and they sailed back up the Archipelago by a route that kept them away from deep water. Ash insisted they stop at Goldenrock, where they took on bales of the weed the islanders call *dekany*. She sat cross-legged on the deck, stumpy fingers knotting a five-stranded web. The *Wind's Eye* sailed, the web grew, and before midsummer's day passed they anchored off Orindol. Ellis and Dinu were there to greet her.

'It's taken ships as far north as Shabelit itself,' Dinu said, limping up the shingle beside her. 'We thought we'd lost it to Bazuruk's coast, then it was sighted off Sephir, and a few days ago here at Orindol again. Half the Council's here.'

'And in a panic, I'd lay bets.'

'You'd win, lady.' He glanced behind, where the shaman woman was being ferried ashore by Spurlock's guard. 'Is that . . . can she help us?'

Spurlock avoided the question. 'Ellis, I want all the animal carcasses you can find and spare, on the nearest islands too, as well as Orindol. Dump them where the current will take them out toward the Western Ocean. I want that beast fed.'

'We'll do it,' Ellis said.

We must be close to it, Ash had said. You must help me, sister.

Spurlock refused to acknowledge her fear. 'When you've done that,' she said, 'find me a small boat – one that can be crewed by two.'

Her legs felt loose behind the knees, and her stomach churned. It was a long time since she'd sailed a boat, and she was clumsy. This isn't nerves before battle, she thought, remembering the dry-mouthed excitement that changes to exultation. This is fear.

The boat slid down a hill of water. Waves smacked the bows,

and spray shot into the air. Sunlight refracted rainbows. As they
came into deeper water the swells calmed. Orindol slid east
away from them.

Ash sat with her back to the coffin-sized cabin, checking the
knots. Stones weighted the net. It was smaller than even an
Orindol fishing-boat's net.

'You must cast it,' she said. 'I will chant the protection on us.
If I fail in that, then it will take us.'

Spurlock was lashing the tiller. 'You haven't seen it. It's the
Kraken! That net wouldn't hold a rock-devil or dire-shark,
never mind . . . ah, what's the use.'

Ash smiled.

'You might as well hope to net Orindol itself.'

'Then why are you here?' the shaman woman asked.

'Those credulous fools on the Council would tell you I won't
send someone else to do what I wouldn't do myself – and it's
good for me they think that. I won't tell them we're sisters. But
believe me, if you didn't need blood kin to help you, I'd be
ashore with those others, cheering you on.' Spurlock recovered
confidence when she heard Ash laugh. 'Stand away. We don't
need the sail now; we'll drift.'

She lashed the sail tight. She went to the side. The ship was so
low in the water, she could have dipped her hand in it. The sun
shone down, picking out grains of silt. Clear water for a few feet,
then murkiness; gold, gold-green, dark. She strained her eyes,
searching for movement. A shoal of minute fish darted past,
sparking briefly in the sun.

Behind her, Ash breathed in sharply. '*Arak-sha u elish tu—*'

The chant continued urgently. In the depths there was movement. A dark sliding: rising to the edge of vision.

Spurlock saw brown scales crusted with barnacles, clotted
with weed; brown scales edged with black. Plate-scales the size
of a man's body. Sliding past under them, endless. She stared
down into the clear water, searching.

There was no end. To either side the scaled body glided by, a
scant few feet under the surface. Seeing it from the beacon hill,
one had no idea of its size. Its shadow darkened the sea as far
as she could see. The boat was a wood chip floating above it.
Crusted flesh gliding under them, bulking in the depths. The
boat so fragile, so easily shouldered off into the water—

She was on her knees, her hands knotted on the rail. They were out of sight of Orindol, of any of the islands. There was only the empty circle of the horizon, the tossing boat, and the monstrous body of the Kraken under them. She saw it curve; they spun like a chip in the whirlpool of its turning.

One of the carcass-loaded rafts drifted ahead of them. Spurlock saw the darkness rise. It broke the surface, curving above them, a sliding hoop of flesh that streamed water. The pale underside was puckered with rosettes of suckers. Gently, scarcely seeming to brush it, the loop of muscle closed over the raft. Wood creaked, split with a sound like gunshots. The raft broke up.

'. . . *anu-elish geir u turaksha ke—*'

Ash's voice rose higher. The weights of the net rolled against Spurlock. Her hands locked on the rail. A lurch of the boat nearly jerked her arms from her shoulders. Spray flooded them. A wave burst over the side. Salt water burned her mouth and lungs. She choked.

'—*shansa ke anu* – Spurlock! —*anu keshta kerasha—*'

Ash clung with both hands to the edge of the cabin, chanting, her face twisted with concentration. The coiled net spilled across the deck. Spurlock saw it. She should move, cast it.

The dark behind her eyes was speckled red. She flattened herself against the deck, clinging to ropes, to the mast, to anything. Nails broke, rope-burn scarred her arms. Wood was rough under her cheek.

'—*kazarak u elish-nar—*'

The begging appeal in Ash's voice forced her eyes open. A hill of flesh reared up against the sky. Crusted with weed; white foam spuming down, slicing

Ash let go the ship, swept and cast the net. The sheer effort halted the chant. She stumbled with the words, missed the rhythm.

The deck slammed against Spurlock's head. She tasted blood. Her eyes clamped shut. She clung to the rail. Under her the world shifted on its foundations. Ash screamed.

The beast came.

Wavelets slapped the side of the boat. All else was silent. The heat of the sun dried her and left salt caked and cracking on her skin. Her hands bore the raw imprint of rope. She stood, slipped down on hands and knees, shaking so violently that she couldn't get up again.

The sea was calm. Snagged on the prow of the boat, the *dekany* weed net was full, stretching with the weight of its catch. Darkness coiled and thrashed in the meshes. At sight of that transformation, she made a dry, unrecognizable sound. It was laughter, relief at being alive, at having survived.

Ash lay cramped between the mast and the cabin. Blood soaked the soft skin tunic, now ragged. Shoulder, ribs, hip and leg were torn with bloody disc-imprints.

Spurlock crawled across to her. The woman was breathing shallowly.

It's over, Spurlock thought. Hoist the sail and go home. Go home and tell them when Spurlock of Shabelit, First in Council, fought the Kraken – she fell down and cried like a newborn brat. Tell them that, Lady of the Hundred Isles.

She lowered her head and shut her eyes, hot with shame and despair at this final failure, where success was most needed. All the hard years between a beggar-brat's childhood in Tulkys and the High Council of Shabelit fell away as if they had never been, as if she had never fought her way up, never imposed peace on the Hundred Isles.

Ash's pulse was irregular. The blood pulsed slower now, soaking the deck. Quick attention might save her. If they reached Orindol . . .

If I'd awakened a little later.

Spurlock cursed, driving the thought from her mind. It returned. Sister she might be, liar she could never be: Ash would say, when anyone asked her, precisely what had happened here in the Western Ocean. And they would ask. And they would spread the story from one end of the Archipelago to the other: Spurlock has turned coward. The peace is ended. Each island turning against the other.

Spurlock saw very clearly what would happen to the First in Council who had betrayed them.

Ash's eyes opened, sought her face.

'I may be corrupt,' Spurlock said, 'but I'm the best chance the islands have. What about Ellis and Orindol? They won't care about the truth. All they want is to live in peace.'

The shaman woman tried to speak and choked. A thin line of blood ran out of her mouth and down her neck.

'I didn't work all those years,' Spurlock said, 'to give up what I have now.'

She sat by the mast, leaning back against the lashed-down sail, and waited.

It was Dinu Vanathri who found her. The celebrations in the great palace at Shabelit were in their third day and showed no sign of slackening. Spurlock was being hailed as the greatest hero since Bran Double-Axe. He found her in the inner court-yard where fountains tumble into a marble pool deep as a well.

'Lady?'

She was looking into the water. A lean aging woman, court clothes uncomfortable on her as battle-gear never was; a sandy-haired woman with a lined face, and the first hints of age in her movements. Dinu stood beside her.

In the black depths, scales glinted. He saw a coiling far down in the water, glimpses of the Kraken seen as if through the wrong end of a spyglass. He thought of it as he'd seen it off Orindol, and his skin crawled.

'The delegation from the Cold Lands is here,' he said. 'They would like to take the body of the shaman woman back to Tulkys. The lords of the Council say she should be buried here, since it was she who aided you, and so aided us too.'

'She was a brave woman,' Spurlock said. 'We will set up her image in the Great Hall. Let them take her. She loved Tulkys. It's fitting she should lie there.'

'She was your friend.' Dinu absently ground his knuckle into his aching hip and shifted his stance. 'It's a bad thing when friends die.'

'I wouldn't be where I am without her.'

Down in the shadows, the Kraken stilled.

'Come on,' Spurlock said and clapped him cheerfully on the shoulder. 'Let's go back to the celebrations. It's what Ash would want us to do, isn't it?'

Afterword

So, people have strange phobias, right?

I'm phobic about big fish.

You can stop laughing now . . .

It's not just fish, I have to say; whales will do it, and dolphins, and giant squid. It's the knowledge that, from a ship's rail, you're looking down a *long* way – deep enough that, if it was 'high' instead of 'deep', people would be terrified. And the sea is, in European waters, mostly murky. Beyond a few yards, you can't see what's down there. You just know it *is* there. Huge; under the surface; rising up to the edge of visibility. . .

So, okay, it's not like it gives me problems eating whitebait, or hoovering my way through fish and chips. Far from it. But the Kraken in 'A Shadow Under The Sea' was in part an attempt to make that phobic feeling visible in a character. I don't know if I succeeded.

Spurlock's another early version of a character that fascinates me: the person who betrays. Betrays for whatever reason – but usually 'for the greater good', because therein lies moral ambiguity. Choosing good over evil is easy. Choosing evil-in-this-way over evil-in-that-way isn't so easy, but it's just as likely to be the choice that needs taking.

The story takes place in the same fantasy world, or section of it – the Hundred Isles – that 'Anukazi's Daughter' does. Despite the publication dates, 'A Shadow Under the Sea' was in fact written second. Spurlock is a general and a powerful politician, whereas Rax was a soldier and otherwise powerless; I wanted, I think, to see if moving up the ladder of power would make the 'swordswoman' story end up any happier.

Not this time around . . .

Human Waste

My child is a pet substitute.

I designed it to be male, to get my own back on men in general. I see nothing wrong in this. My therapist advised me to get rid of my aggression.

The sun is slanting through the window, striping the polished floorboards. The room smells of beeswax. Little Thomas is pulling at my hip with chocolate-covered hands. He stinks of ammonia. I haven't changed him for days.

'Mummy? Mummy? Mummy? Mummy?'

He hits the same pitch every time. Exactly the same questioning whine. I didn't have to alter the basic design specification for this, it seems to come to all of them with their DNA.

'*Mummy? Mummy? . . .*'

The creases of my black denim jeans at my hip are marked with melted chocolate. I hate that. I hate it so much.

'Muh—'

As I have done so many times before, but with no less satisfaction, I lift Thomas by his little romper-suit collar, pivot in the swivel chair, draw my foot back, and kick.

It is satisfyingly solid, like kicking a warm sandbag. Even painful, given how solid a two-year-old is. Nothing else, however, gives the right trajectory, the right *thump*! on landing.

'Whaaaaaaaaaa—'

The small body impacts with the floor on the far side of the room. I can see at a glance that he has broken his neck, and that the downy hair on his skull is matted with blood where he has fractured the fragile bone plates. I lean my elbow on the desk and watch.

Nanoscopic structures scurry across the body of my baby.

They ooze from his pores, micro-machines crafted so small

that their gears are atom-sized, their manipulators capable of juggling basic matter. Nature gave us the prototype of such machines a milliard ago: the organic cell. My nanoscopic devices are merely non-organic improvements.

The grey goo flows, tide-like, as if a time-elapsed mould were growing on the little corpse. In thirty seconds it flows back, vanishing into his bone-cavities that are designed specifically for nano-constructors.

Little Thomas, stiff-armed and stiff-legged, pushes himself up onto his feet and patters back across the floorboards.

'A'gen!' he demands. Breathy. ''Gen! Do it 'gen!'

I didn't say I designed him to be bright.

He pulls at my thigh. This time the kick is a reflex, the anger something bright and shaded and brilliant to go with. So far as I'm concerned, the pain he gave me getting out of my birth canal entitles me to anything I do.

Whomph!

'Whaaaaa—'

Thud.

Patter, patter, patter.

''Gen! 'Gen! 'Gen!'

The day he starts getting intelligent is the day I'll reprogramme him. I shouldn't have to. The nano-repairers in his body are extremely specialised – part of one of the medical projects for which I've earned such astonishingly large amounts of money. One of their design-tasks is to continually maintain a constant state of body and brain from day to day. Thomas is chronologically six now, but biologically he is still two.

I'll keep him this way. He might grow up to be one of those youths outside the apartment in loose shirts and trousers whose bones, ramshackle-tall, always seem on the verge of folding up like a deckchair. At fourteen he could be physically stronger than I am.

He doesn't have much of a memory, either. I haven't quite worked out whether that's part of my design specs, or whether Nature (that outmoded concept whom I flatter myself I somewhat resemble) is being kind. Don't count on it. Nature doesn't care much about individuals. She's not that kind to species, and I have a suspicion the entire biosphere could flip over to a white-state ice planet and She wouldn't be much bothered. As I always tell my students in web tutorials, don't care if you fuck about with Gaia. She doesn't care about you.

My co-workers John and Martin are invaluable in web tutorials. When I say *invaluable*, of course, I mean capable of being exactly valued. I am still paid one third less than they are.

A warm and breathing little body, wet about the crotch, is trying to climb onto my lap.

Whomph!

'Whaaaaa—'

Thud.

Patter, patter, patter.

''Gen! 'Gen! 'Gen!'

Thomas does look like Thomas – his father, I mean. Actually I have nothing against Thomas Erpingham, as such; he is not one of the men I imagine when I break Little Thomas's arms. It's a pity the child has his blue eyes, and his black hair. I would quite have liked it if it had taken after me. I suppose I should have paid more attention to that side of the DNA-twiddling.

I left my various machines talking to the web and went to have a shower. Sometimes I take Little Thomas into the bath and play with him. Sometimes I even don't drown him.

Today I wanted to be on my own, and locked the bathroom door, from time to time turning down the jets so that I could hear the child screaming for food and water. The nanotech makes sure he doesn't die – the micro-machines photo-synthesize for him – but water can be a problem. Dehydration makes him listless. Still, to look on the bright side, I have got good laughs over the web when I remark that I forgot to water the baby.

The shower bounced jets off my freckled skin, warmed, scented and dried me. I don't look at my hands too often these days, although it is a remarkably difficult thing to avoid one's own hands. The scars are gone, nanotech repairers of my own make certain of that. They have, however, the same familiar shape they have always had. Stubby, with strong nails. All they lack is the coarse black hairs.

Familiar, of course, meaning: pertaining to the family. Yes, they are my father's hands. I could alter them. I prefer not to.

'*Mummy!* I want to watch a *vid-yo*.'

I padded across the floor and flipped the wallscreen to the

rolling news channel. There is a small war going on somewhere in the south; they imprison the women in camps and rape them, force them to have the soldiers' babies. Let him watch that.

Sometimes he manages to change the channel when I'm not watching. I keep a thin steel car aerial for those moments.

I continued on into the kitchen and opened the freezer.

'*Fat!*' the fridge-demon screamed. 'You're on a di-et!'

It swung on its over-long arms, wide-toothed face grinning up at me. I used miniaturised orang-utan stock for the base model. Today I didn't have much of a sense of humour.

'Fat – *awp!*'

The fridge-demon bounced off the freezer door, smacked face-down onto the floor, and lay still, flattened. I rubbed my knuckles while its nano-fabricators grew it back, plumped it up, like a balloon with air swelling into it. Pop! Demon-shaped again.

It whimpered back into a corner of the fridge, down by the light, sulking.

'You've got nothing to complain about,' I muttered automatically.

The heat-treatment of unprepared foodstuffs is one of my hobbies, sometimes I can lose myself in it quite satisfactorily. Today I lost the better part of one finger to an over-enthusiastic cheese-grater, and stood biting my lip and dripping over the sink as muscle tissue and skin were nanoscopically rebuilt – never quite fast enough to stem the pain. I lost my appetite.

Sun leaked through the kitchen window between the high-rise blocks. Mostly we find it fashionable, here, to use nano-fabricators only on biological things. There are other quarters of the city where inanimate objects are as mutable as flesh. You can never find your way to the same place twice, usually because it isn't there.

'Thomas!'

He stumped up, determined, on his sturdy feet. Pleased to be called by name, I think. Mostly I whistle for him and he comes. For a moment I touched the warm flesh of his arm, then I slipped the collar over his head and tightened the choke-chain leash, and opened the door into Spring.

I love the streets when they smell of grass and petrol. There are three city parks close to my apartment, I chose the nearest. For a while, enjoying the warmth of the sun, I carried Little

Thomas, holding him by one leg and listening to the piercing screams. In the park there are pigeons. I sat on a bench and let him run around in the sun. There is a road crosses the park, and the traffic is not too careful. There's a chance of him being hit by something – a truck, maybe – so comprehensively that all my nanotech couldn't put Little Thomas back together again. It adds a pleasurable tension to the afternoon. I really don't want to have to start at the beginning and give birth again. Twice was enough.

'Ms?'

This one I recognised. He was another pet-walker, a man in his thirties with an appallingly acned skin. I kept an eye on the grass and the pond, where Little Thomas was busy running up to the bio-ducks and running away again, giggling. This guy's pet hung back, eyes wary.

'No,' I said. 'No, I don't want to hear your story. I don't want to hear how your father fucked you and your younger brother for eight years, and you only went to the police when he started in on the baby. I don't want to hear how your uncle and your cousins used to fuck you from the age of five, and how you *liked* it because it was the only time they ever noticed you were there.'

He looked bewildered. I pointed to his pet, with a certain economy of movement. Even today I am chary of wasting energy; you never know when you will need it.

'Male owner, male pet,' I explained. 'Only the details are going to be different.'

He had nice eyes. I thought of when I put my thumbs into Little Thomas's eyes and they pop like fibrous tomatoes. I couldn't attack this man with the pizza skin, he weighed fifteen stone if he was an ounce, and he (being male) had thirty per cent more upper-body strength than I had.

I got up, the afternoon spoiled, deciding to go home for a vigorous play-session with Little Thomas, and a languorous finger-fuck in the afternoon's remaining sun.

'I thought . . .' the man said hesitantly. 'We might have something in common. Something to talk about.'

What he thought he could possibly have to say to me defeats me. *Sorry* would be nice. What would be nice, actually, would be if he took out a rusty breadknife and sawed open his stomach, and sawed off his cock, and let that say *sorry* for him. But, optimistic as I am about life, I didn't think this was going to happen.

I walked off without looking back, whistling, and strolled so that Little Thomas could catch up. One of the ducks had taken his eye out, I saw. The nanotech repairers were busy, a grey iridescent film over the empty socket. For some time I amused myself by walking on his blind side and listening to him cry.

The city rises up around me.

Even if I weren't working on the web, there is no one I would go to meet. No one I would talk to. I inhabit a different planet. Those who could talk, like the man with the diseased skin, I prefer not to communicate with. I have a strong dislike of communication.

I walk back through residential streets, dodging little piles of excrement on the paving stones. A whiny cry of 'Tired!' pursues me. I bend down and pick Little Thomas up.

His clothes are beyond repair. I strip him and drop them in the gutter. He clings, his naked arms around my neck, nuzzling. A warm body, legs locked around my jutting hip. As I said, he isn't bright. He is affectionate.

That is the only thing I fear.

No – there are two things:

One day I'll get bored with Little Thomas – it just won't be enough any more.

Or else I'll start to love him.

Afterword

'Human Waste' got a review when it first came out, calling it the most morally reprehensible biotech story the reviewer had ever read. Being me, I was immensely pleased by this.

If it *wasn't* a disturbing concept, I'd worry.

Some people can have twisted motivations when they have children, but that isn't where the story started in my head – it came from a quite different direction. I was being annoyed by people who don't get the point of animals, and insist on regarding them (loudly) as other people's 'child-substitutes'. To me, the point about animals is that they're animals.

And the first line of the story popped out of nowhere into my mind. Although, possibly not coincidentally, it happened when I was in the town centre, one sunny afternoon on a weekend, amongst the buggy-pushers and toddler-herders and passing crowds and general frustration. 'My child is a pet substitute.' Some people have pets, too, for very dubious reasons.

And nanotech seemed the ideal way to have a child-pet . . .

I liked the voice that came with the story, and how blatant it was: I still do. And the black humour, and the cheerful cruelty. She's bitter, but she's not prejudiced. And she rejects all the comforting lies of therapy and recovery that she's evidently been offered.

It's not the only take on the subject that's possible – as regards both abuse and nanotech – but dark is true, too.

CARTOMANCY: Conclusion

Outside the gallery windows, dawn coloured the air vibrantly peach and azure above Huirac City and the Citadel. A fresh breeze blew in, smelling of overripe plumes and urine.

The halfling barbarian padded close on jungle-warfare-silent feet. She rubbed the grease of a stolen meal from her shining lips, wiped her tiny hand across her silver-chain and chamois-leather breechclout, and stared up at the elf.

'Sieur-Father . . . ?' Zerra purred questioningly.

The Elected Pontiff waved her aside with irritation. His plume of azure hair fell ragged and sweat-stained about his pointed ears, and his white surcoat was stained with the previous day's ascetic consumption of wine and seed-biscuits. Items of discarded armour lay scattered about the gallery, beneath the various maps. Elthyriel's long eyes were green with exhaustion.

For the last eleven hours he had forgotten to eat.

'Don't bother me, halfling!'

She stood, buxom body hipshot, her magnificent mane of dark hair on a level with the elf's sword-belt, and he did not even spare one glance as she preened. The halfling shrugged; a movement also with its salacious aspect.

'I admit one may learn much of evil from these maps, Sieur-Father,' Zerra ventured, testing, 'but the lengthy time you spend here . . . there may be victims in need of Virtue's succour.'

Elthyriel's bleary eyes did not focus. His aquiline elvish face was shadowed with exhaustion, gaunt as a lich. 'I must learn. *I must learn.* All the secrets of Evil, all the weakness of the Dark . . .'

'But, Sieur-Father, suppose you are needed *now*?'

The Knight-Patriarch spun round unsteadily. 'Get out of my sight!'

Zerra moved back two strides with the smoothness of a fighter. Her ankle-rings jingled. 'You owe us our payment, Eminence.'

'Go. There will be none. Be thankful I do not have you thrown in the Citadel's dungeons, for taking my attention from this!'

'But your oath?'

'Don't bother me with trivia!'

Avid, the elven Pontiff turned back to the blue and gold walls. He stared, his thin finger hovering. At last, with a widening grin of anticipation, he pointed a bitten fingernail and murmured: 'I name thee . . . *Thamys-river*.'

Zerra walked backwards with her eyes fixed on the transfixed Knight-Patriarch until she reached the gallery door. There she glanced up at Muscle. 'No payment.'

The orc's misshapen bald skull brushed the keystone of the archway. He shifted his immense mass from foot to taloned foot, furrows appearing in the leathery skin of his brow. A thin line of mucus ran down from one broad, hairy nostril.

'We could loot the galleries as we go?' Zerra took a final look up at the map-lined hall.

The line of dawn's light creeping down the frescoed walls called brighter colour from seas and mountains; from the pinions of an albino crow, painted high above the sooty roofs of temples; from strange vessels landing amid unhuman ruins; from a chapel where a Man is painted hanging from a Green Tree . . .

'Is it worth what we went through, we two, to create this, to bring it here?' She looked thoughtful. 'Sweet heart, such tales we could tell.'

The orc reached down to rest a gnarled arm around the halfling's tanned waist. He removed the cloth head-band he wore, blew his snout on it, and in a cultured baritone voice, he remarked: 'Our tale will be told, my barbarian princess of the south.'

She snuggled under his arm. Muscle continued:

'Under what strange circumstances we met, and for what purpose; and how a blind Swordsmaster freely gave the secret of cartomancy . . . The Sieur Elthyriel may name the correct name and learn all this, if he does not collapse through lack of food first, or is not carried off babbling into confinement by his fellow knights. We *have* our payment. My dear, see the ruler of the Knights of Virtue – he is our Dark Master's, now.'

'Or at least, out of the battle on indefinite notice.' Zerra reached up on tiptoe and ran a caressing finger under the orc's jutting lower jaw; flicked a protruding tusk playfully. 'Have I done well?'

'As you were taught.' Muscle smiled, revealing a disturbing length of fang. The orc flexed bulging rock-like shoulders. 'Learn from this, apprentice Zerra, recruiting for evil is simple. It is not necessary to use violence, or destruction, or even corruption. No. Subtle evils are the best. Humour. Empathy. Entertainment. Truth.'

They watched Elthyriel's growing paralysis. The orc, smiling, said finally:

'All you have to do is get them *interested* . . .'

Afterword

The corridor of maps can be found in the Vatican. It's stunning (though its maps are naturally more Earthly in subject than shown here). And the 'bang-out' aqueduct, too, can be found close by – more than one Pope has galloped across it, full speed, on his way to absolutely-anywhere-but-Rome . . .

So why is *Cartomancy* like it is?

I happen to have the kind of mind that puts elves and orcs – and helicopter-dragons – in the Papacy.

It was Dean who gave me the word for map-magic. The story itself – actually, that came about because of a different story entirely:

As part of the Midnight Rose company – a bunch of us who got together to edit fantasy and SF short story anthologies – I'd come up with the idea for *Villains!*: genre fantasy as seen from the bad guys' point of view.

At the start of the 1990s that was still a new idea. And I thought that, as well as editing, I might have a go at a short story for the anthology . . . from the viewpoint of orcs . . .

It turned into *Grunts! A Fantasy With Attitude*.

This was not my fault. It was the orcs' fault! I keep *saying* this.

However, the short story turning into a novel left me shy of a story for *Villains!*. I ended up doing the editorial framework – and *Cartomancy* appeared.

This is a slightly re-vamped version of the original, with different worlds in the maps. First time around, you got a number of notably twisted and devious writers, writing notably devious and twisted stories. This time, I can only offer me. Which I guess is one way of being a bad guy.

It's not like I really think that reading the stories in *Cartomancy* – or reading *Ash*, or *Grunts!*, or *Rats & Gargoyles*, or *1610* – will rot your mind and turn you from the paths of righteousness. Frankly, I should be so lucky . . . or so good a writer. But Plato chucked poets and fiction writers out of The Republic for a reason. However the world is arranged, fiction says 'it can be some other way'. And SF – where the 'S' stands for 'strange' – more than most.

But you've been safe here, haven't you? Nothing nasty has leapt out of the woodshed?

There. You see?

Pay no attention to the orc in front of the map . . .